A
Map of
Paradise

Emily Eagar

Also by Linda Ching Sledge

Empire of Heaven

A
Map of
Paradise

Linda Ching Sledge

BANTAM BOOKS
New York   Toronto   London   Sydney   Auckland

A MAP OF PARADISE
A Bantam Book / August 1997

Book design by Donna Sinisgalli.

Library of Congress Cataloging-in-Publication Data

Sledge, Linda Ching, date.
A map of paradise / Linda Ching Sledge.
p.   cm.
ISBN 0-553-37890-2
1. Chinese Americans—Hawaii—History—19th century—Fiction.   I. Title.
PS3569.L355M3   1997
813′.54—dc21   96-40075
CIP

Published simultaneously in the United States and Canada

Bantam Books are published by Bantam Books, a division of Bantam Doubleday Dell
Publishing Group, Inc. Its trademark, consisting of the words "Bantam Books" and the
portrayal of a rooster, is Registered in U.S. Patent and Trademark Office and in other
countries. Marca Registrada. Bantam Books, 1540 Broadway, New York, New York 10036.

PRINTED IN THE UNITED STATES OF AMERICA

BVG   10 9 8 7 6 5 4 3 2 1

To my father and mother,

Lammy and Connie Ching

Contents

ACKNOWLEDGMENTS

A Map of Paradise was written during hours stolen from my other life as a full-time professor at Westchester Community College. This undertaking could not have been accomplished without the encouragement of my colleagues and friends at WCC. While other academic institutions claim to prize creativity among faculty, I am fortunate to work at a campus that actually does so.

Grateful appreciation is also due the following: my longtime editor, Beverly Lewis, whose judicious vision kept this manuscript on course; Una Shih, reference librarian at Westchester Community College, for hunting down obscure materials at a moment's notice; the historical societies at Fiddletown and Locke (California), for preserving rare artifacts, documents, and buildings relating to the Chinese of central California; the Hawaii Chinese History Center in Honolulu, whose scholarly publications greatly aided my understanding of this period in Hawaii; my cousins, Douglas and Curtis Yee of Honolulu, for keeping alive the story of our grandfather's struggles to build a fortune based on *mui;* my sons, Geoffrey and Timothy, for traveling every inch of this manuscript alongside their mother; and finally my husband, Gary. *A Map of Paradise* is his as much as mine.

PROLOGUE

Hong Kong, 1865

"*Fusan*. The Blessed Isles on the rim of the eastern sea," the ragged soldier announced to the woman who had ceased to believe in paradise. "The greenest one will be our home."

A wind was stirring the clouds above the bay, and the air smelled of salt and monsoon. Crickets in the reeds kept up a rapid report, warning of rain. About them in caves burned the fires of other hunger-marchers like themselves, peasants driven by famine, drought, and war toward the southern-most ports of Kwangtung Province as the great peasant rebellion sputtered and died.

Pao An and Rulan had come on foot, hundreds of miles from Nan-king, the ruined rebel capital, to this makeshift shelter in the barren hills above Hong Kong bay. There was no place left in China to which an escaped concubine and a peasant general with a price on his head could run. "Except the Blessed Isles," Pao An insisted.

"You're a fool to believe the lies that poets tell," Rulan said bitterly. "I believed in dream kingdoms when we went to war. Nothing will make me believe again."

"*Fusan* is real," Pao An insisted. "Men from Kwangtung knew those isles long before the *bak kuei* white devils claimed them. We sailed along those shoals and mingled our blood with the dark people there. Only when the empire closed itself to the world did we forget that lucky place." He began to draw a crude map in the dirt with his fingers.

Rulan watched the firelight blaze up in his eyes. Surely this battle-scarred soldier did not believe *Fusan,* the lost paradise of legend, existed! Surely he was inventing a haven for a woman who had traveled rivers clogged with corpses, seen village after village laid waste by war . . .

"Some say that *Fusan* is California, the mountain where Tang men dig for gold," he went on in a rush. He stabbed at the dirt, creating islands with pebbles and sand. "But I believe the Blessed Isles lie closer, in the heart of the eastern ocean, the place sailors call 'Hawaii.' A man can rebuild there. Trade his labor for cash."

"Not Hawaii!" Rulan declared, understanding immediately the price he intended to pay for paradise. "Not where Tang men make themselves slaves cutting cane."

"You sell your labor, not your life! A few years' sweating in the cane fields—then you are free to reap the riches of those islands! No village headman to order you here and there. No imperial official to put a cangue around your neck for not bending low enough. A new earth for people without home or village or clan—"

"But we have old enemies there! What about the man and woman who still own me? What if the magistrates of that place force me back to them and put you in chains?"

They sat in silence awhile, each turned away from the other—until she moved closer, pulling him down so he might seek only the paradise that her body could bestow. His lovemaking, always ardent, seemed more reckless than before; and afterward, he slept as though slain. She lay beside him, watching the fire die slowly away. A log burst in a shower of sparks, rekindling a flame in the midst of the embers.

*A*t sunrise, Rulan was roused by a whirring of wings. A bird with a golden crown and scarlet feathers leaped across her line of vision to the top of a nearby thornbush. Even wrapped in slumber, she recognized it: the crimson bird, the herald of good fortune. Comforted by the omen, she put her face into the warmth of Pao An's neck and gave herself up to sleep.

When she awoke again, there was no bird, no man beside her. Only the marks of his fingers in the dirt mapping imaginary islands floating in a phantom sea.

p a r t 1

Green Valley,
Gold Mountain

1

SLEEPING WOMAN

Honolulu, 1866

An ancient mule cart rattled along the dark, waterfront road, past broken lava stone walls of long-abandoned taro fields and fishponds, up the winding trail to Kapukaki Ridge in the center of the island of Oahu.

The night wind was blowing down from the mountains to the sea, carrying with it the scent of *maile* vines and wild ginger blossoms. Again and again, from her perch at the back of the cart, Rulan urged the driver faster. Yet Nalani, the stolid Hawaiian woman at the reins, was wary of her companion's frail condition and kept to the same steady pace. The destination Rulan had set for them was the sugar mill in the small plantation town of Waialua, an arduous overland journey from the port of Honolulu for any traveler, let alone a woman eight months with child. But longing had made Rulan reckless; word had come via Nalani's cousin, a field boss on a cane plantation, that a "big *pa-ke*"—a Chinaman—had entered camp with a contingent of contract laborers from Peru.

"Is his name Chen?" Rulan asked, praying that this might be Pao An who had sold himself into the coolie, or "pig," trade to buy their passage to Hawaii. He had signed on for a sugar plantation on Oahu, but as shipboard experience proved, he might as easily have been sent to California, Mexico, or Peru at an immigrant agent's whim.

"*Ae, ae,* sounds like," the overseer replied with a dismissive shrug. "*Pa-ke* names alla same, *eh*?" Then he lapsed into a spate of grumbling. "Too many *pa-ke* come Hawaii. Jus' like too many *haoles* come, boss aroun' Hawaiian king!"

Rulan knew that the overseer was voicing a growing native hostility to all foreigners, not only to the Chinese, who were competing with Hawaiians for jobs cutting cane, but to the *haoles,* or whites, for attempting to undermine the powerful *alii* nobility who held the reins of the kingdom. And she was grateful when Nalani rose furiously to her defense, arguing that immigrants like Rulan were seeking only honest labor at any price.

Rulan had met Nalani at the home of a childless American couple named Bosworth where both worked as *wahine hana,* live-in maids. There was good reason why Rulan had chosen to earn her keep among the *bak kuei,* the "white devils" whom her people and Nalani's distrusted, and not in Chinatown. Li Liang Mo, the man who had held her contract of concubinage, was a merchant there with enough money and influence to lay claims on her and her unborn child. And even if Liang Mo no longer felt the sting of her betrayal, Li Mei Yuk, his shrewish wife, would gladly take revenge on the woman she blamed for her family's ruin. The animosity between Mei Yuk and Rulan was both deeply personal and rooted in the enduring hostility between peasants and their gentry landlords. The China that Rulan had escaped was awash in internecine strife, with village pitted against rival village, emperor's minions ranged against a rebellious people, and the *tongs,* or secret Triad societies, clashing with all. Rulan had no desire to see old feuds flare up again in her new island home.

Thus it was Nalani, a woman of an alien race, to whom Rulan confessed her terror of bearing a child. Nalani, from whom Rulan took comfort as month followed month without news of Pao An. Nalani, who bore the brunt of the household labor as Rulan's health declined. The terrors of a two-month ocean crossing aboard a sick and smelly scow, and a bleak tenure on Quarantine Island in the wake of a cholera epidemic on shore had already taken their toll on Rulan before the rigors of pregnancy set in. By her eighth month, the bloom had faded from her cheeks, and her normally sturdy limbs had grown thin, for the child was voracious, intent on taking more than its share. Taller and bigger-boned than most women of her race, Rulan, even in pregnancy, was dwarfed by the massive Nalani. The Hawaiian woman stood six feet tall, with wide shoulders, dark hair that fell to the backs of her knees and hands powerful enough to lift an iron kettle filled with steaming wash, deft enough to bind the pieces of a quilt with nearly invisible stitches. Nalani's strength had not come without cost: She had buried two husbands and five adored babies in the epidemics that were ravaging the native population after the coming of the foreign ships. Now she turned the full force of her great heart on her friend.

The sun had barely thrust itself above the surface of the sea when Nalani whipped the tired mule up the long, rugged incline of Kapukaki Ridge. At a precipitous turn of the trail, one of the cart's wheels dropped suddenly down into a ditch. Rulan, sprawled on rice sacks at the back, uttered a sharp cry. She clutched the rail hard enough for the rough wood to press its grain into her palm until the spasm of pain had passed.

"You *pupule*-crazy for make me come so far!" declared Nalani in worry and exasperation to her friend. "Mo' bettah turn back now!"

"Then I'll walk to Waialua alone!"

"*Auwe,*" Nalani grumbled. "Sit down. *Keiki* get born too quick!" Nalani was convinced that the search on which they were embarked was as futile as capturing one particular fish with a blind cast of the net.

At the summit of Kapukaki Ridge, Nalani drew the tired mule up to rest. Seen from this height, the island was a single organism throbbing with what Nalani called *ola*—teeming life. The great bowl of the sky wrapped itself around the women in a panorama of color and light. Dark, shifting curtains of rain swept the Waianae Mountains, while masses of white clouds streaming in from the sea scudded above the vast expanse of the bay named Pearl for the sea treasures sought by native divers. At the edge of the horizon, the red earth was dotted with neat green checkerboard squares of cane. Black puffs of smoke rose from faraway fields set aflame to burn off the razor-sharp leaves and make the stalks easier for cutting.

Slowly, the women began the journey across the plateau of Leilehua. By dusk, they were close enough to the mill to smell hot molasses from the boiling vats and the fumes of distant cane fires. Smoke curled into the sky and blew like a shroud against the distant mountains.

Rulan gave a soft groan, her stomach churning at the cloying stench of singed cane. Nalani glanced back into the cart with a worried frown. "See that mountain?" Nalani demanded to distract Rulan. "She alla time sleep." Nalani's finger defined a configuration of hills to the northwest in the shape of a reclining woman great with child. The dark purple mountain, she recounted, was bursting with powerful *ola,* for it had once been the woman Lahilahi. Abandoned by the god Lono, Lahilahi had been turned to stone by tender-hearted spirits called *akuas* to keep her from old age until her lover's return. Nalani let her lively imagination shape the talk story, adding embellishments, collapsing one fable into another—anything to fill the silence. Anything to avoid talking about the fruitless chase on which her friend had set her heart. Half-poet, half-warrior, this Chen Pao An seemed concocted out of a lonely woman's yearnings. If he existed at all, he was undoubtedly dead at sea or had given himself over to whatever pulled men to the next shore, the next ridge of hills, the next woman. How easy it was for a wandering man to forget the one who had warmed his body for a few brief hours, even though she might carry his child.

"Did Lono go back?" Rulan asked.

"Sure," Nalani retorted with a wink. Laughing, she gave a vigorous shake of her head that set her long hair dancing. "Him working China camp Waialua-side!"

Rulan sat up to take in the shape of the stone face, neck, breasts, and belly silhouetted against the darkening sky, then lay back upon her mattress of rice sacks, her body aching. Until Pao An's return, she, like poor Lahilahi, was calcified by waiting, her heart turned to stone.

They continued in silence, Rulan's discomfort mounting with every bounce of the rickety cart. Soon the ache in her back had spread to her belly, but this time, the soreness seemed sharper, deeper than before. Quick to sense the change in her friend's condition, Nalani began to chatter again while scanning the landscape with anxious eyes. A woman facing childbirth need never be afraid, she assured Rulan, for *akuas* were ever present in the earth and sky. "Mo' bettah you get eyes like me, can see two way, like one Hawaiian," she soothed. Suddenly, she brought the mule up short. "Look that side," she ordered. "We call that place Kukaniloko. In old days, Hawaiian ladies born babies there inside the rock. Good kind magic. Baby plenty strong."

Rulan peered at the spot near the horizon indicated by Nalani, but saw only the feathery tops of coconut trees rising out of an ocean of cane far, far away.

In the end, the journey she had taken so unwisely proved as vain as Nalani predicted. The husky newcomer at the mill was not Pao An but a gap-toothed chicken farmer from the Four Villages who had signed on to cut Hawaiian cane after gambling away the stake he earned raking guano in Peru. Rulan sat in the stable yard of the mill, watching the sky grow dark and listening to the giant gears chew up the brittle stalks.

To Rulan, weighed down with woe, the road back to Honolulu seemed more pitted and winding than before, the journey infinitely longer and fraught with peril. The cart descended into a small gully, then began the bumpy ascent. By the time they had found level ground, the evening air was shimmering with heat from a flaming cane field nearby. A line of fire came racing in their direction, sending a thick curtain of smoke across their path. Overhead, birds were screeching and insects were leaping into the narrow road, chased by an errant wind that stirred up the cane like a mighty hand. A stone's throw from the cart, a clump of dry stalks burst into flame. Burning ash fell around them like the charred remnants of temple offerings. Frightened by the smoke and the crackling of fire, the mule swung its head, reared up on its hind legs and set off at an ungainly gallop. Rulan was sent tumbling from the cart into an irrigation ditch. *"Auwe!"* wailed Nalani, who scrambled down after her onto the road.

Clambering out from the muddy ditch, Rulan felt a dull, insidious ache at her back and the rush of water upon her thighs. A wave of pain brought her to her knees. Nalani, her broad, brown face knit in alarm, caught Rulan around the shoulders to prevent her from falling. "No," Rulan cried out to Nalani. "It cannot be coming now!"

Flames were hissing around them, singeing their hair and their clothes. Rulan found herself dragged out of the road into a field hissing steam. Nalani seemed to be traveling familiar ground, for she took the lead, pulling Rulan through the acrid haze. A searing heat was spreading across Rulan's loins, tearing at her from within. Pain clutched at the mouth of her womb, leaving her breathless and spent. And still Nalani continued to spirit her deeper and deeper into the smoking fields, across dirt trails crowded with prickly *kiawe* bushes, through ditches half-full of brackish water. Soon they were beyond the fire's reach, surrounded by the cool, green density of cane. And still Nalani pulled Rulan forward between rows of sharp leaves that cut her hands and face and hid the sky from view. "Good, good, mo' bettah you walk," Nalani declared.

Night had fallen. When it seemed as if Rulan could go no farther, the cane plants dropped away. Beneath her felt slippers, she felt smooth earth pressed down by the feet of many generations. She leaned on Nalani's strong shoulder, cursing her weakness and looking with wonder on the strange place they had entered—a clearing ringed by coconut trees in the center of which forty odd-shaped stones shone forth in the moonlight.

"These rocks *kapu,* sacred. Plenty *akuas* here," Nalani declared, and even the skeptical Rulan felt the eerie power of the place.

Nalani had led her through mist and darkness to Kukaniloko, the sacred birthing stones set down in the very center of Oahu between the mountains and the sea. "Mo' bettah sit down here," she ordered, pointing to a formation of lava that was human size. The stone fit the contours of Rulan's swollen body with uncanny accuracy. In seconds, the agony had begun again; Rulan pressed herself into the rock, grateful for its solidity, then tensed for another contraction, but . . . nothing.

"The pain is gone," she whispered, grateful for the unexpected respite.

"Walk some more," Nalani ordered, pulling her up and across the hard ground. "Baby stuck."

"Please," Rulan begged. "Let me rest, let me sleep." But Nalani was shaking her rudely, slapping her face so she could not succumb to the darkness growing before her eyes, kneading the hard muscles of her belly until she cried out in agony.

Suddenly, the child heaved and turned over. It struggled inside her, pressing with savage force against her body's effort to contain it. When Rulan felt she might break apart, Nalani pushed her into a squatting position over the stone. Again the child moved, and in an answering effort, Rulan's body opened and gave way.

With a cry, Rulan pushed the child forth, and in the next instant, collapsed upon the coolness of stone. A moment later, Rulan sat up terrified, for the child had not uttered a sound.

A small creature lay in the hollow of the rock. A child encased in a pale membrane, a caul, like a damp cocoon. "Is it dead?" Rulan whispered.

"No, stay good this one. You like see?" Nalani wiped the child clean with her skirt and held aloft a tiny girl whose perfect limbs and wet black hair bore the faintest traces of blood and wax. She cut the cord with a sharp stone and gave the child into Rulan's arms.

A gentle rain began to fall, washing the agonies of the night away. An infant hand flailed in the darkness, then closed on its mother's finger. The small mouth sought and found its mother's breast. When Nalani tried to shift the child to a more comfortable position, it burrowed deeper, clamping onto its mother's body with a blind, stubborn intensity.

"Nothing, not even ghosts from the old country," Rulan promised the daughter born of the rock, "will steal you away!"

2

SON OF WATER

San Francisco, 1865

Chen Pao An composed a poem as the British clipper *Caledonia* entered the mist-shrouded mouth of San Francisco Bay:

This morning in swirling fog, I saw as the gods see:
Five elements—water, fire, metal, wood, earth—
Melting one into another, forging a new land.
I reached out for the treasure of Gold Mountain.
My fingers closed on air.
I have lost my beloved in another world.

Bitter fate! For the ship he had signed on was not bound for the sugar fields of Hawaii at all, but for the floodplains of California's Central Valley, where Chinamen were digging levees to reclaim the land from the rivers.

The sea voyage had taken seventy-two days, thirty more than anticipated, for the wind had died a week out of Hong Kong, leaving the crew and the three hundred Chinamen in steerage stranded for ten blistering days on a glassy sea. Head winds drove them off course to Indonesia, delaying them further. By then, Pao An had witnessed twelve deaths from heat prostration, dysentery, and fever.

He himself had not suffered like the others aboard the evil-smelling scow. Water was his natural element. He had spent his life half-submerged in it. As a youth in On Ting village, he had worked the huge bucket wheel that lifted water from one rice paddy to the next, dredged fishponds with his bare hands, patched dikes along the immense system of canals that crisscrossed the Pearl River Delta. As a soldier in the rebel army, he had swum across White Heron Bay with an iron chain tied around his waist. Now he would scoop a mountain of mud from the bottom of the *bak kuei's* rivers, endure interminable days in the stinking hole of the *Caledonia* if it bought sanctuary for Rulan.

She, he prayed, had had clear skies and brisk winds to bear her to Hawaii, the Blessed Isles of his imagination. He would write her of his new destination, save his money. What was five years' servitude in Gold Mountain when a lifetime of happiness awaited?

Like Pao An, each man crowded into steerage had been born in Heungsan County in the Pearl River Delta of Kwangtung Province, the southernmost region of the empire. Most were yeoman farmers driven into destitution by war, flood, and famine; fifty were kinsmen from the same village, sharing the surname Liu. Among them too were fishermen, tailors, barbers, peddlers of cloth, bell-doctors, bricklayers, sons of scholars fallen on hard times, fatherless boys, and in a handful of cases like Pao An's, ex-rebels fleeing the empire in the wake of the failed Taiping Rebellion. Whatever their age or trade, all risked losing their heads for violating the emperor's ban on immigration.

The exiles called themselves men of Tang in commemoration of the dynasty when sailors from the southern tip of China ventured as far as Persia and the California coast. Clannish and contentious, these southern Tang men, like Pao An, had little love for the northern Han or the foreign Manchu emperor in Peking, even less for their Hakka rivals, competing for a share of American gold. White devils who had hired Chinamen to dredge swamps for farmland and level mountains for the railroad—dangerous work that no European immigrant would undertake—had no notion of the South China feuds that divided Punti "oldtimer" from "newcomer" Hakka or one district or village from another downriver, much less the complex hierarchies of birth, learning, and custom that separated brothers within a single family. Scholar, merchant, fisherman, or peddler: to the *bak kuei,* all Tang men were as faceless and expendable as ants.

It took hours for the *Caledonia* to dock, hours more before the Tang men were herded out of the stinking hold clutching their bedrolls and bags of clothes and precious foodstuffs, sole reminders of loved ones overseas. Frigid winds whipped the waters of the bay into white froth and cut through their ragged cotton tunics and cloth shoes to their bones. The health official in the newly built holding shack looked each one in the eyes, lifted the lids to peer at the inner membrane, and made them stick out their tongues and pull up their shirts to check for pox or leprous lesions.

This was the closest most of the Tang men had been to a *bak kuei*. Appalled by the inspector's bad manners and sour smell; his pale, flyaway hair; florid face, and gigantic hands, they whispered together like prisoners awaiting the executioner's sword, suspicion twisting their empty bellies into knots.

"If he sends me back, my old mother will starve," an emaciated youth from the Liu clan whispered to Pao An.

"You could have twenty kinds of death in you, but as long as you look clean of skin, they'll let you drip your sweat into their earth," Pao An replied, pitying the boy for his terror. He remembered how the boy had spent hours curled into a tight ball of pain on the bunk below Pao An's or bent over the foul and overflowing chamber pot. The youth was obviously too poor to count in his clan, for his cousins and uncles seemed embarrassed by his agonies. When the boy opened his mouth to show Pao An the blisters on his swollen gums—sure signs of scurvy—Pao An warned, "Roll your eyes and laugh like a madman when the white devil tries to examine you. He will think you too ugly to bother with and send you along."

Away from the endless rolling of the waves and the stench of the hold, Pao An's body felt substantial and sure, poised to pit muscle and bone against whatever trials awaited on this slippery mountain of gold.

"You! The puny one," the inspector shouted at the youth. "Shut yer yelpin'!" He brandished the tied-and-tarred end of a short coil of rope. The Liu boy seemed to shrivel in his skin at the rebuke. "Get them Chinks in line, China Jack," the inspector scolded his companion, a weather-worn, fat-faced Tang man of indeterminate age, dressed in Western pants and boots and a red shirt with wooden buttons. The belly hanging over his trousers showed that "Jack" was a Chinaman who did no fieldwork.

The examination was hasty, intended to humiliate more than diagnose. In an hour, all the Tang men were perched on their ragged bedrolls at one end of the dock, while the Chinaman in Western dress hectored them in the niceties of behavior among the barbarians. "My name is Ah Jack," he bellowed. "Not the name my grandfather or my old schoolmaster gave me, but the barbarians massacre all Tang names and yours will be mangled too." His accent was a rural dialect of Cantonese that the Chinamen of the *Caledonia* barely managed to follow. His laugh was bitter.

"To the white devils, we are not men of Tang but *gu li*." He pronounced the phrase again with elaborate care—*gu li,* the Cantonese transliteration of the despised Anglo-Indian term *coolie,* or "rough man for hire"—to emphasize the level to which they had fallen by the simple crossing of an ocean. "Put no faith in the *bak kuei.* Believe only in Ah Jack. I am your headman in Gold Mountain, your mother and your father. You utter the wrong word in the white devils' world, they gouge out your eyeballs and feed them to the dogs. Tomorrow Ah Jack will take you upriver. Soon you'll all be rich men!" A feeble cheer went up from the exhausted Tang men at the long-awaited promise of reward.

Pao An observed wryly that Ah Jack's power derived from one thing alone: knowledge of the white man's tongue. For without Ah Jack, the newcomers were as helpless as ducks with clipped wings.

Using his cudgel, Ah Jack prodded the Tang men past boxes of fish, bales of cotton, and sacks of grain piled as high as the outer wall of a village mansion. The noise was deafening: yet above the grinding of ships' engines and the piercing shrieks of boat whistles came intelligible sounds—words of welcome in their own Heungsan dialect shouted by men driving horse-drawn carts.

Holding tightly to the edge of the teetering cart, Pao An eagerly scanned the outlines of a city huddled against the vast bowl of the bay. He rejoiced to hear his own tongue spoken on these shores and to find himself on solid ground again. This "city"—if the unpainted wood buildings and square stone structures scattered along the bay shore and up the sides of hills could be called that—was just an outpost compared to Nanking or Shanghai, where he had served as a soldier in the Taiping wars. Stranger still than San Francisco's small size was the absence of an outer wall, as if the builders in their haste had lost sight of their chief duty: to protect inhabitants against thieves and marauders. It gave every sign of having being assembled haphazardly just the day before, with more elaborate construction still to come, for even as the lamps were lit and dark clouds blew in from the bay, the sounds of hammering continued.

The line of wagons pulled up at a cove where scows filled with sand had tied up for the night. Ah Jack sent half the wagons in the direction of the ferry to Oakland; the others he commandeered inland. At the foot of a hill, the wagons unloaded their cargo of Tang men who shuffled up an incline so steep that their bodies leaned head first into the ground. Pao An and fifty others followed Ah Jack past narrow wood dwellings perched at odd angles and cavernous halls echoing with discordant, brassy barbarian music. They traveled streets so newly dug that the marks of wheelbarrows and shovels were still visible on the tightly packed earth. Most were wide enough for several carts to pass through; some were lined with cobblestone, others with rough planks.

Pao An found his attention leaping from one bizarre scene to another. A colorless barbarian woman, whose plump body was squeezed by her fantastic costume into an odd, unnatural shape, embraced a man in full view of passersby. Two men rolled in the muck of the streets, throwing punches and grunting like swine, while their drunken companions goaded them to more ferocity. Packs of hungry dogs and one dazed mule wandered untended and unclaimed.

These glimpses of a half-civilized society excited him in a way that more ancient cities like Canton did not. Who could be free with centuries of custom and duty hanging on one's shoulders like a cangue? His entire life had been spent struggling against whatever authority—clan or class or empire—sought to turn men and women into oxen. A rebel's life had suited him far better than tilling a tiny plot of earth, and so he had risen from peasant to soldier to general in the Taiping army. He had commanded thousands of men, only to lose his power at the massacre of the Taiping army at Nanking. And from that fall, he had fallen farther still in Gold Mountain, where he was once again an ox, a *gu li* rough man. And yet, he told himself in wonder and delight, one might rise again in this barbaric land where all were outsiders and as clanless as he.

Then Ah Jack was pushing them away from the brightly lit square and up a narrow street that wound uphill past two-story houses with flimsy wooden facades and balconies lined with flowering narcissuses and irises. Incredibly, the faces peering down at them from the iron balconies were Chinese. Beyond the houses was a warren of open-air stores where boxes of fruits, vegetables, and fresh fish were stacked Chinese market–fashion on the cobblestone walk. Signboards and flags hung down into the street announcing merchants' wares in ungainly calligraphy: flowers, dried ducks shiny with oil, noodles and spirits, sky blue *ya hoo lam* cloth, blue-shelled crabs squirming in baskets, duck eggs packed in boxes of black sulfur, medicinal herbs, knobs of gingerroot, and twenty kinds of tea. Every food or trinket sold in the market towns of Kwangtung was offered in the secret Chinese heart of this savage city. Home, decided Pao An, and not home. The strong aroma of frying fish led them to an enclosure marked with a triangular yellow flag where dozens of Chinamen were eating noisily at plank tables. "Two bits, Yankee dollar. All you can eat," shouted the proprietor, a Tang man with a dirty apron who was lifting a steaming bucket of rice onto the table. The smells rising from the platters of food nearly brought the famished Tang men to their knees. But Ah Jack would not let them tarry. "No time, no time," he scolded.

Pao An was assigned with fifty others to a one-room barracks erected by the Liu clan for their menfolk overseas. There were already thirty men in the room sleeping on rough-hewn bunks stacked four high and laid end to end in rows. In one corner of the barracks a giant tin teapot steamed upon a cast-iron stove; nearby were two wooden buckets of cold rice, not nearly enough to feed the hungry men.

Before the arrivals could rush to fill their bowls, Ah Jack shouted, "Listen, you! Any Liu man can stay here, even when they are sick or have no job. Those who are not Liu clan stay only one night. Rice is free, meat or fish costs a few coppers, nothing tonight since the cook just died. Liu men pay clan dues to me. The rest of you pay something too."

There was an angry murmur among the Lius. "Why do we have to pay dues if we aren't staying? All you offer is a bed and nothing to flavor our rice," a young man complained. "I have money to buy something to eat outside."

"Do you think the white devils want men of Tang gazing like bump-kins at their ugly red faces and hairy noses? No, they kill any man of Tang who ventures out alone. They believe that all Tang men hide their wealth about their person. If a Tang man has nothing, they tie his queue to the tail of a horse and use him to sweep the dung from the street."

"We are safe on these streets among other Tang men," challenged that same youth.

"Safe?" mimicked Ah Jack. "One block too far down Dupont Street and you go over the boundary of Chinatown. No Tang man, not even Ah Jack, can protect you if you meet with *bak kuei* rowdies. Better stay inside, learn the rules in Gold Mountain. Tomorrow you stuff your mouths with decent food!"

"And what if a man wants to gamble or drink wine?" a youth shouted above the din.

Ah Jack's fleshy face split into a broad grin that showed his one gold tooth. Pointing to his chest, he announced, "For all in life that gives a man pleasure, Ah Jack is your man. You like *ma jong, fan-tan, pai ngow* gambling? See Ah Jack! Is your sack so tight you need to find a civilized woman in this land of foreign devils? See Ah Jack. You want something to drink that doesn't taste like piss? Ask Ah Jack!"

"A *tong* pimp!" an older man snorted to the others, the very uncle the sickly youth feared most aboard ship.

In a flash Ah Jack had struck his detractor a blow on the side of his head that sent the older man reeling. The Liu men were aghast at the insult inflicted upon an uncle. Yet before they could move against him, Ah Jack screeched, "In Gold Mountain, strength, not age, carries the day! The same *tong* brothers give you what you want and need. Show respect!" He shoved his detractor onto one of the board beds. "Too many Liu men here.

You sleep in shifts. You first, Uncle. We get up at four tomorrow to go upriver. Ah Jack has got you jobs working for the devils in a hydraulic mining camp. Think of the riches you will send home from Gold Mountain!" With that, Ah Jack used his cudgel to prod the sullen men into separate groups. The Liu uncle rose slowly from where he had fallen, averting his face as Ah Jack strode by.

Pao An claimed a lower bunk at the back of the barracks on the first shift. He took his other shirt out of his cloth bag to cover the straw-packed pillow, the casing of which was stained with the sweat of strangers, and lay down. He understood what Ah Jack meant by "dues." Not satisfied with controlling gambling, liquor, opium, and prostitution, the *tongs,* through henchmen like Ah Jack, took a portion of every man's money through clan or village fees. This was payment Pao An could ill afford if he were to send money to Rulan. He closed his eyes. The bed was as hard as his pallet aboard ship, but because it did not pitch and roll, Pao An fell asleep immediately. So deeply did he sleep that he did not hear the cacophony of snores and moans around him; nor did he dream, even of Rulan.

3

THE HOUSE OF REST

Honolulu

"A child beneath our roof!" Emmanuel Bosworth exulted, when Ru-lan, with her daughter at her breast, stepped down from the wagon of the Hawaiian farmer who had found the women along the cane road. He drew Rulan and Nalani into the parlor and peeked at the tiny frowning face crowned by black hair that stuck straight up like sea grass. Turning to his wife, Lucy, Bosworth kissed her with as much tenderness as if Lucy were presenting him with a child of their own. So elated was he that he did not see, as Rulan did, the envy and misery in Lucy's face.

Lucy Bosworth, mistress of Hiamoe, did not like babies because she could not have one. Other women had children by the wagonful; why not she? Thus betrayed by the very unfortunate she had embraced, Lucy felt her store of Christian charity rapidly drain away. She had agreed to house one, not two new mouths, certainly not a fatherless infant who squalled and spit and stank and, moreover, usurped the attention she had come to expect from her husband.

Rulan observed with trepidation Lucy's mounting dislike for her and the infant. She was defenseless and alone. Where could she go if Lucy turned them both out? Not to Chinatown where her old enemies, the Lis, held sway! Survival now meant biding her time among the *bak kuei,* saving her money until Pao An returned or she could strike out in a business of her own.

Rulan had earned a powerful ally in Emmanuel Bosworth, former Congregational missionary turned editor of the *Pacific Dispatch,* who had earned the nickname "Blunderbuss" as much for his booming voice as for his pugnaciousness in print. Yet within the confines of his home, he was a supplicant, a dévot, a slavish toady to his mercurial wife. Bosworth had never regretted abandoning the Mission to marry Lucy, an Episcopalian; the newspaper was profitable enough to keep his delicate wife in comfort while supplying him a powerful pulpit for converting souls. Yet Lucy was never satisfied with the presents and attention her husband rained on her. She complained incessantly of the heat, the spitefulness of the Mission wives, the meanness of their cottage compared to the mansions of diplomats or planters, the shabbiness of her wardrobe. The more demanding his wife's complaints, the more yielding the man whose editorials could rock the kingdom would be.

Thus when Bosworth's attention shifted momentarily to the child, Lucy took to her bed, sick with envy and convinced of her failure as a woman. How else to explain Lucy's sudden hostility toward Rulan, her dramatic bouts of hypochondria when the infant was most demanding, or her failures with pie dough or quilting needle, skills at which she normally excelled? That Lucy was clearly intelligent, and a beauty besides, made her self-doubt all the more puzzling to Rulan.

Rulan had encountered *bak kuei* women briefly on the streets of Hong Kong, florid heavy-boned creatures with bulbous noses and loud voices to match their menfolk's; yet the delicacy of the woman who had greeted her at the wharf in Honolulu took her breath away—the tiny uptilted nose, the small perfectly oval face, the skin as pale and immaculate as cream. Lucy's hair, too, was as pale as new silk pulled from the cocoon. Tiny strands had escaped the mountain of tight coils and ringlets and made a radiant frame around her face.

"Oh, Manny, here!" Lucy had trilled. "Goodness, how tall she is! Is she well? Poor thing must be terrified to be so alone!" The brightness of the woman's manner was unnatural. She seemed to Rulan like a musical instrument with the strings wound too tight.

"She speaks English!" blared the red-haired, mustachioed man in a voice as loud as a horn. "Tried out my textbook Cantonese on her and all she did was glare at me! Then replied in the King's English! Joke's on us ignorant white devils!" He laughed so uproariously, his freckled hands pummeling the side of the carriage, that Rulan thought she had landed in a household headed by a madman. Bosworth's tender solicitude toward his young wife, however, quickly convinced Rulan that if he was insane, he was made so by excess of love.

The house Bosworth had built for Lucy and to which Rulan came as *wahine hana* was a testament to the depth of his husbandly devotion. Constructed to her specifications on five prime acres that had once belonged to the chiefs, or *alii,* of Oahu, the house lay at the mouth of Nuuanu Valley where the road out of Honolulu began its winding climb up the steep precipices called the *Pali.* Bosworth had named the cottage Hiamoe, or "Rest," for his hope was that high-strung Lucy, whose disastrous encounters with disapproving Mission wives had nearly broken her health, would find peace there.

Nestled against a stunning backdrop of green cliffs streaked with silvery waterfalls blown skyward by the wind, Hiamoe gave the illusion of grandeur. Yet to Rulan's eyes, the house was as insubstantial as the Bosworths' marriage; it was dangerously, almost callously exposed to noxious elements that threatened to topple it from its flimsy foundation. No high walls shielded its inhabitants from public view; no spirit screen deflected malevolent *kuei* from entering the house. Instead, the road drew up to a wide gate, broad verandas; and not one, but two entrances open to wandering spirits or unhealthy bursts of cold or heat. A few wisps of fabric, as filmy as a woman's undergarments, separated the inhabitants from the eyes of curious passersby. In place of wall slits, immense windows let vagrant valley breezes into the heart of the dwelling. The house was built of thin wooden boards painted white and set atop a foundation of coral stone and lava rock. Two levels crowned by a roof of wooden slats directed the eye upward to the very symbol of the Bosworths' instability: a metal rooster that turned its beak in whatever direction the wind blew—not unlike the response of husband to wife.

Rulan liked to believe that her affection for Pao An did not waver with every shift of temper or circumstance as did the wifely ardor of the volatile Lucy. Whenever ill winds blew, Rulan simply grew more firm in hope. Nothing could change her conviction that Pao An was alive. He would return and reclaim her, take her from this unhappy house where she was so despised into one of her own.

Lucy was miserable. A new mistress reigned in her place at Hiamoe: a small, red, willful thing with a voracious appetite. No longer did Bosworth pass the evening in conversation with his wife; instead, he was sawing and hammering small rocking toys out of koa wood. So engrossed was he in numerous new "projects" for the child that he forgot to write his column.

Rulan was relieved temporarily of her duties in the kitchen to tend to the child, who cried day and night to be fed. Convinced of the efficacy of native cures, she allowed Nalani to rub crushed sweet potato onto the soft spot on the infant's head. And when her milk was slow coming in, she ate what Nalani concocted: a rich broth made from a chicken cooked with yellow-flowered *kookoolau* and crushed *ilima* blossoms.

The attention given to the new mother's comfort and the child's feeding heightened Lucy's hypochondria. She was alternately hot and cold, frenzied or on the point of a faint, complaining of vague ailments that only Emmanuel's awkward ministrations could assuage. Rulan saw that Hiamoe could not tolerate two infants within its walls; sooner or later, the counterfeit child must be made to change, or she and her daughter would be forced too soon on their own, and thus brought face-to-face with the vengeful Lis.

4

THE HOUSE OF LI

Chinatown, Honolulu

The servant girl turned the steaming platter so that the head of the fish pointed at her master, Merchant Li. A naked play for Liang Mo's affections, his wife, Mei Yuk, observed, by a lowly bond maid who aspired to the rank of minor wife. Such snares had been laid for Liang Mo before. The man's taste in women was insufferably common. That small miscalculation would cost the girl dearly, for if Liang Mo's attention turned in her direction, Mei Yuk would sell her to the oldest and poorest vendor among the fish stalls, as she had others who had labored in her husband's bed and in her kitchen.

A wife of a certain age, Mei Yuk believed, had to be ever on guard against rivals, to be ruthless in maintaining her place. And her place, though nothing to compare with the luxuries she had known in China, was this block of ramshackle shops, vendors' stalls, and tenement houses in the crowded Chinatown quarter called Tin Can Alley over which she ruled as *Tai Tai,* matriarch of the wealthiest family enterprise in the islands.

Mei Yuk glanced surreptitiously at her epicene husband, sweating as he always did from the effort of eating. Did Liang Mo know how zealously she guarded their good name and her role as *Tai Tai* of his house? The week before, she had heard the news that her husband's former concubine had dropped a child. Years after fleeing their house in China, the woman had washed ashore on these islands like ocean-borne offal. For six months Mei Yuk had contemplated the movements of her former rival from afar: Rulan was seen strolling through Chinatown with a fat Hawaiian woman, buying fish or breadfruit or fresh *poi* from the stalls owned by the very family she had betrayed. In fury and fascination, Mei Yuk watched Rulan the way a hungry cat studies the movement of a bird perched just beyond reach. She had waited for the inattention, the small change in behavior that would carry the bird within the swipe of her claws and bring to an end that old feud once and for all.

Liang Mo dipped his chopsticks into the watery sauce and touched them to his tongue: cheap oil again, he concluded unhappily. A peasant meal, cooked by calloused peasant hands that could not even brew a proper cup of tea. Mei Yuk, at least, shared with him the memory of being rich, so rich that one had a servant for chopping vegetables, another for carrying hot water, and another for massaging one's feet. For that bond, and for other services Mei Yuk rendered to his family, he kept her as *Tai Tai* long after her beauty had faded and his passion had cooled. It was a fair exchange: his favor for her cleverness at trade. And if he slept with a lowly servant girl, Mei Yuk did not lose what she did not value.

Why then, he wondered, did Mei Yuk force her household to eat like paupers, when the family's accounts showed profits in every venture and the stalls owned by the Lis were stocked with delicacies sent at great cost from China—dried oysters, rice noodles spun into billowing translucent threads, sharks' fins, bears' paws, red dates to tame a fiery dish and to cool the blood. He pulled a handkerchief from his sleeve and mopped his damp forehead. He had always suffered an excess of heat, and that imbalance of elements made him languish in the sweltering, mosquito-ridden atmosphere of wharfside Honolulu. He decided that he had not eaten well since his Second Lady had left his house and his bed years ago. That lady, Rulan, had known the medical properties of food and could brew soups to cure a fever or stir a jaded appetite or relieve the pangs of overindulgence. That lady's unexpected appearance in the islands was a stroke of fortune. He had decided to take her back, to forgive her insult to his name, if she could restore balance to his household and lessen the influence of this harridan who usurped the part of a man.

Hiding his ill-humor under an exaggerated show of politeness, Merchant Li broke off the tender flesh behind the gills with his chopsticks and put it on his wife's plate. Mei Yuk raised it absentmindedly to her lips. She now preferred business to the pleasures of the moment—music or food or conversation. She even insisted on making their daughter, Lily, their only surviving child, take her meals with the bond maid in the kitchen, so the two of them could talk earnings and rents as they ate.

"Husband," Mei Yuk chided, "the accounts for the contract laborers must be settled. If we adjust the numbers, we can claim new losses because some men perished on the voyage and some were turned away by the barbarian doctor because of disease."

The servant girl returned with a fresh pot of tea, and they lapsed into silence. Liang Mo studied the girl's plump figure as if she were another dish set before him.

Although she had fled from him years ago, Rulan was still by contract his possession under Chinese law, as much a part of the family's inventory as the field hands aboard the *Mei Foo*. Liang Mo doubted that the Hawaiian courts would interfere with his prior claims on Rulan: Hawaiians and *haoles* never interfered in matters between Chinese. For even if Rulan sued for release, the courts, dominated by the powerful sugar lobby, were bound to favor master rather than servant. Rescinding a labor contract made in China could throw the planters' own lucrative contracts with immigrant laborers into question. No, law was not a problem. Releasing Rulan from the white devil's protection posed a greater complication . . . and of course, there was the monumental obstacle in the person of his wife. He suspected that Mei Yuk, whose network of spies was as extensive as his, had known earlier than he when Rulan had set foot in the islands and was intent on some secret mischief. She never could abide a rival.

"You are dreaming again," Mei Yuk scolded.

"Only about how we made love in the garden at my father's house. Have you grown so old that you forget young joys?" he added sullenly.

"Your *old* wife forgets nothing," Mei Yuk snapped, her pinched face clouding over with resentment. "I remember that in the same year our son wrote his first eight-legged essay, we sent his body back to Kwangtung to be buried. I remember our daughters' graves in the garden. I remember how old I have grown sacrificing for this family!" Impatiently, she ordered the bond maid to clear the table, and when the girl proved too slow, Mei Yuk threw her papers over the piles of fish bones and puddles of tea. "Here," she said to her husband with white-hot hatred. "You finish the accounts. I am old and useless."

Mei Yuk waited in the dark for Liang Mo, a habit of hers after a row, for he was a soft man who hated quarreling. Yet Liang Mo did not slip into her bed to beg forgiveness, as he always had before.

5

THE WHITE DEVIL

San Francisco

Words were spinning around him. Foreign words, a dizzying rush of guttural hawks and clicks that seemed more the language of beasts than of civilized men. Pao An had learned some English from his American comrade-in-arms in the rebellion, though Rulan had mastered it far quicker than he; yet conversing with a single plain-spoken *bak kuei* was one thing and being assaulted by the random noises of an entire barbarian city was another.

The world too was spinning with the gaudy colors and frenzied movements of barbarian life. Dray horses lifting their hooves out of the sticky mud, leaning into their harnesses as they pulled wagons uphill. Carriages rocking on squeaking springs. And a race of giants—more *bak kuei* than he had ever seen—roaring like lions in deep, stentorian tones, careening into each other in wild abandon. He had known that this was their part of the earth, but who would have guessed that they were so many and so abominably ugly? Most were of the same pasty color, some redder or darker than others, with hair and beards of such outlandish hues that one might think that the custom of the race was to dye itself like birds. There were men with whiskers the color of flame. Men with blue-black hair that curled down the neck like seaweed. Men with gray eyes, green eyes, blue eyes, or eyes with no color at all. The dress too of these giants was as bizarre as the color of their hair and skin! Pipestem pants of coarse material and shirts of square-patterned cloth dyed red or blue and hung with great round buttons or breast patches into which they stuffed knobs of tobacco. Leather boots that rose as high as the knee with heels as high as the "boat" shoes of imperial courtesans so that manly men moved their hips like women. Hats of straw or leather with wide brims that shaded their florid faces like fans. Kerchiefs tied around hairy foreheads like bandages. Some men wore black coats that hung open in the front to show masses of white ruffles. Others walked around naked to the waist, with grizzled hair that sprouted from arms and necks and chests like fur. No man had modesty. No man was deferential. No eyes were cast down.

What astonished Pao An most was that no marks of rank separated one barbarian from the next—no jeweled hat buttons of status, no peacock feathers or painted fans, no servants obsequiously trailing behind. No man was carried on another's shoulders. No criers ran before to warn the crowds to give way. Each man bore himself on two strong legs as if he were a king. Each stood on his piece of cobblestone as if he owned it and lifted his chin defiantly as if to demand more.

Pao An's head swam with the newness and the noise and the sheer magnitude of Gold Mountain. He scarcely minded that Ah Jack drove them along the streets like a gang of prisoners, for there was so much to see. Unlike the other Tang men, who kept their heads down, too appalled to look upon such hellish faces, Pao An stared about him in fascination. Here was a place vast enough for a man to make himself anew.

Pao An tried to pronounce the name of the foreign city as Ah Jack had. "Saan flaan siss ku," he said aloud, studiously flattening the syllables to eliminate the Cantonese tones and dividing up the stream of sounds into smaller notes for his memory to seize and store. The odd noises rolled with surprising ease off his tongue. His ears strained to pick out recognizable barbarian words as he walked down the street. The sound for "water." "Run." "Bread." "Horse." "Gold." More words materialized out of the incomprehensible babble like faint brush strokes across a blank sheet of paper. He whirled around whenever he heard a man uttering a word he knew and studied that face as if it belonged to a friend.

Ah Jack screamed curses at them, hurrying the Tang men along. A knot of white devils blocked their way on the planks laid down to create a makeshift road. "Go around the turd-eating bastards," he yelled. As the Tang men stepped into mud, Ah Jack bowed obsequiously to the white men, shouting, "Keep your eyes down, don't look into their ugly faces. Hurry up! We got to get to the ferry."

Seeing Pao An gaping, a white devil spat a brown wad of tobacco juice in his direction and muttered something with a face full of rage. Pao An understood one of the words in his tirade: "damn." And although he knew the man was cursing him, Pao An smiled, delighted to decipher another sound.

Ah Jack led them down a mud-slicked hill toward the great bay, which to Pao An's eyes was as vast as a sea. Nature in the land of the white devils was appropriately marvelous and gargantuan. Everything—from the great dome of the sky to the steep hills upon which the city was built to the bay itself—was gouged out in gigantic proportions.

"There's the *Jung-sam-mee-tee!*" Ah Jack screeched pointing to the huge barbarian letters painted above the wheelhouse. "That's the wooden bucket that will carry you pigs to market."

A marvelous apparition, which Pao An took to be the ship *Yosemite,* lay at a crude plank dock at the bottom of the road. This vessel was bigger than any sampan or square-rigged lorqua, grander even than the aged clipper ship that had brought him across the wide ocean. It was white and black with huge gold trim snaking across its sides, a flat wide bottom, two decks rising above, a graceful beam and prow, and two great red wheels within a white circular sphere on either side. At the top of the decks, two smoke-stacks spewed twin columns of acrid fume. The forward decks were crammed with passengers, while cattle, crates of mining equipment, hard-ware, stacks of rough-cut lumber, vegetables, and pens of live chickens filled the stern.

"Go up the gangway," Ah Jack shouted. "Then down the stairs to the lower deck." He used his cudgel to prod the exhausted Tang men along.

"I'm not going inside that beast," cried the youth from the Liu clan.

"Move you, dead boy, or I'll fry your testicles in oil," Ah Jack ordered and gave the sick boy a shove with the ball of his fist that knocked him to his knees.

As he stumbled with the others to the stern of the paddle wheeler, Pao An felt as if he had walked into the entrails of an engine far more complex than the great waterwheel he had worked in the rice paddies of On Ting village. From the look of the passengers, such marvelous crafts must be common in the barbarian world. None of the *bak kuei* passengers showed the least trace of fear; they were as carefree and garrulous as if they were on holiday.

A tall white man wearing a black suit and a wide-brimmed hat came up to talk to Ah Jack in pidgin English for a while.

"This ugly devil is 'Mistah Creel,'" Ah Jack announced to the Tang men huddled in the stern, "as hard a taskmaster as any imperial guard. Do what he tells you, or when we get to his farm he'll feed your right eye to the black dog he keeps for that purpose alone. The right eye only, so you can watch it being devoured with your left. Understand, *hai ma?* Then kowtow," Ah Jack commanded.

The men imitated Ah Jack's subservient posture. Pao An's young friend performed extreme obeisance, striking his head upon the wooden deck as if he faced the emperor himself. Pao An, however, kept both eyes on the man while bobbing his head in perfunctory courtesy, and thus bore witness to the naked contempt that flickered over the white man's face.

After Creel stomped away, Pao An filled his lungs with sweet, cold air. He heard the ferrymen cast off their lines with good-natured shouts, then felt the deck shudder and the boat begin to move. The *Yosemite* pulled away, blowing steam as the great paddle wheels whirled and the water at the sides of the boat foamed like a mountain torrent. Then a frightful caterwauling, as if the souls of the damned were being roasted on the spits of hell, erupted from pipes on the upper deck of the ferry. The Liu boy shrieked and even Pao An cringed in surprise. When Ah Jack saw the Tang men holding their ears, he laughed uproariously.

"Does a barbarian fart scare you?" he jeered. "That's *ka-lai-oo-pee,* a big teakettle that plays devil music by blowing air out of its snout. *Aaiiee,* you Tang warriors would make your ancestors proud."

Pao An saw in astonishment how the barbarians nodded their heads and kept the beat with their feet or hands in obvious enjoyment of the horrific noise. To block out the fearful din, Pao An held his hands over his ears and turned his attention to the ridge of hills to the east, where, as Ah Jack promised, Gold Mountain's secret treasure lay.

*A*s the boat sped swiftly across the pearl-colored waves, Pao An saw for the first time the immensity of the waters upon which he was traveling, for the bay stretched south as far as the eye could see. Thousands of Tang men had preceded him along this water route since 1848, not all of them impoverished peasants seeking to fill their family's rice bowl. The *tongs,* Triad secret societies brutally suppressed in China, were sprouting underground appendages overseas. Rival branches of *tongs* fought for control of the Tang men laboring in the gold fields, the levees, and as the Chinese took over work from the Irish, the Central Pacific Railroad.

The ferry churned north against the current before veering east into the mouth of a gigantic river coursing between rounded hills that plunged steeply to the water's edge. Then with a surge of the engines and a quickening of the giant paddle wheels, the boat headed upriver into an expanse as wide as the Yangtze at Nanking. The air had turned sultry, and the land too had changed. Live oak trees became less plentiful and the hills were as brown as oxhide. The boat swept past a small town on the bluffs of the northern bank, and several more on the southern shore before entering a vast region of low-lying islands, marshes, and stagnant sloughs. *Aaiiee,* whispered Pao An to himself in astonishment, seeing laid out before him a replica of the floodplain of the Pearl River, half-land, half-water, which he had planted and dredged as a boy. There were traces of China everywhere—in the ghostly mist that rose from the earth, in the reflection of the sky shimmering in the shallow pools on which the islands swam. In the ancient willows and tule grasses, he saw the same web of foliage that anchored his home village, On Ting, to the Pearl River. But whereas every inch of water and earth along the Pearl overflowed with people and the bones of their ancestors, here there was no sign of human use. It was as if he were seeing the first burst of life emerging from primordial mud.

In the late afternoon, the boat turned up a channel in the direction of a town built of raw wooden buildings.

"Rio Vista!" called out the pilot on the quarterdeck. The passengers crowded to the rails in preparation for going ashore.

None of the Tang men had eaten for hours, and hunger had given them courage enough to forget their fear of the raucous calliope, whose caterwauling had at first caused shrieks of terror, and of the rushing water churned up by the paddle wheels. They complained bitterly to Ah Jack that if he wanted their labor he had better have a feast in store.

"You'll eat," he assured them, "in Rio Vista. Tang men selling proper food, not like the barbarian swill you'll soon be eating." He spat on the deck to show his contempt for such food, adding jovially, "I myself have arranged for you to eat civilized food by deducting a small portion from your first month's salary."

While the Tang men gathered in angry bunches, loudly protesting Ah Jack's avarice, Pao An leaned over the railing to scan the shore as the boat tied up. Fifty passengers disembarked, while a hundred more were waiting on the dock and in the street ready to board. Most were farmers holding baskets of tomatoes and asparagus for market. It pleased Pao An that a few of the farmers were Tang men in Western hats and boots who were selling their own produce.

Ah Jack hurried the Tang men down the ramp before the people on shore could push themselves aboard. "Only two hours to eat before we go on the river again. The Double Happiness Restaurant is down the street. Owned by my cousin. Best food outside San Francisco."

The parade of bedraggled, half-starved Chinese crossed a dirt road and turned down an alley that led them past a maze of small vegetable gardens and the backs of stores. At the end of one small lane stood five long wooden plank tables with a cook shed at the rear of the yard. A clay oven with open holes held three blackened woks in which gingerroot and onions were already sizzling in hot oil. The familiar aroma made the men faint with hunger and homesickness. They rushed to the tables as the cook boys began throwing chunks of raw meat and sliced vegetables into the sputtering pans. A few, however, slumped silently upon the stones of the yard, their heads between their knees, as if realizing for the first time how far from home they were.

Pao An too was famished, and as soon as he sat down, a huge bowl of hot white rice materialized before him. In the next instant, the cook boys banged down upon the table platters of sliced pork gleaming with oil, soy-soaked chicken feet and white cabbage, crisp white onions and Chinese leafy vegetable, and *ji tu,* the prized middle section of the pig's stomach. It was village food, poor man's food, the kind they had all been raised on. For a single moment, the men were silent, lost in private reverie, for the food stirred up memories of clan and family and holidays now lost to them. And then they were gobbling madly.

Ah Jack stalked proudly between the tables as cook boys in greasy aprons ran before him, refilling the platters with the contents of sizzling woks. "Did Ah Jack tell a lie? Best food in Gold Mountain here. Real food, not barbarian shit!"

All too quickly the platters were scraped clean. The men had barely enough time for a final swallow of scalding tea poured into empty rice bowls before Ah Jack was cursing them into line for the walk back to the wharf. The sun was low, and the shadows of the shops fell across the street as the Chinamen arrived at the gangplank behind a troupe of actors and musicians. One man carrying a huge drum with the words *McGuire's Theatre* painted on it was talking to Creel on the passenger deck, and Creel was laughing, his head thrown back in abandon. His smile froze when he saw the Chinese lingering on shore.

"Get them damn yella niggers below deck before they scare the women and children!" Creel yelled to Ah Jack. He made a gesture of apology to the man with the drum.

Pao An was rushed along the main deck, which was crowded rail to rail with passengers. A dwarf wearing a porkpie hat was sitting on a bale of hay next to a little girl with two blond braids tied with green ribbon. The midget was playing a banjo and singing to the delight of the small girl and the crowd. Reluctant to reenter the foul-smelling hold, Pao An had paused to watch when Ah Jack shoved him in the back, making him stumble down the first two steps to the lower deck. "The ugly barbarian who pays our wages says 'move.' You move!"

In one swift movement, Pao An leaped to where Ah Jack was standing, grabbed the open flap of his coat and yanked him forward. His other hand shot out to grasp Ah Jack by the neck, and in the next second the wriggling overseer was hoisted into the air. "A righteous man leads by example," Pao An said quietly.

Ah Jack opened his mouth as if to scream curses, yet for an instant, he could not utter a sound.

"Treat us as men, and we will follow you. As for me, I will go back above." He flung Ah Jack on the boards, ignoring the overseer's loud groans. "Will you come too?" Pao An asked the young man named Liu who was trembling at the bottom of the stairs, the sole witness to their struggle.

"No. Not I," the frightened boy replied.

"Suit yourself," Pao An said curtly and went up. His stomach was churning with anger at himself as well as at Ah Jack. He had not only made an enemy, one who could use the full force of the Triad gangs who managed the "pig" trade to break him down, he had also insulted the only Tang man who knew sufficient English to get a message to Rulan. His anger, which had betrayed him time and again in war, had betrayed him once more. There was no apologizing now.

The engine hissed and the great joints of the drive mechanism creaked into movement; the paddle wheels on both sides of the *Yosemite* spun and caught the water in their teeth. Slowly the ferry moved away from the dock. The calliope screamed to life again, and the banjo player on the top deck strummed along on his tinny instrument. Pao An climbed up to the top deck and pushed his way to the railing for a breath of air, shaking with the effort of suppressing his rage.

"Where ya think yer going?" a voice bellowed. Pao An turned and found himself nose to nose with Nathan Creel. "Get the hell down below!"

Pao An understood the man's intention if not the words themselves. Anger poured forth. He was tired of being ordered around by puffed up fools and vicious white devils. Tired of being forced to bend. He would *not* go down below! He planted his feet on the boards, fully aware that he was attracting attention. The midget was pointing the arm of his instrument at them, a large grin splitting his chubby face in anticipation of the fight to come, and the little girl was staring at him with frightened eyes. Just then,

Ah Jack came racing up the stairs. Creel reached nonchalantly inside his black jacket and brought out a long-nosed, Confederate officer's revolver, gleaming and well oiled.

"No, Mistah Creel. Ah Jack takee Chinaman down, no worry you," Ah Jack shouted. In Cantonese he yelled at Pao An. "Cut your head, dead boy. I should not even help you . . ." But Pao An could not hear him for the unearthly din that rose from the boiler below. All heads turned toward the source of the deafening squeal that was making the floorboards shiver beneath their feet. The noise rose higher, higher than the notes of the calliope . . .

In the next instant, the world split apart. The roof of the ferry blew skyward; the sides of the boat burst asunder. Wooden splinters shot in all directions, boards flew like spears, metal fragments cut through flesh with the deadly force of grapeshot, and human limbs were blown away like chaff.

The report filed to *The Sacramento Bee* blamed the tragedy on the ferry's defective boiler, which had exploded below deck, killing "over 100 men, women, and children" and "fifty Chinese bound for the Delta farms."

6

THE CURSE

Honolulu

Two weeks after Rulan's baby was born, Lucy was prostrated by a migraine brought on by the child's incessant crying. She ordered the windows and doors of her room covered with heavy crepe and draperies.

"You know how noise upsets me," she told her anxious husband and began a long litany of her woes.

This time, however, Bosworth turned a deaf ear to the complaints of his wife, whose rosy features belied her claims of illness. "This is the way with infants," he returned. "And now the child is sleeping and making no noise." There was a new note of impatience in his voice that his wife was quick to perceive.

A tear fell down Lucy's pink cheek. "How cruel you are," she lamented. "How could you take to your bosom this creature of an alien race? You simper and fawn over it as if it were your own flesh and blood! Such an attachment is unnatural, perverse—"

"We're talking about a child."

"That child is killing me!"

"You yourself are doing so!" Bosworth exploded. "And you forget your part in accepting these refugees of war. What better way to show Christian charity, you told me, than to bring someone from a maligned race within our walls! It was your words I borrowed in that week's essay in the *Dispatch* when I wrote about 'shoring up the dying Hawaiian race with a stronger strain from Asia.' "

Lucy turned white with astonishment. Never before had her husband gone against her wishes or lifted his voice in censure. "Emmanuel! We are quarreling! You see what they've done to us? Send them away! I see the reproach in your eyes whenever you come near me. How long until the child's presence awakens gossip among the missionary families who laugh at me for my barrenness? I cannot abide the shame. I shall die of it!"

Lucy's childlessness had never failed to awaken his pity before. This time, however, Bosworth sensed the danger into which Lucy's self-deception was leading them both. "My dear, look to your better self," he entreated. "Yield to your sense of mercy and justice, not to envy. Surely you will not ask me to turn mother and child out!"

"I do. I demand it!" she cried, angrily dashing away her tears and throwing her damp handkerchief to the floor.

Bosworth turned on his heel and quit their bedroom, torn between sympathy for his suffering wife and horror that she could charge him with committing such cruelty. Yet long habit eventually led him round again to Lucy's will. He was a tenderhearted man, and the thought of losing Lucy's love was unbearable to him. A flurry of visits between Hiamoe and the Mission had the expected result. Another benefactor was found—a ship's captain-turned-trader who had brought his wife and children in from Connecticut. The suspicion that the captain's generosity was motivated less by Christian charity than the necessity for a cheap servant gnawed at Bosworth. Nor did Lucy seem appeased; on the contrary, her migraines intensified along with a new round of turmoil in the household, for Nalani was muttering dire imprecations in Hawaiian and threatening to give notice. Moreover, Bosworth could not help showing a new restraint in his dealings with Lucy; he had glimpsed a side of her that made him ashamed, and he wondered if he had married care rather than comfort. And still he was unable to tell Rulan that she must go.

Rulan knew. She felt Lucy's envy and Bosworth's grief, and had already decided to leave before they thrust her out. She would find a fellow Hakka to take her in. The Hakka, who had feuded for centuries in South China with Punti clans like the Lis, would never let their own starve. Yet she did not relish having to make her way through the dangerous factions of Honolulu Chinatown alone.

Three days after her bitter dispute with her husband, Lucy took to her bed again, incapacitated this time by a nervous stomach. Since Bosworth had gone to arrange for the transfer of mother and child, Lucy screamed for

Nalani to bring her a bowl of porridge. The Hawaiian woman was more recalcitrant than usual, and Lucy waited impatiently for Nalani's footfall on the stairs. To her great chagrin, instead of Nalani, Rulan appeared at the doorway.

Lucy sat up with a start. "Oh, it's *you*," she blurted out rudely. "I didn't want you."

"Nalani cannot come."

When Lucy saw the child cradled in a sling around its mother's shoulder, she grimaced and closed her eyes. "Take it away. You know how ill the crying makes me."

"Baby just sleeping, make no noise," Rulan said tersely. She took Lucy's pulse at the wrist, then lightly passed her hands over Lucy's limbs to gauge the heat of her body. "Not sick," she announced.

By way of answer, Lucy began to shriek for Nalani. Her shrill cries roused the child, who began making small mewing sounds. With a groan, Lucy turned her face into the covers and pounded her fist into the quilt.

Lucy's expostulations were interrupted by an unearthly scream from below and the clang of heavy iron falling on the stone hearth where Nalani had been thrashing about in the kitchen. Anger and apprehension had made Nalani careless and now she had burned her hands in the flame and dropped the pot of boiling water.

"Auwe, auwe," Nalani was lamenting. She called for Rulan with more impatience than Lucy had called for her. Rulan pushed the child into Lucy's arms, and ignoring the woman's protests, rushed downstairs to rescue Nalani from whatever disaster awaited in the kitchen.

Thrust from the warmth of its mother's body, the child began to whimper. "What shall I do? I am not a mother," Lucy wailed, her face as twisted with astonishment as the child's. She held the baby stiffly at arm's length as if it were a small cat about to scratch.

Not a mother! The words set in motion the familiar internal litany of shame. An accursed, barren thing. And why had she been punished so cruelly? For the sin of loving herself too well and her husband too little. Lucy had told herself that being loved was almost as good as loving, yet the wages of that sin was death-in-life, for Emmanuel's delight in a baby that was not of his own race was a blade thrust daily into her bosom.

Unnerved by the jostling, the child began to wail. "Stop it, you nasty creature," Lucy ordered. All her unhappiness seemed the fault of this squalling brat who had turned her household awry. When it continued its frenzied shrieking, Lucy scrambled from bed and shook it so hard that the small head wobbled back and forth. "I despise you!" she cried. The child was hardly heavier than a rubber ball. Nearly weightless, insubstantial, an annoying excrescence whose only reason for being seemed to ruin her comfort and ease. Lucy thought about flinging the squirming thing across the room to stop its noise and to quiet once and for all the pounding at her temples. "Stop it!" she shouted into its face, and shook it even harder.

Terrified, the child hiccupped and went suddenly breathless and rigid, its legs and arms flying out like knobby twigs. She looked at its face, which was frozen in a masklike expression of death! Had she killed it? A burst of wicked glee flashed over her like a passing flame . . . quickly followed by a wave of self-revulsion so profound that it brought her to her knees. She clutched the baby to her breast.

"Good Lord, what have I done!" she gasped.

The baby was inert, silent. She had not really wished it ill. No, she had only wanted to remove the agent of her shame from her presence. But now . . . Lucy Bosworth began to moan and rock the small, stiff creature in her arms.

She had clung to self-loathing as an undersea creature cleaves to a corrosive pearl; now fear melted that acrid lump away. Hugging the child tightly, she willed her own life into the baby, kissed its mottled, contorted face over and over, blew her own breath into its small open mouth.

The child shuddered, gasped, and howled into angry life. And now Lucy was tasting her own tears. "Oh oh, little minx, how you frightened me!" she said, pressing her face against the hot wet cheek, which was now as pink as her own.

When Rulan came through the door with a bowl of porridge, Lucy was lying with the child's head tucked against her chin. The baby was sleeping soundly against her breast. Now and again, Lucy kissed the soft spot at the top of the child's head where she could feel with her lips the tiny heart beating within.

"*H*ow plump our precious girl is getting," Lucy said fondly. The baby churned the air with her hands and feet, mad with delight at the sound of Lucy's voice. "Emmanuel was quite right to quit the Mission and begin the *Dispatch*. Otherwise, we might never have built this house away from Honolulu. Old Queen Kaahumanu must have intended to test your brothers and sisters of the First Mission Boat beyond their endurance when she gave them that dry wasteland for a compound. No wonder so many missionary children are colicky and weak." She put her face down to nuzzle the child tucked into her cradle in the kitchen. "I shall call her Molly," Lucy announced. "Her Chinese name is impossible. No matter how hard I try, there are notes in your tongue I simply cannot imitate."

"But you say my name," Rulan observed while stirring a boiling pot of jam made from orange *poha* berries.

"Not well, I suspect," Lucy retorted, and put a spoonful of the hot jam onto the bread. "Anyway, 'Molly' is the name for a heroine as militant as Molly's namesake, your warrior woman Mulan. Our own Molly Pitcher manned her husband's cannon when he succumbed to the heat during our Revolutionary War." She bit into the bread and grimaced. "More sugar."

"So many names—" interjected Rulan with a frown. "How will this girl know who she is?" She took a knife and cut a large wedge from a brown cone of raw cane sugar on a shelf. The Bosworths' immense appetite for sweets appalled her.

"All island children have two names. *Haole* name for go church and school, family name for love," Nalani interjected. "So the dowager queen is Emma to you but we Hawaiians call her Kaleleonalani, a sad name for a sad lady. And you call me Nalani, but church folks call me Ruth."

Rulan decided that as confusing as it was, the Hawaiian system of double names pleased her. With two names for her two heritages—one of blood, the other of place—her daughter was rich indeed. Gravely considering the options, Rulan broke the cake of sugar over the simmering pot and watched it melt into the steaming jam as little Molly began clamoring to be fed.

Lucy was overjoyed that she need not wait a year to make a party for Molly. A Chinese child's birth was celebrated after it survived its first month, Nalani had told her. "We'll bring the ladies in Chinatown up to Hiamoe to celebrate our girl's one-month birthday," Lucy enthused. "What's that family Rulan has talked about, the one that owns the fish stalls near Nuuanu Stream?"

"Li family. Them fella no good," Nalani declared sourly. "Leave alone. No make party."

"Don't be absurd. How could old friends not share her joy! Manny says all the Chinese in Hawaii come from a few districts in the Pearl River Delta. That makes the Lis practically her relations." Lucy laughed delightedly at the thought of another "auntie" and "uncle" for Molly.

"No!" Nalani said. "Two kind Chinese folks—Hakka and Punti. Both hate each other. No eat same, no talk same. Rulan Hakka, Li family Punti."

"Vain stupidity to cleave to these old rivalries," Lucy declared primly. "How can the Chinese dislike each other, since they are by appearance and custom one people? Do I, a woman from New Hampshire, turn my nose up at Dr. Hunnicut from Boston because I pour my syrup on pancakes and he bakes his with beans? Here in Hawaii, all of us from the States acknowledge each other as American."

"How Yankee call fella from South? How you call that Gibson fella work for the king?" scoffed Nalani.

"Mormons like Walter Murray Gibson are not Christians, and Confederates are beneath contempt," Lucy shot back.

"Li fella no like Rulan alla same."

"Well! 'Alla same' make peace between those parties," Lucy declared, and she coaxed Emmanuel into digging out his Chinese dictionary and copying out the appropriate Chinese characters on red paper invitations that she sent to the matriarch of the Li family and the handful of merchants' wives of Chinatown. Each envelope came back with the seal broken, the invitation intact, and no reply.

*A*t the turn of the year, the weather grew humid and dank. Thick clouds, great-bellied with moisture, hung over the parched earth. Having no cranberry or pumpkin, Lucy strained the black seeds out of wild *lilikoi* fruit and stirred the orange pulp into holiday pies, while in the China quarter, one sold whatever one could for cash to pay off old debts, as custom decreed, before the end of the Chinese calendar year. Soon the steaming rains beat down mercilessly upon Honolulu. Following the riotous Honolulu holiday season, marked by parades by the court and the usual round of holiday parties in the local embassies, came the Chinatown bachelors' desultory marking of the lunar new year. A few of the wealthier merchants hung paper lanterns outside their stores and set off strings of firecrackers to mark the passing of one year into the next. Yet without women to take charge of the holiday cooking or the painstaking nurturing of bulbs, the festival passed without the usual fried sesame buns and narcissus flowers forced into early bloom.

Molly celebrated her one-month birthday surrounded by a *hanai,* or adopted, uncle; two *hanai* aunties; and her own mother. There were spice cakes and a pie of mashed sweet potatoes for the grown-ups, a spoonful of *haupia,* a pudding of sweetened coconut milk for Molly, and presents: a doll with a porcelain head from Lucy, a quilt sewn by Nalani with a patchwork design in the shape of a *hala* tree, a miniature rocking chair built by Bosworth, and two tiny shoes of red satin sewn by Rulan.

In the late afternoon, mother and child went out into the yard to sleep off the effects of the birthday feast. The sun, which had sprung that morning from behind the razor-edged *Pali,* had soared past its zenith on its way toward the sea. Far below, a lone whaling ship floated as idly as a leaf on a silent stream, and in the channel beyond, the steamship *Kilauea* carried rum and molasses and a load of ebullient passengers on its weekly run between Maui and Oahu.

Despite the joyousness of the occasion, a melancholy had descended upon Rulan like a curtain's gradual effacing of light. Lately, her body ached continually for the absent Pao An, just as an amputee still feels a tingling in the place where the severed limb had been. Hidden away at Hiamoe, she had become as immobile as rock-bound Lahilahi sleeping beneath the moon.

The sun warmed her back as she drowsily stroked her daughter's downy black hair. *Molly,* she whispered, putting down her face to smell the infant's cheek, as fond mothers do in China. This tiny creature was all she had of him. What kind of world had she brought Pao An's child into? She had bathed Molly in rainwater scented with a medicinal leaf whose Hawaiian name she did not yet know. There were so many things in Hawaii that reminded her of China. The same fish darted in the ponds; the same plants grew along the canals; even the mist rising off the red earth reminded her of the waterlogged tropical terrain of Kwangtung. But in these islands, the essence of things had altered; the forms might be familiar, yet things had new properties, unpredictable consequences. She clutched the child to her breast, wishing that flesh were not so fragile. Soon mother and child were half dreaming in a garden hung with banana, breadfruit, hibiscus, and red torch ginger.

They dozed uneasily through a shifting curtain of rain. The sun began its long, slow arc into the sea. The whaling ship, which had chased the ocean in vain for the disappearing leviathan, had now dropped anchor and was met by outriggers piled high with rope and rice, salt beef and cakes of brown sugar. Nalani came out from the kitchen to hang a load of wet clothes on a line that stretched from the trunk of a coconut tree to a nail in the side of the house. She peeked at the sleeping child, pausing to tuck the blanket tightly around its bare belly before going inside. And still mother and child slept.

The breeze from the sea changed direction. The scent of wild ginger, *maile,* and the crushed petals of plumeria blossoms floated down from the *Pali* as the sun slipped behind a thick bank of clouds. Rulan awoke with a jolt, the child heavy and wet against her chest, and found herself in a circle of fallen breadfruit black with flies. Diapers, shirts, and trousers danced and snapped on a nearby clothesline and for a moment, Rulan thought groggily that she was back on the battlefield with the Taiping flags flapping in the wind and the warrior women calling to each other. Then the voices coalesced into a string of piercing cries, like the shrieking of a seabird. A small Tang woman dressed in a black satin coat and embroidered slippers was shuffling across the yard, calling *"Wei, wei."* The face was an angry apparition: crimson lips and kohl-darkened eyes that glared out from a visage powdered stark white. Rulan shook herself out of her torpor and turned to face Li Mei Yuk.

"You hide among the barbarians to conspire against me," Mei Yuk said in the high-pitched, breathless voice Rulan remembered so well. "And the hairy *bak kuei* with the voice like a gong goes into Chinatown to ask impertinent questions, stirring up old troubles!" Mei Yuk pursed her lips and uttered a string of ugly nasal sounds, Cantonese with a mock-"barbarian" accent. " 'Who knows Chen Pao An? A big *gu li,*' your *bak kuei* says. 'His wife and child are waiting in the big house up Nuuanu.' " Mei Yuk grimaced, as if the foreign-sounding words made her ill. "You mean to shame me, but I will not give satisfaction!" With a quick movement of her fingers, she yanked away the child's blanket, exposing the small sleeping face and rosy foot. "I came to inspect the creature."

"Don't touch her," Rulan declared angrily, pulling the child close. Jarred suddenly out of slumber, the infant began to cry. How foolish to think one could escape old hatreds simply by taking ship to Hawaii. The old world, a jealous harridan coveting even the children it despised, had found her.

Mei Yuk's fingernail stabbed the place where the small foot had dangled. "Is it his?"

"Ours." Rulan uttered the word with great care, knowing that her own happiness had been won at Mei Yuk's expense.

"My son is dead!" Mei Yuk blurted out. "You have a worthless girl, I have a worthless girl. Which one will be the beauty?" Her painted mouth was an ugly slash of red, and her eyes darted from mother to child. Drawing an anguished breath, she murmured, "I ask myself, why did our Second Lady come to Hawaii? Does she know Liang Mo is rich again? Does she come to steal my money, my business, my place, just as she once stole . . ." The outburst ended in a strangled sputter, then her voice rose again, thick with hate. "But I am *Tai Tai* in his house! You were never more than our bond maid, our slave, so the creature is ours to take, to sell . . ."

Rulan shoved Mei Yuk aside. "Don't touch her!" she screamed, and still Mei Yuk pressed closer.

Their angry shouts and the baby's terrified cries brought Lucy Bosworth hastening across the muddy yard. "Here now, Rulan, give Molly to me," she demanded.

As Lucy gathered the child into her arms, Mei Yuk pulled the blanket away. "Pletee gel, so nicee face. So bew-ti-ful," Mei Yuk purred in broken, singsong English.

"Yes, we think our girl quite lovely," Lucy replied warmly. But at that moment, Mei Yuk began a rhythmical chant in Cantonese that turned Lucy's blood cold. The long scarlet fingernails brushed the child's fine features.

With an anguished cry, Rulan slapped the woman's pale, powdered cheek. "Get out," she ordered. "Get away from my daughter!"

Instantly, the chant died in Mei Yuk's throat. "Pletee gel, so nicee," Mei Yuk repeated. Her lips parted in a dazzling smile even as the marks from Rulan's fingers spread upon her face. And then she was gone, moving faster on her mutilated feet than Lucy thought was possible.

Lucy bounced the wailing child on one hip. "What was that awful person saying to the child to make you act in such a way?" she asked in bewilderment.

Rulan was trembling as hard as Lucy. "It's the way Tang people curse," she said gasping. "After a child is born, mothers scold and insult it, complain out loud of its ugliness so jealous demons, *kuei,* will pass the child by." The terrible knot of grief inside her suddenly burst, and Rulan began to weep. "But this woman was calling on the *kuei* to punish this child, *my* child, for her beauty. 'Such beauty,' she said, 'must be paid for in suffering.' She asked the *kuei* to make sure Molly will never be welcomed by the one she loves, never find comfort in a man's arms, never find a proper home."

All color had drained from Lucy Bosworth's cheeks. She was a woman of the West, holding fast to a God of justice and mercy; something shrank inside her at the notion of ghosts and curses. "She cannot hurt you," Lucy assured Rulan shakily as the child's frenzied wailing echoed in her ears. "You are far from that world of superstition now."

"This is how you will know your father," Rulan said while tracing a pattern with her fingertips on her infant daughter's face. Lying together in their little room that night, Rulan spoke in her native Hakka dialect to the infant whose wide, wondering eyes drank in the healing words that would repel the malediction uttered by the vengeful matriarch of the Lis.

"In the broad planes of his face you shall see the deltas and plateaus of the Land of Flowers," she said while touching the tiny ridge of bone beneath the milk-soft cheek. "His forehead is marked with two creases like the rivers that cut across the empire."

When the infant smiled toothlessly and made soft bubbling noises, Rulan kissed the mouth that was a small replica of Pao An's. "He spoke with kings," she said. "Before we two fled, he was the fiercest of the rebels." She saw again in memory Pao An riding at the head of the rebel army, his long hair tied at the back, holding a twelve-foot pike as easily as a staff. "His skin is worked by sun and wind, his body scarred by war," she told the child proudly.

Her fingertip tickled her daughter's small nose. The child shivered and made a small plosive sound. Startled by her own voice, she began to cry.

"No, no," scolded the mother softly, "you must not fear that warrior face. This man is gentle. This man is good. He will hold you safely in the circle of his arms."

7

THE WHITE WOMAN

San Joaquin River Delta

Pao An was weightless, tossed skyward on a column of noise. An instant later, he plunged downward, crashing into the churning river. Brackish water filled his nose and mouth, burned his eyes. He fought wildly against the deadly tugging of the current, hearing the *slap, slap, slap* of objects striking the water. When his head broke through to the surface, he sucked down air in painful gasps and saw through sore eyes that pieces of wood, bits of ash, jagged shards of metal and glass were plummeting out of the sky like broken birds. A dozen yards away, the ferry's shattered and burning hull was slipping below the surface of the river.

The little girl who had been dancing with the dwarf floated toward him. Pao An grabbed her by the hair, rolled her face out of the water, then wished he had not. Quickly, he let go of the bright strand, and watched her drift away on a sheet of reddening foam. Her braids bobbed behind her like pale seaweed.

He reminded himself that in war and devastation, one survived carnage only by an effort of indifference; so he made his heart grow numb, disengaged his mind from the blood and screams and the acrid smell of burned flesh. Thinking only of his next breath, he struck out for shore. A searing pain shot through his right arm whenever he lifted it. Still, he drove his broken body on.

Twenty yards from the beach, his left hand struck the body of a man. It was Creel, knocked unconscious by the blast. A cloud of dark blood rose up behind him as he drifted past. Remembering the gun Creel had pointed at him, Pao An was sorely tempted to let the man drown, but at that moment, Creel's eyes fluttered and he gave a frightful groan. Wearily, Pao An hoisted the wounded man up on a shattered section of the hull, wishing it was the golden-haired child he could have saved.

Pao An paddled with his awkward burden through smoke and ash and the ruined timbers of the *Yosemite* toward shore. Half-conscious, Creel coughed, retched, and dragged his right leg slowly onto the float. The toe of his black leather boot was hacked out, as if some beast had taken a bite of leather and flesh. A shred of woolen stocking hung down, dripping blood.

They were not the first survivors to reach the safety of the riverbank: Ah Jack was already there, planted in the shallows where the blast had hurled him. The overseer was seated with arms akimbo and legs outspread, staring at an object bobbing toward him like a ball. Suddenly, he began to laugh maniacally. He reached down, plucked a plate-shaped object off the ball and stuck it on the shaved dome of his head. Pao An saw then that Ah Jack had put on the banjo player's porkpie hat and what was floating between the overseer's spindly legs was the banjo player's head.

*O*nce ashore, Nathan Creel came sputtering and cursing to life, but the agony of his wound sobered him instantly. Still, he refused to let a doctor treat him. "Seen more men die in the war from dang fool surgeons than Yankee guns," he muttered to Pao An, white-lipped with pain. "I'll do my own doctorin'."

Creel made the two Chinamen drag him to the general store to buy tin snips, a bottle of whiskey, and three cigars. Then he limped outside and sat on the wooden walk with his mangled foot stretched before him. Uncorking the whiskey, he drank half the bottle in long gulping swallows, wiped his chin, and leaned his head against the side of the building for a long moment. Then he took the cigars out of his breast pocket and passed one to each man. "We're in this together," he said, and lit one for himself.

His speech was already slurring from the whiskey when he shoved the tin snips into Ah Jack's hands. "Cut that bastard down, Jack," he said. The overseer, haggard from his ordeal on the water, cut the thick leather boot from top to bottom with trembling fingers. When the boot and sock were off, Creel took another long draw on the whiskey bottle and examined the damage. The tip of his big toe to the quick of the nail was gone; only a splintered bone projected from the raw and oozing flesh. He wiggled the bloody stub slowly, tears coursing out of his eyes.

"Still good to the joint," he gasped. "We gonna cut it there." He motioned to Ah Jack to begin, but the overseer could only stare at the wound, unable to move.

"Goddammit," Creel said. "I ain't gonna rot away 'cause you're too damn squeamish." Ah Jack flung down the shears and backed away, shaking his head. "All right, you, then," Creel ordered Pao An, struggling to keep the desperation from his voice. "It's 'cause of you I shot my toe off in the first place. Right there," he said. "Do it!" and pointed to the lacerated joint.

When Pao An picked up the shears, Creel hastily pulled on the bottle and inhaled deeply on his cigar. Pao An mimicked Creel, grateful for the tobacco's dizzying hold, then positioned the jaws at the joint.

"Do it clean," Creel gasped out, shaking with pain and whiskey, "or I'll cut your balls off." Creel put the cork of the whiskey bottle in his teeth and bit hard. The scream began deep in his gullet, rose higher and higher, and was suddenly choked off in a series of animal grunts. Soon, he lay twisted against the building, his mouth and lips bloody where he had bitten the cork clear through. Moaning, he took another draw on his cigar, kept sucking until the ash glowed red at the tip. Then he pushed it onto the stub of his toe and passed out.

*W*hile Creel was still unconscious, Pao An poured whiskey over the mangled foot and wrapped it in a torn piece of Creel's shirt. Creel awoke an hour later, vomited out the whiskey, and turned his attention to the business of replacing his team of dead coolies. "You got to get me a new crew," he ordered Ah Jack.

"Where find? No can go back China," Ah Jack shot back wearily.

"I don't give a Yankee's damn where. Steal 'em from the railroad. You get me fifty workers in two weeks," Creel muttered, sick to his stomach and groggy with pain. Ah Jack went off cursing ferociously at the tightfisted white devil. Once signed, Tang men's contracts were not negotiable, and the railroad was not about to part with good men. Yet there were ways. A railroad man could die at night in his tent, yet turn up elsewhere in a day or two having conveniently changed his name. Tang men always "died" after monthly pay day; that way there were more dollars to spread around.

With the survivors of the explosion stampeding out of Rio Vista, Creel had to fight off desperate men and women to reclaim the rig he had left behind in the livery stable. Struggling into the seat, he ordered Pao An to take the reins, then directed him out of town toward the marshy Delta. They passed the night rolled up in the back of the buggy in their torn, bloody clothes.

Pao An awoke in a cold sweat, too exhausted to care that the man who had aimed a gun at his head was snoring and mumbling in delirium beside him. An owl moaned in a stand of trees: an evil omen, a harbinger of death. How much death could one man stand? Pao An wondered. Creel's foul smell and feverish mutterings made further sleep impossible. Pao An watched the stars until the dawn snuffed them out. The weakest died first and finally the strong.

When the sun reached the peak of the doubled-horned mountain, Creel awoke, complaining of cramps and fever. Yet despite his weakness, he insisted that they push on toward Invictus Island, half a day's journey away.

He talked without pause. "Three hundred twenty acres of pear and peaches. Planted fifteen years ago by a Swede," he whispered feverishly, without bothering to ask if Pao An understood or not. "A crazy old cuss who got crazier living out there alone in the middle of a shit swamp. Swedes ain't got the guts for muck. They can eat snow and iron-sided trees and hardscrabble for breakfast, lunch, and dinner. Swedes be about as tough as men get. But it ain't heart it takes to live in the swamp. Ain't brains neither. It's a good gut. Kind don't come down with dys'ntry, 'skeeter poison, snakebite, sweat fungus, foot rot . . ."

It was not simply fever that made Creel talk to a despised Chinaman, Pao An surmised, but some need to justify the fact that he had not died with the others on the river. He was telling himself an old, old story, reinventing himself out of the struggle of men to tame the waterlogged land.

"First white men been working here since the forties. Right after the Rush some smart forty-niners figured land was better 'n gold. My neighbors, that's Reuben Konrad and his family, started shaping Grand Island out of what was no more than muck between sloughs. They built levees. Puny, thin little things at first, but he pushed 'em up each year. 'Bout fifteen years ago the State Reclamation Commission got over a million acres of bottom land from the federal government and plumb give it away to anyone who claimed they build levees. Naturally the speck'lators poured in, and just as naturally I missed sucking off'n the public tit.

"But the speck'lators got washed away in the floods of the year after. Ripped hell outta the Sacramento levees and tore like a steamboat through the Delta islands. There was nothin', hear? Nothin' left between Sacramento and the bay but muddy water. Reuben told me he and his slept in rowboats tied to the strongest tree for a week while the rain beat down."

Without knowing all the words themselves, Pao An understood Creel's meaning. He too came from people who had been rained on and washed out. He too had suffered the destructive power of a river and recognized the attempts of men to control, however vainly, the angry waters.

"When we got here in '62 there was grain as well as trees on the island. Pears, peaches, grape arbors, furrows of vegetables as far as your eye could see. We put in a garden, missus did. Puny little garden. Onliest damn thing that made money first year. Put in potatoes, the next. Potatoes command a good price in Sacramento and the downriver towns, but that's the kind of dirt-scrape farming I hate." He spat in disgust. "Vera did it. Worked like a mule, that woman. I did too. Set out little apricot trees in back, be good crop in ten years more, she says. In the swamp you gotta build in waiting time. *Long* waiting time. I can't stand staring at the dirt, waiting for green to come up. Money so scarce I took a contract with a hydraulic mining company. I got a share, short share, of the gold we washed out. Now I'm building levees too—and there damned well gonna be profit come hell or dead coolies! Unnerstand?" His cheeks burning with fever, Creel turned to Pao An in an unexpected burst of fury. "All this time I been talkin' and you don't understand shit, do ya?"

In fact, Pao An did understand *shit*. It was one familiar word in his rapidly growing vocabulary. Moreover, he could read Creel's anger better than Creel himself.

"I could tell you just what I think of you yella bastard and you'd never be the wiser, would ya?" Creel asked. He gave Pao An an evil smile and lowered his voice. "I think you ain't human. You're a rat stretched out to the shape of a man. You're a shit-eatin', piss-drinking, peckerless . . . Hell," he muttered, "who the hell are you that I should waste my breath," and lapsed into a sick, sullen silence.

What Pao An understood of Creel's spiteful declamation were the words *man, shit, gold,* and *hell* as well as the speaker's hateful intent. It mattered little to Pao An that Creel despised him and his race. What did matter was that the man to whom Ah Jack kowtowed owed him his life. An angry man who carried such a debt was the easiest character to predict.

The richness of the low-lying waterlogged earth did not escape Pao An's notice as he drove the buggy down the rutted dirt road that followed the Sacramento River on its winding course south, then west to where it joined the San Joaquin. The peat-rich soil could have supported ten thousand villages in South China; yet except for a few humans as rash as Creel, only beaver and waterfowl inhabited it. Like the Pearl River Delta where Pao An had eked out a meager living with his father, water was more scourge than blessing here.

After they had traveled a few more miles, Creel awoke from his intermittent sleep and pointed to a small dwelling beyond the flat expanse of tules and reeds. It stood by the riverbank, solitary and unpainted, in a copse of blackjack, sycamore, live oak, and drooping willow. In the distance lay a mound of black earth in too aberrant a shape to be anything but manmade. "That there's a Indian graveyard," Creel said, seeing Pao An eyeing the knoll. "Some say there's gold in it, but they that says it are as dumb as dirt. And hell, I didn't come here to dig gold anyways. I come to plant. All gold is fool's gold, far as I'm concerned."

Creel's farm lay on the apron of Invictus Island, a low-lying bar of mud fronting the river for a mile. The trees were small and still bare of fruit. Pao An took note of the garden, the neat plots of potatoes and the six cows in a rail-fenced pasture behind the barn. A rude dwelling of bare plank walls rose upon a stone foundation. But the garden was well tended and from what he could see of the barn, someone kept tools and supplies in good order.

Creel had told Pao An everything but the part of his story that really mattered: how he came to the Delta and why, despite all his failures, he stayed. The Swede had a daughter who seemed to come with the farm. The Swede was tired of living like Noah, and the daughter wasn't going anywhere with that mean old bastard, she said. Creel told her she could stay on.

Vera was twenty-three and he thirty when they threw in with each other. They never did marry "proper"—but proper didn't count for much in the swamp. So Creel bought the place for a thousand dollars, and he and Vera worked the farm themselves for the better part of a year. She worked, this woman, he'd give her that. Together, they tilled the deep, dark Delta land, so like the land he had left behind in Mississippi, with rich soil laid down over the eons by the river. In some places, the peat was ten feet deep. Perfect for raising anything, Creel believed, even though nothing seemed to grow for him. Money ran out quicker than the fruit came in, and then the fungus came. Although he dug irrigation ditches through the orchards and tended the trees as if they were his children, the trees were slow in giving fruit. Only Vera's potato patch brought in a little cash. So Creel tied up with a small construction outfit, a limited stock company formed by a San Francisco bank. Bossing coolies was lucrative work, yet Creel despised himself for having to stoop so low.

As they drove around the house and tied up in the back near the barn, a tall woman in a dark dress walked slowly out of the house. She had broad features, wide shoulders, and work-reddened hands, which she was drying on her apron. Fine, light strands had come loose from the bun at the back of her head and rose above her brow like a halo. Her eyebrows were almost invisible in the bright sunlight, making the shadows around her eyes all the more pronounced.

She walked slowly up to the horse and patted its head, studying her husband's hastily bandaged foot dispassionately. "Ferry came downriver last night, some feller yelled out 'bout that 'splosion." Her lips were parted in an expression that made her seem dull-witted. "Ya hurt?"

"Not much," Creel replied. Climbing down from the buggy, he tried to stand and found himself grimacing in pain. But he forced himself to walk to the house unaided. He gestured toward the barn. "Put the team inside," he said to Pao An.

The woman's face darkened. "That one staying? You know I can't stand his kind."

"He's staying," Creel snapped, without bothering to wait for a reply.

Day in and day out, Vera wore a long skirt and white blouse gathered at the yoke with a high buttoned collar and long sleeves. She carried a bit of old flannel tucked in the waistband of her skirt for wiping her brow or blowing her nose. She was not as plain as he first believed, Pao An observed, merely disdainful of ornamentation. It had been a long time since he had been near a woman, and he found Vera dexterous and neat. One morning, she used a hot fluting iron, which rested on a crimped iron pad. Working quickly to smooth the edges of a clean blouse, she moved the tip of the iron skillfully in and out of the corners of the pleats without singeing the cloth.

What eloquence Vera possessed was in her hands, for she seemed entirely uninterested in anything beside the immediate task she was performing. Neither husband nor wife had much to say to the other, and Pao An could not tell if it was resentment or simply reticence before a stranger that made the house so silent. But listening to the Creels' halting, uneasy conversation, Pao An pieced together a working knowledge of the foreign tongue.

Creel was soon hobbling about the farm trying to repair what had gone awry in his absence. He took Pao An into his toolshed and taught him the name of each implement. Pao An recognized the ax, the chisel, and wooden mallet that drove the sharp flat edge into the wood; but Creel's shed held enough iron tools for a man to build himself an entire city out of Gold Mountain's forests. There were digging tools; cutting tools; boring tools with spoon bits and twisted bits and round bits; a solid iron device called a plane in the shape of a small boat, which shaved wood as smooth as a woman's skin. Huge devices with iron teeth for cutting wood—the largest with handles at each end so that two men could rip an entire log into boards for building—and most interesting of all to Pao An, iron nails: a round head fitted over a sharp square shank, which Creel said were once made by hand in his grandfather's time from horseshoes and were now stamped out by the thousands in factories on the east coast. Then Creel sent Pao An out to clear irrigation ditches with a shovel, to prune trees with hook and saw, and to fix fences with a posthole digger.

The sun had gone down behind the twin purple peaks of Mount Diablo and the more distant shadow of Mount Tamalpais when Pao An came back after a day of dredging the marshes alone. Creel was on the front porch looking out despondently across the levee to the sloughs, the marsh-lands that covered the Delta, with his leg propped up on the rail. The foot had never quite healed and now the torn joint pained him incessantly; he stuffed wads of paper into the toe of his boot, but his balance was still bad. The smell of frying meat came from Vera's kitchen, and Pao An remembered that he had not eaten the entire day.

"This'll be a damn fine country someday," Creel said, by way of greeting. "Men got to die in it first, though. Way it always is. Got to put bones in the earth before it be worth anything." He glanced quickly at Pao An, as if he had showed too much about himself. But Pao An, who was squatting against the wall looking out over the river, showed neither emotion nor understanding. Creel shrugged, acknowledging the futility of communicating with such a dumb beast, and sank back into reverie. "I was born in river-bottom land near like this," he murmured to himself.

"I too," Pao said.

"That so?" Creel shot back. So astonished was he to hear the coolie respond in his own tongue that he blurted out, "Somehow I figured China was all mountains and deserts. Seen a map of it onct. Colored all yella, just like y'all. Figured it was all sand."

"Three river go 'cross China," Pao An said. He stretched his arms wide. "Big like so." Although he could mime the size of the immense waterways that cut across the empire, he had no words to tell Creel how ancient were the Hwang Ho, the Yangtze, and his own Pearl. "Here my house," he said pointing to a knot on the porch boards. "Here river." He drew an imaginary line in a great curve about it indicating with additional swipes of his fingers the streamlets and canals that cut across the soggy land.

"Don't that beat all. You and me mudflat boys." Creel leaned over the edge of the porch and spat out a mouthful of tobacco juice. "You had a farm?"

Pao An nodded. How long since he had thought of the tiny plot that he and his father worked in On Ting, the Chen clan village?

"Don't guess it's still standing or you wouldn't be here. What happened?"

"War come." Pao An brushed his hand across the knot on the board, signifying how rebellion had blown the farm, the village, and all the inhabitants away.

Creel shivered. "I had land too. Lost it all, three thousand acres, in the war." Turning, Creel saw the Chinaman's face outlined by the setting sun so that the bones of his skull were visible. "How big your farm?"

Pao An pointed to a tree on the riverbank, then to a rock on the far shore, an expanse less than three acres.

"That's pitiful small," observed Creel. Suddenly embarrassed by the fragile connection forged between him and his hired hand, Creel said brusquely, "Best go in. Missus'll have gravy and biscuits out by now."

And Vera was indeed at that moment spooning flour and lard from the tin bucket of drippings into a sizzling pan. There were boiled potatoes and great slabs of side meat and a pot of rice that she put out for Pao An with undisguised contempt. The rice was overboiled and too soft for his taste, but he accepted it politely, saving the remainder for eating cold, rolled into balls, as his midday meal.

They ate in silence, and when the meal was over, Creel ordered his wife to make coffee. She took a tin down from a shelf and held it out to her husband. "Not enough for the two of us, let alone three. Need salt and flour too, now that we got a guest from *Cathay*," she said with mocking emphasis. It was the most Pao An had ever heard her say.

"I didn't ask for no damn shopping list. I asked for coffee," Creel roared.

Vera rose, her cheeks flaming, went to the cupboard and took down the grinder from the shelf where she kept her tins. She scooped out the coffee beans, making sure that Creel heard the spoon scraping the bottom of the canister, then measured out the "stretchers," two spoonfuls of barley and two of rye, into the mill and ground them fine. She worked slowly and deliberately, emptying the fine powder into the big tin pot, measuring out water from a jug and setting the pot on the fire. Then she came back to the table. Sat, said nothing.

When the coffee had boiled for five minutes, Vera poured out one cup for Creel and sat down with the other. There was none for Pao An, her actions made clear.

Creel sipped his coffee reflectively. "I was thinking tonight," Creel said, " 'bout ol' Terry, friend of mine." He blew across the steaming surface of his cup and sucked loudly at the brim. "How a bear come up against us one winter when we's sleepin' in a cave and . . ."

"That idjut don't know what yer talking about, and I heard it before," Vera said sharply.

In a flash, Creel had leaned across the table and struck her across the mouth. "Don't you dispute me, woman. Don't *trash* never dispute me," he shouted.

Vera rushed out of the kitchen and slammed the door of their room. Creel continued to sip his coffee noisily. After a moment, Pao An went outside. He walked down to where a willow grew at an odd angle out of the riverbank and slumped down on the damp soil. He would find Ah Jack. He would bribe, even fight the overseer to end his contract with this loveless couple who played out their hatred like two angry parents before a silent child.

Passing the house on his way to the barn, he heard the flat slap of leather on flesh, and Vera's muffled cries, then, something that sounded like a man strangling with agony, and a woman moaning with pleasure or pain.

"*I* can't stand to eat with that one gawkin' at me," Vera whispered angrily to Creel at dinner the next day. "You know how them Chinks is with white women."

Creel's chuckle was devoid of humor. "Take a look-see in the mirror lately, Clementine?" he growled through a mouthful of ham. "Nothin' there for a man to get too het up after. Anyways, everybody knows China-men got no juice. They go for years without studdin'. Made that way." He poured a moat of maple syrup around a small mountain of sweet potatoes and mashed it down with his fork. "Set down and eat," he ordered Pao An who stood at the far end of the kitchen behind a table groaning with platters of overcooked vegetables and bloody slabs of meat, wondering how he could swallow such unpalatable fare without insulting his employer. "The missus ain't much to look at, but she do know how to set a table."

Vera's face seemed to crumple from within. She ignored Pao An during the entire meal, and for a while thereafter, made no complaint about his presence at the farm. At the table, she averted her face and pointedly refused to hand anything to him directly. Pao An's continued courtesy confounded her. Vera would have been astonished to know that what passed for rudeness in her culture was proper feminine modesty in his. Given his wife's decorous behavior, Pao An was puzzled by Creel's continued ill treatment of her. Husband and wife came together only in bed, and that juncture, Pao An judged, was less than satisfying, for within days of his

homecoming, Creel began spending long evenings playing cards and drinking homemade brandy with the Konrads, whose property lay on Grand
Island across the river from Creel's Invictus Island farm.

*I*t was a fallow time between seasons of growing and harvesting; the
repairs went quickly with Pao An carrying out the backbreaking labor
under the ferocious supervision of the increasingly debilitated Creel. His
wound had festered, and a doctor had had to come out from Antioch to
amputate the now gangrenous toe. With Creel laid up for a week, Pao An
dug out irrigation ditches, cut down trees that had died over the winter,
caulked the windows of the house with clay dug out of the riverbanks.

On a day so overcast that one could not tell where the dark sky ended
and the low-lying Delta islands began, the two men set traps for gophers
whose tunnels weakened the levees, then returned famished and mud-
splattered to the house. Vera was making butter in a rotating churn. She
had hitched up her skirts, revealing one white leg to the thigh, and was
grinding the iron handle in a steady rhythm. Damp tendrils of yellow hair
had fallen across her sweaty brow and her face was red with exertion. When
the backdoor opened, she whirled around, almost knocking the churn off
the counter.

"You!" she said to Creel.

"Who the hell you expecting?" Creel retorted, dragging his foot to the
stove to pour himself a cup of coffee. Pao An stood at the door, staring at
the firm white flesh of her thigh, not knowing whether to enter or go to
the barn.

"We're hungry," Creel stated and motioned Pao An to sit. "Fry us up
some eggs."

Vera's face took on a mulish look. She brushed down her skirts and put
her hands back on the churn. "I got to finish up this butter or it'll curdle on
me," she answered and began cranking the handle again.

Creel's face reddened. He raised his cup, about to fling the hot coffee
into the back of her head, when Pao An moved between them. "I do it,"
he said, putting out his hand for the churn.

Vera's eyes flicked over him as she relinquished the churn into his
grasp. "Eggs is in the cellar," she said dully to her husband while wiping
her hands on her apron. "I ain't goin' down there myself. Cold weather
done run the field mice in. You know what that means."

Creel smiled. "Means the serpent's in your house, Mrs. Adam. Means
temptation's knocking on your door. Means your man wants some takin'
care of," Creel said, in high good humor at her acquiescence. He had spent

his recuperation fashioning choke traps for mice by drilling holes with an augur in a wooden block and setting handmade wire springs. Vera wanted the traps everywhere: behind the stove, in the cupboards and especially in the cellar to eliminate the rattlesnakes that fed on the mice.

"Fetch me them eggs and I'll cook 'em," Vera repeated warily.

"I'll fetch you more than that, darlin'," Creel said, brushing her ample bottom as he passed. He stumped down into the root cellar and came back with eggs and part of a salted ham hock.

Along with the eggs and side meat, Vera stirred up a batch of biscuits, which they spread with the butter Pao An had made. They wolfed the food in silence, as was their habit, and when they had done eating, Pao An went out to make up his place in the barn while Creel took his unwilling wife to bed.

Why, Pao An wondered, did an otherwise strong woman capitulate to a man she clearly despised? Why didn't she leave? Yet after watching Vera at her household tasks, he decided that enduring Creel's unwelcome caresses was the price Vera paid for the house she clearly loved. He saw the care with which she plucked the dry husks from the bean stalks in her garden and how lovingly she polished her kitchen implements. She could never pass a shelf without touching the articles set out upon it—a crock of sugar, a line of tin mugs—as if comforting herself with the fact of her possessions. She seemed happiest in her kitchen, banging pots and pans in a cloud of fragrant steam. The black cast-iron stove, which had come around the Horn, was her pride. Standing on lion claws, it had three doors in front, six lidded pot holes, and a side well for heating water. She cooked for Creel and Pao An three times a day, and when she was not stirring up dishes for the next meal, she was salting, preserving, canning for the starving future.

The dirt cellar that she was afraid to enter held potatoes, knee-high crocks of black and green olives, green tomatoes packed in brine, ironstone jars of beets, string beans, wax peppers, cucumbers—all the remains of the summer's bounty. She also stored preserves of peaches, apricots, and wild grapes, which Creel dearly loved. Every morning he took his coffee with a thick slice of bread toasted on a wire rack over the open lid of the stove, and slathered with a half inch of yellow butter and Vera's preserves.

In Pao An's daydreams, Vera was always associated with food.

"We need some rabbits kilt," Vera said to Creel one morning over the remains of their breakfast. She brushed back a loose strand of yellow hair that had fallen out of her kerchief, adding with studied nonchalance,

"Maybe that 'un can do it." Her eyes flicked without emotion over Pao An. "A dozen pelts can buy me a barrel of sugar."

"Don't reckon you ever skinned a rabbit, have ye?" Creel asked Pao An, rising with a satisfied groan from the table.

Pao An shook his head, wondering why the woman always talked as if he weren't there.

"Come on then. I'll show you onct. You do the rest." Creel hobbled out to the hutches that were kept on the wind-protected side of the barn. The pungent odor of rabbit feces assaulted Pao An's nose as they approached. The little beasts seemed to shit more than they ate, for mounds of round pellets stood under each wire cage in which the rabbits were kept. The rabbits began leaping over each other in frenzy as Creel opened the door of the hutch. Reaching in quickly, he caught a black-and-white one by the hind leg. It beat its other leg frantically and scooted away, its eyes wide and terrified, but Creel held on, got hold of the ears with his other hand and yanked the fat buck out.

"You have to do this sweet or there's a damn mess later," Creel said. "Watch right close." He held the kicking, twisting animal over a tree stump, and hit it sharply behind the head to break its neck. Instantly, it went limp. Next he took it to a spot at the side of the barn where he had nailed up a skinning board. The board had two three-inch-long square nails pounded through from the back. He took the rabbit's hind legs and forced the nail through the ankle joint. Then he made a clean circular cut around the feet, loosened the skin with his knife and pulled down, pinching hard to hold the wet, bloody skin. He worked the skin around the leg until he had sufficient purchase and then gripping tightly, he ripped the skin away in one red wet piece as if it were a sweater pulled inside out over a man's head. Blood ran over Creel's hands and down the weathered skinning board and puddled into the soft black earth at his feet.

"Right here," he said pointing to the earth between his legs, "is where I have my worm bed. That spout off the barn keeps it wet in summer . . . wet as ya can in the dry summer heat ya get around here. That spot breeds up the best damn red crawlers in the Delta, though. Deep-hole bass love 'em." Deftly, Creel peeled the pelt right over the ears, slit it and nailed it on the barn side to dry. "You do eleven more." He held up ten fingers, then one. "Savvy?"

Pao An nodded, his stomach churning with distaste. Slaughtering animals was the one task he avoided as a child in the village. On Ting, like every village in South China, bred ducks and dogs for eating, and Pao An was convinced that any animal about to be slaughtered sensed its impending fate. Even now, he saw that a current of fear coursed through the rabbit hutch at his approach.

After much wasted effort, Pao An managed to seize one by the ears, pulled it out of the hutch and took it, kicking and pedaling, to the stump where he crushed its neck with the heel of his hand. It was dead, or so he thought. He had the skin ripped off down to the neck when it began to twitch and kick. And now it was flailing in unspeakable agony, making an unearthly sound that broke his heart. His hands dripping with blood, Pao An tried to grab it, but it kicked off the nail and fell to the ground where it flopped around blindly with its skin peeled over its head. Finally, he caught up with it and was able to break its back with his boot. After that, he was more careful that his neck-breaking blow was "sweet."

But he could not eat the fried rabbit Vera served and that night, his dreams were full of blood. He was back once more in the midst of war, hearing the women screaming as they were savaged by their conquerers, relentlessly and without mercy, one by one. At dawn, angry shouts pierced his uneasy slumber. Was he dreaming or had he heard a woman's high-pitched cries? He rose groggily and groped his way to the barn door in time to see a man galloping his horse into the blackness of the Delta. Pao An washed quickly at the pump and walked up to the kitchen door, which stood wide open. A fire blazed in the stove and a tiny bit of water was hissing in a large pot. He had just taken the pot off the stove and set it on the table when a sound, more animal than human, floated down the hall.

Vera lay half-conscious on the bedroom floor, her nightdress in disarray. Her eyes were bruised and swollen shut, her nose bloodied, and her face and neck covered with purple welts. "My fault," Vera gasped. "Clumsy. Fell down and hit my face . . ." She rolled back on the floor, nearly undone by the effort of raising her head, and too weak to protest when Pao An knelt beside her. He only intended to pull the torn dress down around her, but one touch was enough to make the front of her bodice fall away. Before she could cover herself, he saw that her breasts were large and heavy, crowned with tiny flat nipples set within large pink aureoles. The whiteness of her skin was shocking to him.

"Oh God, no," she cried, clamping her legs together and twisting away in revulsion.

Pao An ignored her frightened mewing. Ugly, stupid woman, he thought to himself. Vera had crawled into a corner of the bedroom. Her dress was hiked high enough to reveal the fist-sized bruises on her thighs and her eyes were bright with terror.

"He'll kill ya for touching me," she snapped.

Pao An wiped the blood from her face and neck with a corner of the pillowcase. Then lifted her onto a chair. She watched him slowly putting the room to rights: the chair that Creel had kicked apart was reset and placed beside the window, the broken shards of glass removed, the torn bedclothes gathered up into the washbasket and fresh bedding wrapped around the mattress.

When he had closed the door behind him, Vera stripped off her night-dress, grimacing with pain, and inspected the bruises on her body. She was painfully conscious of the slackness of her belly and thighs. She was beginning to gain weight. How she hated getting old. Men had touched her out of desire, anger, need, frustration, but never before out of compassion. Her skin burned where the Chinaman's hands had been.

*F*or two weeks, Vera kept to herself. When Pao An next saw her, she was stirring a bowl of sticky bread dough. His appearance at the back door seemed to startle her.

"You," she blurted out, nervously flicking a shred of dried dough from her apron. She averted her face, but not before Pao An noticed that the bruises on her face had faded into yellow splotches.

He stepped through the door without invitation. "Missy not sick . . . ?"

"I ain't planning no more accidents if that's what you mean" was her derisive reply. With furtive, sidelong glances, she studied this alien intruder as if seeing him for the first time. He had a full head of hair, not the bald pate and ridiculous pigtail of his compatriots. His costume was typical of his race—bare feet and black cotton pajamas that were much too small for his lean, rangy body. There were angles to his face that revealed the fine bones beneath, and his eyes were not narrow slits but long and large, his skin more bronze than yellow.

"I ask help," he said finally.

Still holding the spoon, she retreated to the stove in suspicion.

"I have woman," Pao An blurted out. "She stay Ha-wa-ee. Ho-no-lu-lu side. She stay house, how you say, teacher." He pronounced the words with elaborate care, trying to imitate Ah Jack's accent. "You write letter, send money for me?"

Vera studied him in silence before replying. "I don't know. Maybe . . . well, hell with him. Come tomorrow evening, after supper. He's going over to Konrad's to arrange for the crops to be lugged to Sacramento. Come to the front door. You savvy? That one," she said darkly, pointing toward the parlor.

Pao An did not understand why Vera had turned his simple request into an elaborate scheme that pit them both against Creel. Yet he could not alienate his only source of aid, so he waited until Creel had left before coming to the front of the house. In the darkness of the porch, he did not see Vera sitting in a ladderback rocking chair until she spoke.

"Rockin' feels good. Can't seem to get my strength back . . ."

The mention of her injury made him uneasy. "Maybe not work so hard," he replied politely.

"All I know is how to go hard, Mister Chinee," she snapped.

"Yes. Can see."

Vera swallowed, embarrassed by the compliment. "Well, what's this here letter business?"

Hers was the first offer of help in all the lonely months in Gold Mountain. How he wanted to pour out his longing for Rulan, his desperate fear that he had lost her. "My woman need money. She stay Honolulu, teacher house." He handed her a wrinkled and dirty piece of paper with Bosworth's address on it.

"Teachers'n me don't git along, but I'll write this feller on your say-so. What you want me to say?"

He had thought all night about how to shape the next words. "Say, 'Here is money for Chen Rulan, my wife.' Tell her I work California, contract finish, go Hawaii. Write my name, Chen Pao An."

"That yer name?" she said softly. She closed her eyes and whispered the syllables, trying to imitate the singsong tones. "Funny how I never think of ya havin' one. Creel never calls you nothin' but 'Hey.' " Her eyes narrowed. "You bring the money?"

He held out ten dollars, all he had left after food and fees and society collections.

She studied the handful of coins with a frown. "He ain't payin' ya much, is he?"

"You write? You send?" he said curtly.

"Yeah, yeah. I'll do it. Don't know why I'm so good to ya," she grumbled.

He wondered if he should take her hand to seal their bargain, as he had seen barbarians do. But since she gave no sign of doing so, he merely bobbed his head in awkward acknowledgment of the successful transaction and slipped back to the barn.

With Vera as ally, Pao An allowed his hopes to soar. The few years' servitude would pass in a heartbeat, and he would have money at the end to build a business with his wife. There would be sons, too, in short order, and perhaps a girl in the image of Rulan.

8

THE WIDOW

Honolulu

"There's been an accident," Bosworth said stiffly, as he handed Rulan a torn envelope. "This came from California addressed to me, but it's yours really."

A crumpled bit of newsprint fell from the envelope like a dead leaf, and as Rulan's eyes scanned the words of the letter that marched backward in bizarre barbarian fashion from left to right, her mind screamed alarm.

"A Mrs. Creel writes that a ferry carrying your husband and a team of Chinese laborers exploded on the Sacramento River. He was gravely wounded. They took him to her husband's farm. He died there three weeks ago of his burns."

Rulan sat as if turned to stone, too stunned to speak or weep, although Molly, swaddled tightly in Lucy's arms, suddenly burst out in furious wailing.

"Don't cry, don't cry," Lucy soothed, jouncing the baby frantically in her arms. "You are safe with us here."

Rulan's grief poured out with her milk, for the infant's wracking cries filled the cottage with the very sounds of mourning she herself had no strength to utter. Then her milk went dry. Molly clung stubbornly to her mother's breast, and although Nalani plied her with a napkin dipped in sugar water, the child clamped her lips stubbornly shut and turned away, flailing the air with her arms. The child's suffering seemed to grow out of a nature so sensitive that it absorbed the unruly passions around her as a mirror swallows up the slightest displacement of objects before it. Eventually, Bosworth hired a Hawaiian wet nurse, and although this alien presence made Molly scream with rage, she did at last begin to suck.

Long after the routine of work had blunted the edges of her mother's grief, Molly remained a finicky eater who gave up the breast at nine months with the same stubborn resolve with which she had once clung to it. *Poi,* the thick purple paste pounded from cooked taro, the staple of the native diet, proved to be her preferred substitute for mother's milk, and sometimes the soft inner flesh of young coconut or rice boiled into a thick paste. No one could predict, however, when Molly would spit out the very food she had downed the day before.

"Whassamatta this *keiki,*" grumbled Nalani after Molly had upended a bowl of *poi* and rubbed the sticky stuff into her hair. Nothing the women had offered had induced the child to eat that day.

"This *keiki* is Chinese," Lucy pointed out, breathlessly lugging the howling, squirming, *poi*-spattered child to the basin. "Maybe we should try something imported." Although Rulan warned the women that foodstuffs from China were horribly costly, Bosworth was dispatched by his wife straightaway to Asam's General Store in Chinatown for something "sweet that a baby might enjoy." He came home with a bagful of dried foods in torn packages that reeked of incense and fish, all that remained on the shelves from the previous month's shipment from Hong Kong.

"What were you thinking, Emmanuel, when you purchased these?" Lucy declared in exasperation, peering into a small bag. She shook the contents into her hand and held out her palm where four small desiccated objects rolled about. They were vaguely of the vegetable kingdom, and smelled both sour and sweet. Odd-looking edibles were no novelty to Lucy, an adventurous cook but a wary eater. At her husband's urging, she had sampled far uglier morsels than the small black disks in her palm. At least these were dead rather than alive, unlike the slippery black and yellow barnacles called *opihi* that Nalani insisted on eating with her *poi* and that Bosworth himself relished as a side dish.

Rulan snatched them up with the first trace of eagerness in weeks. These were *mui,* she told them, dried plums, a rarity in overseas ports like Honolulu where merchandise from China was meager, costly, and limited to basic items like tea and common medicines.

"What does this awful-looking medicine do?" Lucy said doubtfully.

"Not medicine," Rulan replied. "Like candy."

The women each placed a dark plum on their tongues. Lucy choked and spat it out at once. "I don't know why one would ruin a perfectly good fruit! If you want to eat a plum, eat it ripe," she grumbled.

For Rulan, however, the salt-sweet taste of the plum evoked a surge of childhood memory and sensation. She felt again the warmth of her mother's hand on her shoulder as they strode through the bustling village market, heard the cry of the vendors hawking myriad varieties of preserved plums in outdoor stalls. Ignoring the protests of the women, she peeled a bit of the dry flesh from the kernel and pressed it between the child's lips. Molly's face instantly contorted into an unsightly grimace.

"Auwe," cried Nalani. "You poisoned her! Here, here," she cried, holding out her hand for the child to spit into.

Molly twisted her head away from Nalani, her small mouth bursting with the pungent mouthful, and continued to chew with relentless concentration. Then she opened her mouth and began to wave her tiny hands for more.

Lucy burst out laughing. "Little minx!"

Rulan fed the rest of the plum to Molly, then put another onto her own tongue, welcoming the familiar sweetness that purged the bitter taste of sorrow and flooded her mouth with a wave of remembered love.

*E*arnestly espousing the aphorism that honest toil in behalf of one's neighbor was the surest antidote to grief, Lucy, an earnest disciple of the Anglican Church of Hawaii, which had shaken the hold of the Congregationalists in the islands, pushed Rulan into a dizzying round of philanthropic activity. The indulgent Bosworth normally welcomed his wife's sudden and harmless "enthusiasms" because Lucy seemed happiest and least self-pitying when in the thick of some grand cause. He was not unaware that the wives of his own Congregational brethren disapproved of his marriage to an Episcopalian and dismissed Lucy's religious zeal as social climbing, a harsh but not unworthy assessment given Lucy's penchant for publicizing her "projects" through dinner parties with those Anglophile royal patrons who favored the Anglican rite. Her present enthusiasm was the native hospital founded by Dowager Queen Emma, the widowed sister-in-law of King Lot Kamehameha and the most popular royal of that day. Since public health was Queen Emma's cause, Lucy had made it the very banner under which she too did battle. This time, Lucy's enthusiasm led her into the foulest, most sordid sections of the city to bring social enlightenment in the form of strong brown soap—Lucy intended no less than to give Honolulu a scrubbing behind its ears!

Lucy's well-meaning efforts would have proved typically innocuous, except that a new strain of typhus was moving among the native populace as the result of an influx of infected rats off a ship from Sydney. This rat-borne variety of typhus was not generally fatal for whites and Chinese, who sweated through the illness; yet it was lethal to the more vulnerable Hawaiians who developed skyrocketing fever and delirium and died within a week. In its perversity, typhus chose the young and strong. In an epidemic eight years earlier, two of Nalani's children had been felled by the disease while Nalani herself had passed unscathed and thus had been declared immune.

As Queen Emma's foot soldiers against the plague, Lucy, Rulan, and Nalani were sent by the queen's hospital to a warren of huts not far from the harbor where several rural clans lived crowded together with their Honolulu cousins. The women's tasks were to convince the families to stop dipping water buckets into the polluted end of Nuuanu Stream; to hand out packets of poison to kill the shipborne vermin invading the huts; and to urge the women to refuse any man with sores, for syphilis, rampant among the sailors, took a particularly virulent form among the Hawaiians. Those whom it did not disfigure outright, it rendered sterile and prone to other diseases.

In one small compound at the end of a lane, they encountered an ancient matriarch named Malia whose granddaughters' popularity with sailors kept the entire family supplied with *poi,* breadfruit, and an occasional roast pig. Malia saw no reason to stop her girls from going to the ships and dance halls. "Nobody sick this family," Malia maintained, her lips pressed stubbornly together.

Although she refused their advice, Malia did take the packets of poison because rats bit the little dogs raised for eating. Nalani carefully described how to place the poison-laced grain out of reach of domestic animals and children. Then the women walked back to the harbor road and waited dejectedly for Bosworth to pick them up in the cart. They were hot, sweaty, and dirty; nits had gotten into their clothes; and they had failed to convince a single of Malia's granddaughters to reject the glamour of the harbor for the dusty safety of the country.

What worried Rulan most was the growing assumption among the king's health officials that every fever was the fault of immigrants from Kwangtung. Even those inspectors who had traced this new infection to the ship from Sydney grumbled about the "pigtailed scourge" that had brought plague into their midst.

"There's talk of burning the Chinese quarter down," Bosworth warned Rulan one night as he drove the exhausted women home. "The worst areas for typhus are the vermin-infested warehouses and the fish market where vendors throw the offal into the canal."

The next morning, Rulan went alone into the Chinese sector of the wharf. She wrangled with the vendors of cloth, meat, and fish; the merchant at Asam's store who kept her supplied with preserved plums; the bachelors who played dominoes and the lottery and smoked two pipes of opium each day. She scolded them in village dialect about spitting on the floors, ordered them to dig their privies away from the wells, to put out poison for vermin, and to wash down their stores and barracks with brown soap. They grumbled and made ribald jokes, but in the end they took the items Rulan handed out, although they did not promise to use them.

Once in a rice warehouse, Rulan saw dark shapes scuttling across the floor. "Rats," the rice merchant affirmed. "One or two hide in the boxes that come off the ships, pretty soon they're everywhere. Everything in Hawaii grows wild, even rats."

"*S*o you have finally come, Second Lady," Merchant Li said when Rulan entered his shop. The afternoon was humid and dank, and Li Liang Mo was dipping a spoon into a bowl of *leong fun,* sweet black jelly drenched in syrup, and fanning himself vigorously. She remembered how in the great house overlooking the Pearl River, he had whiled away the fetid days before the summer monsoon, avoiding his studies for the imperial examinations and gorging on cooling foods, and how the heat and the cloying sweets invariably brought him round to making love.

"You went to every Tang merchant before me," Li Liang Mo said fretfully. "You, who once lived in my chambers!"

She tried to hide her distaste for Liang Mo under a rebuke. "Your stores cover an entire city block, the busiest in Chinatown. Yours was the most difficult case for me. You would do well to scour the area when the king's inspectors come."

Her acknowledgment of his wealth pleased him. "Such a commotion over a few drums of fish guts. I'll pay the *bak kuei* a squeeze," he declared contemptuously. He gestured grandly with his plump hand at the proofs of his prosperity: baskets of shiny-skinned dried fish, crocks of bitter cabbage packed in brine, quantities of dried abalone and scallops stored in glass jars. Dried ducks, their beaks glistening with droplets of oil, hung down from the ceiling on fishing lines. A row of unpainted shelves held stacks of papers and leather-bound account books, writing instruments, and a schoolboy's ink slab.

"You cannot end the matter with bribes," she told him severely. "The *bak kuei* are threatening to burn Tang men's shops and barracks to end the sickness. We have to convince them that Tang men are not to blame for the new fever. That means cleaning up the streets, streams, and stalls." She took a packet from her bag and wrote quickly on the wrapping where and how to use the contents.

Merchant Li took up the bowl with a frown, spooning the *leong fun* noisily into his mouth. He studied her over the rim of the bowl with a faint trace of surprise. "When did you last serve me food?" he said finally. "It must have been the night before my mother married me off to that harridan. I was quite distraught at the thought of not waking up next to you—" He swirled the melting *leong fun* in his bowl, studying the patterns left by the sticky substance on the sides of the bowl, before drinking the syrupy leavings in one swallow, as if a much-awaited course of action had been revealed at the bottom of the bowl. Picking up the packet with a sigh, he scanned the writing absently and tossed it upon the counter. "Filthy barbarians," he muttered. "Must you do whatever they tell you?"

"I do what I please," Rulan retorted, making ready to leave. "I am no longer your property to dispose as you choose."

Liang Mo cursed softly and began to ladle more *leong fun* into his bowl. "You were not unmannerly in my house, so I blame that man for your bad temper. No decent Tang man would allow his woman to wander abroad in the streets. Or let his daughter grow up among *bak kuei* and *kanakas*."

The sorrow that Rulan had so ruthlessly suppressed choked off her angry reply. "My man is dead," she said finally. "In Gold Mountain."

A flicker of contempt passed over Liang Mo's smooth face. "I, for one, do not intend to die in this wilderness," he declared. "I have made enough money to rebuild my father's house in Kwangtung. . . . Remember that house? How it spilled over the mountain like a scroll rolled down from heaven?" His eyes grew soft at the memory. "Second Lady," he said, uttering the title he had no right to use, "come back to China with me!" Taking Rulan's shocked silence for assent, he reached out for the woman he had once owned, confessing, "I have waited so long for you to set my house in order—"

A shrill laugh floated across the room. Mei Yuk stood in the doorway, her painted lips set into a brilliant smile. "Chen *Tai Tai*," she purred, "how good of you to call. I hope your daughter is not as naughty as my rascal girl who cries for her father to rub her sore feet." Gliding to Liang Mo's side, she pried his hand from Rulan's wrist with a coquettish laugh. "What a trial we women are to our men, *hai ma?*" she murmured, as she drew Merchant Li, red faced and protesting, away.

Rulan's feckless encounter with Liang Mo in Chinatown was matched by Lucy's failure to stem the onslaught of typhus in the community-at-large. It was not the Hawaiians' fault that centuries of isolation had made them more vulnerable than whites or Chinese to every passing scourge. Or that the native custom of *aloha* by which every newcomer was embraced was proving tragically fatal to their race. History seemed to be cruelly effacing the Hawaiians from the earth as easily as footprints washed away by the tide.

Unwilling to believe that God might ignore her ardent ministrations, Lucy pointed a zealous finger at the Hawaiians themselves. Surely, she asserted, typhus might yet be conquered if not through an attack on filth or rats then by an assault on the primal syphilitic source: rampant fornication! Determined to launch a frontal attack upon the dance halls, Lucy gathered the Anglican churchwomen who dubbed themselves Queen Emma's Companions to march with Rulan, Nalani, and herself into Alexander Street to convince the tavern women to give up their lucrative trade. Each morning, they positioned themselves with a sign proclaiming free health care just as the gangs of barefoot Hawaiian women ambled through the narrow lanes; they wore tight taffeta *holokus* with dusty trains and as they leaned on each other, sleepy from lovemaking and rum, they plucked broken blossoms out of their tangled hair and tossed the petals onto the dirt road.

Some women held fresh fish wrapped in bloodstained paper and calabashes of *poi,* for there were old people and hungry children to feed. Cash rich from their trade with the sailors, the women could afford now to buy fish and *poi* from Chinese vendors, rather than wait for their menfolk, who were themselves weary from work at the docks or plantations, to throw out their nets or pound the taro corms by hand.

Nalani knew many of the women by name, since in the loose kinship system of the islands, every Hawaiian shared a cousin or two. They spoke of nephews, aunts, and lovers; of who had gone to California to work in the gold mines and who had been found with *mai pa-ke* and sent to the leper colony at Kalawao on Molokai; and of which *hula* dancer had played the ball-of-string game in the palace and now slept every night in the king's bed. At a convenient point, Lucy would begin to hector the women about their livelihood. Invariably, then, the women would saunter resolutely away. In one particularly disappointing encounter, a fifteen-year-old girl burst out in furious indignation when Lucy chided her for going with a seaman with the hesitant, flat-footed gait of the syphilitic.

"They hate me for being a *haole,* don't they?" Lucy asked Rulan angrily. "They reject my message for spite!"

One afternoon, the women were traveling the waterfront road, when their cart was blocked by a line of Tang men marching in the direction of the China quarter. Some of them wore black Triad armbands; others wore bankers' coats of shiny black sateen and black skullcaps upon the shaved domes of their heads.

The far-off wail of a Chinese flute and the *dok-dok-dok* of a drum made Rulan shake her head in tired exasperation. "A funeral," she told the others wearily; there was nothing to do, she added, but wait for the procession to pass, for the dead personage, judging from the din and the size of the crowd, was wealthy and the funeral parade long. Two chanting monks in saffron robes led the line of mourners, followed by several men holding huge lanterns and a name banner curled tightly around a pole by the rising wind. The parade wound directly in front of the cart. Before Rulan's eyes, the name banner unfurled with a snap, and Rulan saw for the first time the character crudely brushed upon the white cloth: Li.

"Which one in the family died?" she called to the bearer of the banner. Her hopes soared. Let it be Mei Yuk!

"The big man," came the answer. "Merchant Li. Caught typhus three nights ago. Died vomiting blood and screaming for his grandmother in China."

Spitting up blood? Rulan thought in horror. Typhus? A bleeding stomach wasn't a mark of the disease! Nor had Liang Mo seemed ill at their encounter the week before when she had placed in his hands the packet of poison meant for rats. A horrible suspicion blossomed. Rulan leaped to her feet with a cry, but the bearer had already moved on.

Behind him came the casket carried on the shoulders of six brawny men, one from each of the family societies, followed by a gang of hatchet-faced roughnecks from the *tong,* and finally the widow in white funeral robes, stumbling awkwardly on her tiny bound feet behind a servant holding a large portrait of the dead man. Mei Yuk held her four-year-old daughter by the hand, her head hanging down in an attitude of profoundest woe. When she passed Rulan, the widow pulled back her hood with a small white hand. A smile of triumph spread slowly over her face. Then with a sorrowful wail, Mei Yuk yanked her daughter's arm and they passed in a cloud of incense and dust.

"What do you see?" Lucy called from the back of the cart.

"My old life," Rulan replied. What folly it was to think one could start anew, when the past sprang back upon itself, and fresh crimes were begotten upon the carcasses of the old. Liang Mo would never rebuild his cliffside mansion, never restore the name of Li to glory. His bones would lie unmourned in a strange land, far from the ancestors he loved better than himself. And her hands had helped him die.

9

THE PHEASANT HUNT

Invictus Island, California

A stack of weather-worn wooden crates a dozen feet high sat against the side of the barn in anticipation of Creel Farm's first crop of pears. Pink with exertion, Vera was hurrying across the yard laden with an apronload of ripe fruit as the newly hired gang of Chinamen came up the levee road. Her face lit up with welcome at Pao An's approach.

"Did letter come?" he asked, the same question he had put to her for months.

"Sure did," she replied panting, "but it ain't good news." Her expression turned sour when Creel limped into view behind the last of the crew. She blew an unruly lock of hair from her cheek. "Come around tonight after he goes next door to Konrad's."

Harvesting pears was easy compared to the arduous task of dredging the river, which still lay ahead for the fifty Tang men in Creel's work crew. Too easy, for Pao An's mind wandered all day, and he worried about the letter. Was Rulan angry at his long silence? Had she fallen in love with another man? The afternoon seemed to stretch forever, and dinnertime proved a tiresome ordeal. While Creel barked orders at her, Vera killed a brace of chickens and set up a makeshift cooking station for the men outside the barn with a quantity of rice, oil, onions, and chard from her garden, enough for the men to make an ample meal to their liking. Pao An could not eat for worry. At nine, after inspecting the sacks of rice to make sure that no man was taking more than his due, Creel took his leave and Pao An slipped away to where Vera awaited in the darkness of the parlor. He hated that she had turned them into conspirators.

"I got the letter right here," she told him. "Come on in."

A kerosene lamp was burning behind the parlor's closed curtains. She waved a piece of paper, beckoned him closer and ran her finger across a line of incomprehensible script. "See? Says it's from this feller Bosworth to Chen Pao An." She held the letter against the lamp and began to read. " 'My dear Mr. Chen. I'm sorry to say your wife died not two month ago. She took to working with sick natives and caught their fever. The money you sent was enough to bury her. Yours truly, Mr. Bosworth.' "

The words had a devastating effect on Pao An. Invisible filaments, like descending cobwebs, seemed to wind themselves around his flesh. He found himself wiping his cheeks with his hands to stop his face from crumbling. He stopped when he noticed Vera staring.

"Bad, eh?" she observed.

"Yes. No," he mumbled.

"It's not like you'n she was together much," Vera returned.

He nodded, anxious to take his leave.

"Never took you for a moper," she declared. "Yer such a damned sight different than most men I know." A harsher edge crept into her voice. "Need ya to move some fruit into the cellar tomorrow," she told him, all business now. "Come round 'bout noon, hear?"

The night was a sleepless torment in which half-formed visions of Rulan materialized in the blackness of the barn. Now and then, a Chinaman called out in sleep: wordless cries steeped in loneliness and longing that echoed Pao An's loss. Even the owl's familiar moan took on a terrible, human note. He gave himself up to grief, allowed it to sap what remained of his dwindling resolve, to drain from him every hope that had made his exile in Gold Mountain worthwhile.

*W*eeks passed. The pears were harvested. The men worked steadily on the levees carrying away acres of mud with wheelbarrow and clamshell diggers. The kindness Vera continued to show him drew him out of the orchard and back to the house every afternoon. She always had an errand or two for him in exchange for a bit of extra food. One day, Creel had been particularly brutal all morning, roaring out of the house at dawn and hounding the crew onto the levees without their typically huge morning meal. Then he rode off to Sacramento in tearing bad humor. Hours later, Pao An found Vera sitting on the packed-earth cellar sorting out jars of preserves.

"What kept ya?" she said without looking up.

"Work. Forgot," he replied listlessly.

His reply seemed to enrage her. "It was him kept you away. He don't want even a Chinaman to come near me!" Unbuttoning her bodice, she lowered the cloth to reveal fresh bruises on her neck and shoulders. "Look what he done this time," she moaned and began to cry. Great, gasping sobs that tore at his heart. Her white shoulders gleamed in the light shining through the solitary window.

Stepping toward her, he knelt upon the hard ground of the cellar in a circle of swirling dust motes. His fingers moved of their own accord across the marks left by Creel's fingers and fists. It seemed entirely natural then for her to embrace him and for his hand to slip from shoulder to breast. His head was spinning with the heat and the smell of the damp earth.

The pears at Creel's farm were sweet; the flesh soft, white, and yielding; the aroma heady and inviting. The trees gave abundantly in the first harvest, so much so that Vera entertained visions of groves all along the levee.

Pao An observed wryly to himself that Vera taught him much, not the least of which was English. The surprising thing was his effect on her. Her bitterness and taciturnity melted away: in the earthen pit packed with the summer's bounty, she was wild, talkative, bursting with ribald wit. Sometimes, however, a casual aside would reveal the horror of her years with Creel. "Ya don't have ta worry none about gettin' a child off me," she announced after their second lovemaking. "I can't have none. Which is one reason he hates me. Now that his leg's gone bad, the rest of him's bad too, and he can't be a man no more. That's the other reason he can't stand the sight of me."

Pao An's mood in those days was as somber as hers was gay, for he acknowledged what she denied: the danger into which their reckless passion thrust them. Yet by then, Vera had become a need that he could not abandon.

Partly to earn his crew's respect, partly to elude the increasingly careless Vera, Pao An spent each day on the levees laboring alongside his men in the brackish water. He always selected the site for the digging, measuring out the pan of river wall that they hoped to fill that day by swinging his leg wide in the unit the *bak kuei* called a "yard."

In the late evening when the men were bent over their evening rice, he tarried alone upon the levees, finding pleasure in retracing their slow but relentless progress along the river. Waterfowl nested among the grasses he had planted to anchor the sod, and fish darted in the dark water below. Loath to return to the farm, he took out the remains of his midday meal, cold rice balls and a piece of jerky wrapped in a handkerchief, and sat down with his back against the trunk of a live oak.

Pausing now and then to drink boiled water from a clay jar, he listened to the insects in the weeds and watched shifting patterns on the surface of the river. They had put in a thousand yards in a single month; a mound twenty feet at its base, eight feet at the top, and fifteen feet high now stretched over a mile beyond Vera's pear orchards. Soon, an earthen wall would surround Creel Farm and intersect with the levees that other farmers on the island were building with crews of Chinese. Nothing but complete encirclement would protect farms like Creel's from the inevitable overflowing of the river from its banks. On the day when the Delta was entirely crisscrossed by interconnecting levee walls, what was now thirty miles of waterlogged earth would become the richest soil in Gold Mountain. But how high would the walls have to soar in order to keep pace with the vagaries of the river? And then there was the silt and tailings from the hydraulic mining in the foothills. The miners in Columbia County were blasting apart a mountain of dirt for every pound of gold, leaving the farmers of the Central Valley with tons of runoff from the mines.

Pao An scanned the distance covered by water and reeds, orchard and potato fields. To the southwest the horned peaks of Mount Diablo lay silhouetted against the setting sun. He felt as weary as a man trying to scoop out the sea with a spoon.

A breeze whispered along the sloughs, carrying with it the odor of salt and rotting vegetation. A family of wild ducks rose from the rushes and soared westward; the sight filled him with excruciating loneliness. It was his dead father's habit to turn moments of sorrow into poetry, but Pao An had always been too conscious of his own ham-fisted view of the world to mimic his gentle, scholarly father. Now, however, hearing the plaintive cry of the birds, he felt words forming patterns in his mind.

The green-headed duck knows its way home.
No nest is too far for him.
Even a peasant, staggering drunk,
can find his own door.
I sit on the narrow wall I have built
with my bare hands across this alien river.

When I am done, who will care
if the wall will stand or fall?

The poem was crude, the language labored; yet chanting it lifted his spirits. Then he rose from his solitary perch and walked back to the farm, intending to join the crew's nightly gambling only to find that Vera had hung a lantern on the porch, her sign that Creel had gone to Konrad's. Pao An's body began to tremble with an urgent need for connection. When the rest of the men were snoring on their pallets, he descended the stairs into the underground storage room where Vera entwined her limbs around him, pulling him down upon the damp earth.

The rot started as a mere blister on the stump of the missing toe. Over the course of a month, gangrene set in again and eventually Creel had to have his leg amputated at the knee. Now he hobbled around on a stump of wood strapped to his thigh. The ebbing of his strength made him cling more stubbornly to his plan to vanquish the river. He had come so close, he declared to Vera, that God in His heaven would not dare prevent him.

Impatient with the painfully slow pace of the levees' construction, Creel embarked on a cooperative scheme to treat the Delta as a single vast tract with the farmers united in a war against the Sacramento and San Joaquin Rivers. He convinced his neighbors that none of them were safe unless they encircled the island with levees, and he took up a fund from his lowland neighbors. With the two hundred thousand dollars collected and new teams of coolies Ah Jack sent, Creel commenced the building of levees on a grandiose scale.

Soon hundreds of barefoot Tang men were scurrying across the Delta, scooping silt into buckets, climbing over the ramparts with wooden levelers to tamp the waterlogged peat down, as their levee-building forefathers had done for centuries in the Pearl River Delta. Creel had told him that the high-water mark in 1857 was seventeen feet above the flood line. Yet Pao An, who directed the coolies, soon realized that the unexpected problem of runoff from the gold mines in the nearby Sierras, which had altered the level of the river bottom, had changed the scope and urgency of the project. When winter rains came, the channels would be unable to hold the extra volume of water. He directed the coolies to critical bends in the river where the torrents were most likely to plow straight into an earthen dike. Here they built gigantic bases fifty feet thick and twelve feet high with crests five feet wide. They took fill from the river to lower it and pushed the walls even higher. To shore up the loose soil of the riverbank, they drove two lines of stakes into the mud and filled the gap with sand, dirt, and rock.

*I*t took two long years, but the army of Chinamen eventually worked their way around the twenty-nine-mile perimeter of Invictus Island, yard by backbreaking yard. And when the levees were finished, the farmers threw a grand celebration. *The Sacramento Bee* reported that they "dined like kings" that night on what they harvested from the river and the rich Delta soil: corn and tomatoes, pears and apricots, crayfish and trout and bass, asparagus and lettuce.

Although their own feast was not reported in the *Bee,* the men of Tang also ate like kings, or at least like the gentry families whose wealth they coveted in China. Ah Jack brought an all-male opera troupe to Creel Farm and six prostitutes from Sacramento. He also hired his cousins, the cooks of Rio Vista, to prepare food in outdoor woks set up on clay pits.

"This is a great day," Ah Jack declared over the shouts of Tang men playing raucous drinking games. "We men of Tang have made land out of nothing for the *bak kuei!*"

"When did you make anything but more debts?" Pao An hooted over the din. "Go home, Uncle!" He saw that Ah Jack was not nearly as drunk as he pretended and was undoubtedly planning some new chicanery; whenever Ah Jack made a speech, it ended in emptying the men's pockets.

"I would gladly go home," retorted Ah Jack, "unlike the headman of this job." He paused dramatically. "Maybe this headman is a wanted man. Maybe . . ." An angry murmur swept over the crowd, for Pao An was respected by his crews. Quickly, Ah Jack veered down a different rhetorical path. "What Tang man doesn't want to go home to die in his own ground, *hai ma*? Not earth that the white devils pissed on. What happens if a boulder smashes into you in the river and you drown? What if you break your neck falling off a muddy wall? You think Devil Creel will ship your body back to the village so your bones can lie in clan soil, *hai ma*?"

The answering murmur told Ah Jack that the notion of a lonely death in Gold Mountain was too horrible for the homesick Tang men to contemplate. Now the flute was too shrill, the painted faces of the actors tawdry and gross. Even the feast seemed an empty shadow of what wives and mothers were cooking in the village.

"Who wants to die in China, like decent men of Tang, with sons and daughters to pour out wine and set out rice for our ghosts?" A roar went up from hundreds of throats. Suddenly, Ah Jack was all officiousness. "The society is opening a bank for Tang men. Put in money. The society feeds you. Buries you too."

The Tang men surged forward to hand over to Ah Jack the cash set aside for gambling in the hope that their bodies might not lie in this barbarous soil. Ah Jack collected eight thousand dollars that night, something from every man present but one: the headman of the digging.

*F*or a while, at least, farmers like Creel could claim a victory over the insatiable waters of the Sacramento. The Tang men wandered off to other rivertowns and cities along the coast, leaving miles of earthen turrets to mark their sojourn in the Delta. Inevitably, however, without a sizable workforce to maintain the levees, the river had its way. In places upriver, the wind and rain quickly toppled those mounds that were not secured with piles and stone breakwater.

The owner of Creel Farm was disintegrating at the same rapid pace as the levees themselves. He no longer kept up a pretense of working but gave himself over to drink and self-pity, breaking his bitter silences only to rail at his wife, whom he blamed for his repeated defeats.

Sensing that Pao An stayed only to fulfill the terms of his contract, Vera clung ever tighter to him. "He means to kill us," she warned. "I swear he knows," and she begged Pao An not to abandon her to the man who had twice in drunken fits held a loaded gun to her head.

One morning, Creel limped into the kitchen as Pao An was wolfing down his breakfast of coffee and cold bread. "You know how to hunt pheasant?" Creel demanded.

Pao An grunted his assent. There was never any reason to elaborate. Creel didn't want conversation, only acquiescence to his plans.

"Good," Creel said. "Me and some fellas around here going to kill us some birds. You and a coupla Konrad's boys'll be the beaters."

The hunters arrived at Creel Farm hours before daybreak the next day and stood in the yard with their host passing around a jug of home-brewed whiskey and talking in low, conspiratorial voices. When Pao An approached, Creel gave a drunken whoop, which made the others laugh with malicious glee. Ragged cheers went up as Creel bellowed out his plan: They would work the half-mile area between the dry cornfield and the marsh from the levee to the Indian burial mound. Pao An and a young field hand from Konrad's ranch would act as beaters on the flanks, but the main force would be the hunters themselves stomping through the corn stubble and undergrowth five rows apart. The men clambered onto horses only recently unhitched from the plow. The drunkest piled into Creel's buckboard, where the jug was passed around once more.

Within the hour, the hunters had taken their positions across the field as the sun peeked through a pale cheesecloth of fog over the eastern levees. Creel gave a high, piercing whistle, and slowly, the men began their relentless drive through the tall grasses. A dry wind pulsed against Pao An's cheek, carrying with it the heat of danger and the rank scent of the river. Now the most innocuous sounds bore the threat of imminent slaughter: the hunters' boots crunching on the dry earth, the frenzied chirping of the crickets in the reeds, a wild duck shrieking a warning to its mate overhead. Suddenly, Pao An saw an enormous rooster pheasant striding down a furrow with the comical, high-stepping gait of a trotting horse. As if it sensed the hunters' guns upon it, the bird turned, bracing its body on a wing, then darted unexpectedly across a furrow into heavier cover.

A cry of disappointment went up from the hunters; yet in the next second, a gray-green bird burst from cover and soared upward—neck bent with strain, wing and tail feathers fanned and distorted by the violence of his effort to hurl his three-pound body aloft. The bird rose higher and higher, his body angled, his long tail whipping violently, before leveling off. With beak pointed straight ahead, he shot across the horizon at twice the speed of a galloping horse.

Pheasants fly only to hide, and thus go no farther than the flight of an arrow. So Pao An waited, his heart pounding, for the bird to begin its inevitable and precipitous plunge to earth. Yet the terrified bird swept on and on, catching the air currents under its heavy wings in a frantic bid for escape. Two rifles roared as the bird swung left across the line of men. The bird veered as if wounded, plummeted to the ground, then disappeared in a mound of broken earth and decayed leaves.

Somehow Pao An and the field hand missed him. There was no bloody trail, no crushed twigs to mark its fall. The next three hours were given to fruitless thrashing about in the brush, for the hunters, having worked their way to and back from the burial mound without another flush, were forced to drive through two more fields downriver. Without a single kill, the hunters' mood had turned sullen. By midmorning, they were cold, dew-soaked, and cranky from drink and disappointment. They sprawled on the levee griping about the empty jug and glaring at Pao An, whom they blamed for their bad luck.

Finally, a downriver farmer named Murphy, who had lost badly to Creel at poker, burst out angrily, "Your Chink is letting them birds walk through his legs."

"Damn right," Konrad echoed, his wide, flat face red with resentment. "That Chinaman put the Jonah on the hunt."

"Jest his mean kinda luck too," Creel assented with more malice than Pao An had ever heard. "Ever'thing bad come to me the minute I set eyes on him." And he told them how he had been poised to shoot Pao An when the boiler blew on the *Yosemite,* leaving him forever maimed.

"Whyn't ya shoot the bugger now?" Murphy yelled in disgust. "Hell, I'd he'p you out and do the job meself."

"Don't know how you kin stand having him so close to ya. I hate having 'em near me, even to dig mud," Konrad announced. "Specially now they's taking white men's jobs, jumpin' claims up Columbia County way, raising ever' kind of heathen hell in San Francisco."

The next moments were given over to vivid recollection of this Chinese atrocity and that. One farmer recounted how a crazed Chinaman with a cleaver had slaughtered several of his compatriots at a camp near Fiddletown. Murphy told of a cook in a lumber mill who had butchered the beloved camp dog and served it to the unsuspecting lumberjacks for Sunday dinner. What unnerved the hunters most was Konrad's recitation of what his brother-in-law had seen in the streets of San Francisco Chinatown. "They get Chinee girls and stick 'em in cages, see? Dope 'em up so's they can go at 'em night and day. A hunnert men on one. I tell ya no white woman is safe a mile of any Chink."

While the hunters joined their voices in bitter denunciation of all Chinese, Pao An sat watching the river as if turned to stone.

"Hey, you all quitting?" Creel shouted with forced hilarity. "C'mon boys, up and give her one more try." He got uneasily to his feet, for pain was snaking up his bad leg, then limped a few steps and declared dramatically, "I says we go back to that field we walked on first this morning. I know there's birds in there. If this here Chink don't let 'em get around him," he added with a spiteful wink. Complaining of his bad leg, Creel offered to take the horses to the burial mound, their final destination, and wait with gun in hand for any birds that the hunters might miss. The rest would return to the bank where the hunt had begun and take up the watch once more.

Now the hunt took on a savage, holiday mood, especially when Konrad pulled out of his knapsack a new jug of whiskey. One youth took out a harmonica and began to play a rollicking tune. To Pao An the odd comb-size instrument sounded like the squealing of the calliope on the doomed *Yosemite:* shrill, unearthly, ominous.

"Swaller that thing, Pete," Konrad shouted impatiently after a while. "You're scaring the birds and giving me a headache."

"But the foreign gentleman there likes it," the boy retorted slyly. "Up to Bode, fellers caught a couple o' Chinks sniffin' round their claim and tied their pigtails together. Made 'em dance the six-shooter high step." He laughed and blew an antic reel.

"Kin you dance, China boy?" Konrad demanded. "I can he'p you out if you don't know exactly how." He had just swung his shotgun off his shoulder when an enormous pheasant rose up from the weeds a scant fifty yards away. The harmonica player whooped, and soon the men were scrambling unsteadily off the levee after the bird. Pao An retreated into the marsh in anger and relief, tromping the ground in a moon-shaped curve in hopes of flushing the bird toward the advancing line of hunters. Figuring that the farther he got from Konrad, the safer he would be, Pao An made two long loops, intent on bringing any living thing within the men's firing range to divert their frustration away from himself.

He was twenty yards from Konrad when a shot blasted the tops off cattails not three feet from his own head. Diving into the mud, Pao An let fly a string of Cantonese invective that culminated in curses he had heard the *bak kuei* use themselves. "Goddamn you sonabitch!" he shouted. He rubbed the mud from his eyes and spat out a mouthful of dirt, disgusted by the gales of laughter his angry outburst provoked. More Cantonese epithets fell from his lips: white devils, long-noses, turtle-dung red-faced barbarians.

Pao An stalked toward Konrad, shaking his fist. "Damn you, watch you shoot!" he yelled.

His face pink with excitement, Konrad whooped and aimed his weapon at Pao An's groin. "Better start runnin' the other way, boy," he said almost kindly. "We mean to bring us a yeller bird home." In the next second, the ground exploded at Pao An's feet. Another blast flew so close that the dirt from the passing pellets stung Pao An's ankle.

Turning across the cornfield, Pao An crashed through the dry husks while bursts of gunfire erupted behind him. Stupid, he told himself, to walk into a trap as obvious as this! Already he saw flashes of color from the shirts of the hunters who were scrambling on the levee beside him, driving him along the very path intended for the birds. Pao An's feet pounded the broken earth. Sweat poured down his face as he crawled along the edge of the marsh. Dry stalks scraped his skin and insects climbed over his hands. In the distance, he spotted the burial mound and the crooked figure of Creel upon an ancient levee that had once separated the errant river from an Indian cornfield. He could hear the beaters coming closer and the insane wail of the harmonica. They were driving him straight to Creel. Creel intended to make the kill!

"Here he come, Nathan," Konrad whooped. "Get yer gun ready."

"Ya hoo!" chorused the men.

Creel lifted the shotgun to his shoulder, bracing his good leg in the ground like a scarecrow's pole, and sighted down the barrel at the rustling of the dry stalks as Pao An moved within firing range.

So this was how the drunken Creel planned to avenge the dishonor done to his house. Well then, Pao An decided, he would not perish like an animal stupefied by fear. He burst out of a running crouch and raced toward his executioner. Behind him, howling and cursing, swept the drunken farmers.

"Gut shoot 'im!" Konrad yelled. "Do it!"

But as Creel was about to squeeze the trigger, Pao An stopped running. He rose to his full height and glared at Creel with contempt. "You want shoot me," he said, "shoot quick."

At the last moment, Creel tipped the barrel slightly and let fly three blasts that ripped inches above Konrad's head and the line of drunken men. The hunters screamed and rolled pell-mell in the dirt. "What the hell you doing?" Konrad bellowed. "You s'posed to shoot the Chink, not us!"

"Changed my mind!" Creel yelled.

"That ain't no way to be neighborly," Konrad retorted, shaking with indignation. The liquor was wearing off, and with it the hunters' thirst for blood; they were tired, bloated, and furious at Creel for spoiling their fun, but when Creel cocked his rifle, they backed away. In the flood-ravaged Delta, a man could not make enemies of neighbors, for he might need a loan of seed or tools or a strong hand against the river. With sullen faces, they drifted toward the wagons.

"If I thought you come at her for real, I woulda blasted your balls off. 'Cept I figured she lied to get back at me," snapped Creel. "Gonna throw you off anyhow. So pick up your bedroll and git. You savvy? Sold your contract back to Ah Jack. He owns you now." Then he mounted his horse and rode after the others, leaving Pao An to make his way to the farm alone.

10

FANNY HOLT'S DRESS

Honolulu

Out of the ashes of Lucy's brief career as public health nurse rose yet a new enthusiasm: education for women. For if, as Lucy believed, the present generation of Hawaiians was doomed by disease, then salvation for the next generation must lie in molding the minds of future mothers and wives of Hawaii. Fired by this vision of the "new" woman of Hawaii, Lucy joined Queen Emma's Companions to rally in support of the dowager queen's plan for a high school for native girls sponsored by the Church of England. She urged her husband to launch a series of editorials on women's education and, with Emma's approval, planned to hold teas and receptions for potential donors.

The first party would be an intimate gathering at Hiamoe for the Ewells and Hunnicuts, prominent citizens from whom she intended to extract large contributions for Emma's building fund. Yet high-minded Lucy was still vain and frivolous at the core. Three days before the party, her greatest affliction was that she had nothing to wear! A shopping trip to Leland's Emporium for sewing notions and to Fanny Holt's for a new dress was planned with Rulan, who, in Lucy's eyes, was even more in need of proper attire than she.

"I would not treat Rulan as a doll for dressing," Bosworth said carefully as he lifted his wife into the rig for the trip downtown. "Perhaps she prefers her own costume."

"Nonsense," Lucy snapped. "The shirt and pants she wears are cut like a man's. Besides, I want her to astonish that old hen Pamela Ewell, who despises the Chinese."

Lucy's anecdotes during the long ride out of the valley had a painful similarity: all focused on the failure of her enthusiasms to produce beneficial results, ending with a confession of inadequacy. "God knows I am blessed with neither wit nor strength of purpose" was her rueful refrain. In the pause between stories, Lucy bemoaned her shabbiness. Although Bosworth's income from the *Dispatch* had outfitted her home and her person in a manner far more lavish than the women of the Congregational Mission, still Lucy was lacerated with envy for the wives of prominent British and American planters, merchants, and foreign diplomats who would always possess more than she.

Countering Lucy's flood of self-deprecation were bursts of hearty reassurance from her husband. Rulan had never known a husband who listened to women's talk with such attention as Bosworth. Despite his intransigence in public, he was at heart a soft, uxorious man, as only an ascetic, who surprises himself by the ferocity of his ardor, can be. Lucy, on her part, rewarded her husband's devotion with a demanding petulance that left them both dissatisfied. What a difference leisure and abundance make to a couple, Rulan reflected. In China, conjugal passions as complex as the Bosworths' were unseemly. Poorer couples worked too hard to concern themselves with matters as unproductive as love; while in rich gentry families, the relationship between husband and wife was a practical transaction with male heirs as coin. And yet, she reminded herself, she and Pao An had come together out of choice and passion; if he had lived, would that spark be crushed by custom and the need to survive?

Their carriage bounced past a cluster of open-air stalls where vendors sold freshly butchered pigs and dogs, fish thrashing their tails in iron tubs, and wooden crates of *limu,* seaweed drenched in brine. Lucy took a tuzzy-muzzy filled with herbs, flowers, and spices out of her sleeve and held it to her nose. In seconds, a cloying fragrance filled the tiny cabin, assaulting the senses of the Chinese woman who preferred the sharp smells of the fishmarket to Lucy's ball of artificial scent.

The women disembarked at the end of a long row of shops at the corner of Hotel and River Streets near the busy terminus of the mule trolley. At Leland's, the women searched through bolts of Indianhead cotton and calico, inspected yards of ribbon and lace, and peered through glass tables at tiny government-issue sewing kits of hammered tin emblazoned with the Union flag. Lucy decided on several yards of unbleached muslin for petticoats, a packet of needles, and a supply of good silk thread. But nothing at Leland's would do for a party dress. "Fanny Holt would never choose such plain stuff as Leland's sells," she grumbled as they made their way down the row of stores with their packages. "Straight off the ships, and first choice too. All her own suppliers are from Canton and Valparaiso." She brightened when she came to Fanny Holt's shop, a whitewashed structure at the end of the row of narrow stores, with a horse tethered outside and a lady's mannequin perched on the bare boards.

Lucy pronounced the frilly gown adorning the dressmaker's model as "perfectly cunning." "I must warn you, though," she confided as they stepped through the wide entrance, "Fanny is notorious. She's been the mistress of at least three kings. And she's smart, our Fanny. She went to missionary school to learn to sew. Now that she's too old to 'entertain,' she works a new trade, and at the same extravagant prices as the old!"

The store was richly appointed with China rugs on the floorboards and armchairs upholstered in red velvet. In one corner, a bolt of brilliant yellow silk was unraveled like a flag upon a flat table; two Hawaiian girls were laying out a brown paper dress pattern on its shiny surface. On the wall behind them, colorful gowns festooned with tassels and feathers hung on pegs. A tall *hapa haole,* or half-white woman, in an orange dress cut close to her shapely figure was moving slowly toward them, calling out, *"Aloha, aloha."*

From a distance, Fanny Holt looked more *haole* than Polynesian, for her skin was the mellow shade of weathered ivory. Yet unmistakable traces of her high-born *alii* mother showed in the generous shape of her nose and mouth and in the sensuous grace with which she moved. Her voice, too, if not her accent, was purely Hawaiian—warm and inviting with languid, musical cadences. *"Aloha,* how good of you to come," she said to Lucy. And to Rulan, *"Aloha,"* she said again, infusing that native greeting with such affection that Rulan felt embraced.

"What cloth has come in?" Lucy asked breathlessly, her gaze darting from one shining garment to the next.

"A piece of lace from England. Black bombazine for Princess Pauahi, which is all she wears now that she is Mrs. Bishop, wife to a banker. Good Canton silk, but already claimed by Princess Liliuokalani for a ball gown. Six bolts of violet satin for Princess Ruth—enough, barely, to cover the royal stomach." With a wink, she added, "And the filmiest pink lawn specially ordered by a man for his newest lady. Worn without a lining, next to the skin," she whispered. "Not exactly suitable for Sunday meetings at Kawaiahao Church—"

"Oh I know it is far too frivolous of me to ask," Lucy interjected with a nervous laugh, "but if there were something *en vogue*—nothing in that ugly bombazine but still respectable, of course. Something different, no, *daring* enough to set a particular lady's teeth on edge . . ." Lucy pleaded. "Something with great style. And of course," she repeated, "not too costly." She looked longingly at an elegant frock of turquoise silk and peacock feathers on a dressmaker's model.

"That dress is for a court lady with royal needs and royal means . . ." Fanny Holt replied gently. When Lucy's face fell, Fanny Holt added, "But if you do not mind something already worn, I have others on hand. Some are my own things, and some are gowns that did not quite suit the wearer. Everything *en vogue,* as you say."

"Oh do let me see!" cried Lucy. Fanny Holt entwined a graceful arm around Lucy and led her toward a small trunk of dresses at the back of the store.

Lucy, with Fanny Holt's encouragement, tried on gown after gown behind the teakwood screen. A costume for herself was farthest from Rulan's mind, however. Carefully, she inspected the bins of buttons and laces, counted the yard goods neatly laid out on the shelves and the brown paper patterns piled upon the cutting table. After a while, Fanny wandered languidly to where Rulan awaited.

"How can a woman open a shop like this?" Rulan asked Fanny eagerly.

"I have backers," Fanny replied with an enigmatic smile, and dabbed daintily with a handkerchief at her damp temples. She seemed at the point of exhaustion; her dark eyes were glazed and a bright spot burned in each of her cheeks. "Women are willing to pay because I know what men like, and men come to choose pattern and cloth because they can see with their own eyes what will please them." Pointing to the two young *hapa haole* seamstresses stacking up pieces of yellow silk, she said, "Those girls are from good Hawaiian families fallen on hard times. They are good girls, bred for a gentler life than what the dance halls offer. Nor do they wish to waste their youth dusting and sewing for *haole* women. So they come to me. Here they learn a trade and are seen by men who shop for their wives and . . . Ambitious girls do not stay long. Two became favorites at Queen Emma's court and found generous protectors. Another lives in a cottage on Kauai given to her and her sons by a planter."

The candor with which she described her situation impressed Rulan. Fanny Holt was a shrewd businesswoman who prospered because of and despite her indeterminate status between the races—the nuances of that status were not entirely clear to Rulan. Perhaps, Rulan thought, she might break free of the Bosworths' charity and join the exuberant interracial parade of entrepreneurs that was changing the face of Honolulu. "I see shops in Chinatown. Can a Tang woman do business like you?"

"Depends on what you want to sell," Fanny replied archly.

"China things," Rulan replied. "Medicine. Food. Tang people don't trust *haole* goods."

"A sensible plan," Fanny Holt replied. "The real problem is money to start. You Chinese have what we Hawaiians call *hui,* associations. You could petition your *hui* for aid."

"Would a *hui* lend money to a *wahine*?" asked Rulan skeptically.

"Why not?" Fanny pressed, her cheeks aflame. "You'll be notorious, not a bad thing for business. Chinamen would come simply to stare at you. One Chinese woman already owns several stores, although you rarely see her on the selling floor. A termagant, the widow of a Chinatown merchant, Li by name. She owns the block off Nuuanu Street where the fishermen set up their markets. . . . Ah, you know her?"

The eager smile had slipped from Rulan's face.

Fanny inclined her head. "I see you cannot count on her," she murmured, and put a hand on Rulan's shoulder. "If you leave Hiamoe, come to me. I will see that you have your chance to prosper." Fanny Holt's touch was surprisingly warm.

Lucy cried out with giddy abandon from behind the partition, and Fanny called back, "Hurry and show us what you found."

Lucy emerged in a billowing white confection of ruffles and lace, twirling her full skirts like a schoolgirl. The dress was cotton eyelet, with handwork at the sleeves, coral buttons, and a neckline low enough to show Lucy's full breasts. Rulan thought it quite indecent for a married woman.

"How much? I must have it!" she cried.

"And so you shall," Fanny Holt said warmly. "But mind you, my girls and I have worn it."

"Oh, who can tell?" said Lucy, unable to take her eyes off her reflection in the mirror. "Since you are all dark and I am fair, it is not the same dress when I put it on."

"She forgets we have friends in common," Fanny Holt whispered slyly to Rulan, "though only that dress can tell who they are."

A price was set, higher than what Lucy had intended to pay, but far lower than any of the dresses that hung on the walls. Lucy rejoiced that she had found such a bargain.

•   •   •

The silver gleamed, the claret-filled goblets cast crimson shadows on the damask tablecloth. Lucy glowed like a bride in her white gown, her cool beauty set aflame by the red *lehua* blossom pinned into the tower of ringlets Nalani had shaped with a curling iron. Next to their vivid hostess, Pamela Ewell and Emily Hunnicut paled into invisibility. Lucy's health was drunk so many times over that by the time the puddings were served, she had pledges of two hundred dollars from each of the men for Emma's school fund and was more tipsy from the men's admiration than from the wine.

Rulan spent the evening in the kitchen dishing out platefuls of biscuits, Haleakala beef, bowls of savories, and mashed sweet potatoes, which Nalani set out on the sideboard. The company's tastes ran to the sweet and unctuous, for the stewed Lahaina mangoes, the jugs of molasses, and the homemade marmalade disappeared rapidly. Although Bosworth urged that Rulan's presence in the dining room would help secure Ewell's imprimatur on a project dear to the *Dispatch*—the repeal of the penal clauses against Chinamen—Rulan declined to meet the guests directly, for the Englishman Ewell was a well-known opponent of Chinese immigration, which he viewed as ushering an unsound race into the islands and as blatant capitulation on the part of the king's party to the sugar interests. But near the meal's end, with Nalani serving the puddings, there was no one else to bring out the brandy but Rulan.

Rulan entered with the decanter and tray of glasses just as the ebullient Lucy was describing her recent encounter with the headmaster of Oahu College over her proposal to teach calisthenics to the missionary daughters. "The gray hairs from the First and Second Boats do not see as Manny and I do that the day of strict Calvinist discipline is over. Ask the young people, and they will tell you how they hate long hours poring over Greek grammar or digging potatoes in the school farm. They want sea-bathing and chorus and lessons in Hawaiian! Where do they go on weekends? To tea dances and horse races to do all the things their grandparents railed at! No one was brought up with more rigid Congregational standards than the young *alii* at the Chiefs' Children's School, and all except Pauahi Bishop rebelled. Emma and her husband, King Alexander Liholiho, turned Anglican because you Puritans could not satisfy the Hawaiians' need for ceremony. The Kalakauas, David and Lydia Liliuokalani, make music in their native tongue because it was so long denied them. I say, give children amusement, and they will come round to virtue of their own accord."

"Hear, hear," Ewell boomed, and raised his glass to Lucy, who blew him a kiss. Flushed with wine and good spirits, Ewell seemed far less formidable than his dour wife in lace cap and stringy gray ringlets who was scraping the crumbs from her dish of plum pudding, all too conscious of her husband's attentions to Lucy.

"My congratulations on your experiment," Ewell said genially to his host as Rulan came round with the decanter of brandy again. "I had not thought it possible to make a heathen Chinee decent in so little time."

Bosworth moved his utensils noisily around his plate in a vain attempt to drown out Ewell's words. His huge mustache quivered with the attempt to guard his tongue. "She was already decent when she set foot on shore," he replied frostily. "So dear has she become, in fact," he growled, "that she is much more than mere servant. What would you call her now, Lucy? Companion? Sister? And her child is as much our own!"

Ewell burst out laughing. "We British have never understood why you Yankees refuse to recognize what your Confederate brethren accepted as a law of nature," Ewell continued, shaking his head with a jovial grin. "By that I mean the natural distinctions between peoples. It's the same in Hawaii as in Canton or London or Calcutta, for that matter—some are made to serve, others to rule. Not with whips or sticks, mind you, though a good caning sets many a miscreant on the rightful path! But you and your Unionist, abolitionist cohorts *will* insist on blurring the boundaries between ourselves and the lesser races, a misguided principle for which you were willing to kill a hundred thousand kindred in your own land."

"My principle is God's own. Men and women *are* created equal," replied Bosworth with frosty politeness.

"Are you not confusing Holy Writ and your Declaration of Independence, sir?" retorted the British Consul General. He winked at his wife while taking a sip of brandy.

"A man of science might say that both are separate pages of one book, that of natural law," interjected the physician Hunnicut while holding out his glass for Rulan to fill.

Ewell did not relish the role of minority opinion. "You Americans assume mistakenly that law is holy, not common," he said sourly. "We British wrote the text."

The frivolous mood of the party had turned partisan and sour. In the debate that ensued among the men, discussion moved with alarming speed from race and law to the future of the Hawaiian Kingdom, on which neither Hunnicut nor Bosworth nor Ewell could agree.

"Reciprocity with the United States will secure our prosperity," Hunnicut pronounced. As a medical student he had sat out the War Between the States in libraries; now that his career was blossoming, he was an ardent advocate of diversified trade. "Crude oil can be gotten from out of earth. No use for whalers anymore, even if by some miracle the whales fill the seas again. The new California markets for Hawaiian sugar are the only salvation for the islands' tottering economy," he averred.

"Yes, but exclusive trade with you Yanks will seal this kingdom's demise," Ewell stormed. The Englishman punctuated his speech by stabbing his fork into the pudding that remained on his plate.

"But there has to be an affinity between this kingdom and the United States. Our destinies are linked not only by need, but by affection and, to a significant degree, by religion," Bosworth thundered, his voice taking on the familiar pulpit cadences of his editorials in the *Dispatch*. "And there is a destiny in the affairs of men beyond mere propinquity or economics that bind the islands to America!"

"My father had a saying, 'Keep giants at a distance,' " Ewell intoned. "That is the only sort of arrangement that will ensure the Hawaiian Kingdom's safety and independence."

This last comment set the spark to Bosworth's volatile temper which, for Lucy's sake, he had held in check all evening. "Then perhaps it is propitious that these islands are at the antipodes from Great Britain, for that imperial glutton has an appetite of unparalleled voracity!" he shouted.

"You are impertinent, sir!" Ewell exploded. He was mollified only by Lucy's begging "forgiveness for my husband's frontier temper."

Rulan went round the table once more with the brandy decanter, which prompted Pamela Ewell, primed for combat in her husband's defense, to comment on how well "the Chinee *served*." This time Lucy's angry flush mirrored Rulan's own. "Rulan is indispensable to us," Lucy asserted. "*And* she understands everything, including innuendo." As the final cap to her defense of Rulan, she added, "The puddings were kneaded by her very hands."

"The native concoction of course?" replied Ewell's wife, moving the untouched slice of *kulolo* on her plate.

"No," replied Lucy with prim assurance. "The plum pudding. I gave her my mother's receipt, and she added touches of her own."

"But plum pudding is *English*," interjected Pamela Ewell in a voice laden with offense. "Hiring these people for washing up and serving is one matter. Making them privy to one's family recipes is another."

"Oh," blurted out Emily Hunnicut, glancing anxiously at her husband. She was twenty-two, easily tongue-tied, and greatly perplexed by the strange foods tasted that night. "Has she been vaccinated?"

"A question one might well ask of any hired hand in the kitchen," Pamela Ewell snapped, "considering that these newcomers from the Orient carry any number of diseases." Bosworth noticed Rulan's hand trembling as she put back the glass decanter onto the tray.

"I examined her myself, Pam," Hunnicut added heartily. "Had pox before, so she's clean. But damn, Bosworth, Emily's got a point. There's a new strain of pox just come into the islands, so we all need to watch who's putting hands into our food. Only four cases along the waterfront so far, all in the last two days. Just did in Fanny Holt this afternoon. My guess is that she was hiding her sickness for at least two weeks, afraid to ask for help, poor creature. Her white blood carried her through five decades of plagues. But once the fever began to climb, the native weakness finished her off in a matter of hours. I myself gave the order to burn her shop, pattern and cloth, just before we drove here. Holt's is just a scorched patch on Hotel Street now."

A wineglass fell, and a crimson stain spread across the white cloth. "What is it, dear?" Bosworth exclaimed.

Lucy's fingers were plucking at the white lace around her bodice as if it were a noose. "My dress," she stammered. "Fanny wore it before selling it to me."

The air in the room suddenly turned stifling. Emily Hunnicut covered her nose with her napkin.

"You were vaccinated in '53," assured Bosworth, an empty remark, for all at the table knew that that vaccine, rushed into emergency use, had proven notoriously unreliable.

"But the dress . . . !" Pamela Ewell insisted.

"The infernal dress," echoed her husband. "There is no vaccine for that!"

"Well, and who will have more brandy?" demanded Bosworth angrily. He motioned for his wife to take the decanter out of Rulan's hands, but when Lucy went around the table, the brandy was refused with an embarrassed shake of heads.

By the time she reached her husband's side, Lucy was trembling with humiliation. "Fill it, my dear . . . to the brim," her husband boomed and quaffed the drink in one angry swallow. Lucy burst into tears and ran from the room.

Seconds later, the guests were fleeing Hiamoe. Hunnicut's carriage careened out onto the road and just as suddenly stopped. The doctor jumped out and ran up the stairs to where a stunned Bosworth stood on the veranda.

"Burn the dress and wait, old man. She might be one of the lucky ones. The incubation period is twelve days. After the fever comes the eruption—papule, vesicle and pustule, scabs, and finally—"

"Scars," Bosworth interrupted. "Oh, my beautiful Lucy," he cried, putting his head into his hands.

"Fanny had two half-Hawaiian girls working for her. One had fever, which peaked last night. She's holding on. She'd been vaccinated in '53 and had a severe reaction then, so the immunization must have taken. The other girl had no vaccination. She got toxic rash with the fever, massed confluent mottling with hemorrhages like a thousand insect bites. She was dying when I left her this evening. If Lucy gets the fever, hers might be like the first."

"I haven't the heart for this," Bosworth said near tears. "God cannot possibly try me in this way."

"I do not know what God may do, but I know what you must. Send the two women and the child away, and leave immediately yourself, or be quarantined with Lucy," replied Hunnicut.

"Abandon her?" Bosworth replied angrily.

"I know you would not. But once the fever comes, then the pox is spread upon the air, by touch, by any contaminated object, and no one can leave. Notify me at the first sign of malaise. I will set a mark upon the house. Terrible, terrible luck, old man," Hunnicut added. He ran down the steps to where his terrified wife waited in the rig with a handkerchief pressed to her nose.

After burning the dress, Bosworth came back into the kitchen. The clutter of plates and food looked to him like the ravages of war. Rulan and Nalani could not be persuaded to leave, but the child, Rulan agreed, would go that very night with a neighbor to Nalani's cousin on the leeward coast.

Bosworth reached out to touch Molly in farewell, but his hand stopped inches away from the small head. Pox had now turned every gesture of affection into threat.

The next morning, Rulan found Bosworth fully dressed and wide awake at his desk with copies of the *Dispatch* strewn about, and his pen frozen above a blank piece of paper. "Words have abandoned me," he told her.

"I'm afraid too," Rulan said. She brought him a cup of oolong tea, brewed strong and black and laced with sweetened milk, a *haole* addition that no longer made her gag. He sipped the tea gratefully. "Nalani would suffer more than you or I," she observed. "Why do so many Hawaiians die?" she asked.

Bosworth replied at first in hoarse, measured accents, and then in a great torrent of facts and figures. "They were cut off, as it were, from the sins of civilized men. My God, Rulan," he said angrily, "the history of disease in Hawaii is astounding! When James Cook sailed into Kealakekua Bay, there were six hundred thousand Hawaiians! From then on, it is a record of unmitigated horror how these gentle people have had to suffer! Only eighty years after Cook's landing, the Hawaiians numbered seventy thousand. Syphilis brought by Cook's men has laid them open to every other scourge. It afflicted the children in the womb and rendered men and women infertile. Do you know that not one of the younger Kamehamehas has produced an heir that lived through infancy except Alexander and Emma? And the little prince perished at four! No wonder the poor father went mad!"

"Nalani told me how all Hawaii wept when Emma's son died."

"That child was the last hope of Hawaii. And now the melancholy Lot Kamehameha sits alone on the throne—there is no heir. 'Speak Hawaiian,' the king orders educated Hawaiians. He sells licenses to anyone who wants to bring back the *hula* and the old chants. He blames us *haoles* for his people's demise, seeing us as a single party, although among us *haoles,* there is finger pointing too. The whalers hate the missionaries for stopping the girls from going down to the ships. The planters hate the whalers for taking good *kanaka* men out of the fields to the sea. The merchants see their profits vanish when the women go back to the villages. The Congregationalists hate the Anglicans, the Lutherans despise the Catholics. The British despise the French and the Portuguese, and all hate the Americans. . . . And in truth there are those of my American brethren who take the cruel position that God has brought upon the Hawaiians fit recompense for their sins. Yet to those who blame the missionaries, I say disease was here and rampant before the first mission boat arrived! From the time Captain Cook came, until the Missionary Board sent doctors, there was no message of salvation and no medicine to heal . . ."

"Tang people use plants for smallpox," Rulan ventured. "I can find some for Lucy." She did not know the English word for the small pitcher plant used by village bell-doctors to prevent scarring. And there was a salve one could make from hibiscus to ease the itching, and a tea out of chrysanthemum to lower fever.

"No, Rulan," Bosworth said firmly. "Superstition is no more effective in combating this scourge than those ignorant native priests, the *kahunas*."

When Rulan tried to convince the skeptical journalist that all avenues of healing must be used to protect Lucy, Bosworth rejected Rulan's counsel out of hand and began a long litany of the disease's offenses in the island.

"Listen," Rulan said.

Upstairs, a woman wept. Bosworth sat down suddenly, terrified. He had railed in the pulpit and in the pages of the *Dispatch* at the idea of disease. Now he was a man come face-to-face with the fact of smallpox invading the body of his beloved.

"*Auwe*" was his only utterance.

Auwe, auwe, auwe: the sound of woe.

*O*n the fourth day of quarantine, Bosworth rejoiced, for the incubation period had passed without a pimple to mar Lucy's skin. The vaccination had taken; Lucy was safe. Yet on the afternoon of the thirteenth day, Lucy complained of headache. By early evening, despite the heat, she developed chills, and in the middle of the night, fever struck. The next day, Hunnicut arrived with salts for the fever and tied a yellow rag to the weather vane upon the roof, prompting the Hawaiian families on the neighboring homesteads to flee their huts. Now Hiamoe was cut off from the world as surely as if its inhabitants had died.

Rulan mixed the salts, for it was agreed that she only, having been twice poxed, should attend Lucy. Hunnicut's medicine did no good. At the height of the fever, Lucy screamed her rage at a world that had conspired to deprive her of her beauty. She argued with invisible missionary wives, remonstrated with Bosworth over the tropical hell to which she had been consigned by marriage. When Rulan came in, she found the bed empty except for a mass of tangled sheets. At first she thought Lucy had fled out the window until she saw a small foot sticking out under the bed. Having taken refuge from the heat searing her body in the coolest place she could find, she was curled in a fetal position, her gown as soiled as an infant's.

Rulan tore the clothes from Lucy, washed her with a sponge held in gloved hands, and let her sleep as the Hawaiians do on a mat of woven *lauhala* leaves upon the floor. Then she locked the door so Lucy would not wander in her delirium. In the second week, the point at which most victims died, the fever subsided, but the disease itself struck with alarming ferocity in the form of purple pustules that covered Lucy's face, neck, arms, and thighs. Bosworth had secluded himself in his study to mourn and pray and write, having given his wife up for dead.

Realizing that both husband and wife would take no further action to combat the disease, Rulan took Nalani aside to propose a desperate plan. "There are plants in China that look like a bell," she said. "The kind that eats insects. Do you have these in Hawaii?"

"We have," replied Nalani. "Where alla time get rain. This plant good?"

"Insects fly into the mouth of the plant. They move down to drink and fall in. The dead flies make strong roots. If you boil the roots and drink, the scars will not be so deep."

They rose after twilight, in order not to be caught breaking quarantine, and walked into the heart of a valley lit by the moon, avoiding the main road for vine-laden gulches and ravines. In a small declivity, Nalani found a stream running through a grove of thorny *kiawe*. After searching for hours, they found seven small yellow-and-white trumpet plants hidden in the moss. The roots were shallow, however, and Rulan was not certain there would be enough to boil into a potent tea.

Bosworth was waiting on the front porch, unkempt and distraught. He did not ask where they had gone, saying only, "Thank the Lord, you have not run away. She is locked inside with a mirror and sewing shears," and for the first time since their siege had begun, he wept.

Rulan ran upstairs, and called to Lucy through the door. "Nalani and I have new medicine. If you take it, maybe no scars."

There was a shattering of glass against the wall. "Liar," Lucy cried. "No medicine will make me beautiful again. I am useless, a Medusa. A hag. A woman so ugly deserves to die!"

Rulan pleaded through the door, "You wait. I make medicine." She ran downstairs to prepare it. And while the herbs steeped in a blue teapot, she and Nalani ground hibiscus blossoms into a salve for the sores. Then she went upstairs and knocked once more. This time, the door swung open into a room smelling of sweat and sickness. Lucy was lying motionless on the bed. The rash had turned from red to scabrous, pustulent sheets, mottled dark brown and yellow, and as stiff as the bark of a tree. "Can you fix this?" Lucy cried bitterly. Then she erupted into piteous weeping. "Help me, because I swear I will kill myself if you lie."

There was no way of knowing for sure if the medicine would work at all. Rulan fed Lucy the potent tea, then gently applied the salve with wet cheesecloth. Three more times she and Nalani went hunting for pitcher plants and hibiscus. Three more times she anointed Lucy's face and body. The final time, Rulan found the sewing scissors under the pillow and carried them away.

In two weeks, the scabs fell off. Waiting made Lucy sick at heart. "Take every mirror out of the house and break it," she ordered Rulan. She vowed never to walk in the light again.

A month after the fever had first struck, Hunnicut came to call. Although Lucy hid from him, the doctor pronounced her case a success for she had not died, and he ordered all the furnishings in her room to be burned. Even the smoke was believed to be virulent, and as the wind bore the last taint of the pox away, the neighbors closed their windows. The surfaces in her room were washed with formaldehyde. He examined the three other inhabitants of the house and found them whole, though exhausted, and Bosworth himself gaunt from the ordeal. Only then did Hunnicut untie the yellow rag from the spire.

But Lucy would not open the door to her husband. Desperate to reach her, he slipped a message under her door. "I will do whatever you wish, only let me speak to you alone."

The next morning, she called down to him, "If I am a horror, if I am repulsive to you, I ask that you simply turn away and shut the door. I will know then what I must do."

"My dear . . ."

"Don't speak! If I am too abominable, divorce me. Send me away. But say nothing!"

Bosworth trembled from the effort of containing his unquiet emotions. "Yes" was all he said, for his greatest fear was that his feelings would betray him and send Lucy fleeing from him forever. Looking up, he saw her skirts appear on the landing and a tiny bare foot descend upon the stair. Her form was as graceful as ever, though she had lost weight, judging from the looseness of her gown. She stepped down slowly, her hands covering her face. A cap hid her shorn hair.

She stopped at the bottom of the stairs, so it was he who gently pried her hands from her face.

The disease had melted the soft contours of youth away. Her skin was shiny and raw in places, as if it had been burned. Rulan's medicine had healed the deepest scars, but there were dark pits over her cheekbones that flared like bat's wings and furrows upon her brow that not even paint could hide. Her once perfect nose was marked with reddened welts, and her eyelashes and eyebrows had fallen out. Never would women envy that face. Never again would men look upon it with favor.

Although she threw up her hands to stop him, he swept her up and kissed her face, her hands, her neck, her shoulders, wherever the disease had marred her flesh. Loud, raucous, unruly kisses. The kind he had never presumed to inflict upon her before. "Oh my dearest love," he cried, holding her tight as she sobbed with loss and relief. "You have come back to me."

11

A FIDDLETOWN WELCOME

Sacramento, California

Pao An went to work as a lookout in a Sacramento gambling hall of which Ah Jack was part-owner with the head of his *tong,* a Gold Mountain veteran of legendary toughness and indeterminate years called Old Chun. The work was easy—policing the door for rowdies from rival Triad societies and breaking up fights at the gaming tables. The money was good too—two dollars more a month than Creel had paid, and for far less labor. More important, he found a companion among the regular customers at the lottery window, a jovial former gold miner named Ah Lock, who dubbed himself "Lucky." Yet as much as he enjoyed the camaraderie at the gambling hall, Pao An disliked playing even a peripheral role in Ah Jack's profiteering. His only comfort was in avoiding entanglement in opium and prostitution, that part of the business run by Old Chun.

Old Chun, a boxer in his youth, moved with the splay-footed, precise gait of a *t'ai chi* master and could send a man flying with a lightning-fast snap of his hand. The considerable power in his still muscular body was now concentrated on business, for rumor held that Chun had never been bested in any deal. All this was changed, however, on the afternoon that Pao An met up with a bizarre procession on the street beyond the gambling hall. The parade had the marks of a raucous village wedding, from red cloth banners and musicians piping tunes on Chinese flutes to the veiled bride, a wonder herself given the scarcity of wedding trappings and accoutrements in the China camps of rural California! A crowd of men and boys were making merry as they bore the bride aloft in a stout captain's chair.

"Who's getting married?" Pao An asked a youth who was clapping his hands to the *dok-dok-dok* of the drum.

"Old Chun, the invincible, got his *yang* caught in his own trap. He's taking his harlot to wife!" the boy hooted. The one called "Big Mouth, the ugly Fukienese."

Greatly amused, Pao An decided to follow the parade into a two-story building at the end of the block that served as saloon below and brothel above. Inside, men were playing *ma jong* and drinking tea at round tables. With much crude joking about the weight of the bride, the bearers set the captain's chair on a table, upsetting a wall of ivory tiles, and loudly petitioned her to remove her veil.

The bride stood up, threw down her fan, and pulled aside the heavy red cloth to reveal an unruly mane of hair; a round, flat, sunburned countenance with broad cheekbones; narrow eyes; and thick lips in the center of which a small red rosebud of color had been painted in the style of Manchu court ladies. Big Mouth was neither young nor particularly good-looking despite the wild applause that greeted her unveiling, yet she was possessed of considerable aplomb, for she simpered and fanned herself in a perfect pantomime of a dainty Chinese beauty. She was well known among the denizens of the brothel for her loud, coarse voice and her horrible temper. When a dish failed to please her, she'd smash it on the ground; when a customer complained of inattention, she'd throw herself on the floor and scream until he pleaded for forgiveness. She was vain and ambitious too, seeing plots against her everywhere. If she thought a rival had bested her, she set up a whispering campaign to bring that unfortunate woman to ruin; and if gossip didn't work, she attacked with her nails, accusing the other of jealousy so that Old Chun never had a moment's peace with his whores.

Someone had thrust a lit cigar into her plump hand, and after easing her ample bottom into the chair, the bride shook loose her wild mane of hair and blew smoke rings at her admirers, urging them in raucous tones to greater heights of foolishness.

"I had her twice for a single price," a youth boasted.

"Once before his belt was undone. Once at the entrance of the heavenly gully. Rains that came and went in a lightning flash," the bride retorted to the delight of the crowd.

"Remember me? You said you had never seen such a weapon as mine," another called out.

"A woman never forgets little things," came the curt reply.

Old Chun sat hunched over a glass of whiskey at the far end of the bar, his craggy features set with a look of silent mortification. Once Big Mouth walked over to him and, draping her skirt over his head, asked whether it was true that if old men looked up, they could see heaven. Chun sat unmoving, his long sinewy arms hanging limply, while his customers loudly demanded to know where he had gone. When the bride turned her attention to the other end of the bar, Pao An approached Chun.

"She is very witty, your wife," ventured Pao An.

"The only one of my girls who wouldn't let me ride her. Fought and swore at me like a cur" was his hoarse reply. "I had every other girl in the house, all of them younger and prettier, but she kept her legs together. Curiosity has undone me!"

Seeing her husband's attention diverted from her, the bride wandered down the bar and put her leg across Pao An's shoulder. Old Chun's face turned scarlet with humiliation at the sight of his wife's large foot displayed under Pao An's nose. But before he could protest, the woman was already flirting with another group of men. "When an old man makes a fool of himself, there is no place to hide," he croaked to Pao An. "Give me ginseng and rhinoceros horn."

Chun had shrewdly supplied the guests with whiskey but no food. In due time, the celebration began to break up. Pao An went across the street to a noodle stall and ordered a bowl of freshwater clam soup. He ate his meal standing beside the steaming kettle while the owner of the stall, an old man as thin as a fence post, crouched silently on his haunches eating watermelon seeds, one by one. Pao An sipped from his bowl, prolonging the meal in order to watch the old man expertly crack open the seed between his teeth, lift out the small flat kernel with his tongue and spit the splintered husk into the street. This was what housewives did while they gossiped and played with their children around the village well. Except that in Gold Mountain there were no women and children, only silent old men.

At a hardware stall run by Tang men, Pao An bought nails, wire, a crosscut saw, and other tools needed to repair a burned-out wall in the kitchen of the gambling house. The house crowd was thinnest at midweek when regulars like his friend Lucky hauled their fresh fish and produce to the open markets in the Delta. Pao An worked until the gaslights were lit in the darkened hall, wishing Lucky were there to share his merriment in the absurd nuptials. Then with the evening stretching before him like a desert, he returned to the saloon for more amusement. But Old Chun was sweating in his marriage bed upstairs and the revelers had gone elsewhere; the only noise was the clicking of ivory game tiles on the green felt cloth and the hissing of a brass teapot on its cast-iron stand.

Presently, one of Big Mouth's sisters-in-trade approached daintily on her small feet and plopped herself on Pao An's knee. The girl was as beautiful as Old Chun's wife was plain, although her sunken eyes and hollow cheeks could not be obscured by the layers of powder and rouge.

"Shall I sing for you upstairs?" she asked coyly.

"I have no ear for music," Pao An replied.

"Listen," she called out gaily to three men at the *ma jong* table, "this one thinks I actually sing!" Her tinkling laughter ended in a spate of coughing.

"Hey you, Phoenix!" called one of the gamblers. "I was before him." He wore a bloody butcher's apron and barely glanced up from his small shelf of game tiles.

The woman put her face to Pao An's ear and said in a hurried whisper, "If you don't come up, I'll have to go with the butcher. He's rough and I can't stand his smell."

"Then tell him no," Pao An replied. He hated being drawn into the woman's game.

"I can't. I have to earn at least four dollars tonight," she replied. "Do you have four dollars? Never mind, come up and I will forgo my share. You can have me all night for three, so I won't have to go with the butcher." The effort of whispering set her coughing again. Her hand brushed Pao An's leg. "You are a scholar surely," she told him, her painted lips touching his ear. "I see your brush is ready for work."

Her cheap sexual banter was practiced and silly and left Pao An feeling far too sober to play along. "Save your money to buy yourself out of this life," he told her abruptly, then pushed her off his lap and walked across the street to the clan house where he paid twenty-five cents for another night in a room of foul-smelling, snoring men.

The vicissitudes of Old Chun's domestic life, while furnishing the Tang men with weeks of amusement, inevitably undermined the operations of saloon and gambling hall, for Old Chun's wife was soon poking her flat nose into every aspect of the business.

Two months after the nuptials, Ah Jack accosted Pao An at his station at the door of the gambling hall. "That fat whore is acting like the empress dowager," Ah Jack complained. "She accused me of skimming off profits and she wants to get rid of Phoenix, our best moneymaker, because Old Chun favored her."

The mention of Phoenix's name drew Pao An's attention.

" 'Sell her off!' Madame Big Mouth screeches night and day," Ah Jack sighed. "Chun says no, no, but I say, what's a dollar or two lost for a few months' peace? Besides, the woman is sick, though there's still good work to be had out of her. So the deed is done. I need you to take the girl back to the brothel in Fiddletown."

"Why me?" Pao An asked.

"I can't trust anyone else with the woman! I've watched you with horses and dogs. You don't beat or kick them"—Ah Jack gave a sigh of resignation—"and this whore has a son, who she won't let out of her sight. So take the mule cart. Pretend you're married. Stick to back roads. If you're lucky, the white devils will leave you alone. I'll give you ten dollars, Mexican gold, for your trouble."

When Pao An refused, Ah Jack admonished, "Listen, someone is going to earn the money and abuse her all the way. At least you're a man of virtue. Think of this as a good deed." What ultimately swayed Pao An was not money but an early release from his work contract if he delivered the "goods" undamaged to Fiddletown.

With great reluctance, Pao An set off for Old Chun's saloon. First, however, to soothe his sore conscience, he bought a quarter pound of rock candy at a general store. Then he walked to the dingy, unpainted shack behind the saloon where the women lived. A small boy with straight black hair falling over his eyes opened the door at Pao An's knocking. Phoenix had never shaved the boy's head or plaited his hair in the requisite Manchu-style braid, an act of rebellion unusual for such a timid woman. Pao An, who courted treason by eschewing the queue himself, wondered if he had misread her diffidence.

"Go away to hell," the small boy cried out and tried to push the door shut.

When Pao An pushed himself in, the child retreated warily. "Go away," he repeated. "My mother is sleeping!" The child spoke an odd mix of rural Canton dialects, gleaned, Pao An supposed, from the men who passed through these rooms.

"I'm here to see you," Pao An said gruffly.

The unanticipated overture seemed to confuse the child, whose small eyes darted from side to side in alarm.

Pao An knelt beside the small boy. "I heard of a Tang boy who was obedient to his mother. Are you he?"

The child was silent for a long moment. "Sometimes," he said in a whisper, then hung his head. "But sometimes when bad men make her cry, I cry too, so that she does not get the tips we need," he said miserably.

Without a word, Pao An placed the brown paper bag of hard candy on the earthen floor.

The child tried to ignore the bag, as good manners warranted, but curiosity defeated him. "What is it?" the boy cried. His face lit up with delight when he peered in and beheld the sweets. Yet at the moment when his lips closed over a chunk of sugar, a burst of coughing came from the adjoining room.

"Go away," came Phoenix's breathless voice. "Didn't Lin Kong tell you that I'm not receiving guests?"

Pao An stood up. "I'm not a guest," he called out. "I'm the ox Ah Jack ordered to bear you to Fiddletown."

Phoenix came to the open doorway. "Oh, it's you," she observed with the ghost of a smile. "The one who refused me three dollars now takes me back to hell." Her next words were drowned in a fit of coughing that made her slump against the door. The boy put his arms around her hips in a vain attempt to hold his mother up. In the harsh light, Pao An saw that Phoenix's beauty had withered in the last weeks. Illness was melting away her flesh, leaving her skin as translucent as rice paper. After the spasm had passed, the boy wiped her mouth tenderly with a towel, and Pao An saw that the cloth came away with a trace of blood.

"I'm ready," she whispered finally. "I want to go."

*T*hey spent the first night in a copse of live oak with the woman and boy taking shelter in the wagon while Pao An slept on the hard ground between the wheels with a gun by his hip. The wind blew constantly on their shivering bodies. Pao An could not sleep listening to Phoenix's hacking cough. Her meekness made him furious.

"You have customers. You make money," he accused her in the morning. "You could have bought yourself out a long time ago!"

She replied with surprising heat. "Do you think a small-foot woman can walk unprotected in this world? What man would have me? Who would take in my no-name boy?"

"Buy yourself a husband," he retorted.

Her brief spark of defiance vanished in a burst of coughing. "And even if I wanted to buy such a one as you, I have no money!" she said with a sigh of resignation, wiping her mouth neatly with the handkerchief tucked in her sleeve. "Everything's gone—spent!"

"On 'dirt'?" he blurted out. Her refusal to change her debased state enraged him.

"I bought my boy," she retorted. "Do you think Chun keeps extra mouths for charity? He ran the brothel in Fiddletown then. When I refused to kill the child in my womb, he made me pay for every day I did not work. It took everything I had earned in two years. And I still pay to keep him!" Her voice sank to a whisper. "Lin Kong is all I have. I pray the merciful goddess Kwan Yin will let me live until he is old enough to make his way alone."

After Phoenix's revelation, Pao An felt more her executioner than her guard. He was pensive, furious for Phoenix's sake, inventing myriad reasons for not delivering her to Fiddletown at all. The road rose past Hangtown, then turned south along a ridge of hills that stood like sentinels before the ramparts of the Sierras. The dry, cool air in the higher elevations seemed to revive Phoenix, for she coughed less and even smiled now and then. Pao An thought the suit of plain blue cotton suited her far more than the tawdry silks she had worn in the brothel, and when she removed her conical straw hat, her face had an ethereal glow. Perched on a bundle of clothes with the boy in her arms, Phoenix chanted nursery songs in a high, breathless voice as the cart lumbered hour after hour along the rutted road.

He half expected her to come to him. On the second night, she crawled beneath the wagon after the boy was asleep. "You've been kind to us," she said, reaching for him.

"No," Pao An said firmly, stopping her hand.

"Then keep me company while I smoke," she pleaded. "I cannot sleep, and I have just enough dirt for one pipe." She retrieved the ceramic pipe from among her belongings, then came back to lie beside him. Her fingers rolled a chunk of raw opium into a ball small enough to fit into the bowl. A match glowed in the darkness, and soon, the opium was hissing and the frigid air was thick with sweetish fumes. Whenever she moved to place her lips around the pipe, the sleeves of her tunic fell back to reveal arms that were pitifully thin.

The bowl glowed red with every inhalation, and a dry ticklish cough accompanied each puff. Presently, and with great reluctance, she put down the pipe and began to drowse. Once she spoke sharply out of a dream. "Not that," she said, then fell silent. When she drew her knees up to her chest, he put his arms around her and felt her shiver. The crown of her head fit under his chin and the tips of her lily-feet brushed his knees. He had heard about places to the south along the coast where a Tang man could make a living catching shrimp or growing vegetables. With luck and his protection, Phoenix might elude the *tong's* reach awhile. This way, at least the boy would have a chance. Phoenix's hair smelled of dust, camphor, and the sweet sandalwood fragrance of her combs. Soon he too fell asleep.

The next night, the weather turned wet, and Phoenix began to cough up blood. This time, the bleeding did not abate, and she begged Pao An to turn toward Fiddletown despite the danger of falling back into the hands of her persecutors. She had a friend, she assured him, an apothecary esteemed for his skill, who had given her sanctuary when Lin Kong was born. He alone knew the remedy to purge the poisons in her lung meridian and make her whole again. Although she spoke without conviction about her chances for survival, she displayed the singleness of purpose one sometimes sees in the dying, which made Pao An accede to her reckless plan, rather than escaping south, as he intended. There was something Phoenix was seeking in the place she had first known shame, Pao An sensed. Some business she was determined to end.

The road to Fiddletown ran up an arroyo dense with live oak and pine to a ridge denuded of trees. Outnumbering whites four to one, four thousand Tang men lived in the dusty hillside camps below Main Street, digging, crushing, sifting, and washing ore, while the whites claimed the more verdant area uphill. Main Street, however, made no distinction between races, for there, the most substantial buildings were Chinese-owned and Chinese vendors vied with Irish blacksmiths and Italian saddlers for every inch of selling space.

Pao An had timed their arrival for the shadowy hour after sunset before the lamps were lit, calculating that the exhausted Tang men would be far too intent on their bowls of rice to notice three vagabonds slipping through the China camp. Wood smoke hung in the air, and a low hum, like the droning of bees, rose from the tents and alleys and vendors' stalls as Pao An drove the mule cart along Main.

Where the road turned uphill, Phoenix pointed out the apothecary shop, a cottage of rammed earth adobe. Directly across from it was the gambling hall, a two-story brick structure with a massive iron door. Narrow floor-to-ceiling windows on the floor above the entrance were fronted with iron shutters. Here, Phoenix told him, the women were kept in tiny cubicles. A sign above the entrance read *Dai Loy* ("Welcome") in black characters a foot high. "Paradise for men, the gates of hell for such as I," Phoenix said bitterly.

As the shadows deepened, the oil lamps hung from the ceiling winked on one by one, turning the cavernous gambling hall as bright as day. The hall looked merry and inviting now, with its doors and windows thrown wide to reveal house dealers stacking up tiles on the green felt tables. Pao An guessed there were at least ten tables, far more than in the gambling hall in Sacramento: the square ones were for *fan-tan* and the round tables for *dow ngow* and *pai ngow* dominoes, each table already crowded with Tang men yelling out bets. At the rear of the hall, he glimpsed gamblers studying the chart of characters for the next day's drawing posted outside a tin-plated lottery cage.

He tied up the mule behind the apothecary shop, warned Phoenix and the boy to keep inside the cart, and entered the adobe building. He had seen such dwellings in the Delta countryside built by the Spanish or by mission-trained Indians, but never one built by Chinese. The shop was as humble as the gambling hall was grand, yet in its own way, its workmanship was far more impressive than that of the brick hall. Earth rich in red clay had been dumped into square frames and rammed with wooden stampers. The massive walls had been replastered many times over to perfect smoothness, as if the proprietor refused to let wind and rain mar his handiwork. As a consequence, the shop was dark, cool, and inviting; tiny drawers built into the walls stretched from floor to ceiling, and the clean, sharp smells of herbs and incense chased away the sickly sweet opium fumes issuing from the hall across the road.

"Wait one minute, stranger," called the owner, an ancient Tang man with a stringy beard and scholar's skullcap. His long, thin fingers were weighing herbs on a tiny scale for a Chinese miner whose face and arms were covered with poison oak lesions. "Don't burn the vine," the apothecary warned. "Even the smoke gives you rash." The herb doctor counted out several packets, reciting the prescriptions for each, and received as payment seven small spoonfuls of gold dust which the miner scooped out of his purse onto a brass plate.

"How may I serve you?" the druggist asked Pao An when the customer had gone.

"I have a sick woman outside who says you know her."

The old man's hand shook loose a thimbleful of gold upon the countertop. "The lung meridian?" he asked gruffly.

"Yes. Coughing up blood."

"Phoenix," he blurted out in a strangled voice. "She must be dying."

The old man fretted over her as if she were his own sick child. He spread a salve of camphor onto her temples and forehead, and made her drink a strong, black medicinal tea to relax the muscles of her chest. When she began to shiver, he rubbed her body with raw peanut oil warmed between his palms. The attention as much as the medicine soothed her irritated lungs, and Phoenix fell into an exhausted slumber in a room plastered with Chinese newspapers advertising import goods on Dupont Street in San Francisco.

On the second day, she was well enough to eat a bowl of thin rice gruel; on the third, she took a few halting steps with the aid of her son. On the morning of the fourth day, as the apothecary had feared, she began suddenly to sink. Yet even in these last moments, her thoughts were only of Lin Kong.

"This old uncle is your mother and father now," she whispered to the boy. "Uncle will teach you to read and write and to doctor with herbs. Obey him as you would me."

"Could I go with the other one?" the boy asked timidly.

Phoenix had not expected this. "No! You will be a scholar. Not a *gu li* with dirty hands . . ." She was too weak to cough and her frail body shook as a spasm seized her lungs. "Obey," she whispered finally, hoarse with exhaustion. "Promise me!" When the boy began to sniffle, she rasped, "Don't cry!"

The boy buried his face into his mother's neck by way of answer and hugged her close.

"Promise me!" she gasped. She did not touch him except to brush a long tendril of hair off his forehead.

Death gave Phoenix back her beauty. The long sleep that surpasses sorrow smoothed the marks of illness and despair from her ravaged countenance and showed her as she might have been if men had cherished rather than misused her. While the grieving old man washed and dressed her body, Pao An went across the street to the gambling hall to report her death.

"Don't expect me to pay for a funeral," the owner of the gambling hall complained. "Ah Jack didn't tell me the whore was sick! Throw her in the dump."

The apothecary paid the fee for a plot in the Chinese cemetery and Pao An dug the grave. The next morning, in the stillness before cockcrow, he strode onto the porch of the gambling hall, pulled down the wooden sign that said *Dai Loy,* smashed it with his fists, and threw the pieces in the dump on the way out of Fiddletown.

Three nights later, Pao An made camp on the same desolate stand of wild oak where he had first stopped with Phoenix and the boy. The lights of Sacramento burned in the valley below, yet he felt no joy at his journey's end. He had fallen into an uneasy sleep when an eerie sensation set the hairs at the back of his neck tingling. A log burst apart in the fire, sending a shower of sparks skyward, and beyond the curtain of flame, the reeds were swaying crazily as if stirred by an invisible wand. He had just drawn the gun

Ah Jack had given him when Lin Kong stumbled out of the darkness toward the fire.

Pao An caught the boy as he fell. His small, wizened face was dirty and scratched; his clothes were torn; his hair was thick with burrs and leaves. The soles of his homesewn shoes had worn through and his feet were bloody. He had been running a long, long time.

"*W*e can do it! We can be rich men!" Lucky's eyes danced in his brown, leathery face. He had sought out ten of the regulars from the *pai ngow* tables, all Gold Mountain veterans who had finished their contracts, all bachelors with no women or aged parents in China to feed, all ambitious enough to share Lucky's hunger for riches.

"Pao An here has been to Fiddletown where Tang men outnumber the *bak kuei* four to one!" Lucky asserted. "Up Courtland way, Tang men run their own farms and sell what they grow in the open market. All this because they put aside clan loyalties and pool their money. We all know something. I can repair tools. Pao An knows waterworks. Even the boy is good for something—"

A grizzled man from the Four Districts who had spent fifteen years mining scoffed, "You think you can rewrite *bak kuei* law? You can't force the banks to lend us money or sell us land! You can't stop the Irish gangs from coming after us with pickaxes and guns!"

Lucky interrupted, "The *bak kuei* are afraid because we work harder and for far less pay. I am sick of bending and scraping to an overseer. Let them beat me up, set my queue on fire! This one time I want something of my own!" He went around the group, hastily tallying up their cash. "How much money can you put in to rent tools, buy a little bit of seed?"

The querulous miner refused to part with a single Mexican dollar, but Lucky quickly won promises of cash from six Tang men, including Pao An. Each alone had pitifully little, yet together, there was enough capital for what the *kanakas* who had worked side by side with Tang men in the gold fields called a *hui,* an informal partnership, that would transform seven men and one boy overnight from laborers into businessmen.

The first winter, they nearly starved. Only Lucky's relentless optimism and Pao An's firm hand kept the men working. All their money had gone for seed and rent for ten soggy acres of river-bottom land hired out at exorbitant rates by a German who had run out of money after purchasing twenty-one parcels of wetland from a reclamation company in Oakland. The eight members of the *hui* built levees and drained the swamp using a foot-pedal bucket lift like those they used in South China. When the land was ready, they planted asparagus, potatoes, and onions, living in tents to save the cost of lumber and nails and eating only what they caught in the river in nets. The boy had a knack for trapping wild fowl, cleverly providing them all with a bit of meat for their table every day.

Unable to afford an animal, they took turns pulling the crude iron plow as their ancestors had done for centuries along the Pearl. The asparagus crop perished in the scorching heat, yet the ground yielded enough potatoes and onions to fill six barrels, which they took up to Sacramento by wheelbarrow. With the money from that sale, they were able to rent an ancient horse and rusted trap, and this Lucky proudly drove up and down the Delta as far as Courtland and Rio Vista to the open-air markets run by other Tang men operating subsistence-level farms.

All too soon, March, the month of floods, was upon them again. So close were they to failing that they had cut their rations of rice. The horse ate better than they. And although they were often so weak that they could barely pull the plow across the muddy soil, they put their small profits not into food but into renting five more acres of land from the German.

Lin Kong was as stoic as the men. He had not spoken a word since his mother's passing, nor shed a single tear. Pao An worried that the child's silence sprang from guilt for having renounced the life his mother had chosen for him. His behavior was impeccable: he did all the chores assigned him by the Tang men—pumping water for the horse, feeding the ducks and the nanny goat—in a kind of exhausted stupor that was excruciating for Pao An to behold. And yet, the child, though somber and mute, was not without feeling, for sometimes at dawn, Pao An would awaken to find Lin Kong staring out the ragged entrance of their tent, as if the far-off play of shadows and light would yield some trace of his lost mother.

One evening late in the second spring on their land, the boy could not be found. Lucky claimed not to have seen him. "Think he's run off?" he asked with a worried frown because, by now, all the men considered themselves Lin Kong's uncles.

Sick at heart, Pao An raced to the spot at the corner of the pen where Lin Kong set out the scraps for the pair of ducks each morning. The water bowl was half-empty. The trough for the horse, too, had been pumped full at least once. He hurried out to the marshy fields blanketed with a thin carpet of green, the first new onion shoots of the season. Beyond the fields, the swift-running Sacramento rose as high as their newly made levees, carrying mud and silt and pebbles from the Sierras. Pao An ran along the ramparts above the angry brown waters for several anguished minutes. Had the child sought this dreadful route back to the mother he could not bear to mourn? The notion was appalling, yet common enough in the starving villages back in China where orphans often "disappeared" by design. Pao An ran back to the pen where the milk goat was kept, wildly calling Lin Kong's name. The pen was empty, but small human tracks in the mud led to the hay shed—the only wooden structure on the farm, a building fifteen feet long and five feet high. At the entrance of the shed, Pao An saw a tunnel the size of a large dog dug into the damp, pungent straw.

"You in there, boy?"

The sigh that escaped from the straw made Pao An sick with fury. He kicked down the pile of hay and dragged the boy into the open. "Why do you hide?" he cried, jerking Lin Kong so roughly that his teeth chattered. The goat by the child's side jumped over his arm and darted away.

By way of answer, Lin Kong held out two stillborn baby goats. The sorrow that the child had tried to hide now burst forth in a fit of violent trembling. He jerked and twisted in Pao An's arms, gasping out strangled syllables, "nuh–nuh–nuh . . ."

Pao An held the boy by the shoulders in a vain attempt to stop his shaking and the awful noises that issued from his throat. Why had circumstance foisted this pitiful creature on him? Pao An did not know how to talk to such a one; he could only shout again and again with a sternness that belied the pain in his breast, "Stop! You did not kill the lambs! Stand tall! Be a man!"

*T*hat night Pao An dreamed of his dead father, a scholar transformed by necessity into a farmer. "I approve of that monkey you caught," the old man said. "He is as worthless as you when I found you abandoned in the cane and, therefore, must be loved for himself alone." Then the old man walked over a rainbow arching across a river and disappeared into a mountain.

Pao An sat up with a start. A fragment of moon hung above the opening of the tent. In the pallet next to him, Lin Kong's sad, pinched face, half buried in the torn and filthy bedding, was drenched in silvery light. The child seemed in the midst of a dream, for his limbs twitched and his mouth worked as if sucking on a vanished teat. A wave of tenderness made Pao An nearly cry out with longing and regret. How many Tang children were there in this vast tract of mountains and forests where thousands of Tang men had come to lay rail or dig mines, tunnels, and levees? A dozen? Twenty? Here lay the rarest treasure of Gold Mountain in this small, wretched form beside him. He felt like crushing the boy to his chest. Instead, he reached out with hesitant fingers and brushed a loose strand of hair off the child's forehead as he had once seen Phoenix do.

12

SECRET PLACES

Honolulu

"Mui," demanded the little girl. *Plum.* There were several kinds of preserved fruit that Asam's in Chinatown stocked, and these Rulan kept in ceramic crocks in their room, carefully apportioning them out piece by costly piece to her greedy daughter. There were the hard salty plums that made the lips pucker; the moist, black, soft-fleshed plums with splintered seed that smelled and tasted like honey; the powdery sour-sweet plums that lasted a long time in the mouth. Just as there were several ways to say the word.

Mui mui, the girl repeated insistently, the tone falling instead of rising, so she said not "plum" but "girl." Devouring the child with hungry mother-eye as she carried the plum with both tiny hands to her mouth, Rulan found the unintentional pun delicious.

That unforgettable burst of salty-sweetness upon the tongue was the earliest imprint upon Molly's burgeoning consciousness. *Mui. Me. Molly.* Sound and taste were one with the splendid image of herself. She was the sweet plum girl, the unexpected and cherished fruit of her mother's sorrow. With one cheek bulging with the soft plum, the child lay in the curve of her mother's hip, sucking noisily as Rulan spun tales of the lost father. Sometimes Molly would fall asleep in the middle of her mother's story, and

Rulan would push a finger inside the small pink mouth to remove the sticky seed, yet the sleeping girl continued to suck even in sleep, her eyelids trembling with visions of warriors and fox-spirits, cliffside mansions, and rivers running bright as pearl. She dreamed of a China of light and illusion—a brilliant phantasm her mother had conjured to block out the memories of war and fire, abandoned women and dying men.

The rainy winter season was one long round of celebration, with Christmas at Hiamoe slipping easily into the Chinese New Year. Even as Lucy was taking down the palm fronds hung with polished *kukui* nuts that served as a Christmas tree, Rulan was clearing her accounts for the year and sewing new clothes for herself and her daughter in anticipation of the gala celebration in Chinatown, an event that drew Tang men from across the island chain to Honolulu. Driven by homesickness, Tang men turned their one paid holiday into a two-day riot of feasting and fireworks. By day, fireworks crackled along the muddy lanes like gunfire; at night, the dingy storefronts were awash in the glowing light cast by lanterns strung on wire. Planters hated the holiday, for the number of runaways surged during the New Year festivities, and some workers would invariably return blinded or maimed from fireworks or the inevitable brawling between competing Triad societies or rival Punti and Hakka clans. Yet by Rulan's arrival, the surname societies were intent on ridding the holiday of its violence by devising strategies to bind the disparate factions of a bachelor society together. Thus was born the tradition of the Lantern Queen, a commemoration of what Tang men in the islands missed most: women.

Molly had been three when she first went with her mother to the Lantern Parade, a ragtag affair complete with rented pony carts, second-rate musicians, and youthful cane workers pressed into service as tumblers and dragon dancers. With the child astride her shoulders, Rulan had pushed through the crowd to the corner of Fid and Merchant Streets at the far end of Chinatown where the smell of gunpowder and burned paper was not as oppressive. Rulan cleared away a place on the dusty floorboards of a warehouse entrance and sat down with Molly to wait for the marchers to appear. The child had escaped her mother and was waddling on chubby legs toward a lantern swinging on a peg nearby when a string of fireworks burst across the street, sending her hurtling back into her mother's arms with a wail. After the long succession of explosions ended, Molly peeped out from the safety of Rulan's embrace and went rigid with amazement as a creature far more frightening than fireworks appeared. Dancing down the street in her direction snaked a dragon with golden head and shuddering body, which writhed and curled in a cloud of dust to the *dok-dok-dok* of a dozen drummers.

Seeing Molly, the dragon stopped, shook its silvery head and pranced stiffly for a moment or two—while Molly hid her face against her mother's breast—before passing on down the street.

"Bad and bad," Molly said, escaping her mother's arms to run after the monster and shake her finger at him as he was swallowed up by the noisy crowd.

Rulan saw with amusement that the papier-mâché head was cracked and broken, and that under the flimsy covering of burlap rice sacks, the dancers were kicking and tripping each other up. Yet Molly's eyes were huge. "The dragon danced for you," Rulan assured the child. "You are a very lucky girl this year."

The spectacle of the dragon was quickly eclipsed by the entry of the Lantern Queen, a beardless youth in women's clothes, bobbing awkwardly in a pony cart. It mattered little that the mock-queen's dark, field-roughened skin wasn't quite concealed by the heavy makeup or that his queue had fallen down the back of his headdress, for the onlookers cheered as lustily as if they welcomed a real queen.

Caught up in the frenzy of the crowd, Molly waved her arms at the gaudy apparition. The boy simpered and put his fan before his face in a comic imitation of a shy maiden, driving the field workers to uproarious cheers. Merchants began to throw coins from the doors of their stores, which the boy, to the crowd's delight, snatched out of the air with a sure, quick hand, or trapped with his knobby knees in the lap of his skirts. As the wagon passed the storehouse of the Lis, the boy signaled to the driver to stop in anticipation of the gift to come. The door of the store opened and down the steps tripped a girl of six dressed like a miniature bride in festival red. Her tunic and pants were red satin, her blue-black hair was braided and dressed in red ribbons, and her cheeks and lips were painted crimson. The crowd gave a collective sigh of admiration as the girl glided with mincing steps on feet encased in white bindings down the stairs and across the street to the pony cart.

"Thank you, Uncle," she piped to the boy, and handed up a coin. The twenty-dollar Spanish gold piece, which the boy held up, set the crowd cheering. The child's remarkable beauty had stirred up in each lonely bachelor an unbearable ache for what was best and most beloved of home: children, sweethearts, wives. Alarmed by the crowd's noisy attention, the girl hastened back to the porch where her mother awaited, but the mother pushed the girl back out into the street and made her stand in the halo of light cast by the lamppost so that all might see clearly her flawless white skin and porcelain features. Mei Yuk, wearing a Buddha's enigmatic smile, stood in the shadows, taking her daughter's triumph as her own.

By the third year of the Lantern Festival, Chinatown, a makeshift city of unpainted lumber and corrugated iron, sprawled out to engulf the waterfront. There were enough newly arrived merchants' wives to meet for weekly *ma jong* at Mei Yuk's mansion, a few steps away from the Lis' expanded fish market, which supplied most of the freshwater mullet and deep-sea *ulua* that Honolulu ate with its Chinese-manufactured *poi*. Tang children too appeared in enough numbers for the surname societies to bring in two tutors from Kwangtung, one for the children of Hakka and another for Punti.

At the New Year, Hawaiian youths in Prince Albert jackets took their sweethearts to dine at the noodle shops and gawk at the dragon dancers; the children of missionaries and whalers, who made their living in sugar or shipping, came too in anticipation of the moment when strings of firecrackers were ignited in lucky batches of three to usher out the evil spirits of the new year.

In honor of the parade, six-year-old Molly was decked out in a new, high-collared suit of yellow polished cotton. Her thick, unruly hair was brushed to a high sheen. Giddy from the noise and the lights, and the heady smells of incense and festival food, Molly preened and strutted, and did a mad little dance in her new red satin shoes in the dusty street as she and her mother waited for the parade to pass by. Like all citizens of Honolulu, Molly adored parades! This year's Lantern Parade promised to be particularly riotous, since the selection of the Lantern Queen had been hotly contested, with rival societies putting forward candidates of their own.

The *dok-dok-dok* of a tympany sounded, a Chinese flute wailed mournfully, and presently, the parade wound by. Molly climbed up the banister of a storefront to see the dragon dancer hold aloft a new and costly dragon's head sporting whiskers of real fur. Behind him shuddered the dragon's body, a length of shiny red satin fringed in silver. Beneath the shimmering satin, the dancers' feet beat a rhythmic tattoo in identical black shoes on the hard earth. No one tripped or fell.

In the wake of the dragon came the Lantern Queen, carried in a cart pulled by two sorrel mares. At her approach, cries of delighted surprise rose from the throats of the Tang men. "A woman! The queen is a woman!" they shouted as one. Not exactly a woman, observed Molly in astonishment, but a girl a few years older than herself. That same young beauty who had won the men's admiration three years before. Lily, Mei Yuk's nine-year-old daughter, was arrayed in silver brocade with a headdress of

metallic fringe and pearls. She stood in a cart lined with blooming narcissuses. The Tang men surged toward Lily, tossing coins at her tiny feet and
setting the cart dangerously rocking. Yet the girl never broke her pose. She
stood as stiffly as a temple statue with two fingers raised in blessing.

The cart stopped at the corner of Fid and Merchant Streets, now a
major intersection, where a merchant in a black banker's coat placed a *lei* of
orange *ilima* blossoms around Lily's neck. Hidden in the shadows cast by
the rooftops, Molly watched the queen with envious eyes, her own home-
sewn finery forgotten. Next to the shining Lily, she felt ugly and awkward
and brown.

Only Rulan saw that the Lantern Queen's glitter was store-bought and
suffered to think that her daughter was blind to her own bright beauty.

A true child of the islands, Molly could name in Hawaiian the separate winds that blew through Nuuanu Valley by the time she was seven.
Nalani had taught her to breathe with the earth, to feel the *ola* that coursed
through land and sky and sea, to see *akuas* hidden in the mists, to trace the
footsteps of tiny creatures called *menehunes* in the ancient ditches and canals
that crisscrossed the hidden reaches of the valley and thus to make herself
one with the spirit-infused land. Wisdom came to her from diverse sources:
her mother's talk story; the tales of Rip Van Winkle, Homer, and Aesop,
which she read with Lucy in the spacious library at Hiamoe; and the heroic
chants of old Hawaii with which Nalani had filled her dreams.

Molly's playmates were the Hawaiian and part-Hawaiian children from
the homesteads, who lived in shanties stuck on poles in the crumbling taro
patches in the valley, joined occasionally by an adventurous *haole* child from
one of the new cottages that had sprung up along the wide cobblestone
avenues. Now that the mule trolley ran to the entrance of the valley,
Nuuanu had become a fashionable place for newly prosperous citizens to
build homes. The airy mansions of downtown merchants and advisers to
the king dotted the hillsides, and Dowager Queen Emma herself had built a
spacious summerhouse where Lucy often took tea with the Companions
on the veranda in the very shadow of the *Pali*. So similar were the houses in
some parts of the valley that a visitor might think he had come to a town in
Vermont or New Hampshire, until the children leaped off broad verandas
or darted out of banana groves where grass houses were hidden; white and
brown, ruddy and golden-skinned, they called to each other in a singsong
tangle of English and Hawaiian and Cantonese.

Molly inhabited a far different valley than the one populated by
wealthy *haoles*. Nuuanu to her was the ancient playground of vanished *alii*.

Ducking past broad avenues lined with coconut palms, she ran through rain forests where the ground oozed water. Water dripped off ferns as tall as a man's head; in the rainy season, silvery waterfalls cascaded down black cliffs. Once within the valley, she made her way through shifting curtains of rain and thickets of wild ginger and fern. There were birds in the valley that one rarely saw in the islands nowadays: the tiny brown *o'o,* whose single yellow feather once adorned the capes and helmets of kings, had a secret nesting place here. *Nene* geese waddled along hidden trails. In the gulches lay the remains of ancient fishponds lined with stone walls built by *menehunes* who still came by night to repair their handiwork.

All year, Molly and her playmates waited for the rains, for then, the mud was slick enough for sport. She went with a gang of neighborhood urchins to the steep slope at the base of a gorge where a torrent of water poured out from the rock. Ancient stepping-stones allowed the nimble-footed to climb to the top of the gorge where patches of glossy *ti* plants bloomed along the hillside. The ritual for *ti*-leaf sliding was simple: clear a muddy path of stone, snap off the head of a *ti* plant and, holding the broad, thick leaves between your legs, push off downhill. Molly screamed her delight as she hurtled down the slide, then tumbled headlong into a chilly pool at the base of the gorge where she washed herself clean of red mud. Long ago, the slide had existed for the pleasure of chiefs. Now, however, the descendants of these same *alii* had forgotten that their fathers and mothers ever went there. Even the children who came every rainy season forgot once they left the valley.

Half a mile from the slide, a path through a thicket hung with fragrant *maile* vines opened on a crude stone altar, or *heiau,* tucked among the ferns. Unlike the mud slide, the altar had never passed from use. Molly often found small tokens left upon the surface of the stone by Hawaiians in the homesteads: usually a bit of raw pork wrapped in *ti* leaves, a bottle of whiskey, a coconut left in an egg-shaped hollow, and once a cock with its neck twisted. A groove at the base of the altar provided a hiding place into which she crept whenever rains lashed the valley. Molly could not name the precise reason why she returned again and again to the comforting shadow of the altar. Perhaps because she was, in Nalani's cryptic words, "a child born of the rock." Perhaps because she needed a sanctuary from her mother's bouts of desperate sorrow. Perhaps because the place itself seemed holy. For after a rainfall when the grove was bathed in rainbows, Hina, goddess of the mist, walked beside her, and the place seemed charged with *ola;* so much so that she could almost feel her dead father among those benevolent spirits Nalani called *akuas.*

When Nalani told her that priests, or *kahunas,* once raised the dead upon *heiaus,* seven-year-old Molly determined to pray her father back to life. At the altar, she said an incantation in Hawaiian, fixing her mind on the image of her father's face, a countenance her mother had described as scored and pitted as China itself. For good measure, she said the Lord's Prayer, the Twenty-third and One Hundredth Psalms, and added a petition to the god Kwan Kung, the patron saint of Tang men, whose warlike image was carried with great fanfare in the Lantern Parade.

As surety, she set down on the rough stones her most precious treasures: the porcelain doll she had slept with since infancy and a handful of *mui* stolen from her mother's jar. Then she sat down to wait for her father to appear through the curtain of *maile* vines. Hours passed; she saw no shape, heard no footsteps. Nor did any *akua* spirit her offering away.

From that time on, the *ola* seemed to drain away from the secret green places in Molly's valley. Molly forgot her mother's stories and Nalani's chants. Soon gentle Hina no longer came to her out of the rainbow, and *menehune* voices ceased to whisper on the wind.

13

THE BROKEN WALL

The Sacramento Delta

Each new year was ushered in by a season of torrential storms that pounded the spongy, peat-rich soil of the Delta into sludge. Unlike the Delta islands, the farms near Antioch were built high enough above the river to be spared from flooding. What was once useless swampland was now an expanse of neat furrows and hand-tended mud ramparts that yielded bushels of onions, asparagus, and potatoes. The *hui* formed by Pao An and Lucky had grown to twenty-five men and the farm to fifty acres.

Seeing the transformation of the land, the German had raised the rent yet again. Now the interest from their debts exceeded even the profits they had projected for the next year. How would they pay? the men demanded of Lucky, the official banker of the *hui*. Lucky cheerfully quoted them a village proverb: united in heart, mountains become jade; united in strength, dirt becomes gold. Some windfall, some miracle, he promised with cocky assurance, was in store that would turn their luck golden. Hadn't their small farm flourished while the acres of sugar beets planted by their Tang brethren in Isleton were washed away by the tide? Wasn't that proof that Kwan Kung, the god of manly men, held them in his favor?

At Lucky's urging, they took yet another loan from Ah Jack to purchase a hundred cuttings of a particularly hardy tomato hybrid from a Tang man in Sacramento to hasten the day when they all would be as rich as mandarins.

In every season on the Antioch farm, Pao An had awakened at dawn for an hour of solitary exercise and meditation, a luxury he allowed himself now that he was his own master. The dancelike calisthenics of *t'ai chi ch'uan,* at which he had excelled in his days as a Taiping soldier, helped to build up his body for the physical exertion of fieldwork. *T'ai chi* also offered him a way to recapture the discipline of his warrior past at a time when his life seemed in deep disarray. He had fallen so far, wasted so many years, lost so much. Whenever he gave himself over to the complex sequences, his mind threw off its perpetual unease and his body its pains. Mind and body moved upon one tether, beautifully, harmoniously. He could almost forget that the years spent as Creel's ox had earned him a pittance and that his woman had perished alone.

The day after the meager New Year's feast, while Lucky and the others were sleeping off the huge amounts of beer they had consumed, he stripped off his shirt, rubbed his bare chest and arms to get the blood flowing, and went out into the crisp Delta dawn to practice the slow circular movements of *t'ai chi*. Faint rays of light pierced the sky and swelled into a ruddy glow across the horizon and long shadows slanted toward the barn where the plow horse, sensing Pao An's presence, whinnied for his morning feed.

Pao An closed his eyes, lifted his shoulders, and straightened his spine. He let his neck and arms tighten, then relax, willed the muscles of his face to ease. He filled his lungs slowly, sending energy coursing through his body. Even before the first gesture, he had so completely shaped the movements in his mind that the river of motion had the inevitability of an afterthought. Then concentrating on the axle of power deep in his gut, he lifted hand and foot simultaneously and swung into the first sequence. Dubbed "the effortless art" in an ancient treatise by Cheng San Feng, *t'ai chi ch'uan* was originally an attempt to imitate the movement of animals at play. Now he was a deer leaping, now a monkey, now a bird, now a tiger slouching, tensed with power. Each movement had its complement, and so Pao An stepped right and then left, turned and lifted, lowered and turned. His gestures were as round and rhythmical as the contending forces of the surrounding water, the river flowing against the tidal surge of the far-off ocean into the Delta wetlands.

Halfway through the first sequence of movements, he noticed Lin Kong sitting on a box in the shadows just inside the barn. The boy was studying his movements, and he saw by certain small physical signs that without actually stepping through the ritual, Lin Kong was mimicking him. Pao An completed the set and called the boy over his shoulder. Lin Kong froze in terror.

"You've watched before, *hai ma*? Spied on me!"

Lin Kong hung his head in shame.

"Why didn't you ask?" Pao An demanded.

The boy flinched, as if he were about to be struck.

"What do you like?" Pao An probed sternly. "The rhythm or the power?"

Lin Kong shrugged, wishing he could disappear into his shadow in the dirt.

"A boy your age would like the power," Pao An observed in an offhand way. "You want to know how to fight and fling your enemies around, break bones and noses. Maybe jump up high like a cat and tear the ears off an enemy."

Lin Kong said nothing, but a small smile played on the corners of his mouth.

"Well, then," Pao An said, "we will exercise together, you and I. First, you must make your body strong. Then you will have to memorize the sequences. Dozens of them, each one harder than the other. And when I say you are ready—hear me, boy?—when you are disciplined and graceful and strong, only then will I teach you how each movement can be used against an enemy. Agreed?" He held his hand out to the boy the way the white devils did when they struck a bargain. Without a word, Lin Kong took the man's scarred and calloused hand and lifted it upon his head as a disciple might a master.

From that morning, whenever the press of work would allow, man and boy would exercise in the yard at sunrise before the summer heat rose from the dry earth, and then in the barn as the winter rain hammered down on the tin roof and turned the dark Delta loam into slippery clay.

*T*he first weeks of 1872 were unusually mild; the fields were blanketed with thick green alfalfa plants, and gnarled branches of infant fruit trees thrust up from acres of rich earth. With profits coming in, the men of the *hui* began to dream and plan. It was Pao An's idea to invest in milk cows, having seen from Vera's example how *bak kuei* used milk in every aspect of cooking. The steady profits from the sale of milk confirmed the wisdom of the venture, yet because the smell of milk revolted the other Tang men, it was left to Pao An and the boy to shoulder the burden of tending the cows.

Then the rains came. On a dreary March morning, after a long month of driving rain, Pao An roused Lin Kong for the first milking. Halfway across the muddy yard, a thunderclap shattered the vaporous silence, followed by a deluge of water, which hit the ground seconds later with the force of a waterfall. They dashed to the long, narrow shelter built of precious wood and corrugated iron, struggled to open the heavy door and stood upon the steaming hay, watching the darkness melt. So loud was the rain upon the tin roof that the cows, their udders heavy and swollen, swung their broad, bony heads against the stalls in terror. Lin Kong clucked his tongue and crooned to them in strangled sounds, his private language for animals, feeling a surge of power from the furious pounding of the rain. So much had hard work in the outdoors changed him that except for his uncanny silence, Phoenix would not have recognized this sunburned, sturdy boy as hers.

When the rain slackened and the cows calmed down, Pao An took out the milking stools and seated himself at the end of the line of animals. He leaned his head against the cow's warm flanks while the boy claimed a creature nearby. Pao An's practiced fingers closed automatically on the leathery teat, but it took long minutes of tugging before the cow let down her milk, for she was finicky and reluctant, unsettled by the downpour. He dozed, his fingers moving automatically, until the first spray in the iron bucket jolted him awake. Soon, two pairs of hands had fallen into an easy rhythm, and Pao An had drifted to the edge of sleep, his fingers working of their own accord, when the door of the barn was flung open by a pale-haired woman dripping wet and covered with mud.

"I know I shouldn't of come," Vera was saying. "You don't want to see my face no more, I reckon, and if Nathan knew he'd like to kill us both."

Frightened by the entry of this stranger, the cows stamped their feet and bawled their protest. Lin Kong leaped up from his stool, knocking over the bucket of milk. Thick spurts of foaming liquid hissed into the steaming hay.

"Better you stay away," Pao An said.

Vera seemed aggrieved by his lack of warmth. "I been stickin' my fool nose in every damn tent in the China camps. I jest about give up when someone said some Chinks was farmin' out here. Soon's I saw the cow barn, I knew it was you," she blurted out. "He's been fightin' the river for a week. Gone crazy, screamin' at the river like a madman, yellin' how it won't get him this time. He's still up there sandbaggin' and haulin' in timber by hisself." A sob strangled her momentarily. "He fell in last night just when I come out with the lantern. I ran down the levee and hauled him out at the Point. And you know what he done?" Tears sprang into her eyes and rolled down her sallow cheeks. "He didn't even curse at me. He climbed back up without a by-your-leave, hobbled over to his wheelbar-row and started baggin' again like I wasn't there. I took off then. Every-body took off. Ain't hardly nobody left on the island 'cept one crew of coolies workin' for the Konrads. They's all afraid it's goin' under!"

"He'd shoot me if he saw me coming," Pao An snapped.

"Not if you bring him a gang o' Chinks. He hates you, sure, like he hates me," she replied, "but he hates the river more. Anyways, he ain't the same man. . . . He's old now." He flinched when she touched his arm in supplication, and her hand sprung back as if burned. "I ain't got no pride, ya see?" she said weakly. "You got friends here, they do what you tell 'em to. If it's money ya want," she whispered, "the Reclamation Company jes' made us a loan. I saved up some money of my own. We got more'n enough to pay." She added with a shame-faced look, "And I got plenty stashed away that even Creel don't know about. Money I was fixin' to use if you ever come back."

Lin Kong watched in consternation as the woman came up to Pao An and put a hand on his bare chest.

*L*ucky greeted Vera's offer with wild glee. Here was the windfall that Kwan Kung, the god of manly men, had provided! Rapidly calculating in his head, he announced that twelve of them would accumulate enough cash in a month to pay off the entire year's debt to the German. How much more quickly would the debt be expunged if all twenty-five pitched in?

"Let the *bak kuei* drown," shouted a youth from the Four Districts. "We have our own farm to look after. Anyway, we're free men now. Why should we hire ourselves out for slaves?"

"Not slaves," corrected Lucky. "Businessmen!"

"We *are* free men now," Pao An added. "Not 'pigs' from Kwangtung. We sell our services for top-dollar wages. I say let's take the money and save our own farm!"

After Lucky negotiated a deal with the desperate Vera, which netted the *hui* a substantial sum more than she had first offered, the men agreed to go. But Pao An, knowing the danger posed by the treacherous river, ordered Lin Kong to stay in Antioch.

The rain stopped at noon, began again two hours later when their boats were halfway across the river, then dwindled to a feeble drizzle. By the time the Tang men reached the farm, a rainbow had broken through the clouds over Mount Diablo, whose broad slopes were touched with fire from the setting sun.

"What the hell you hangmen's dummies doing here?" Creel cried when the haggard, wet men appeared on the levee road. He was hobbling on his wooden leg and awkwardly pushing a wheelbarrow full of rocks to dump along the river's seething edge. Creel struggled stubbornly on. Wild-eyed and emaciated, his lank hair hanging in long damp locks, he seemed driven by an uncanny strength.

"I brung 'em to help," said Vera,

"Help who?" he snapped. "Help you put canning in the cellar?" With a heave, he jarred the wheelbarrow loose from the mud, and shoved it farther along the levee, barely glancing at Pao An.

"Believe what you want," said Vera, exhausted, "only let 'em help you."

When the wheelbarrow ground to a halt in the mud, Creel gathered an armful of rocks, lugged them out onto the side of the bank and cast them down into the river. With a painful effort, he straightened himself and squinted into the darkening sky, muttering, "Damned Mexicans run off. Ain't finished raining yet, neither. River fixing to make one last charge." Creel shouted to Pao An, "Go tell them pigtailed sonsabitches to get workin'!"

Just as Creel predicted, the rains came again. A slow, passionless drizzle, one without outward significance or force, but as the hours rolled by, it kept up its unrelenting rhythm, the way a throbbing in the temple presages agony to come. The men slogged through the knee-deep mud, shoring up the levee.

The second day, the rain turned savage. Where it had been a capricious thief, stealing one farmer's field but leaving another, now it was a famished animal intent on devouring everything in its path. It came down in a rush, great flat sheets of it, winding through the sky, obscuring the hills and Mount Diablo above them, and roiling the river into angry brown froth. Having gone for days without sleep or food, Creel seemed to forget who was master and who was hired hand. He labored side by side with the Chinamen, lifting stone and timber to raise the ramparts higher in a stubborn attempt to stem the river's assault upon his cherished land.

In the middle of the night, as Pao An's team was taking its first long rest in three days, word came down the levee by rider. One of Konrad's boys on a plow horse, splashing through puddles a foot deep along the road, reined up at the farmhouse, yelling, "Levee's down at Potter's ranch below Free-port!" Then he rode on like an antediluvian Paul Revere.

Creel yelled for Vera to rouse the men. Wearily, she shuffled out in her nightdress to where the crew slept on straw strewn with burlap in the barracks that once held the pallets of a hundred men.

"It done broke," she said in a voice devoid of hope. "And I ain't fixin' to stick around when this place goes under . . ."

Lucky had already fled out the door to collect the promised wages from Creel; the rest of the Tang men flung their meager belongings into knapsacks and raced after Lucky in preparation for the trek through the muddy sloughs back to Antioch. When Pao An tried to order the men back on the levees, Vera gave a bitter laugh. "It ain't their land," she said wearily. "Wish to God it weren't mine neither. He never got a damned thing outta this 'cept sweat and cursin' and now maybe dyin'. I ain't stickin' around long enough to see."

"A man has to fight, not run," Pao An retorted roughly. "All a man got is pride."

"That's pitiful little. Don't a man got a woman?" she ventured.

"You're *his* woman."

"I ain't," she declared, measuring the effect of her words on Pao An. "He got a chain on me. But that don't mean I belong to him." She looked at him pleadingly, and when he didn't respond, she said in a rush, "You 'n me could figure sumpin'," she said, tripping over her words in her excitement. "Leave the bastard be. I got money saved, enough so's we could go up Canada way, where no one knows us. Who'd think twice about a widder woman and her Chink? Some of that money's yours, you know," she added breathlessly. "That time you was sending wages to that Chinee woman, I stuck 'em away. Saved it up for a *rainy* day," she said with quiet pride.

"You never sent the letters?" Pao An asked stonily.

"Sent the first one. Give them some cock and bull so's they wouldn't bother you no more. After that, made up the replies myself."

"My woman is alive?" he asked, hardly daring to breathe.

Vera shrugged. "Who knows by now? I figgered you'd fergit about her so why waste good money. . . . Come with me," she begged. What she saw in his blazing eyes brought her up short even before Lucky burst through the door.

"Devil Creel's paying triple wages to any Tang man that stays to fight the river!" he cried. "Enough for a hundred acres and a year of opium dreams!" This was more money than a fisherman could make in a season of hauling in salmon, more than twice what a Tang man was paid for a year of blasting through the Sierras with nitroglycerine. This offer, moreover, falling on the ears of the debt-ridden *hui,* quickly transformed the Tang men's mood from exhaustion to exhilaration. Pao An followed Lucky onto the ramparts.

"Damn you!" screamed Vera; she stumbled after Pao An, confounded by his undisguised contempt. Her hair, matted and darkened with rain, hung down around her face like the reeds of the river and her mouth was as twisted as a cat's. "Damn your kind to hell!"

*A*t daybreak, two Tang men passed in a wagon with the news that Ah Jack, with ghoulish but uncanny ability to sniff out potential profits, had come aboard the steamer *Hercules* to hawk coffins and grave suits to the scores of Chinamen hired by desperate Delta farmers to fight the river. Once again, fear seized the *hui*. Ignoring Creel's curses, three men threw aside their shovels and rushed down the muddy bank in the driving rain to the place where the *Hercules* had made a landing. Yet Ah Jack, fearing the river more than he craved profits, stayed only long enough to collect a handful of coffin fees in his strongbox before pushing off to Sacramento.

Creel stuck a pistol into his belt and, propping himself up with a long black cane to balance his tricky wooden leg, vowed to shoot the first Chinaman who tried to flee. They stayed only because they had nowhere to run. Bent like oxen in yokes, their legs freezing in the water, Pao An and the men of the *hui* carried railroad ties to a breach and, wading into the powerful current in a human chain tied together with rope, built a front-line breakwater. On the shore, they were joined by other gangs of Tang men hired by the farmers who had stayed to defend their ramparts; they labored all night, Chinaman and white man side by side, to fill the yawning gap with wood, stones, and bags of wet sand, and by midmorning, just as the rainfall was subsiding, the breach was sealed.

No one could tell Tang man from white man now, for all looked more like mud-covered monkeys than men. And when word came to Creel and the farmers that the levee had broken at Sutterville and that every man able to lift a stone was needed, all who had labored to shore up the Delta levees, white and yellow alike, lay down upon the wet ground and stubbornly refused to move. Only Creel had energy enough to bellow his rage at the fools who could not muster their own neighbors to fight the river. "Look to your own!" he shouted back to them. And in a renewed burst of frenzy, he persuaded the captain of the steamer *Hercules* to ferry the work crews up to the wing dam on Old River, where the tricky play of currents incessantly undermined the earthen walls.

And again, with little food and less sleep, Pao An and Lucky and the men of the *hui* were ordered to shore up the levees at the curve of the river where danger of erosion was greatest. Because the rain had abated, they were able to set up a caravan of wagons to and from the nearby farms, commandeering all the bales of hay available to wedge between the stakes and railroad ties they had sunk into the levee. Then from the deck of the steamer as it lay idling like an immense bird on the turbulent water, Creel directed the Tang men onshore to dump driftwood, rocks, gravel, fallen trees and bushes, anything that would slow the water's undertow. Creel's mad hatred of the river had begun to infect them all.

By midnight, the rains began again. A gale-force wind blew from the west, driving up from San Francisco Bay and across the northern valley. The *Golden Hind,* a sternwheeler out of Oakland, passed the *Hercules* at daybreak, making for Sacramento with forty thousand board feet of lumber and seven thousand sacks to fight the upriver breaks.

"How's things downriver?" Creel yelled into the undulating curtains of rain.

"The levee broke at Deadman's Drift and at Robert's Track," the boatman's voice resounded through a brass horn. "Just lakes behind the levees there. Murphy's place washed away as we was going by. Dike done busted fifty yards upstream of his house. It come through like a stampede, hit the house and knocked it clean off'n its foundations. We saw it tip like a funnel and the river pour right through it. The house is on its side driftin' south in twenty feet of water now."

"Anybody get out?"

"No tellin'," the boatman yelled back, and then the rain and the wash of his wheel drowned him out, and the great lighted platform, beating heavily against the current, vanished in the dark downpour.

At noon a lone rider slogged through the fog and rain, bearing a terrifying message to the twenty-five Tang men working like muddied ants on the levee mound: the river had broken through the levees upstream, sending mile after mile of hand-raised earthworks toppling into the swirling waters. In a matter of minutes, the rider shrieked, the flood would engulf them. Lucky called to the others to lay down their shovels and pickaxes and, wading into the angry waters, signaled to Creel. When the boat did not respond, Pao An took a line and, tying one end to a locust tree and the other about his waist, plunged into the river, fighting the angry current until Creel fished him out with his cane.

"What the hell you do a fool stunt like that?" Creel screamed down at Pao An, who lay shivering and limp on deck. "I heard the message that rider brung. What he say don't change nothing. We keep hauling rock, dumping in timber until the levee holds."

Pao An was on his haunches, retching and coughing up river water. He rolled over and sat with his back against the rail. "My men are done. Finished," he panted. "By now the gap is a thousand feet wide and the water is behind us. My men will be standing on a mud wall between two seas. Take them off!"

"You mean *quit*? There's a damn sight more to do. I never heard of you men of Tang giving up, especially at wages like I'm paying you." Creel was leaning over him, his eyes red and wild, pressing the sharp cane hard into Pao An's side. Whereas Pao An and the rest of the Chinamen were staggering from exhaustion, Creel's energy seemed boundless.

"Men of Tang?" Pao An repeated slowly. Here were the words for which he had waited so long for Creel to say. But the words were as false as the deceiver who uttered them. He rose painfully to his feet, hating Creel for all the years of degradation and deception, hating all *bak kuei* deceivers who had ground him down. "Are we finally *men*?" he bellowed. "Not 'yella niggers, dogs, bastards, prickless apes, heathen devils, shit eaters'? Are we *men* now that you need us? What good is a pile of dirt in the middle of the sea?"

"It's a place to stand and fight!" Creel shot back in return. "I already had one piece of land took from me. I ain't figuring to let go my land a second time. Not one inch of it."

"It's your land, not ours. I'm taking my men off!" Pao An insisted.

"Yella, just like I said!" Creel bellowed in disgust. "I figgered you wrong, Tang man. If you can't boss your own kind, then clear out! Go! Git!" He raised his cane and struck Pao An so hard a blow to the head that he fell to the deck, stunned and bleeding. By the time Pao An staggered to his feet, Creel was at the prow, brandishing his cane in one hand and the revolver in the other and yelling at the captain to bring the boat close enough to the shore for a plank to be lowered.

Creel was already climbing down, pivoting on his bad leg with the ease of an acrobat, before the tip of the plank touched land. "Men of Tang," he yelled over the roar of the waters. "With your own hands you built the Great Wall for your emperor. Now build me a wall against this infernal river!" The speech was framed in the same flowery, nonsensical diction that *bak kuei* typically used to approximate Chinese, except that none of the Tang men seemed to hear. Their faces were ghastly, twisted by terror. Lucky, who feared no one, was screaming, waving his arms, shouting for Pao An to save him. Pao An looked behind and saw that the levee had broken a hundred yards away; water was sucking through the breach with the noise and force of a mountain cascade.

"Hurry, hurry," Pao An yelled to the captain. "Get them off. It's breaking up!"

At that moment, the levee-side wheel caught a submerged tree stump. It grated, clamped, stuck. The river-side wheel spun, turning the prow into the makeshift barricade the men had been building for the last hours. With a sickening thud, the *Hercules* hit the barricade, knocking out two tall railroad ties. As if a gate had been lifted, a small trough of water poured through the gap, and at that moment, Lucky, who was closest to the gap, began to scream. In the next second, another tie gave way. And another. Lucky leaped to the edge to steady the ties with his bare hands, yet they fell away like a line of ivory game tiles. Frantically, he scrambled to the eroding crest of the levee to where Creel stood roaring and cursing at the foaming river.

With a jerk, the wheel broke free of debris, tearing loose a section of sandbags and opening another spillway in front of the stranded men. There was no time now to bring the men on board. Pao An ran to where a small boat was turned upside down on the deck, and dragged it to the rail as the *Hercules* spun and listed. He was about to throw it over the side when an entire section of the levee sheared off. The noise came first. A thunderous blast, like the sundering of the ground beneath them. Then the under layer of earth slid out from beneath its muddy surface. Pao An watched in horror as Lucky sank out of sight, his cries drowned out by the roaring of the water. One by one, the Tang men dissolved into the muddy water, their mouths open in a wordless scream, their hands flailing in a mad attempt to ward off the avalanche of water and debris.

Creel, who stood at the highest point of the levee, was the last to slip into the vortex of the river. Slowly, he sank to his knees, up to his chest, then as the monstrous wave curled over him, he raised his cane above his head to plunge it like a sword into the oncoming wall of water. Creel's arm hovered above the flood, unyielding and unbent, then it too was swallowed up by a huge brown current of broken ties, haybales, and rock.

For a moment it seemed that the *Hercules* would be carried sideways through the gap, but the wheels caught hold and pulled the boat slowly into the safety of the channel. Except that no channel remained. In its place was an immense, foam-flecked ocean sweeping across the entire Delta as far as the eye could see.

Pao An put his head on the rail and wept for all the good men swallowed up by the pitiless river.

Only he, the son of water, remained.

Sherman Island. Brannon Island. Fagin Track. The river had effaced them all. Cows stood forlorn and frightened on tiny atolls of sodden earth, all that remained in some places of the vast stretches of levees that had crisscrossed the Delta. Sometimes, only the tops of pear and peach trees hinted at the acres of drowned orchards underneath the tide. Chickens, perched on sycamore tops or the roofs of barns, cocked their heads at the bloated corpses of cattle and barnyard fowl floating by. The water pole at Steamboat Slough read twenty-six feet above the flood, the highest the Sacramento had risen since white men had measured it. And still the rains fell.

*A*fter two weeks in Rio Vista waiting for the waters to recede, Pao An started back to Antioch. There in an elbow of the river he came upon the battered corpse of Ah Jack caught in the roots of a sycamore tree; he was still clothed in a black satin banker's coat, though the rocks had torn the expensive garment to shreds, and the body was distended with gases. Filled with revulsion, Pao An attempted to kick the corpse out of the tangled roots, yet it would not budge. He was about to turn back upon the road when a glint of metal aroused his interest. Had Ah Jack, greedy even in death, carried away a cargo too precious to relinquish to the river? Certain now of the reason for the corpse's odd, immovable position, Pao An leaped into the brackish water and rolled the corpse over, searching for the chain around Ah Jack's waist. This done, he pulled at the slippery metal and felt the answering weight of the iron strongbox dragging on the river bottom. In minutes, he had tugged it ashore. The lid was broken; the box was empty. All the coins taken from the Tang men had floated away.

*O*n the steamship *Sequoia,* bound for Hawaii and Rulan, Pao An made a poem to honor gallant Lucky and sorrowful Phoenix, Ah Jack, Devil Creel, his brothers from the *hui,* and all the rest whose bodies were sown into the soil of the Delta. And when he and Lin Kong reached the immigration station in San Francisco, he borrowed an ink brush and painted the words onto the walls of the shed so other Tang men might read how Gold Mountain was being made:

I pull apart black loam with my hands:
Earth holding earth.
Long netted threads of peat entwined;
fat brown worms and blue beetles writhe and run,
segmented ants, white beads sprouting on yellow tubers
cling to my fingers.
Like the men sent by Emperor Chin to build the Wall
these dark warriors build and swarm.

Nothing for them is waste.
Even a homeless man has purpose.
The unsung man will be remembered;
the no-name man, scratched from the clan tablets,
will find a home in the earth below the river.

part 2

Plum Girl

1

THE RETURN

Honolulu, 1873

"Where is my father?" Molly wanted to know as soon as her growing consciousness brought his absence to light. Other children had fathers, why not she? Instead, she had Uncle Emmanuel and two busybody aunties who bossed her around as much as her real mother.

That question never failed to plunge the aunties into uneasy silence. Her real mother, by contrast, had too many answers, some flippant, others obscure. "He is gone buying *mui*," she would tease. Or "He is away making rainbows." That answer pleased Molly the most. She loved to think that somewhere on the rugged green *Pali*, her father was mixing pigments against the sky—as Auntie Lucy did with watercolors and brush on soft, thick white paper—and letting the bright colors melt into the mists.

Eventually, she came to understand the true significance of her mother's obfuscations: her father was dead. Now the stories disturbed more than comforted her. What was real and what was not? Who was this shadowy figure who shaped her mother's life from the grave? Her mother answered with more stories.

"Your father was a soldier," Rulan might say. "In the season of rain, when thunder echoes across the *Pali*, you can hear him rouse his warriors as he did in China when the farmers and boatmen took up arms against the Dragon Throne."

Molly wanted to believe her. In bed at night, listening to the hot, wet wind raging up from Kona, she would listen for her father's voice in the thunder echoing from valley to valley.

If her father spoke out of the thunder, her mother's face was etched on the surface of the moon. Like the Moon Lady, Molly's mother was always sad. Molly did not know any other mother or any other face than the sad one. Whenever that smooth Moon Lady face seemed in danger of cracking, Molly would whine or cry or pretend to be sick so that her mother would go looking for sour plums or sticks of licorice root or a brush to loosen the tangles in her hair. It was for her mother's own good, Molly decided, that she was so demanding. Her chief duties were to keep her mother from dreaming too much of sad things and to furnish the heat and light that kindled the wan Moon Lady smiles.

*S*even years and an ocean between them. Pao An stared down from the ship's rail at an island devoid of beauty. He saw a dilapidated dockside, the tin-roofed shacks of Chinatown spilling over with Tang men as shabbily dressed as he. Hawaii was only a bedraggled copy of Fiddletown or Stockton and hardly the "blessed" isles of village talk story. He prayed that Rulan had survived.

Yet if she lived, would she want him back? Maybe she had taken another. Perhaps she would know just by looking at him that he had betrayed her with Vera. Perhaps they would meet only to have love die!

He and the boy found a two-story boardinghouse of unpainted wood with an outside stairway and balcony that leaned precariously over a narrow, fetid alley. A tinderbox like the other tenements in the Chinatown district, he observed, built for quick profits in rents rather than durability or safety. The landlord, an ex–cane cutter, demanded a week's rent in advance and posed a dozen questions to discover Pao An's character, fortune, and clan. And after having determined that the new tenant was a free laborer with money in his pocket and, moreover, a Punti from his own home district of Heungsan in the Pearl River Delta, the landlord urged him to register at the *tong* clubhouse down the lane. "You take the oath, pay dues, the brothers find you a job or stake you to a business," he avowed. "No need to mingle with those filthy Hakka."

"I don't keep the old feuds," Pao An replied brusquely. "A Tang man is a Tang man," and he went about the shops and tenements making inquiries of his own about Rulan in as offhand a way as he could contrive.

He had paid the landlord for a week's rent of two narrow wooden beds covered with straw mattresses in a roomful of ten men. The silent Lin Kong, exhausted by the rigors of the ocean voyage, fell asleep immediately, but Pao An lay awake for hours listening to the sharp cries of *ma jong* players in the gambling hall across the street and the clatter of game tiles. When sleep came at last, his dreams were unexpectedly sweet, pulling him back to the first heady days of the great rebellion before he and Rulan had become lovers. He heard again the voices of the horsewomen calling to each other as they rode their swift ponies from one end of the column of foot soldiers to the other. Rulan was leaning over her mount to touch his face when suddenly, he awoke with a jolt and found himself surrounded by snoring men in a room thick with the sour smells of alcohol, stale opium smoke, and urine. He groped his way past the line of cots, trying to hold on to the vestiges of the dream, but once having set foot on the stairway outside, he felt the night air sweep clean the images from his mind. The streets were blanketed in darkness so deep that he felt suspended in a void. He heard the rhythmic murmur of the sea, the lonely cry of a seagull. What if he had come all this distance to have Rulan slip away? He stumbled blindly downstairs in search of someone, anyone to talk to.

The landlord leaped up in terror when Pao An peered in at the doorway of his tiny kitchen. "*Aiya,* it's only you," he blurted out, visibly relieved and as glad of companionship as Pao An. "I thought you were a thief! Here," he told Pao An, "I just made tea. Iron Kwan Yin. I pay top dollar for it, Mexican gold coin," and pulled two cups from a stack of crockery upon the table.

The man's teeth were chattering as he poured water from a brass kettle into a cracked ceramic teapot encased in a bamboo carrier. He had not slept in days, the landlord confided, out of fear of thieves. When the dark layer of tea leaves swirled up to the surface of the pot, he banged down the ceramic cover and filled the cups to the brim.

The brew was thin and yellow, but Pao An gratefully put the steaming cup to his lips. The landlord's agitation seemed to mount. He made small, darting movements with his hands as if he could not decide whether to flee or stay.

"You going to open a business in Honolulu?" he asked after a while.

Pao An nodded and kept drinking his tea. The hot liquid seared his tongue and throat, sending a welcome wave of heat coursing through his tired body. A small shuffling sound assailed his ears: sandaled feet slapping against the wooden boards of the veranda. He turned, expecting to see Lin Kong, sleepy and distressed, when the door flew open and three men burst in from outside.

Before Pao An could move, a machete was at his throat and a knife was slashing in the landlord's direction. The landlord shrieked and flung the teapot at his attackers, hurling himself through the door. But he was dragged inside and wrestled to the ground.

Pao An's attacker peered into his face, then released him with a contemptuous shove. "This is not your concern," he barked, and turned his attention toward the unhappy owner of the tenement who was flailing his arms and limbs wildly and wailing, "I paid the Widow last week. I swear I gave her all I had!" But his pleas fell on deaf ears, for two men dragged him by the pigtail across the table until his head lay like a duck's on a chopping block, while the third let fly with his knife.

The man with the machete slammed his blade hard into the wood, each time closer to the landlord's head until the queue was severed from the skull. Then he swept the hair onto the floor where it lay in the steaming puddles of tea like a dead black snake. "The Widow says one more week. Pay what you owe, or I swear by the god of waste that I will slice the head from your body and kick it into the canal."

When the intruders had departed, the landlord began to moan, "Oh my mother and father, your foolish son is dead." His head was bleeding where the machete had nicked his scalp. Matted, bloody bits of hair clung to his shirt.

Pao An had never believed the landlord's story about "thieves." He helped the landlord off the table, saying, "They're from the *tong, hai ma?* The Triad brotherhood you wanted me to join . . ."

The landlord nodded with a groan. "I don't blame them for doing their job. They didn't put the pipe to my lips. This year I smoked more 'black dirt' than I could afford. I put more beds upstairs to bring in cash, and then the bachelors stopped coming to town. Profits are bad in sugar, and no cane cutters come over from Gold Mountain or the village in three months. . . . *Aiya,* I curse the day I heard the name Li!"

Pao An grew still. "I know this name. Is Li the headman of the *tong*?"

The landlord shook his head. "Merchant Li is dead. It's his wife, a demon from Buddhist hell, who runs the business now. The Widow is ten times worse than the husband. She used to own the opium license. Now that the king outlawed that trade, she sells so much that she has an army of *tong* henchmen as her collectors. It's this house she wants. She thinks if she squeezes me enough, that I will sell it to her cheap. *Aiya*," he groaned, rubbing his bleeding scalp, "maybe I will! When my neighbor was late in paying the Widow, she made the *tong* take his store. But when the store didn't pay enough, her thugs took his ears too." He began to cry.

Pao An took five silver dollars from the bag at his belt, pressed it into the man's hand, and left him mourning the enormity of his debt and the immensity of his folly.

*T*here were less than a hundred Tang women in the islands, thirty wives, daughters, concubines, and bond maids in Honolulu Chinatown alone. All of them except the Chinese woman living with the *bak kuei* met regularly for *ma jong* and gossip. A man could not inquire about the most recalcitrant member of this elite sisterhood without attracting the attention of the Widow, its most powerful member. Li Mei Yuk heard about the Tang man in Western boots who had cut off his queue and how he was going into the shops and restaurants asking about her rival. That he had found lodging with a man who owed her money was fortuitous. It was easy to coerce the landlord into searching through the stranger's things. The man found little to identify the newcomer except a handbill from an apothecary shop in Fiddletown. By then, Mei Yuk was already certain that the peasant-rebel who had once been her lover had come to the islands to claim the woman who had stolen him away.

The prudent thing to do was to have Pao An killed; the secrets he knew could easily bring her down. But when it came to the rebel general, Mei Yuk had always been rash. As a young wife in the house of Li, she had risked exposure and death to keep him close, her secret solace in a loveless marriage. She desired him still. So she sent Pao An a letter by messenger inviting him to her shop the following evening. Who could predict how the simple crossing of an ocean had changed them both? she told herself. An impossible union in the old country might prove propitious in the new, since all that mattered among the Hawaii Chinese was money. Pao An must see the advantages that a liaison with Chinatown's wealthiest citizen could offer.

Mei Yuk waited alone for him in the pale light of evening. She had put on a good dress, not her best. The pink shade of the gaslight cast a ruddy glow over her skin. He would see instantly how the years had usurped her beauty. Still, she was rich. That fact alone would tempt him, as it did all the no-name rascals from the *tong* who had thought to lift themselves up by offering for her after Liang Mo died. When she heard his footsteps on the wooden walkway outside, her heart beat an excited tattoo. She felt the sudden gust of air when he opened the door and remembered how he always entered a room as if to invade it. And then he stood before her, as massive as a tree, squinting in the gathering darkness in her direction, like all the times he had returned to her after a season of war.

"*Aaiiee!*" she cried, when he moved into the light. "What have the filthy *bak kuei* done to you? You are old now!"

His eyes roamed the room, taking in the ivory figurines on the huge koa wood desk, the teakwood screens inlaid with mother-of-pearl, the painted scrolls, the ink stones and brushes gathering dust. The abacus within easy reach of her long fingers.

"Don't stand there staring at me," she told him, although he had scarcely glanced in her direction at all. "You make me nervous. Come, sit by me," she said, pointing to the chair drawn up beside her.

Pao An pulled the chair toward him, moved it farther away from her, turned it backward and plopped down.

"Are you afraid of me?" she pouted. "It is I who should take care. You were always rash—who knows how desperate you are or what you might do! I'm a widow now, you know . . ."

He let her talk, observing without interest or affection the familiar quick movements of her fingers and head. Nothing had changed about her. She was still as nervous as a crimson bird—jumping, turning, cocking her head coquettishly. Impossible, he had once thought, to snare, yet now his for the taking.

"Did you make your stake? Where did you travel?" she demanded eagerly.

"Gold Mountain. I built levees for the *bak kuei*." He held his hands out before him, as if releasing the years into the air. She saw that they were scarred, calloused, stained by labor.

"A *gu li*!" she said with a mocking smile. "How low the proud general has fallen!"

Her barbs had no more sting for him. "Rulan . . ." he asked impatiently. "Does she live?"

"*Aaiiee,*" Mei Yuk said softly, the color draining from her cheeks. "Well, *that* one is quite alive! Lives with the *bak kuei,* puts on *bak kuei* airs, talks and dresses like them. We in Chinatown hardly see her."

"Is she alone?"

"Alone, no!" Mei Yuk said quickly. "She has a child, you know. A girl. A wild-looking dark creature. Obviously Hawaiian."

Pao An looked away. "She has a man then?" he muttered.

"Do I know these things?" Mei Yuk cried out sharply. "Am I to confess all my sister's secrets? . . . If she did, the scoundrel left her. Why else would the *bak kuei* take her in? You know their fondness for fallen Tang women, how they like to use them as examples of their own goodness."

"Where is her house?"

Mei Yuk pulled her chair closer and touched the rough cloth of his shirt. "Let *that one* alone. I own the fish market on King Street, tenements, and stores. I paid a fortune in bribes for an opium license from the king. A good business, but dangerous. I need a strong man to help me run it. Someone who can make the *tong* stop skimming off my profits."

"Tell me where she lives," he insisted.

"A Tang man needs friends to make his way in Hawaii," she pressed on, not bothering to disguise the desperation in her voice. "The king taxes everything so he can have parties and boat races and new uniforms for his guards. The *kanakas* pretend to welcome us, but they blame Tang people for the sickness and taking away their jobs . . ."

He rose quickly from the chair. "I have no time to talk. I must find her . . ."

"She doesn't need you! She goes around with the old queen's companions now." Mei Yuk's voice had turned strident. "The *haole* she lives with up Nuuanu will run you off with his gun!"

When she grabbed his sleeve to stop him, he pulled her hands away, held them for a moment in order not to give offense, then let them fall.

*H*is emotions lurching wildly between relief and fear, Pao An raced back to the boardinghouse for Lin Kong. Alive! In a place called Nuuanu. With luck, by the end of the afternoon, he would lay claim to his woman. And if she had taken a lover in his absence, well, he would not hold that transgression against her, having erred himself with the wife of Devil Creel. He would take in Rulan's "wild, dark" child, raise it as his own, although he wished with all his heart that he had been the one to plant the spark of life inside her!

*I*n the spring of her seventh year, not long after her abortive attempt to pray her father back to life, Molly saw a peddler trudging up the road to Hiamoe. It was 1873. A new king named Lunalilo, whom Lucy reviled as a "drunken lout" for beating her dear friend Emma in the election to the throne, had just been crowned. Bent under a wooden yoke laden with bedding and cooking utensils, the gaunt, sunburned Tang man rattled as he walked, a comical sight. Behind him, carrying a child-size yoke, trudged a boy somewhat older than she, although he was so skinny Molly could not really tell for sure. Molly swung back and forth on the gate, vocalizing wordless tunes and singing the tall stranger closer. She saw that unlike the

Tang men in blue-black field pajamas who hawked fish or crude silk cloth in the valley, this one was dressed in Western breeches and a checked shirt like the kind the Spanish cowboys from the Big Island cattle ranches wore. And instead of a Chinaman's bald pate and pigtail, he had short cropped hair under a broad-brimmed hat that hid his eyes.

She hailed him in Cantonese, and when he failed to reply (her Chinese never came out quite right), repeated the words in Hawaiian. He did not return either greeting but stopped outside the gate awhile in awkward silence. Up close, he blotted out the sun. She swung back and forth on the gate, making the rusty hinges sing, peeking up at him through lowered lashes so the stranger could admire her. She was used to Chinamen staring. Nalani said it was because she was *maikai,* pretty. Too *maikai* for her own good, echoed Lucy sternly. With one scarred hand, the man stopped the gate from swinging. He studied Molly's eyes, her quavering smile, her sturdy brown fingers grasping the top beam.

"Where is your mother?" he finally asked.

There was a rule in the household: no peddlers in the yard, but the urgency in his voice pricked her curiosity and led her to break the rule this time. She leaped off the gate and led him across the yard, around the stand of banana and papaya trees to the back of the house while the boy followed behind like a dumb beast. When the man saw Molly's mother, he put down his burden and stood awhile, watching her bend and lift the wet clothes to the line. The shirts, still steaming from the wash pot, danced in the wind like headless ghosts. Quietly, then, he called her mother by name.

Her mother clutched a dripping shirt to her breast, unable to move.

"Rulan," he said again. At the sound, her mother seemed to lose her strength. She sank down beside the basket of wet clothes and covered her ears with her hands as if to block out the sound of thunder. The man went up to her, knelt down and pulled her hands away; at his touch, her mother jerked so violently that the basket overturned and wet clothes spilled out onto the ground. The man said something that Molly could not hear. She only saw their bodies falling together on the wet clothes and the white shirts swaying above them, and her mother pressing her Moon Lady face into the man's shoulder, and the man turning his face into the darkness of her hair.

So he had finally come. And he was not a king, not a warrior, not an immortal who painted rainbows or spoke out of the storm. Only a *gu li,* "rough man," with lines of care etched into his face, dirty hands and a shoulder yoke loaded with junk.

"This is your father." Her mother's words clanged like a gong in

Molly's head. Terrible words, for having once uttered them, her mother had flung herself with great choking sobs back into the arms of the stranger. Molly wanted to hit him, drive him away, not only because he made her strong mother cry but because now her mother looked only at him, not her. Not her! It was his light her mother now reflected. He from whom her light derived.

From that day forth, Molly measured her life in two great epochs: the first paradisal period at Hiamoe when she was the sole occupant of her mother's heart, and the bleak years thereafter in the Chinatown tenement, shut up by her father like a songbird in a cage. Her father's distant manner struck Molly from their first meeting as an expression of distaste. He did not touch her in welcome; nor did he draw her aside for whispered confidences as he did the orphaned boy Lin Kong. A furrowed brow, a disapproving growl would send her tumbling into black despair. Molly hated her father not simply for displacing her in her mother's life but for refusing to make her the center of his own.

She could not have known that his hapless time among the "Deceivers," as he called all *haoles,* caused him to regard the Bosworths' kindness with suspicion. And because he had striven all his life against weakness, he strove too to suppress his helpless attraction to the child he feared was not his own. Rulan had told him how she had arrived, pregnant and alone. Nalani confirmed how she had delivered the child into a sacred stone. Still, doubt, fueled by Mei Yuk's accusation and born of his time with Vera, lingered in his mind.

*I*t was painfully apparent to all that the newcomers were as out of place at Hiamoe as two scrawny roosters in a covey of plump geese. The times were out of joint. A new epidemic was spreading swiftly among the populace—leprosy, which the Hawaiians called *mai pa-ke,* the "Chinese disease." When the horrible extent of the disfiguring scourge was determined, King Lunalilo commanded that anyone infected must be sent to Kalawao, the isolation colony on Molokai. Everyone, it seemed, now knew someone who had been pulled from their homes into exile and death across the Molokai Channel. Suspicion bloomed at the back of Molly's mind. Who was to know if these two skinny strangers were really who they claimed to be. Perhaps they were bringing *mai pa-ke* into their midst. The boy couldn't talk. Maybe disease had swallowed his tongue or was rotting his brain! But when she asked her Uncle Emmanuel to report the newcomers to the king, he scolded her about speaking "against her own kind."

Her "own kind"? She had not realized until then that she was the same as that foreign-looking waif or the unkempt stranger who claimed to be her father.

Pao An in his awkwardness knocked over Lucy's tea tables and bric-a-brac; Lin Kong stood rooted at the doorway of Emmanuel's library, mouth agape, eyes bulging at the sight of an entire room given over to books and papers. Yet where Bosworth and the women responded with compassion, Molly blamed her father for not fitting in. In his daughter's eyes, Pao An was rough-edged and crude, embarrassingly alien. His village dialect bruised her ears, and although she had heard him speak perfectly service-able English to a *haole* tradesman outside the door, he chose to speak *gu li* workingman's talk to the Bosworths, which he uttered disdainfully, as if they were the outsiders, not he.

The tension at dinnertime in the first days after the newcomers' arrival was palpable under the veneer of civility. At their first meal together, Lucy had set wooden chopsticks alongside the boy's and the father's plates, which Pao An took as an insult, since he was accustomed to fork and knife. He ate instead with the teaspoon beside his cup, to Molly's intense mortifi-cation. Discomfited by the abundance on the table, the boy at first took only a morsel from each tray and bowl, until the women piled his plate high with food. They mothered him because he was hungry and voiceless. Only Molly noticed the furtive way in which Lin Kong continued to take from this bowl and that platter, as if he might never eat again. His sneaki-ness disgusted her. She studied the boy with contempt while grown-up voices swelled around her. They were arguing, using words she did not understand—"houseboy," "free labor," "factory-made *poi* flooding the market," "depressed sugar industry"—so she fixed a gimlet eye on the small thief while her mind sloughed off the grown-ups' words like drops of rain.

Suddenly, Lucy gave an éxasperated cry. "Emmanuel, do something to make the man understand!!"

Amid the crash of silver, she heard Emmanuel's impatient expostula-tion, "Think now, how will your wife and child eat? If you hire yourself out, you'll make next to nothing! Work here for me. We need an all-around houseboy!"

Her father's terse reply punctuated the silence. "I take care of my family myself!"

The men's argument plunged Lin Kong into private humiliation. He set his fork down, his mouth slack with shame, half-chewed bits of sweet potato tumbling from his mouth. The boy was fair game for ridicule, Molly decided, for he was too stupid to defend himself, and she began to imitate his sneaky eating habits until Nalani slapped her hands down.

After dinner, Molly heard odd noises behind the outhouse. When she dashed over to look, she discovered it was the object of her scorn, vomiting up his meal. His pockets were stuffed with bread and there was an uneaten sweet potato still clutched in his hand.

"Ahana, ahana," she taunted, "shame, shame, rotten guts," and raced away, daring him to chase her, imitating the sound of his retching. "That's how you talk," she called.

Lin Kong hid behind the chicken coop until nightfall, waiting for Molly's lamp to be extinguished and the ache in his belly to ease before wolfing down the last of the stolen food. The next day, he wore the hunted look of a beggar boy. He was certain that Pao An would abandon him, for who would keep a foundling with one's real child at hand?

As days went by, he tried to curtail his appetite, but his hunger grew to grotesque proportions, giving Molly ample excuse for further torment. She saw that Lin Kong could not resist the roast beef studded with bacon, the sweet potato biscuits drizzled with lard, the bowls of salt pork and baked beans. The steaming plates of food made his mouth run with saliva, his face flush with desire. She smirked at his greediness when he was at table. *"Ahana, ahana,"* she sang mockingly when she found him sneaking a meat pie from the pantry. Gleefully she reported the theft to the aunties, only to be told to her fury that Lucy and Nalani had purposely put the pie in his way.

The consequence of Molly's vendetta was that Lin Kong soon found reason not to eat with the others. Soon after his quarrel with Bosworth, Pao An also absented himself at mealtime. Both man and boy ate alone on the porch hours after the others, hunkered down on their haunches like field laborers. Eventually, Rulan came to sit between the boy and the man. She held her bowl up to her open mouth, as they did, and took out bits of meat with her chopsticks to put into the boy's bowl.

How had this stranger changed her mother so quickly? Molly wondered. Just by appearing, he had crushed her mother's spirit, turned her into a witless foreign creature.

Within days of his arrival, Pao An had retreated behind a wall of disdain that neither Bosworth nor Lucy nor Nalani could penetrate. Their offers of employment met with cold refusal. He thanked Bosworth with scrupulous politeness for having kept his wife and daughter so well and insulted Lucy by offering to pay for the food they had consumed. When Nalani railed at him in Hawaiian for being a "damn stubborn *pa-ke*," he tossed his yoke over his shoulder and took the boy to town. Molly saw them go and rejoiced, hoping he was leaving for good.

"*Auwe, auwe,*" Nalani was wailing. Three weeks had passed since Molly's father had turned Hiamoe from a sanctuary into a place under siege. Had someone died in the night? Molly wondered, rubbing her eyes sleepily as she stumbled downstairs.

Everyone was already awake; bright sun was streaming through the windows. Her father was gone. The household was back to normal. Why then was there danger in the air? No one remembered that Molly had not eaten breakfast. Lucy was still in her nightgown with her hair loose around her shoulders. Her normally placid face was mottled with fury and her mouth hung open in an angry O as she shouted at Rulan over the clatter of china and Nalani's loud laments.

Molly's heart sank, for from the rear of the house came her father, deaf to the aunties' shrieking. He had returned, after all. Back and forth from storeroom to yard went Pao An, silently piling bundles and bedding onto a wooden frame. Maybe he was going to California, Molly told herself with joy.

Her father picked up an object from atop a pile of garments, looked at it quizzically, and tossed it aside. Instantly, Lucy flew at him like an angry bird. "You know nothing, nothing, about your wife or child! It was better if you never came," she cried.

Pao An spoke sharply in Chinese to his wife.

"What did he say?" demanded Lucy.

"Only that a Chinaman cannot be a man in a *haole's* house," Rulan said wearily.

"That's what we are to him! *Haole? Kanaka?*" Lucy cried. "Look what he threw away." She held up the porcelain doll she had given Molly long ago.

Something inside Molly broke then. She ran away to hide under Lucy's bed, crying herself to sleep among the puffs of dust and straw, until strong arms pulled her out. She felt her mother's lips against her wet face, heard her murmur Cantonese endearments into her ear, and hating herself, burrowed closer to her mother in her distress. Rulan carried her, still crying, out of the house, and followed Pao An through the gate.

Half a mile down the road, Lucy came running after them. "The child must have playthings," she said as angry tears ran down her scarred cheeks. She thrust a small bundle wrapped in a baby-size quilt into Molly's arms.

Inside was the girl's favorite china doll and a book of poetry she had been reading to Molly.

Night fog was rolling in from the sea as the Tang man and woman, bent by the burdens on their backs, led the children out of the mountain valley into Chinatown. Only Molly looked back at the lamps of Hiamoe winking ever more faintly in the distance until the valley mists snuffed them out at last.

2

Outsiders in Chinatown

"I wouldn't have you think ill of them simply because they were our servants in Kwangtung," the Widow told the other merchants' wives.

The women were gathered around the banyan tree in her courtyard on a sweltering afternoon to play *ma jong*—four to play, a dozen more to watch and eat watermelon seeds as their children rolled noisily in the dirt and their bond maids ran back and forth with fresh pots of tea. Mei Yuk's fingers were rapidly stacking the ivory tiles facedown into a wall as thick and long as her arm. "I know *that one* claims to be my husband's old concubine, but I swear to you, she was nothing more than a slave girl with ambitions as large as her feet. And more power to her I say, for why shouldn't any woman be ambitious? Here in Hawaii ambition is the horse that pulls the wagon, *hai ma!*"

The women clacked their tongues in assent and sipped the scalding tea noisily through their front teeth. One by one, the players went back to constructing their tile walls; then, swiftly, they pushed the walls around the table to form four miniature battlements. As usual, the Widow had positioned herself to be chosen "banker." It was she, then, who rolled the dice and began the betting.

All the women, except city-bred Mei Yuk who had been born to wealth, came from one of the dirt-poor villages in Heungsan County in the Pearl River Delta with hardly a good gold bracelet among them. Yet in Hawaii, these same village women were an elite sisterhood. In their zeal to repopulate the island with families from China, plantation owners were paying immigration agencies thirty dollars a head for Tang women, five dollars more than what Tang men nowadays were worth. That so few women chose to make the arduous journey overseas with their menfolk did not surprise the wives already here. What woman wanted to raise her children in this plague-buffeted wasteland without the support of kin? There were no clan schools where sons could be scholars, no bell-doctors or midwives or physicians to help them weather childbirth and plague, no temples unless you counted the upstairs rooms in the *tong* hall given over to the worship of Kwan Kung, the god of war, a man's deity, really.

Still, there were ample rewards for those women who preferred to take their chances in the rough-and-tumble world of Chinese Honolulu. Their menfolk had opened warehouses and concessions catering to the needs of Tang men already in the islands for *manapua* buns or pickled ginger or strong cotton work clothes. Some men had hired out their services as "factors" or middlemen for Chinese rice planters in rural districts of Oahu. Doing business with their own was making the women rich, the Widow the richest of all.

"Some say *he* got his money slitting throats in Gold Mountain," Mei Yuk went on primly, her fingers skillfully arranging the tiles she had selected into sets of matching designs. "I know he had nothing when he left China, but I say, one kind of money is as good as another, even blood money. Who among us did not have brothers or fathers who did things we would never suffer our sons to do in Hawaii? And only because of hunger or envy of our betters. Poor man, he deceives himself that the woman's bastard is his own. So let others look for dirt in that corner. You will not hear a word of blame fall from my lips about *him*."

Holding a watermelon seed between her fingernails, she split it between her teeth, slipped the kernel neatly out with her tongue, and flicked the husk away. "So why then," she said, chewing with casual disdain, "with not a bad word spoken against them, is *that one* pushing her way into the hardware business, taking customers away from an honest man like Aseu, the husband of one of our own sisters here? Isn't one Chinese hardware store enough?" She studied her chosen hand—fourteen tiles arranged in a line facing her, one more than the others because of her favored position as banker—contemplating the next play.

Mei Yuk rolled the dice and reached for a tile atop an opponent's wall as high-pitched voices rose and fell around her, like the angry cooing of pigeons when a crust is snatched away. Mei Yuk cocked her head, her fingers grazing the backs of the tiles, feeling for the coveted "dragon" tile, the blank white board that would double her score. She turned the tile over and frowned. Bamboo. No good. "You might think *he* is the greedy one," she snapped, "but no, I say, look closely at *that one*. She never could leave alone what another person had . . ."

The rest of the afternoon was devoted to the game, a noisy affair, with tiles clicking, children screaming for attention, angry expostulations when a coveted tile was snatched by an opponent. The betting was so heavy that two of the players' back hair had come undone in the excitement of play. At the end of an hour, the battlements were torn apart, the discarded tiles flung down in a huge mound; each player was studying her own neat row of ivory bricks, the final hand, intent on pocketing the winnings.

"Hoi kong!" Mei Yuk shouted, a signal that stopped the game. Relishing her opponents' consternation, she pushed her four tiles face up to display a remarkable run of four of a kind. Four flowers—the riskiest hand. As banker, her score was automatically doubled. *"Ma jeok,"* she declared; the game was over. The Widow was a subtle, unrelenting competitor who disguised her moves with talk and indirection, but who pounced ruthlessly and without warning—and always seemed to win.

*W*hat remained of the money Pao An earned in Gold Mountain was enough to purchase a two-story wooden tenement with an outside stairway and a separate privy on a crowded block near the harbor end of Nuuanu Stream. He hated investing in a building that was so obviously vulnerable to earthquake and fire, but all the buildings were as flimsy as paper. So he immediately began renovating the rooms, substituting hardier materials for walls, floors, and windows, and kept barrels of rainwater in the small yard in case of stray sparks. He stocked the shelves with buckets of factory-made wire nails, awls, hammers, axes, boat-shaped iron planes, wiring, saws of various sizes, and a wide assortment of boring devices with various bits; his store would cater to Chinese laborers experienced in handling Western-style carpenters' tools. His long-range plan was to build a construction business from this small base, for he intended to erect buildings more durable than those stuck into the ground like dry sticks by Tang men who wanted only to make their stake quickly and leave.

Rulan decided that the store had more room than the family needed. "Two rooms behind the shop, that's enough for us," she decided. "The four upstairs, we'll rent."

Pao An was not happy keeping a houseful of bachelors under his roof. Tang men were in the habit of using water pipes for tobacco and lighting small fires to heat ceramic pipes of raw opium, he reminded Rulan. The danger of fire was as great here as in the Chinatowns of San Francisco or Sacramento. The ancient fire engine that serviced Chinatown was thirty years old, a fire hazard itself, he complained. But Rulan persisted and soon had the upstairs rented to fourteen men. As she foresaw, the rent, not the hardware store, paid their suppliers and kept them from going hungry during the first months when few customers came.

The infant business seemed to languish even before it drew breath. For no matter how generously Pao An stocked the shelves with tools and supplies every Tang man needed and could well afford, few bought. Selling was difficult for Pao An, who could not attract customers by laughing loudly and slapping backs and telling jokes. And there were mysterious "accidents"—crates of supplies stolen off the wharf or spoiled by seawater. Pao An was sure these small disasters were the work of the *tong*. Rulan further suspected that Mei Yuk's hand was orchestrating the boycott, for whenever she tried striking up conversations with Tang women in the market, they would turn away after a simple salutation, as if her time with the Bosworths had made her unclean.

Slowly, however, a small but steady stream of customers came to the shop. These were men fresh from the fields, Punti and Hakka alike, who needed credit to start their own small businesses. When they told Pao An of the rumors passed around in the Punti community about him, he did nothing to counter the evil talk. Pao An would not have believed it, but his business difficulties were islandwide. The bachelor king Lunalilo was dying; with no successor to the crown, British and American warships were poised on the water outside the harbor with cannons primed to assert their national interests. The widespread news that sugar exports for the year before were off five million pounds made businessmen edgy and customers reluctant to part with hard-earned dollars. The pro-American planters had set their hopes on a treaty with America that would allow sugar and rice to pass into American markets duty free. Yet nothing had yet come to pass, and there were no new workers hired to pick cane.

With the business hard pressed for cash, Rulan sold off her last treasures from Hiamoe—a stack of English china cups and plates and Molly's storebought dresses—to keep their creditors from shutting the store down. Molly sulked for days, stirring only to taunt Lin Kong whenever he passed by sticking a finger down her mouth and pretending to gag.

Rulan tried to scold her daughter into becoming an ally of the orphan boy. She stood them both against a wall and hectored them with tales of disobedient children. "We're a *hui,* a family enterprise. For one of us to act independently is unthinkable. Can a finger separate itself from a hand?" Lin Kong was shamed enough to take the words to heart. Molly, from the belligerent look upon her face, made plain her refusal to put the intruder's interests before her own. It pained Rulan to see how Lucy's and Nalani's generous affection had spoiled the girl and to know that Molly did not love her father enough to change.

With so few customers, the family's monthly needs began to exceed what the renters paid. Perhaps they could begin again on another part of the island where the danger from Mei Yuk and the *tong* was less keen, Rulan proposed. Or they could sell off the stock to Aseu, their only competitor, and try something new. But Pao An was adamant: he would not be driven out of business by one spiteful woman harboring enmity from the old world. Chinatown was big enough to embrace them all: Hakka and Punti; merchant and laborer; Li and Chen. He was gathering a small band of men, strong-minded merchants like himself who refused to pay "dues" to *tong* enforcers or to bow down to the Widow. They too had had goods mysteriously pirated, customers threatened. Even more than their aversion to the *tong,* pride in their hard-earned property made them fast friends. They feared fire as much as Pao An and did not laugh, as other merchants did, when Pao An described the steam-driven fire trucks he had seen in Sacramento or San Francisco.

So while Pao An spent his days with his companions, stubbornly waiting for Mei Yuk's whispering campaign to die down and profits to rise, Rulan began a business of her own. She cleared out a corner of the store where she could practice her former avocation of herbal medicine. Between the tools and the lumber, she stored crocks filled with salty *harm mui* for sore throats; boxes of medicinal tea for coughs; an aloe plant for burns and rashes; and a few branches of *longan* (dragon's eye fruit), an antidote for weak eyes, drying on rope hung from the ceiling. She also kept on hand bottles of wine for washing and steeping herbs, and common plants that the Hawaiians used for medicine such as *awapuhi,* or wild ginger bulbs, for cuts and toothache and *kowali awa* vines for broken bones. This was a pathetically skimpy pharmacopeia given the storehouse of herbs at her disposal in the house of Li or the huge kitchen at Hiamoe in which she and Nalani had cooked up herbal remedies for Emma's Companions to distribute among the Hawaiians; yet she had no money for imported goods from overseas and no seed for growing more.

Rulan was convinced that even with her scanty stock, she could serve the bachelors of Chinatown as assiduously as the wealthy pharmacist Asam. Hadn't her cooking kept her family in good health while others in the

China quarter were falling to every passing disease? Under her skillful hands, the contents of her soup pot changed with the seasons and the family's needs. She served a *yin* broth made from young winter melon and dried orange peel, which cooled the body in sultry autumn; a thick sweet stew of lily root and red dates was a winter tonic for lungs and heart. When Asam sent word that he had obtained a rare shipment of medicinal foods, Rulan traded the six live ducks she had been raising for a small box of dried "birds' nests" and a tin of red lycium berries. The birds' nest was a rare treat for herself: when cooked into a viscous soup, the dry, gelatinous secretions plucked from the nests of mountain swallows kept the skin from aging too quickly in the unforgiving tropical climate. The lycium berries had another, more vital use. A handful of berries boiled for hours with a wedge of pig's liver made a potent remedy for Lin Kong whose morning headaches were a result of weak eyes, which he further abused by poring over the one book that Molly had taken from Hiamoe. She also boiled watercress with pork bones into a rich, dark broth for his consumption and pressed sour *mui* on him: both *mui* and watercress soup were antidotes for the throat and lungs, although Rulan suspected that the child's inability to speak had nothing to do with any bodily deficiency. Pao An had told her how Lin Kong had been an intelligent, curious child who had stopped talking only after his mother had died.

Amazed that anyone would go to such trouble for him, Lin Kong for the first time began to show, in his own fashion, the hesitant signs of affection. He made little figures twisted out of paper and put them on Rulan's counter where she would find them in the morning—little birds and cats and rabbits hidden among the dented pots and bamboo strainers.

It was the heady fragrance of the medicinal soup that brought the first old man to the store. He wandered among the shelves, stopping at this barrel and that, feigning interest in the stacks of tin sheets, and drawing closer and closer to Rulan, who was seated on a stool picking through a pot of raw rice for twigs and stones. When Rulan nodded a greeting, he began to boast of possessing a nose so sensitive that he had guessed the ingredients of the pot. "It's earth fairy soup for the eyes, *hai ma?*" he ventured jovially, then blurted out, "*Aiya,* let me taste, Sister-in-law," he begged, squinting in her direction. "These old eyes can barely see your face."

Rulan laughed at the old man's comically hangdog expression. Beckoning him onto the stool where Lin Kong usually took his meals, she ladled a generous portion of soup into a bowl and put it in his eager hands.

The old man remained all afternoon, regaling her with stories of his grandmother, whose medicinal soups were so tasty that one wished for illness just for the pleasure of the cure. "*Poho,*" he said mournfully, "she's dead, and no woman knows the old recipes anymore. Even the bell-doctors have gone overseas to grow rice or pick cane."

The next evening, when Pao An entered the shop covered in grime and with muddy tools slung over his shoulder, there were nine men hanging about the selling floor chatting with his wife. The soup pot was empty, the dinner unmade.

"Who are these idiots?" Pao An hissed in his wife's ear. He glowered at a youth who was smoking a *haole* cigar.

"They are guests," Rulan replied in reproach.

"Send them away. That one is going to cause a fire, and I don't like their dirty eyes on you."

"They're just lonely men who want to be around a real family. See . . . ?" she pointed out, "They're teasing Molly. They made her smile . . ."

Immediately, Pao An sprang to his feet. "Shop is closed," he announced angrily, banging down his shovel and pickax with a clatter, and pushing the men out the door. After the store was cleared, he complained to Rulan, "Some Tang men want everything for free! They see somebody's woman, they think they can stare at her, beg a meal . . ."

"Today guests, tomorrow customers," Rulan shot back. "They eat a bowl of soup. Next time, they remember how it tastes and come for nails and twine. Do you want to run a shop like the Lis where the sellers treat customers as cheats and the *tong* pressures everybody to buy more than they need? Here, at least, a Tang man can sit awhile and feel that he is with friends."

"You gave them the last of the soup!" he said angrily, adding in reproach, "You promised it to the boy!"

This smallness of heart was a revelation to her. "They had more need than he," she challenged.

"You don't know these bachelors. How loneliness sends them out of their heads. They mistake a woman's kindness for something else . . ."

Rulan was disturbed by what she sensed at the heart of his last insinuation—his secret suspicion that she had been unfaithful. "Is every old uncle a lecher in your eyes? Do you have so little faith in me? The girl is *your* daughter, you know. We made her together on that last night in China when you drew a map of these islands in the dirt."

From the blush that rose up his neck, she knew her barb had hit home. "Of course," he muttered, embarrassed, "I have never doubted you," hating himself for that small speck of suspicion that ruined the whole. Still he insisted, "No more serving soup to strangers. You don't know if they're *tong* extortionists come to spy on us! If they don't come to buy, throw them out!''

Rulan rarely defied her husband, but this time, she stood her ground. "I would sell to any man if he was in need! I stayed chaste seven years—I know my own worth, and I know why homesick Tang men come to this store. Were you the only Tang man in Gold Mountain who never longed for a woman?''

Her husband's silence confirmed Rulan's long-held suspicion that it was he who had taken a lover. So she stubbornly continued to serve soup to whoever asked, even those he suspected of taking the *tong* oath. But as a concession to her husband, she charged a nominal sum, a copper or two, depending on the cost of the ingredients. Soon men were venturing into the small store, first filling their pockets with nails, then plunking down more coins for a bowl of soup or tea and a chance to talk to Pao An's clever and welcoming wife.

"Even in this debased society a woman ought to be scrupulous about her daughter. But *that one* uses that wild, dark girl to entice men into the shop! Scandalous behavior! You'd think the hardware store was a brothel. And the girl! Have you ever seen such ugly dresses?'' The Widow was yelling over the clattering of the game tiles, which the women were "washing'' or stirring with their hands in anticipation of a new game.

As the players' fingers flew over the table, creating out of the chaos of fallen tiles a new set of battlements for the siege to come, the merchants' wives admitted that the girl's Mother Hubbard dresses were an affront to the eyes. No decent Chinese daughter would trade pants and tunic of robin's egg blue *ya hoo lam* cloth for the shapeless garment, a native version of the *bak kuei* woman's nightdress, especially when every Chinese mother could sew. These were women who could turn rice or flour sacks into strong work clothes for their men as well as embroider elaborate designs on tablecloths for sale to *bak kuei* women. Even the poorest Tang wife knew how to soak crude silk cloth in the muddy waters of taro patches so that the cheap yard goods were as soft and supple as satin.

The battlements were clicked into place, and the betting began. "I am careful to keep my daughter indoors, as I know you all do,'' Mei Yuk ventured. "With so many bachelors coming into town now from the sugar mills and rice plantations and the brown devils from the wharfs with the urges and morals of pigs, Tang girls are more precious than gold! We mothers must set walls around our own!'' She studied the bird design on the face of a tile for a heartbeat, then tossed the ivory square on the table in disgust before attacking a new subject with her tongue. "Did you hear? A Tang girl was raped in Kula! Daughter of a farmer, one of those Hakka who brought their big-foot wives to cut cane. American sailors found her playing near a saloon at twilight and thinking she was a prostitute, had their way with her, a dozen of them. And the girl only ten years old. Torn apart! The poor mother drowned herself. Even a Hakka has her pride. What Tang man will bring his woman over now?"

The women were silent, their fingernails nervously tapping the tiles, contemplating the horror of Mei Yuk's tale. The Widow went on with a world-weary sigh, "You and I know to take care. But for years now, *that woman* lets her daughter go running about like a *kanaka* through the lanes with no shoes, that ugly dress flapping, and her hair loose like a *kanaka* girl. Be ashamed, I say." She ran her fingers lightly over the top of her opponents' wall, trying to feel for the design on the other side. She needed a flower tile to complete her run. She plucked a tile from her opponents' wall and stood it on its end, like a tiny ancestral tablet on an altar. A niggardly circle design. Not a single flower or dragon had come her way. Her smile was brilliant. The tiles were mocking her. Every one she picked was bad.

The merchants' wives sipped their tea, cracked their watermelon seeds, murmured their assent, and inwardly cringed at Mei Yuk's accusations. The Widow was always most dangerous when she was losing. This time, she was reminding them that they, too, were letting their daughters run wild in streets that were crowded with predatory bachelors. Granted, the women told themselves, Hawaii was not the village, and daughters these days were not as custom-bound as their mothers. Still, each woman vowed silently to take a firmer hand with her daughter, for no one wanted gossip to spread about her family. No one wanted to lose face. No one wanted to be the uninvited guest, the mother whose daughter was too ugly, too poor, or too wild. No one wanted to be the object of the Widow's ridicule at the next *ma jong* game.

3

THE WILD, DARK CHILD

The distance between Hiamoe and the family's present quarters in Chinatown was measured, in Molly's mind, not in miles but in attitudes. For seven years, Molly had lived in an atmosphere where privacy and personal property were sacrosanct, no matter how many guests filled the rooms. Yet in this rickety building of which her parents were so proud, that fundamental right to one's own space was lost. It seemed to Molly that they had slipped through a trapdoor in the earth and fallen out the other side into a South China village.

With all attention fixed on communal enterprise, nothing in the house was Molly's alone, no corner she could claim as her domain. Every space was public, every article intended for the common use. Teacups, bedding, combs, slippers had no permanent owner. An item's value depended on the multiple purposes it served: the house provided not only living space but workrooms, selling floor, and warehouse; a cracked white bowl was for drinking tea, for measuring rice and coffee into gunnysacks, and for grinding medicinal herbs. Molly's underpants were made from her father's threadbare shirts and in time became scraps sewn into a quilt. The head of Molly's china doll, broken off in their move, stopped the top of a large jar

of preserved lemons. Without doors, the three rooms of the shop were one
fluid space through which family, customers, and tenants moved at will.
Molly felt as if she were a changeling kidnapped from her rightful home
and set down among strangers.

She ate her evening rice to the sounds of their boarders hawking and
spitting in the privy outside. At night, she lay as inert as a lump of earth,
feigning sleep, while in the next bed, her father drove himself into her
mother's compliant flesh. Witnessing their silent intimacy humiliated her
even more than the presence of Lin Kong, who slept on the other side of
the thin partition. She imagined that he listened in lascivious silence to her
father attacking her mother with his body. Sometimes, when she rolled
sleepily toward the wall, her skin would crawl at the realization that the boy
was only a few inches away. She heard him cry out in dreams—half-formed
words choked off into strangled sobbing. She felt naked all the time.

Molly relinquished all claim to privacy in order to bear its loss. She
learned to dress with uncanny swiftness in the minute it took her father to
gulp down a bowl of tea. To braid her hair beside the place where her
mother was killing chickens without shrinking from the stench of blood
and hot feathers. To turn her head when the men from upstairs were
outside pissing against the wall. She grew accustomed to the explosion of
male voices throughout the house, quarreling, scolding, boasting, haggling,
although she never learned to speak as they did, using words as weapons in
a commercial tug-of-war rather than as intimations of the workings of her
heart. She taught herself to escape to a sanctuary within, the only private
place she knew. When her father hectored their tenants about stamping out
the embers of their pipes or wrangled with customers over the top of her
head, she didn't hear.

She measured every new experience against Hiamoe's remembered
perfection. Mealtime at Lucy's had been a merry, social affair where lively
conversation prevailed. Now the only silence of the day happened when
the four of them sat down to eat. There was no silver or glassware, only
cheap ceramic bowls used for rice and tea, and chopsticks of bamboo.
Instead of polished koa, their dining table was a cast-off door with one end
resting on a sawhorse and the other on two beer barrels set side by side.
They ate off the raw wood, without napkins or linen, or any utensils
besides chopsticks and bare hands.

The menu was always the same: rural Cantonese dishes, for her father
claimed that his stomach had gone bad from *haole* food in California. And
soup. A hundred kinds of evil-smelling concoctions for which her mother
made elaborate claims, all of which the two interlopers believed.

Even the etiquette at her family's table was wrong. Once the *soong,* or main dishes, were placed on the table (simultaneously rather than in sequence), a strict order of service prevailed: the family waited until Pao An's bowl was filled, then picked on what was left. This was *backward,* just as serving soup last instead of first was backward, Molly reminded her mother, for Bosworth had always served himself last and her first. Her meat had been cut before she put it to her lips; her portion of sweet potatoes mashed up with milk so she need not chew; the aunties even sprinkled sugar onto her *poi* to tempt her to eat. Now, the best of every dish was saved for Pao An: the gizzard of the chicken, the delicate fin meat of flounder, fatty and sweet and dripping flavor, the crisp layer of singed rice at the bottom of the pot. And Molly's father took this deference as his due.

Where, Molly wondered, had her mother learned to cook such odd dishes? Mullet steamed in a sauce of fermented black beans. Swamp cabbage fried in a foul-smelling purplish fish paste. Rulan took the two children on the tram to the rice paddies and duck ponds in Waikiki to gather buckets of small brown water snails, which she stewed in garlic and soy. The utter strangeness of her mother's table filled Molly with indignation. So much so that she often declined to eat. At other times she'd stuff herself with some dish she did, in fact, crave, then caught in the grip of self-revulsion, incomprehensible even to herself, would go outside when no one was looking and put her finger down her throat and vomit up her meal as she had once seen the boy do long ago.

Worst of all was the serving of *mui.* Her *mui.* What had once been a private ritual between her mother and herself was now available to all. For after the communal soup was served, and the common platters scraped clean, her mother laid a bowl of *mui* like an offering before her husband.

Molly watched in mounting chagrin the first time Pao An took a plum with his chopsticks and placed it into his wife's bowl. Blushing, her mother put it quickly to her lips. Molly found the exchange embarrassingly intimate, a wordless prelude to the nightly ritual to come.

The bowl was handed next to Lin Kong, the perennially hungry hanger-on who took his share in typical tentative fashion before passing the remainder to the incensed Molly. *Mui* was good for the throat, Rulan would say, urging the boy to take his fill. Until one evening when Molly in jealous fury grabbed the bowl out of his hands and crammed his share into her mouth, chewing triumphantly and spitting the seed on the table as her mother railed at her. Yet to her horror, Lin Kong's response was to make a gift of her insult. He shook his head when Rulan offered him more.

"Faker," she hissed, furious.

The next day, she took Lin Kong's portion of *mui* again. And again he relinquished his claim, implying that he was too full to eat. Her father's fury and her mother's shame filled her with joy.

Lin Kong loved *mui,* as he did all sweets. He loved Molly with the same sick, worshipful yearning he saved for the rich foods he desired and could never taste. Whenever Molly humiliated him, he would go outside and swallow the tears before they came. He had not cried since his mother died. He would not allow it.

How his life had changed since coming to Hawaii. Food he now had in abundance. Yet the terrible hunger still returned to shame him, calling forth dream visions of the objects of every unfilled appetite. A brown spice cake spiked with raisins he once saw on Lucy's tea table. A marzipan pig in a confectioner's window in Fiddletown. A bowl of black gelatinous *leong fun* perched atop a cake of ice in the back of the gambling hall in Stockton. Pancakes hissing on a griddle in an Antioch farmwife's kitchen. Dozens of varieties of sticky-sweet *mui* packed in glass jars on Asam's shelves.

And still the hunger came, like a hole that would not be filled. And still he would not speak and would not cry!

No longer newcomers in Chinatown, the family found ways to stave off creditors to give the hardware business time to grow. As Rulan predicted, the small business in soup and tea in her corner of the store brought customers to his. For his part, Pao An had found a loyal core of customers among the growing number of shopowners who did not frequent the *tong*-owned gambling houses or throw away profits on opium or borrow money from the *tong* at preposterous rates. Soon these men were going from shop to shop to raise money for the new steam-driven fire engine that they hoped to buy. The Widow made plain her opinion that the project was absurd and the efforts of these zealots wasted. Why put money into safeguarding buildings that were not their home? she asserted to her allies in the *tong* and to the wives at the *ma jong* game. Especially when decent Tang men were saving their cash for the day when they returned to the village as wealthy men. Why worry about a conflagration that would never come? Better to channel excess cash to old-country organizations that protected Tang men in customary fashion.

Although his lack of success made the scanty profits from his wife's medicine business welcome, Pao An's discomfort was apparent whenever he looked over at the knot of bachelors clamoring for tea or for a taste of pickled mango. He had held his tongue, learned to tolerate Rulan's schemes as a way of providing the extra income they needed to survive in these perilous times. He would never compel her to reject the work she loved; that was not his way. Nor would he deny her claim that the wild, dark child was his. He was head of the family and did his best for them all, although he berated her customers when they lingered too long over their soup bowls or took to describing their ailments in too familiar a fashion. He could never forget that she had been seven years on an island of men, and that the child had none of the daintiness or decorum of a China-born girl. His suspicion was all the more painful because he despised himself for it. In the end, the medicine business was stunted at the moment it might have made them rich because the healer herself, unwilling to hurt her jealous husband, held back her art.

In China, as a young woman, Rulan had mastered the arts of needling; moxibustion; and *chi-gong,* healing with the *chi,* or energy, in her hands. She had not drawn on these skills at Hiamoe since Bosworth had made plain his belief that *chi-gong* was witchcraft. Pao An's jealousy proved just as dampening as Bosworth's skepticism. He let his wife give the bachelors food, medicine, and conversation, but he would not allow her to put her hands on them. Her healing touch remained for him alone.

One evening, after having hounded his wife's customers out the door yet again, he was filled with guilty rage and unable to make peace with his wife. He lay down beside her, misery clouding his eyes. Yet later, in the darkness, his body burned with fever and old wounds in his side and on his thigh pricked him like knives. He lay pressed down by pain like a supplicant.

"Silly man," she scolded gently, "you have made yourself ill." Her hands moved above his body, stirring the air in practiced configurations, seeking the break in the channel of *chi* that would signal the area of pain. When she pommeled the air softly, directing a stream of heat into the old scar on his belly and into the muscles that wrapped his rib cage and back like long knotted rope, he began to groan.

She took raw peanut oil and rubbed it between her hands until the heady fragrance was released and held her palm to his forehead for a minute until the heat from her hand moved into his body; and after rubbing his hands and feet gently to warm them, she moved her fingers over the ridges of his shoulders and down the backbone, pulling the muscles smooth and straight across his shoulders, back, and legs.

She shook her hair loose when it came undone from the matron's knot and straddled his buttocks, then leaning, slid her body against his back in order to reach the crevices of his arms and elbows. Rising up, her breasts slipped over the hard flesh of his shoulders, and she felt his hips begin to move against the mattress, smelt the scent of the oil rising up from his flesh. He turned over and as she raised herself to accommodate him, he reached up for her, his body shiny with the warm oil, his hands gripping her waist to pull her down upon him tighter, closer than before.

He groaned, driving himself deeper, muffling his cries in her shoulder. Afterward, he shivered uncontrollably, then slept cradled against her breasts and belly, his heaviness a great sweetness to her.

*M*olly set her teeth on edge and shoved her fingers in her ears against the sounds of her parents' lovemaking. She kicked her feet, turned over in her bed and pressed her face against the wall. On the other side of the partition, Lin Kong heard them too, and finding himself erect, flung himself facedown, flushing with shame at the thought that Molly was only inches away. At dawn, while dreaming of bare-breasted brown women swaying with bent, open knees in skirts of green *ti,* he was jolted from slumber by a spasm of pleasure. He lay awake listening to the raucous chorus of Chinatown roosters, frightened by his body's willfulness, and worrying whether his face would betray his sin to Hoapili, his new school-master, who seemed omniscient enough to penetrate the secrets of even his stupidest pupil's soul.

*E*ven after making peace with his wife, Pao An's anger remained. He was better at war than business, he told himself, and should, therefore, set out to destroy Mei Yuk since she was bent on destroying them. Except that Rulan in her usual feisty manner thwarted the vengeful designs that seemed so clear in his mind. He decided to get out of Chinatown for a brief time, away from the feud with the Lis and the confines of the shop, to try selling in a different way. To that end, he tied packets of tools and supplies onto a shoulder pole with the intent of making a circuit of the island. He would call at rice farms, plantation stores, sugar mills, taro patches, and farms—wherever Tang men had set up businesses—selling his wares and taking orders as he went.

He took the dusty road over the Kapukaki Ridge toward the mill towns and sugar plantations in the interior, the same path that Rulan and Nalani had taken eight years before by mule cart, the only road a peddler could travel. The sun was hot upon his back, and dust mingled with his sweat.

The farther he went from Honolulu, the clearer his mind became.

Bent under his burden, feeling the bundles on his carrying pole swaying, he felt his anger subside. Walking, he discovered, aided reflection. He dismissed his quarrel with his wife as an insignificant thing. What surprised him was how his mind perennially returned to the girl. She made him uneasy, this strong-willed, reckless creature. How strange that the quality he admired most in other men filled him with apprehension when he beheld it in the girl.

He lengthened his stride as the afternoon wore on, leaning into the rising wind, enjoying the effort of pitting his body against the elements. He spent the night in a bunkhouse at the Orbison plantation where Tang men slept twenty to a room. He sold an ax head and two machetes to the Hawaiian headman, or *luna,* and in the morning pushed on across the cool, windswept plateau of Leilehua to the rice farms nearby. On the third day, he came to the China camp at the Waialua sugar mill. A gang of ten sweating, cursing men were loading barrels of bagasse, crushed cane, into a wagon for dumping. Beyond them, six youths were playing Chinese dominoes on the narrow ridge that ran high above a drainage ditch. When the gamblers saw Pao An, they threw down their tiles, rose quickly, and came near. Pao An saw that the tallest of the gang had leather workboots instead of a workman's rush sandals, a revolver stuck into the waistband of his trousers, and was winding his queue around his head as if preparing for a fight. Thin to the point of emaciation, the gunman moved with the splay-footed gait of a Chinese boxer.

"That's him. The peddler. He's right on time," he barked at his comrades.

The workers loading raw cane at the wagon put down their barrels and began to back away. They were hot, ill-humored, and had no intention of losing good jobs with the plantation for breaking the penal code about brawling.

"Eh, you peddler," called out one of the gamblers. "Do you have a license for selling your rusty hammers and broken nails?"

"I did not know that a license from the king was required," Pao An replied coldly. He gave no sign of apprehension.

"*Aaiiee,* you need a license." A smile spread over the bony face. "Not from the king. From the *tong*! You wouldn't want to cheat the brothers, *hai ma*?" He stepped directly in Pao An's path as the others fanned out behind him, all coarse-faced fellows in clean blue tunics with unstained hands. Laborers who, like the reprobate Ah Jack, did no labor.

"I know of only one Tang man who sells tools on this island," the skinny gunman continued. "Aseu pays his license fees. . . . Did you steal goods from him in town to sell out here?"

"These tools are mine. My wife and I have a shop in Honolulu," replied Pao An.

"Aaiiee, that one!" the leader roared. "I know her. Good-looking for a big-foot Hakka. Lived for years up Nuuanu. Came down to Chinatown only when she needed a man. I had her myself a couple of times in the alley." The others echoed his rude laughter, each one calling out the number of times they had had her too.

Pao An looked quickly in the direction of the cane wagon, but the laborers had melted into a field of green cane. He dropped his voice into a peddler's whine. "You want to buy? I give a good price, cheaper than this Aseu." He loosened the ropes, slipped out the shoulder yoke and made a show of opening his cloth bundles. His stomach was churning as he calculated the chances of defending himself against six younger assailants, one of whom had a gun . . .

"What kind of coward won't defend his wife's honor?" the skinny leader asked his companions. "Unless his wife has no honor!"

Pao An felt rather than saw the dark shapes close in behind. In the chaos of his mind, one clear thought emerged, an old axiom of war about choosing the high ground. He bobbed his head in a nervous kowtow, picked up his shoulder yoke with one hand, and with the other dragged his bundles toward the wagon.

"You better bow," the skinny leader warned. "A man who sets himself against the brotherhood is worse than a *kanaka*," and as Pao An turned, he kicked him in the seat of the pants.

Pao An rose with exaggerated awkwardness and rubbed his buttocks in a show of pain. His antics provoked a chorus of jeers. Good, Pao An thought to himself; laughter takes the edge off blood lust. With a roar, the leader yanked a bundle out of Pao An's hands.

"No, no," Pao An shouted, his horror genuine. Cartons of meticulously sorted nails rained upon the ground.

"Yes, yes," the skinny pockfaced leader shouted. "Yes, yes, yes, yes, yes," his companions screamed. Eagerly, they pulled apart the bundles and began to hurl precious supplies into the cane field.

Pao An was already crouched low when the skinny leader grabbed him by the shoulder. In a split second, he pivoted toward his attacker and smashed him in the chest. The shout of triumph became an anguished exhalation and a succession of animal grunts when Pao An hit him behind the head as if he were killing a rabbit with the flat of his hand. Pao An had just time enough to grab up his shoulder yoke and swing it like a club as a second man ran forward. There was a sound like the shattering of pottery, and a howl of pain. Pao An whirled again, his yoke raised, but this time, no one leaped in his direction. He had struck so fast that the four remaining men were still on their knees, smiles frozen on their faces, tools spilling out of the broken bundles.

An instant later, they were upon him. Pao An ran along the earthworks until the ledge was narrow enough for only one man. Then he turned quickly. Momentum drove the first attacker into the arc of Pao An's yoke. He screamed, plunging headlong into the ditch. There was the crack of wood against bone, as the rest stumbled over each other in a vain attempt to escape the swinging pole.

Pao An had just time enough to smash the shoulder of his last assailant when two blasts from below tore into the earth scant inches beyond his feet. The leader cried out as his gun clicked on an empty barrel. Cursing in dismay, he looked down at his weapon, and in that moment, Pao An leaped from the ridge and smashed the wooden cudgel across the man's eyes. The gun flew onto the rocky ground as the leader fell, blood streaming from his ruined face.

Stepping nimbly between the writhing men, Pao An gathered what he could of his merchandise. Several awls, a dozen drill bits, an iron plane. The nails were irretrievable, having been strewn into the fields or trodden into the sodden earth. The assault had cost him a fifth of his inventory, yet the loss was more than compensated by the damage done to his attackers. He doubted now whether the *tong* would waste their soldiers on such a one as he. The Widow would be forced to use more devious methods. He would be ready for her next time.

4

THE BOY WHO COULD NOT CRY

Power was slipping away from the *alii*. Official posts that had once been the birthright of chieftains' sons were now put up for election, among them, the throne itself. When the unhappy Lunalilo died without issue in February 1874, the legislature was forced to choose between two candidates for the throne: Dowager Queen Emma and her former schoolmate David Kalakaua, a colonel in the king's militia. Lucy was confident that her friend would be queen again, but Bosworth made it known in the pages of the *Dispatch* that he sided with the more forceful Kalakaua. The vitriolic campaign exposed the divisions among the native populace that had deepened with the encroachment of foreigners into Hawaiian affairs. The pro-British Emma, descended from the dwindling line of Kamehameha, was a favorite on Oahu, while Colonel Kalakaua, shrewdly playing British against Americans, drew his power from *alii* on the outer islands.

Forty-five chiefs convened at the courthouse a week after the king's death to vote. Convinced of victory, hundreds of "Emmaites" marched to the courthouse to celebrate Emma's accession only to discover that Kalakaua had won thirty-nine to six. Enraged, Emma's supporters stormed the courthouse to attack legislators and demolish furnishings, paintings—even a carriage—until American and British troops came ashore to quell the riot.

The political battles roiling the kingdom did little to change the lives of the Chinese sequestered in the district around the wharf or in plantation villages, except to increase their unease. For power was inexorably passing into the hands of *haoles,* many of whom resented the intrusion of Chinese merchants into the island economy. When the victorious Kalakaua appointed a cabinet representing a "cosmopolitan" constituency, including a Hawaiian minister of finance, an English minister of foreign affairs, a German minister of the interior, and an American attorney-general, missing, of course, was a minister from the second-largest racial group in the islands—the Chinese.

Long before Molly was born, the legislature, after years of prodding by the Congregational Party, had decreed that all children in Hawaii attend a form of grammar school until the age of fourteen. The vast majority of Hawaiian and mixed-race children attended the tuition-free "common" schools run by native graduates of Lahainaluna Seminary on Maui according to mission guidelines. In the crowded, underfunded common schools, learning was conducted in Hawaiian, using dictionaries and Bibles translated by an earlier generation of Congregational missionaries. English, Americans, and Europeans enrolled their children in the "select," or English-speaking, boarding schools established by the various churches along British or American lines.

The handful of Chinese children in Hawaii did not fit into this islandwide system at all. Eldest sons were sent back to the villages in China to attend clan schools until old enough to return to work, except for the sons of wealthy merchants who had private tutors to teach them the Chinese classics. Daughters were hoarded like treasures at home against the day of their marriage.

Since Pao An could not afford a tutor or tuition to the Bethel Mission School, the first of many English-language mission schools that would serve the Chinese so well in the next decades, nine-year-old Molly and eleven-year-old Lin Kong were sent to the Hawaiian-language common school adjacent to Chinatown, an experience for which each was woefully ill-prepared. The only Chinese among dozens of boisterous Hawaiian schoolboys, the mute, awkward Lin Kong was the perennial goat for his classmates' pranks. They laughed at his mouth-gasping attempts to force a response to the teacher's questions, pelted him with *kamani* nuts, smeared cow dung in his hair, and beat him regularly simply for coming too close, as if a frozen tongue were a kind of disease.

Molly, on the other hand, was a model student. Her English was perfect, her Hawaiian fluent, and she affected an attitude so imperious that the Hawaiian girls despised her instantly. She knew the answer to every question, whether posed in English or Hawaiian. And yet, she was as miserable as Lin Kong. Years of being tutored at Lucy's knee had endowed the girl with an unassailable sense of superiority that only sharpened her disappointment at the loss of her former life. The chief target of her frustration was Lin Kong, for she was humiliated by being linked to such a clumsy, stuttering creature.

"*L*incoln . . . ? You mean like that one with the big nose and beard?" Molly asked, her face twisted in comic scorn.

Lin Kong nodded wretchedly. "Nuh-nuh-nuh . . ." he moaned. He had been christened by the schoolmaster that morning, and the preposterous English name hung about his neck like a cangue. Nervously, he pulled at his ear, a gesture that, he remembered, too late, never failed to infuriate Molly, whom he longed only to please.

"Master Hoapili must hate you to give you that bad-luck name! Lincoln, that ugly American president, was killed, you know . . . *assassinated*—" Molly paused dramatically to let that recent addition to her vocabulary reverberate between them. Hers was a perfect performance of exaggerated pity; yet she was clearly delighted to push Lin Kong's nose ever deeper into the muck of mortification.

Lin Kong silently cursed his misfortune. If he had to have an English name to go to school, then why not a gloriously ordinary one like James or Edward or John? There had never been a Lincoln in the class until Hoapili, the newly ordained seminarian who oversaw the class of rowdy boys, had made the alliterative connection between the name Lin Kong and the object of the previous week's history lesson!

Molly repeated the name, drawing out both syllables until the sound became nonsensical. Mocking laughter bubbled up from her slim throat. "Lincoln was skinny and ugly . . . like you," she jibed. She drew her brows and mouth into an exaggerated frown, wiggled her fingers at the base of her chin to make an imaginary beard, then pulled her eyes taut with her forefingers. "Here's you—China Jack Lincoln!" She stuck her tongue at him and danced away on nimble bare feet, saying "nuh-nuh-nuh," to mock him.

Lin Kong had no way to tell Molly that he hated the name too. Especially when his own had been chosen after careful study by the apothecary in Fiddletown at his mother's request. The two characters connoted a concentrated, luminous intelligence; he would be a family's bright star, the apothecary predicted to his mother. What was this Lincoln to him but a dead *bak kuei* whose hooded eyes peered out from a cheap daguerreotype beside the mustachioed countenance of Kalakaua, the new king, on the classroom wall? This time, Molly's naked hostility left him more grotesquely tongue-tied than ever, gagging on his own chagrin. He tried to tell himself that "Lincoln" was at least more euphonious a name than any nonsensical pseudo-Chinese invention like Afong or Asam or Aseu that immigration officials slapped with callous indifference on arriving contract laborers. And yet, how much more would his tormentors at school taunt him now that he carried the weight of history along with his own obvious failings? And what would his dead mother say?

He stayed away from the house until evening, lamenting his ludicrous, humiliating predicament and falling more deeply into black despair. By the time the crickets had begun their mournful serenade, he was as miserable as the time he had discovered the dead lambs. He wanted to die himself and go back, back to his mother, to put an end to his stupid, tongue-tied existence. Hot tears surged up in the corners of his eyes, but he blinked them back. He gave himself no pity. He'd pick through his measly belongings for something to leave his uncle and throw his worthless self into the canal with the seaweed and dead fishes. Except that someone was blocking his path . . .

Rulan was sitting on the back steps folding squares of red and gold mock-paper money into tiny boats to burn at next month's Ching Ming festival in the Chinese graveyard up Manoa way. She saw how the boy started when he spied her before slipping back into the shadows. His look of desperation told her everything. She called him over. Reluctantly, he eased himself on the step below and silently pretended to read the book he had brought from school. This one was a Hawaiian grammar and the words marched meaninglessly before his face.

"Light's bad," Rulan said; her fingers neatly bent the ends of a folded square into a graceful curve. "You'll hurt your eyes." A small mountain of folded gilt paper rose at her feet. She intended to sew the artificial money into strings and feed them into the fire at Ching Ming for her father-in-law's use in the afterworld. The year was now organized by Chinese lunar feast days instead of the Christian rituals of the Bosworth years. The familiar rites were a source of comfort for her husband and herself, providing a welcome stability after years of wandering. "I'll make you soup tomorrow."

Lin Kong grunted in response.

"Here," she said, studying his mottled, feverish face, "I saved food for you."

Beside her, under a clean white cloth, there was a bowl of cold rice heaped with bits of gristly *lap cheong* sausage. Suddenly, Lin Kong was ravenous. But he shook his head violently. He didn't want food, didn't want tenderness from someone else's mother.

"Molly tells me the teacher gave you a new name. Every schoolchild has two names in Hawaii," Rulan ventured. He looked up sharply, but Rulan was tossing handfuls of paper money into an empty oil can. "One for home, one for school."

"Naa, naa," he growled, so famished he felt sick.

Rulan looked up to see him struggling to speak. His face was flushed with the effort. Veins stood out on his forehead.

"Your uncle told me that once you used to speak. Only after your mother died did you cease talking." She saw that the boy's eyes were bright with terror. He shook his head again.

Rulan went on ruthlessly. "Your mother told you to stay with an old apothecary in the mining camp. You disobeyed and followed a stranger. Is that why you cannot speak? Do you feel bad for disobeying her?"

He scrambled to his feet to run away, but she caught his hand and pulled hard. "Look at me," Rulan ordered. "I will not let you go until you look at me."

His eyes darted wildly to one side and the next, his breath coming in sharp, terrified pants.

"You are not the only boy to have lost a mother, but you may be the only one not to have mourned her. I have never seen you cry. Even when you dropped a heavy board on your foot, you did not cry. Why don't you cry?"

Again, he made a strangled sound, more animal than human, *"nanananana!"* and now he was fighting to loose himself from her grasp.

She held him tightly by the elbows, shaking him, forcing him to face her, but he lolled and twisted grotesquely. "You are a terrible, heartless boy!" she rebuked him. "You don't cry for your poor mother! She died so you could have life. Why don't you cry or make plain your grief? Bad, unfilial boy! You have nothing in this world. No family. No home." She went on with redoubled fervor. "Nobody wants you. We already have one child . . . what do we need with two? *La sap!* Rubbish boy! We will throw you into the street!" Then she added gently, "Is that what you tell yourself? *Hai ma?*"

"*Nanana, na . . .*" he shrieked and then the tears began to stream from his eyes and the strangled, animal sound became a human wail of utter desolation.

When he tried to wrench himself free, Rulan held him fast. "When your mother was dying, she forbade you to cry, *hai ma? Hai ma?*"

He nodded violently, gagging on his tears. Tears clogged his nose, ran down his cheeks, down his neck, and wet the front of his shirt.

"I tell you that your mother has given me the power to release you from that vow. You may cry and you may talk," she ordered him.

"Ah, ah, ah," he gasped, convulsing from the effort. He choked on the words he could not bear to say, his teeth chattering.

She pulled his head down to her breast, holding him tight as he shuddered against her. "What is your name?" she whispered against his cheek as they rocked together.

"I am Lin Kong," he gasped, trembling uncontrollably. "Not Lincoln. Not Lincoln! I am my mother's boy."

"Yes, you are," she told him.

He would weep throughout the night. But in the morning, he would speak again.

5

FISTS AND STICKS

The Hawaiian children who attended Molly's school accused her of being stuck-up, of aping *haole* ways. Certainly, she raised her hand too often and talked too much and blurted out the answers, not caring whether she made the other girls look slow or stupid compared to her. She fought to be first in line or at recitation; worst of all, she didn't try to fit in.

One day in the schoolyard, a Hawaiian girl twice Molly's size swung down from one of the half dozen ropes dangling from the arms of a banyan tree and stuck her wide, brown face into Molly's. "Ever'body hate you dis place," she taunted.

"But why?" Molly asked, truly amazed that anyone would think her less than extraordinary. She vaguely remembered answering a question that morning that the girl had gotten wrong. Yet Auntie Lucy had always said that an intelligent girl should never hide her light under a bushel. Was being smart sufficient reason for someone to hate her?

The enemy's reply was swift and crude. "Because you get big mouf', ask alla time too much question, make alla time noise!"

The children streamed toward the antagonists, yelling, "Fight! Fight!"

Those who were swinging on the ropes scraped their feet in the dirt to slow down and leaped forward, shouting with glee.

The Hawaiian girl was already banging Molly's face into the dirt when Lincoln pushed her off. "Stop it! Fighting all finish, *pau*," he said panting, shaking his bony fist at the girl. "Why you fight somebody so small?" Fine words, despite the fact that he was hardly bigger than Molly and for all his appetite no more than a pound or two heavier. With a loud oath, the girl unleashed a roundhouse punch that caught Lincoln in the gut. For a moment, he looked dazed, unbelieving, then he plopped down on his buttocks in the dirt, and gasped soundlessly, his mouth opening and closing like a fish, while the children laughed themselves to tears.

Molly fled the yard holding her ears against the taunts of the children. She crawled under a prickly *koa* bush behind the school, shivering with humiliation, and feeling that she might vomit from shame. When the jeers from the playground died down, she raged against Lincoln. It was his fault, she told herself. He was stupid and weak, and magnified her burden by using his newfound speech to embarrass her. But the awful, inescapable truth that her attacker had uttered fell like a dark curtain before Molly's eyes. *They hate me!* Molly told herself and let the hot tears flow.

In a while the Hoapilis, man and wife, came to summon the boys and girls to their separate classes for the rest of the afternoon. The wife was wide and soft, with clear brown eyes that saw everything at once—from one bullying girl's strutting to Molly's empty chair. This was just the sort of situation that wrung her heart, for Mrs. Hoapili was a gentle soul, Hawaiian to the core despite her Calvinist upbringing. Unlike her more scholarly husband, she liked nothing better than to spend the day leading her charges in Hawaiian hymns for which she devised complicated harmonies and shifting rhythms, like the name chants her grandmother used to recite from memory and that the new king was reviving to the Hawaiian people's delight.

The Chinese girl had easily mastered the singing and the schoolwork after only a few weeks in class. Bright, inquisitive, talkative, the girl was pathetically eager to please. So much so that the wise Mrs. Hoapili was convinced that the other children found her insufferable. So after putting the class to work in their copybooks, Mrs. Hoapili ran out into the yard to undo the damage done by the bully. She spotted Molly's hiding place at once.

"Why aren't you inside with the other girls?"

"They're ignorant, hateful! *Pupule*, crazy!"

"Pupule?" Mrs. Hoapili echoed, with the faintest trace of amusement. "Even the boys?" she ventured; it had not escaped her attention that putting boys and girls into separate classes only sharpened young girls' fascination with the opposite sex.

"Especially the boys. Especially one!" Molly declared emphatically. Angry tears popped into her eyes. "The girls are bad too!"

"Then perhaps I should punish their bad behavior by working them harder," said Mrs. Hoapili with a wry smile. "Which girl needs correction? Come, tell me her name!"

Molly felt a twinge of fear. If her classmates suspected she had betrayed one of them to the teacher, they would make her life a living hell.

"No," Molly said in a small voice, adding, "God will chastise her."

The girl knew her doctrine, Mrs. Hoapili admitted, even as the Hawaiian in her cringed at the arrogance of the retort. She ruffled the top of Molly's sun-warmed hair with her plump fingers, led her indoors, and, to the students' surprise, said nothing for the rest of the day.

Yet at dismissal, Mrs. Hoapili surprised them all by dispensing with the usual benediction. "I was talking today with our newest student," she said slowly. Every head quickly turned down to the desks. "I asked Molly about her welcome here. Had we shown her *aloha*? Had we extended her the good, right hand of Christian fellowship?" Again she paused, longer than before. "And do you know what this new girl said?"

Molly's head was spinning. She was convinced that Mrs. Hoapili was sacrificing her on the altar of some principle. If she punished the class on Molly's behalf, then the girls would stone her like disbelievers did to martyrs in the Bible. Molly didn't want to die.

"And this new student," Mrs. Hoapili continued in mellifluous Hawaiian accents, "said that yes indeed, you had treated her like a sister. That being the case, we are going to put the books away for two days. We will spend the time singing from the hymn book and thinking about ways in which we can be sisters, one to another."

A cheer rose up from the back seats where the big girls sat. Molly's face turned crimson. Even the girl who had pounded her head into the ground was smiling as she sang. But the singing made Molly's head hurt all the more.

"**D**id you hear what *that one's* bad girl did at the *kanaka* school?" the Widow demanded at the *tong* council. "She fought with a Hawaiian! Daughter of the man who owns ten acres of marshland in Waikiki where some of our brothers grow rice and raise ducks. How can we tolerate a

Chinese girl fighting? Something should be said to the parents, or all Chinese lose face.''

The eight men hunched around a long plank table on the second-floor meeting room of the *tong* clubhouse put on expressions to match their somber black coats and skullcaps. Although it was rare for a woman to address the council or to set foot in the society's private meeting rooms, an exception was made for the Widow. She was the wife of the society's founder and the chief source of money and favors. Although she had lost the opium license when the legislature had declared the drug illegal, the Widow had organized a system whereby overseers were paid a fee to include a ration of opium in every bucket of rice served to the men in the cane fields. Business under the Widow was more brisk than when opium had been sold with the approval of the king. Her daughter, Lily, was currently queen in the *tong*-sponsored Lantern Parade, a living symbol of prosperity, which even a Hakka could point to with pride. One did not dismiss such a force in the community as a mere woman come to whine, despite the fact that she sometimes made bad judgments like the disastrously unsuccessful ambush of the rascal Chen. Yet the Widow rarely made such mistakes, and her support was vital at this fragile point in the *tong's* business on Oahu when the brothers were being harassed by rival Hakka *tongs* springing up on the outer islands. It was the Widow's idea to hide its illegal activities under the guise of charity. When public outcry grew too loud against the *tong's* continued commerce in opium, the council's *haole* and Hawaiian allies in the legislature were vociferous in maintaining the *tong's* spotless reputation. Theirs was a *benevolent* association, the council argued, hardly secret at all, certainly not given to violence or crime, and devoted to maintaining the well-being of its members and preserving the harmony between Tang people and Hawaiians. To that end, the *tong* devoted large amounts of energy and money on mundane matters such as settling feuds, lawsuits, complaints against the king or the planters or the Bureau of Immigration, and other breaches of decorum in Chinese Honolulu.

''Let me remind you that Hawaiians regard us with dread,'' the Widow continued. ''The planters wanted families to replenish the islands, and when our men come without wives and children, they grumble about the gambling and 'dirt.' Now the Hawaiians blame us for bringing *mai pa-ke* and smallpox and for taking the best plantation jobs away. Sugar profits are down, and the Hawaiian nobles are trying to stop the shipments of contract workers from China and pressing the planters to hire families from the Azores or Samoa or even''—Mei Yuk wrinkled her nose in disgust— ''Japan!'' When the chorus of indignation had died down, she added, ''We have to keep peace with the Hawaiians. Don't start fights with their children. Make Tang parents punish those disobedient children who do!"

There was a lengthy period in which one council brother after another gave vivid testimony of unfiliality successfully amended by such impressive means as fists, starvation, imprisonment, chastisement with a half-inch-thick bamboo rod. After each had completed his tale, Mei Yuk's argument became more pointed. "Why doesn't the mother or father discipline the girl? Because the Chens themselves are uncivilized! They pay dues to no association or clan! The father, a man from our own county, has refused to pay a contribution or to take the oath and chooses as companions not the good people of his home district but those ridiculous men who hector the rest of us about fires! One wonders, too, why this man is so stupid that he cannot see his wife has made him a cuckold and that the girl is not his own! The woman herself prefers the company of brown devils and white devils, while trying to run honest men like Aseu and Asam out of the hardware and medicine businesses by undercutting prices and enticing lonely Tang men with dirty tricks."

The council brothers agreed that something needed to be done to curb the behavior of the Chens' wayward daughter. Perhaps they should make a case of the family by burning the store down, ventured one brother. Or by fixing it so that the father met with an accident on the street. When one brother reminded the others that the last such encounter had ended in the loss of several valuable *tong* soldiers, another erupted in fury, claiming that the girl's behavior was the fault of this renegade named Chen, who was inviting even filthy Hakka to join his useless fire brigade.

" 'Useless?' Every young man off the plantations who joins with Chen means one soldier less for the *tong*! Burning down his store makes this man a prophet and his cause more sure. No, better to make the young men laugh at him! And what shames a man most? Not broken limbs, but a wife and daughter he cannot control!" scolded the Widow.

The brothers stirred nervously on their stools. They were perfectly willing to design a scheme for extortion or to arrange an accident to destroy a competitor. Yet dealing with unmanageable women required more courage than facing down an angry minister of the king. They were glad to leave this new stratagem to their founder's wife who could negotiate with far more impunity in matters as complex as these.

Thus Mei Yuk arranged to be on the dock one day when a boat from Baltimore was unloading supplies. Pao An was prying open a crate stamped "Hayward Wire" with a Hawaiian longshoreman when she walked past. Seeing her, he flushed angrily and began to pull more assiduously at the boards of the crate with his fingers.

"Don't hide your face from me!" Mei Yuk cried out, walking boldly up to him.

Pao An picked up the crowbar and continued to work loose the boards.

"You don't greet an old friend?" she said.

"I have given up courtesy in these islands," he snapped. "Too dangerous. Friendship can so easily turn sour. I hear a peddler cannot do an honest day's work these days without being waylaid by bandits professing to be friends."

Mei Yuk's laughter was shrill. "You blinded one and the others have broken bones. Island life makes Tang men too soft."

"Next time, I will kill whoever comes against me!"

She turned large innocent eyes on him. "You are a monster," she offered sweetly. "I concede defeat. The council chastised me for wasting good soldiers on you. You have vanquished me entirely."

He continued to work in silence.

Mei Yuk frowned. "I forgive your bad manners. You always took pains to be rude. The council sent me to warn you about your daughter and that mongrel boy. They fought with a *kanaka* girl at school . . ."

"The council concerns itself with weighty matters! I know this!"

"Whoever heard of a decent Tang girl fighting?"

"If she fought, she had reason."

"*Aaiiee,* listen to the foolish man! He wants the girl to brawl like a *kanaka*! She even looks like one—so dark and wild. You'd think she had Hawaiian blood . . ."

Pao An threw down the crowbar with an oath; this time, Mei Yuk's barb had hit home. "She has her mother's blood and mine!"

"Her mother's at least, that much you can be sure of. But you were away when the child was born, *hai ma*? I warned you about going back to *that one*—but you were always foolish when it came to her. Well, the girl has to be reined in for the sake of us all. It's not good business if our girls brawl with the daughter of the *kanaka* who owns land on which *tong* brothers grow rice. You put the brothers' livelihood in jeopardy."

"Your brothers, not mine!"

"All Tang people are brothers against the brown devils," Mei Yuk shot back. "The Hawaiian father is angry. His daughter complains that the teacher favors the Tang girl over her. Now he raises the rents on his wetlands. And he tells his daughter to gather her friends against the girl. Use fists, sticks, knives. Only make the Tang girl keep her place!"

Pao An's face was unreadable. He took up the crowbar and began to smash the wooden crate in.

Mei Yuk's laughter stopped him. "One might think that you were the girl's father, after all. Such fury!"

Pao An did not tell Rulan of his encounter with Mei Yuk. But over his wife's protests, he insisted that Molly be pulled out of school and kept "decently" at home.

$\mathcal{M}$olly wandered the lanes and vendors' stalls of Chinatown, a small girl easily ignored amid the comings and goings of the noisy marketplace. She had been warned repeatedly against lingering too long at the market, for her parents' enemy, the one they called "the Widow," was landlord to the fish vendors and lived in a house nearby. Molly had also been forbidden to go near the *tong's* new clubhouse down the lane from the fish market. The brothers were enemies of her parents too. Molly discounted these admonitions. What did old country feuds have to do with her? And why should her parents' enemy be an enemy of hers? Besides, exploring the area around the fish market was more fun than chopping herbs for her mother in the store. She had nothing interesting to do now that they had taken school away from her except to go where all of workaday Honolulu congregated to buy, to gossip, and to flirt. Even King Kalakaua's cook and the kitchen staff of the new, three-story Hawaiian Hotel on Richards Street came through the market to pick out the freshest catch.

Once, spying Nalani bartering with a vendor for a pound of briny *limu* to eat with *poi,* Molly ran up behind and threw her hands around her auntie's waist.

Nalani swore and whirled around so quickly that Molly went sailing into a tub of silver-eyed *ama ama.* As Molly rose, sopping wet and laughing mischievously, Nalani caught her up in her arms and rubbed her nose against the girl's cheek, crying, "*Auwe, auwe!* My naughty *kolohe* girl!" Nalani recognized Molly's Mother Hubbard as one made over from an old dress of hers, part of a pile of castoffs Rulan had begged not long ago from Lucy. In addition to being ill-dressed and unkempt, Molly looked unhappy, and the faded skirts of her Mother Hubbard could not hide the fact that the girl was far too thin, her bare legs already sprouting beyond the ruffled hem. Nalani sniffed back sentimental tears, recalling the sweet, plump child she had once held to her bosom. Dragging Molly to a vegetable stall, she bought her a length of sugar cane to suck on. "So skinny," she lamented again and again, and called down the wrath of *Ku* and *Kanaloa* on Pao An for taking her girl away.

Molly came again and again to the fish stalls on the chance of encountering her auntie. The gregarious Molly suffered keenly from loneliness. She had not gained a single friend in her short tenure at school. The brooding Lincoln, intent on proving himself worthy of his new namesake, had withdrawn behind stacks of Hoapili's history books and was no fit company for a lively girl. Speech seemed to have granted him the right to think, and the old hunger had transferred itself from stomach to brain. He had already made his way through most of Hoapili's Hawaiian translations of English works and was soon devouring missionary tracts and speeches. Yet sensing that he was dining on tasteless fare when there was stronger meat to be had, Lincoln was now inching his way through Hoapili's copy of Macaulay.

What grieved Molly most was her exclusion from the tiny circle of Tang children her age. Once by chance while exploring the back alleys of the wharf, she peered into the noisy *tong* meeting hall and saw a banquet in progress. The table nearest her held six children in colorful holiday dress, some of whom she recognized from her ventures into their fathers' shops. The sight of the laughing, boisterous children stuffing their mouths with long-life noodles filled her with a desperate yearning to belong.

While she stood in the open doorway, mouth agape, a boy came up behind her and gave her a shove. He was a few years older than herself, tall and thin with a long glossy queue. The front of his head had been neatly shaved and gleamed with sweat.

"Aren't you going inside?" he asked impatiently, brandishing a red paper money envelope in his fist. "I'm a cousin. Who are you?"

"Nobody," Molly replied, scuffing her bare toe in the dirt.

"Oh, you're the Chen girl. Were you invited?"

Molly shook her head.

"I didn't think so. No one likes your family."

"But why?" Molly gasped in surprise.

"Because of you. Everybody says you're not one of us." The boy put his forearm next to Molly's. "See? Dark like a *kanaka*!" he declared in an offhanded way, and pushed past her into the crowded hall.

Molly stood rooted in the sunlight, the smile frozen on her face. She could hear the clatter of crockery and the sounds of revelry from inside the cavernous hall. She wanted to run. She wanted to hide. Except that a hole had opened up inside her, an enormous yearning to taste the dishes the merry children in festival clothes were eating, to hear what they were whispering into each other's ear. Why didn't they love her? What secrets did they know that she couldn't share? She had not a single friend in the world, Chinese or Hawaiian.

The aunties must have been lying when they called her *maikai*.

6

THE CRIMSON BIRD

Pao An's business was taking hold, for new customers were crowding into Chinatown at an astonishing rate as a result of a burgeoning economy driven by sugar. A new treaty between Hawaii and the United States gave preferential rates to Hawaiian over other foreign sugar. Cane was creating fortunes among the planters! Now they were putting their own *haole* candidates up for the legislature against a shrinking generation of Hawaiian *alii* and vying with missionary sons for Kalakaua's ear. With so much wealth invested in sugar, more strong Tang backs were urgently needed to harvest the vast tracts of cane. In the crucial year of 1876 when the Reciprocity Treaty took effect, the numbers of incoming Tang men soared from a few hundred into the thousands and would climb even higher by the end of the century. Chinatown soon outstripped the *bak kuei's* efforts to contain it. Shops and tenements owned by entrepreneurial families like the Lis and the Chens spilled past Nuuanu Stream to the brothels of Iwilei, spreading *mauka,* toward the mountains, block by block. There were enough Tang men in the islands to support several tobacconists, four smithies, cigar makers and coffin builders, a goldsmith and a silversmith, masons who worked in brick and lava stone. Tang men operated virtually all the restaurants, bakeries, and "coffee saloons" catering to the transient menfolk in the islands, *haole,* Hawaiian, and Chinese. There were tailors who made work clothes as well as foreign ladies' dresses, shoemakers and bootmakers, two hardware stores, and two merchants catering to Tang men's medicinal needs. Asam had bought up three stores to create a huge space where apprentice druggists chopped, weighed, and mixed herbs and a China-trained physician provided detailed diagnoses in addition to needling and moxibustion. But Tang men seeking cures also liked coming to a woman's domain dense with the smells and tastes and clutter of a village home. Unlike Asam's more elaborate concoctions, Rulan offered remedies using chiefly island-grown ingredients. Her shelves were stocked with a few imported items ordered in bulk from a supplier in San Francisco, for she was enough of a competitor that Asam would not sell to her wholesale anymore. Her most popular imported item was *mui,* particularly the sweet-sour plums for sore throats. Hawaiians had developed a taste for these and ate them even when they weren't sick.

Rulan also sold several kinds of teas, including a particularly potent dark brew, a remedy for weak lungs, which she served with homegrown Chinese lemons as big as oranges and cured in brine. Many Tang men who came to their shop had croup or bronchitis, and the tea relaxed the muscles of the chest, quieting their coughing. Some lingered among the baskets of nails and wire and tools and sought the advice of Pao An—a good man really, not the brute that rumor painted him—on this repair or that and heard him discourse on the necessity of a fire brigade.

The growing number of inhabitants on Oahu increased the need for drinking water, always in short supply, and decent housing across the island. Artesian wells were tapped and new reservoirs dug to augment the old brick reservoir near Nuuanu and Judd Streets. Soon dry, dusty Honolulu began to sprout small blocks of cottages and stores spreading outward from the older, "downtown" area along the wharf to the outlying districts of Palama, Kalihi, and swampy Waikiki into Nuuanu and Manoa Valleys and onto the plains of Kulaokahua, stretching from Punchbowl Street to Punahou Street.

Buggies, drays, and hacks crowded the downtown avenues and were joined by a public omnibus that ran between Waikiki and downtown Honolulu. By 1878, the "talking wire," or telephone, was in use not only at the palace but by businessmen around the islands as well.

These were good years for Pao An. Business was growing. He had gathered a core of fellow merchants who met regularly for fire protection. Their numbers were large enough to incur the enmity of the *tong,* which continued to harass individual members with clandestine acts of vandalism but, in the main, left them alone. Together, they had organized a protest against the *haole* fire department for failing to respond to Chinatown fires. Convinced now that they had to help themselves, the group collected enough contributions to order a steam-driven fire engine from California. Pao An's success in orchestrating the purchase of the engine coincided with a burst of new opportunities in construction as a result of the new trade agreement. Pao An envisioned teams of his laborers building wooden barracks or flumes for the rice and sugar plantations that were springing up throughout the islands. So when Claus Spreckels, a sugar refiner from California, began buying huge parcels of land on Maui and designed a thirty-mile irrigation canal to bring in water from the north side of the island to his sugar fields, Pao An put in a bid for the digging. He was elated to win a contract to bring in a crew of a hundred Chinese to begin work on what was dubbed the "Haiku Ditch."

Molly rejoiced that her father would be leaving. His disapproving eye never failed to drain away all joy.

*O*ne fall morning in Molly's eleventh year, as she lingered to watch a street tinker transform a metal plate with hammer and awl into a lantern, she became aware that someone was also observing her. Looking up, she spied a small white face peering out from behind the half-open gate of the Widow's compound.

It vanished suddenly behind a wooden slat. Then the gate creaked open a hair's breadth and the same face peered between the crack.

"You, girl. Come here," a lilting voice called in a dialect Molly had heard only rarely around the fish market. It was the Lantern Queen.

Molly went cautiously to the fence and peeked around the gate. What she saw astonished her: a pocket-size garden cunningly decorated with miniature palm trees and pots of narcissuses forced into bloom. A statue of the goddess Kwan Yin stood on a stone lily pad in the center of the pond in whose depths fat, speckled carp swam. At the pond's edge sat a girl a few years older than herself staring dejectedly into the water.

"What's wrong?" Molly called. "What do you want?" When the girl's body began to shake with sobs, Molly stepped tentatively inside.

"I've lost my crimson bird," the girl confided in a rush. "I put a bone in its cage to sharpen his beak, and he flew out over my hand . . ." Her shoulders began to tremble at the memory of her loss. "Oh," she gasped out finally, "my mother will beat me if she finds out . . ."

"But it wasn't your fault," Molly said reassuringly. How terrible, she thought, to have a mother more tyrannical than her own!

The girl sniffed back her tears. "They call you Molly, *hai ma*?" she blurted out. "I heard the skinny Tang boy who follows you around shout out your name one day. I watch you a lot. That boy too. I'm Lily . . ." she continued. "Our mothers know each other from the old country. Your mother hates mine . . ."

Lily tilted her head and smiled, a gesture that stirred a vivid recollection of white satin, crimson lips, and the deafening explosion of fireworks.

"My mother made me promise not to talk to anyone in your family," Molly declared. "I don't understand it, do you? Why should we be enemies?"

Lily brushed a stray lock away from her face with a slender hand. Molly was enthralled. If Lily was lovely when seen by moonlight and arrayed like a goddess, in the unforgiving sun, with her face bare of powder and paint, she was more exquisite still, from the slight swell of breasts beneath her tunic to the tiny, teacup-size feet in black satin shoes that peeked out from the hem of her wide trousers. Lily's daintiness made Molly all too aware of her dirty feet and threadbare Hawaiian dress, her dark skin, and unruly hair. How she coveted the sleek braids coiled around Lily's ears and the tiny cloisonné butterfly that danced on the end of a hairpin. Why shouldn't we be friends? she thought.

Lily pried Molly's fingers from the gate. "Stay with me," she said, drawing Molly into the yard. "No one ever comes to see me. Your mother lets you go where you want, but mine never lets me outside."

"Even to visit the shops?" Molly asked. She studied Lily's smooth face with a puzzled frown. "How old are you?"

"Almost fifteen. Old enough for the go-between to visit. Men have been offering for me ever since I was thirteen. My dowry, you know. But Mama says no bride-price has been high enough, so she is looking for an *exceptional* man . . ."

"She means to sell you?" blurted out Molly. She was appalled and yet seized with curiosity about bride-prices, dowries, go-betweens—and marriage.

Lily cocked her head and asserted flatly, "Men want to marry only rich girls. It helps to be pretty too. You're not as pretty as me. You have prickly hair, your dress is too big . . . and your skin is dark from the sun."

Lily's assessment, delivered without malice, reinforced Molly's long-held conviction that she was ugly as well as poor. Why else would the children in Chinatown treat her like a carrier of *mai pa-ke*? Pao An's disapproval and Molly's prolonged isolation had worked like acid over the years to dissolve her childhood confidence. Now Lily had made Molly's secret fears explicit. She was a schoolyard joke to the Hawaiians, a clumsy, long-legged thing to the Chinese, not at all the kind of girl that an *exceptional* man would offer a bride-price for.

Lily tucked her small hand into Molly's. "Don't worry," she whispered. "I'll paint your face and give you one of my old tunics to wear instead of that funny Hawaiian dress. I'll even make your hair like mine." A narrow section of Lily's front hair was cut and oiled to hang down in the middle of her forehead past her eyebrows "like a swallow's tail," the current fashion in Peking, according to Lily. Lily also confided that the *tong* council was searching for a replacement for her as queen. "I'll make them choose you," she promised breathlessly.

Molly threw her arms around her new friend, her only friend. She wanted nothing more than to be a copy of Lily: dainty, graceful, wholly and unmistakably Chinese.

To Molly's eyes, the interior of the Li house was as elegant as the outside was plain. It was clearly a woman's house, filled with cane chairs that curved around the body and toy-size tables adorned with big-bellied Buddhas and porcelain bowls, which the ten-year-old bond maid kept filled with sugared fruit. The only masculine item was the huge portrait of Lily's long-dead father, a pudgy-faced man in black banker's coat and skullcap, on the wall above the family altar. Lily confessed that she remembered the late Merchant Li chiefly for trying to strip the bindings off her feet. "Thank goodness Mama defied him, or my feet would be as big as yours," she said primly, "and what rich Tang man would marry me then?"

Molly envied everything about Lily: her bound feet, the luxury of her dwelling, her little maid, even Lily's mother. Mei Yuk's apartment was at the back of the house away from the noise and dirt of the street, a sitting room and bedroom smelling of joss sticks, which burned day and night in jars filled with sand. But Mei Yuk herself was rarely there; instead she spent her time in her husband's old office on the ground floor of the building. Lily told Molly that after her father's death, her mother doubled the profits of the family business. Now she owned tenements, shops, stalls and concessions, contributed generously to several prominent surname societies, and held shares in a score of *hui*. She was a meticulous manager, directing stewards, accountants, and foremen charged with the day-to-day running of the Li enterprises with a firm hand and a sharp eye for swindlers.

Molly encountered the formidable matriarch of the Lis on her fourth visit, a rare occasion when Mei Yuk allowed herself an afternoon of rest. Lily took her up the courtyard stairs onto a balcony that ran around three sides of the house and into Mei Yuk's bedroom. Molly at once spied Mei Yuk's tiny feet poking out from a yellow quilt. The teacup-size feet encased in bed shoes of red satin twitched every time their owner, propped up on a bolster with a small table over her lap, flipped the beads on her abacus or made a notation on paper. Compared to this elegant woman, Molly's mother was ungainly and plain. Mei Yuk's jacket was of quilted brocade, not threadbare blue cotton like the one her mother wore, day in and day out. Her hair was done up in heavy coils secured with gold pins, not carelessly tied up with a piece of twine.

Mei Yuk's rouged lips curved into a smile as the two girls entered.

"Tai Tai," Molly stammered nervously, calling her hostess by title as good manners demanded.

Mei Yuk nodded amiably. "Good! Good! A proper greeting from a proper young girl," she said, laughing, and ordered tea and sugared fruit for the girls. They ate by her bedside while she gossiped with them about the women in Chinatown.

Instead of the wicked harridan of her mother's stories, Molly found another indulgent "auntie." Molly loved lying at the foot of Mei Yuk's huge teakwood bed, drinking tea and nibbling on savory dishes while Lily's mother told stories of how she had beat a rival out of a contract or how she had bought a minister's favor by giving money for the king's birthday. Unlike Molly's mother, Mei Yuk was playful, irreverent, bursting with wit and charm. Molly told herself that at heart, she was really more like a Li than a Chen. This was why Rulan did not understand her, and why Molly kept secrets, the most important of which was the number of hours she spent every day with the Lis. I will deal with kings and ministers too, she told herself.

"Your mother is a thief, you know," Mei Yuk confided one day. "We lived like sisters until she took something from me and ran away to join the landless riffraff who burned the great houses along the river. It was not an important thing that she took, but I loved it nevertheless, and because I was a spoiled young woman in those days, used to getting my own way, I hated her for it. Now I am older and age teaches wisdom; but your mother, for guilt, avoids me."

This version was entirely different from the stories Molly's mother told about the noble sacrifices of peasants and the brutality and greed of the gentry. To hear her mother called *thief* and *riffraff* confounded Molly. "What did she steal?" she asked.

"Aaiiee, I'll not bring up old grudges again. Ask your mother one day." Mei Yuk's lips parted, showing teeth as small and pointed as a cat's. "I can never keep up with your father's enterprises. What is he building now?"

"He's taking some men to Maui to build an irrigation ditch for Spreckels's plantation. Father hopes to make lots of money," Molly added with pretended enthusiasm. She was ashamed that her father was little more than a *gu li,* "rough man," a digger of ditches.

"Then won't this rich man be proud to see his daughter honored in the next Lantern Parade!" Mei Yuk purred.

Molly was never sure what her father would think—but surely, he would be glad of that great honor. Winning the title of queen would confer respect on the entire family. Customers would stream into her father's hardware store to congratulate him for his celebrated daughter. Her father might even smile on her!

"Come here, child," said the *Tai Tai,* drawing Molly close. "Let me paint your face so you can look like my rascal girl."

No one knew more about the proper cut of a tunic or how to reshape an eyebrow or how to coax a recalcitrant shock of hair into a tight, smooth braid than Li Mei Yuk. No one could dress down a tradesman with blistering scorn in one moment and in the next charm her way through a complicated rental agreement with a hostile agent of the king. Next to Lily's clever mother, Molly's own mother was a creature from the countryside whose expectations for her daughter were as distressingly humble as herself. Molly realized that her common school education would make her fit only for serving others; Lily, on the other hand, had been trained by her mother to *be* served. Lily had talents no other Tang girl in the islands possessed: she spoke three dialects of Cantonese; could wield ink brush, water pipe, and embroidery needle; could sing ancient laments and coax achingly sad sounds from a moon harp. Molly longed to be just like her!

7

THE LANTERN QUEEN

Molly was as hungry for the secret pleasure she found in the Widow's mansion as she was for *mui*. Everything about the Lis fascinated her—and one thing especially, since it was a secret kept from Lily as well: an old trunk in which the Widow saved treasures from her life in China. Lily was forbidden to open it, and naturally, both girls were desperately curious to see why.

On Mei Yuk's temple day, the girls sneaked into her room to open the battered trunk. As Lily pried open the lid, a moth fluttered drunkenly out of the depths. Molly's eager hands reached inside and found no jewels, no scrolls, no porcelain figurines; in short, no treasure at all. Only a stack of worm-eaten tunics and skirts folded flat and below that, discarded goods of various sizes wrapped in white muslin.

The smallest were three pairs of tiny satin shoes, each a forefinger in length. Up close, the shoes seemed too small even for Mei Yuk's doll-size feet. What did the *Tai Tai's* feet look like? Molly wondered. Her mother was vague about how foot binding was accomplished, and Molly preferred to imagine that Mei Yuk's and Lily's feet were simply smaller copies of her own limbs, not mangled appendages, the instep broken in order to force heel and toe together "like an animal's hoof," as Aunt Lucy's friends in the China Mission's anti-foot-binding league maintained.

Nothing, on closer inspection, looked like "treasures." There was a cinnabar box containing implements of gold. The filigreed spindles were hair ornaments while those shaped like tiny spoons were ear picks, Lily explained. A knobby item that tinkled when shaken and looked like a lantern was damaged beyond repair. Even the gilt rondel, which Lily pulled out of the cloth wrappings, was tarnished and old. "Whatever is that for?" she asked.

"A mirror, I think," Lily said, hesitantly. "I can almost see my face."

"Anything else?" Molly persisted. She was growing nervous, her ears magnifying the most innocuous noises. Even the ticking of a small china clock sounded like a woman's shoes clicking on the wooden boards below.

There were two remaining objects, a gold button rolling about on the bottom of the trunk and a slim package as long as Lily's arm which proved to be not a parasol, as Molly guessed, but a lock of human hair tightly plaited. Gingerly, Molly took the braid and placed it on her lap where it coiled, thick, black, and curiously vital.

Suddenly, small white fingers gripped Molly's shoulder, making her cry out in alarm.

"*Tai Tai* . . ." Molly stammered in fear.

"Did your mother tell you to do this?" Mei Yuk snatched the braid away and leaned forward, her eyes mere slits in her narrow face. "I shall report you to the *tong*."

Molly turned white. "No, *Tai Tai*. My father . . ." She hung her head, shaking with terror. Her father was set to sail for Maui. There would be no one to protect her.

But when Mei Yuk spoke again, her voice was purged of anger. "I know, fathers can be cruel when shamed, *hai ma*? Be glad, then, that you have caught me in a merciful mood. What shall I do with you? Sit, sit."

Molly came at once to kneel beside Mei Yuk, grateful for the reprieve.

Mei Yuk ruffled up Molly's hair affectionately. "You have vanquished me with your curiosity. I will tell you all." Each item, she explained, was a memento plucked out of the fire that had consumed the Lis' Kwangtung country house. Treasure or wreckage, the contents told a far different story than the one the girls had guessed. The shoes did not belong to Mei Yuk but to the old *Tai Tai,* her husband's grandmother, as did the gold pins in the cinnabar box. "She cursed my marriage, but happily she died." Mei Yuk held up the tiny dagger-shaped spindles that had once decorated the old *Tai Tai's* sparse hair. "Your mother was the *Tai Tai's* bond maid at the time."

It shamed Molly to be reminded that in China as in Hawaii, her family occupied so low an estate. Most troubling of all were Mei Yuk's hints at an intimacy of long standing between the two families that her own parents denied. Mei Yuk's allusions to a mysterious curse left Molly more confused than before. Molly was not sure whether the curse was pronounced on or by Mei Yuk, for the Widow's mood veered from rage at unspecified enemies to sorrow for her own losses. As proof of her own bad luck, Mei Yuk held up the mass of hanging mirrors, broken tassels, and faded papier-mâché, not a lantern as the girls assumed, but her bridal headdress ruined during a bandit attack on the wedding procession. "An omen," Mei Yuk asserted, "of all the unhappiness ahead for me."

For with her marriage, the fortunes of her husband's house had begun to sink, and Merchant Li was not the man to raise the family back to its former heights. "The gold hat button was never used, you know," she mused, rolling the shiny disk in her hand. "He failed the examinations, and all the money spent to buy his rank went for nothing."

As evidence of what the family had lost, Mei Yuk held out the brass rondel, an ancient artifact from Shouchou handed down from one *Tai Tai* to the next. Molly dismissed it as too scratched to give an honest image and her mind wandered to the lock of hair on the Widow's lap.

"What about that?" Molly interrupted. "A man's queue, right?"

Mei Yuk stopped short. *"Aiya,"* she said, sighing, and took the braid into her hands. "My lover's," she said simply. The mask of civility dropped from her face, revealing such naked suffering that even Lily did not dare to question her mother more.

When all the items except the mirror were put away, Mei Yuk led the girls to her dressing table.

"Which one will be the beauty?" she asked, all calm and dignity restored, and made each girl look into the Shouchou mirror. Lily narrowed her eyes at her reflection, striking a pose by habit, while Molly stared warily, frightened at what the glass revealed. Her reflection appeared other-worldly and strange. Molly closed her eyes as Mei Yuk sponged on the cakelike powder that made her as pale as Lily.

"Where do you go in the afternoon?" Rulan demanded that evening. "Lin Kong says you slip away for hours before he finds you wandering in the market. What do you do?"

"I look at the stalls." Molly silently vowed to make Lincoln pay.

Rulan stabbed a finger on a telltale spot of crimson on her daughter's cheek. "Is that where you got this fancy color?" she demanded in fury.

Knowing how Rulan hated this sort of adornment, Molly had scoured her face at the pump before climbing the porch steps, though not well enough, it seemed. "A woman was selling it at the market," Molly stammered. "She let me try some for free."

"I don't want you buying face paint. Paint is for lazy rich girls, and you are too poor . . . and too busy. Or ought to be. Go! I left bowls and pots in the bucket for you to scrub."

Molly stormed off, raging at the unfairness of her life. Mei Yuk was molding her daughter into a beauty, while her own parents were turning her into a drudge.

"You do not know how ambition has corrupted *that one*," the Widow confided to the go-between, the woman with the longest memory and the biggest mouth in Chinatown. "How can such a good-for-nothing, *la sap* rubbish mother aspire to such a prize as Lantern Queen for her daughter, when the father has no connections to the *tong,* pays no dues to any clan. All he does is talk against our *tong* brothers and scare merchants into buying his silly engine to put out fires that will not come."

The marriage broker had been widowed three times in Hawaii, and in the course of negotiating for two husbands of her own, had learned enough about the economics of ambition and desire to set up a business as a go-between in Chinese Honolulu. She knew that youth wanted wealth in a mate, whereas age craved beauty and that a clever match could satisfy both a zealous mother and a rebellious son. It was said that she held in her head the astrological charts and family tree of every merchant's child born on Oahu and had a list of possible mates for their parents by the time the children went from crawling to tottering on two legs. This particular part of her legend was of such interest to the Tang girls nearing marriageable age at this time that some had tried to bribe the woman to make a case for the penniless youths whom they favored. But the broker was no fool; she knew that a successful marriage was a victory of economics over sentiment and could frame an answer so that even a lovesick girl came round in the end to her parents' choice.

The broker's purpose in visiting the Widow was to consult about a suitable spouse for Lily. They had met frequently over the last months, for Lily's was a particularly complicated case. Whoever won the girl would walk off with the largest dowry offered in the community and, moreover, supplant Lily's dead father as headman of one powerful branch of the *tong*. Mei Yuk intended the broker to earn her fee. This meant shoring up the Lis' position in order to gain the maximum bride-price. To this end, the go-between had been gathering confidential information for the Widow about leading families with eligible sons—which sons were secretly in debt and which young stallions preferred boys to girls—and dispensing news on the Lis' behalf around the community.

"This bad business about the Chen girl . . . decent people should be forewarned, *hai ma*?" Mei Yuk said. "Why should the girl make herself higher than other daughters from better families? What right does the mother have to put her daughter's name up for queen and reap the rewards that others have toiled for?"

"Indeed such a one should not," the old woman replied, perfectly willing to follow wherever her patron might lead.

*A*ngry clouds gathered over the harbor. Pao An was packing up his gear for his trip to Maui the next day, when a letter came from the *tong*. It informed him that twenty of his crew, all members of the brotherhood, were breaking their work contracts for the Haiku Ditch. The names of the laborers were listed, men Pao An had not suspected of affiliation with the *tong*. No reasons were given for the action. The letter was signed by the eight men who formed the council, and a schedule of public meetings was included if Pao An chose to protest. Cursing roundly, Pao An stormed out of the store to the hall. He would throw the letter back at the council, accuse the cowards to their faces of conspiring to ruin him, and gather a crew for the digging in spite of their meddling!

The *tong* clubhouse was a new two-story building on a side street near the fish market. That morning, the hall was as crowded as on a lunar feast day. Pao An was surprised to find the downstairs reception hall packed from one end to the other with jostling youths, many of whom he recognized as recruits to his fire brigade. There were also a few well-dressed Punti wives among the men, an unusual circumstance, since Chinatown matrons rarely ventured out to market or public meetings. Mei Yuk, he supposed, the founder's widow, was among them. Six middle-aged men in scholars' skullcaps and black satin *ma gwa,* collarless banker's coats, were seated at a table with writing brushes in hand. The secretary of the *tong,* a scrawny man with a self-important air, made a great show of welcoming the women to the meeting and proclaimed that the first order of business would be the competition for a new Lantern Queen.

A murmur rose from the women, all ambitious mothers, Pao An guessed. He was thankful to have been spared marrying one of those. Angrily, Pao An understood that he would have to sit through an interminable public display before he could vent his rage at the council. What right did the *tong* have to intrude into his affairs? he fumed. Such nonsensical bureaucratic acts strained his short supply of patience, just as amateur theatricals like the one about to be mounted by the girls and their mothers filled him with embarrassment.

He squirmed inwardly as a fat woman on ridiculously tiny feet pushed her daughter forward in front of the crowd. His discomfort deepened when two men brought out a chair and moon harp, and the girl took sticks in hand and made ready to play. In the hands of an ill-trained musician, the moon harp gave off sounds that were excruciating to the ear. The secretary announced the girl's name, and after the hubbub had died down, Pao An was surprised by the poise with which the girl bowed to the council members and to the audience. Dressed in a peach-colored suit of polished cotton, she seemed entirely at ease before the rowdy bachelors and played her piece flawlessly, a stream of tinkling sounds that rose and fell like silvery water and made the bachelors long for their women in China. Pao An suspected that years of practice had been compressed into this four-minute performance and applauded the girl's skill as energetically as the rest.

An ominous peal of thunder drowned out the name of the next contestant. Yet from the cheers of the audience, everyone already knew this girl, who had the pink cheeks, oval "watermelon seed" face, and long eyes of the classic Chinese beauty. Her hair hung in a single braid down to her waist and her blue satin tunic and black pants hugged her shapely body. She walked to the front of the room with an athletic stride, gracefully trailing two long red ribbons. While three musicians accompanied her movements with *pi pa* and drum and flute, the girl whirled and dipped and leaped, flinging the red ribbons in amazingly intricate patterns that hovered in the air.

Once again the audience exploded in applause, and the dancer pirouetted, bowed, and ran daintily off the stage. She was the obvious favorite, so far, of the young men in the audience, although the dour men at the table signaled neither approval nor scorn.

The secretary came forward to explain that after the next performer, each girl would be questioned by the council to determine her qualifications for queen. The rain had begun in earnest now, creating a distracting rhythm on the corrugated iron roof. The noise was so loud that the secretary had to order the young men in the audience, still noisily discussing the charms of the ribbon dancer, to stop talking. Then the name of the candidate for Lantern Queen was announced: "Molly Chen, to sing a song from the Chinese opera."

Pao An's head shot up. From behind the curtain, he saw Molly hobble forward in too-tight shoes and a borrowed *sam fu* tunic and pants that hung like a sack on her slim body. The girl made an awkward bow to the audience and took her place in the center of the floor. Then, remembering the council, she dipped her head in a hasty, embarrassed gesture of obeisance to the six men at the table. The men frowned.

Pao An felt hot, and there was a ringing that issued from somewhere inside his head. The girl would humiliate herself! Every eye fixed on Molly seemed to be fastened on him as well.

Molly was the youngest of the three contestants, and her nervousness was obvious when she began to sing.

Pao An could not remember having heard Molly sing before. Her voice was sweet and pure, a child's voice, but thin and artless, like a tune played on a homemade flute. It was a voice suited to a simple ballad, not to the ridiculously melodramatic song she had chosen, a courtesan's lament for her dead lover with complicated flourishes that jumped up and down the scale. Pao An wanted to weep for her, and found himself glaring at the youths in the audience, his hands clenched into fists, ready to strike out at the first hint of mockery.

It seemed to Pao An that the song lasted forever. Molly's voice grew weaker, in a vain attempt to drown out the rain hammering on the tin roof. Periodically, not knowing what to do, she turned her back to the audience and sang to the table of elders behind her and could not be heard at all. When finally the song ended, Molly's performance was met with perfunctory applause. By then, Pao An was drenched in sweat.

Then the leader of the council, a portly man with a ruddy complexion and a voice as sonorous as a bullfrog's, moved his spectacles lower on the bridge of his nose and announced to the assembly, "We will start the examination with this contestant."

A man brought a stool, and Molly perched uncomfortably on the edge.

"Let me say," the florid man with the spectacles intoned to the frightened girl, "that personally I was amazed that you would bother to apply at such short notice and with so little preparation. Had it not been for Li Mei Yuk's insistence that every girl be given a chance to compete, we would have passed you over. So tell us then, what is your father's clan? What did his people do in Kwangtung?"

It was obvious to the crowd that the girl was confounded by the question. Frightened by the acrimonious attitude of her interrogator, Molly ransacked her storehouse of memories, yet was unable to recall any details of Pao An's birthplace. "He came from a village in China," she said nervously.

"Which one?" her interrogator snorted. "There are hundreds of villages in the Delta alone!"

Molly was confused. Her feet hurt, the paint was running from her face, and her hair had sprung loose from its pins—the very ones Mei Yuk had used to anchor the elaborate arrangement of rolls and curls and braids. It had taken every ounce of courage for her to finish the song Mei Yuk had taught her. Now she looked to Mei Yuk sitting in the front row and found no comfort there. The Widow, in fact, was wearing an expression of glee and thoroughly enjoying the girl's anguish.

"This girl doesn't know!" another council elder muttered, incensed. "A daughter who doesn't know who her father is!"

A man with a long whiskery lock at the end of his chin leaned forward. "You lived among the *bak kuei*," he accused. "Why?"

The epithet unnerved Molly as it always did when her father spoke of "white devils" and "deceivers." "Yes . . . with *Auntie* Lucy and *Uncle* Emmanuel," she replied with a trace of annoyance.

Her willingness to justify such preposterous connections—worse, to claim them as kin—spurred her interlocutor to a burst of indignation. "They are not your *real* family. Why do you call them 'aunt' and 'uncle'? Why did your mother turn to *bak kuei*, not her own kind for shelter?"

The angry murmur that went through the assembly was interrupted by several loud expostulations. A few bachelors were regular customers in Rulan's small shop and a handful of others had joined with Pao An in organizing the fire brigade. These allies of the Chens were quarreling heatedly with *tong* members who were following the hostile line of questioning with enthusiasm.

The man pressed on, ignoring the cries of protest in the audience. "We would not have turned her away if she came to us. The *tong* considers itself a benefactor to all Tang people in the islands, and if she had applied to the brothers for aid, we would have been generous. There was no need to go to outsiders if your father abandoned you."

"He did not abandon us," Molly said, her voice quavering. "We thought he was dead, but he was working for seven years in Gold Mountain for a stake to start a business."

"This father who comes and goes interests me," another council elder interjected. "Where did he get this stake? I heard he murdered a *tong* brother in Gold Mountain and stole it off the dead man's body!"

There were loud protests from the back of the room and scuffling in the midst of the crowd. The heavens opened and a mighty torrent of rain pounded on the iron roof. "The father is not on trial here," another said with growing vexation over the angry murmuring in the room.

"Why are we talking to *that one* at all when she is not her father's daughter? Look at her. She's some barbarian's half-breed bastard—*bak kuei* or *kanaka!*"

"No!" Molly blurted out, horrified at this new accusation. "I'm the same as you. My father . . . ," but she was unable to speak for the tears that clogged her throat. When the council leader made an impatient gesture of dismissal, she stumbled off the stool, wishing the floor would open up and swallow her. A strong hand caught her before she fell.

"You wanted to know her father," Pao An announced in a voice that carried over the din. "I am Chen Pao An of On Ting village. I was a general in the rebellion and a general for the provincial army. I earned my stake in Gold Mountain carrying mud and rock to build the levees. I murdered no one for it!" Looking directly into the Widow's white, anguished face, he declared, "This child is mine. And as her father, I withdraw her from the competition. Let no man raise his voice against this girl again, or he answers to me." And as the rain echoed like drumbeats in the cavernous room, Pao An held his daughter in the circle of one arm while fighting a path through the shouting, jeering Tang men with the other.

A new Lantern Queen reigned over the raucous New Year's parade, the comely ribbon dancer whose father was an ally of the Widow in the council. Even from afar, Molly saw that the new queen's front hair was oiled and cut in the shape of a swallow's tail, the current fashion in the capital of China, Molly told her mother wryly. The willowy girl threw coins from her carriage as she went by, accompanied by Lily, who had been Lantern Queen many times before. Rumor had it that Lily was now an almost-married woman, having been promised to the *"poi* king," a former cane worker who manufactured most of the *poi* eaten on Oahu. A huge bride-price had been paid.

While all of Chinatown gathered in the streets to watch the new Lantern Queen pass, an odd thing was happening in the reception hall of the *tong* clubhouse. A long-limbed Chinese youth was strewing over the polished floor of the hall the smelly remains of a catch that had mysteriously disappeared off a fishing boat several days before.

When the queen and her entourage of *tong* officials and government dignitaries arrived for the postparade banquet, they were assaulted by the stink of rotten fish. The Hawaiian guests made a hasty retreat despite the officials' pleas. Even after the slimy carcasses were swept up and carted away to be buried in the backyard, a stench hung over the feast. It permeated the walls, the banquet tables, the red good-luck banners and signs; it clung to the clothes and shoes and hands of the revelers, to the rich gravies and thick noodles that no one could eat for gagging. The queen vomited after taking a bite of a fried oyster. The Widow and her daughter left without putting a morsel to their lips. No speeches were made. Meetings were suspended while the walls and floors were scoured. And still, the stench lingered.

*N*o one enjoyed the reports of the disastrous feast more than Molly. "Even my singing could not smell as badly as that fish," she said with a laugh one night over evening rice. She was quite at ease now about her unhappy bid for Lantern Queen.

"I don't know," Lincoln offered slyly. "The fish were four days old— by all accounts, not nearly as ripe as your singing."

8

PAPER SECRETS

Pitting himself in a public brawl against the powerful *tong* had an immediate effect. Pao An's efforts to gather a crew for the Haiku Ditch failed, and the contract, which would have won him extra dollars for new equipment, was given to another *luna*. Yet ironically, the feud with the Widow had shored up the family's flimsy foundations. Molly was suddenly made aware of the fierceness of her father's love, although that knowledge, however reassuring, did nothing to ease the tension between them.

Pao An soon had matters other than his unruly daughter on his mind. As soon as it became known in the foreign community that the Chinese had purchased a "steamer" manufactured in New England, the king's *haole* ministers rushed to obtain an identical engine. Both fire trucks arrived on the same boat to considerable fanfare on the dock. By then, Pao An had convinced fifty Hakka and Punti to bury their rivalries and form a fire brigade that cut across clan, provincial, and district divisions. So zealous were these first Chinese firefighters that in a matter of months, the volunteer squad with the title of Chinese Fire Company was named an official division of the Honolulu Fire Department. The next year, all Honolulu cheered the bright-uniformed members of China Engine Company No. 2, the last and largest delegation in the annual fire parade.

Despite the stories that the Widow fed regularly to her allies in the *tong* and to her cronies at the *ma jong* table, Pao An's business did not die. Profits kept accruing in haphazard fashion, for Pao An was venturing beyond the environs of Chinatown on small jobs on sugar and rice plantations, and Rulan's loyal core of customers came regularly for doctoring. But there were always bills: a roof broken in a storm, a rotten stair, termite-eaten walls, iron tools ruined by rain. One night, a rope holding lumber came loose and crushed a shipment of Rulan's dried fruit. On the heels of that "accident" there were robberies of supplies newly unloaded onto the docks. Pao An dismissed these as the desperate measures of a jealous and embattled *tong*. For the fire brigade was recruiting strong young men who would in earlier years have taken the oath. The *tong* would like nothing better than for him to retaliate, he supposed. Then his colleagues would be drawn into the fray and Honolulu would witness the kind of gruesome combat fought by rival *tongs* in San Francisco or Sacramento. Pao An decided that he had no stomach for the war the Widow intended to wage. Instead he hired himself out as day laborer on an out-of-town construction site and took Lincoln with him. In the absence of the men, Molly and her mother took charge of both the hardware concession and the herb section of the store.

Molly daydreamed while toiling side by side with her mother, hauling sacks of coffee from the warehouse up the stairs, stacking boxes of merchandise, fixing loose boards with her father's tools. Yet the more the daughter fled into daydreams, the more the anxious mother pursued, enveloping the girl in a cloud of opinion that smothered and stung.

One morning, Molly awoke to find her thighs and nightgown streaked with blood. From that day forward, her mother overflowed with peasant commentary about her daughter's changing body. Nothing Molly did during her monthly bleeding went unnoticed by her mother's intrusive eyes and tongue: an insatiable hunger for sweets, a stray blemish on her cheek, a growing malaise, all would provoke frightening tales of bleeding virgins, dead babies, and pregnancies gone awry.

For her part, Rulan prided herself on knowing everything about her daughter. Her hungry mother's eye was always searching out the slightest physical alteration that would provide a clue to the restless spirit within. Did she sleep well? Did her skin look rough? Was she silent too long? These were signs that needed perusing, for Rulan had no way to express the immensity of her love except through counsel. Then why, the anxious mother wondered, did her girl hide the secrets of her heart from the very one who understood it best?

To shore up her private world, Molly kept secrets. She pocketed coins and bits of glass and metal found in the marketplace and knotted them in her father's handkerchiefs until her mother took to ransacking her daughter's pockets on washday. She flirted with strangers from the ships, stole food from the stalls: sticky *manapua* buns, handfuls of sweet-sour *mui,* a string of expensive dried cuttlefish, and gobbled her hoard in the damp corner underneath the stilts that supported the house. She touched herself beneath the covers until her flesh burned. Too willful to bend herself into her parents' ideal of feminine docility, too clumsy and ill-bred to be a beauty like Lily, she would be like no other Chinese girl at all: rebellious, renegade, wild.

"*I* have business to discuss with you, Rulan," Lucy said when Molly turned fourteen. She had entered the shop that day in her usual brusque fashion, holding a tuzzy-muzzy to her nose and complaining of the smell of stagnant water from Nuuanu Stream and the odors of the fish stalls nearby.

Rulan looked up in suspicion from the corner where she was grinding Lucy's monthly order of coffee beans. The only "business" Lucy ever came for these days, besides her usual allotment of Big Island coffee and oolong tea, was Molly. The friendship had barely survived the move to Chinatown, for Rulan could not forgive Lucy for her antagonism to Pao An or for voicing her displeasure at Rulan's assumption of "Chinatown ways." Yet over the years, hostility had settled back into prickly friendship.

Lucy began to pull nervously at the ball of fragrant herbs with her fingers. It still hurt her that Rulan had taken Molly out of Hiamoe's bright rooms and buried her in this cramped, malodorous space. It enraged her further that the child spent her days in mindless labor wandering the lanes like a stray dog and not improving her mind. She saw too how the girl had become pale and listless, dangerously cut off from other children, and turned inward like the fingertip of a glove. Yet intelligence sparked in the small dark head, for whenever Lucy came with a stack of books, the girl clapped her hands and twirled on the dusty floor of the shop like the Molly of old. Encouraged by righteous indignation, Lucy began the speech that she had rehearsed on the way over. "I have been to Mother Juliana, the new headmistress of the Priory School, on Molly's behalf . . ."

Rulan raised an eloquent eyebrow and kept measuring out coffee with a cracked china bowl.

"Molly's mind cannot be allowed to languish further," Lucy continued, more harshly than she intended.

"She is learning here," Rulan asserted hotly, "from me."

"A young woman of Molly's intelligence and imagination needs more," Lucy replied, warming to her task. "Especially if she is to help build a new Hawaii . . ." She took a breath and plunged on. "Molly needs good teachers to guide her, the very sort that Queen Emma's Priory School can give—"

Rulan frowned in displeasure. "The Priory is a school run by English! My daughter is Chinese," Rulan asserted, as if that fact blasted any notion of a "new" Hawaii.

"—and would be the first of her kind to enter the Priory," Lucy persisted. "She would keep company with daughters of prominent Hawaiian and *hapa haole* families. This is the next best thing to Oahu College, which insists on restricting itself to missionary offspring despite brilliance springing up everywhere, as in Molly and in Lincoln, as Emmanuel so often says. Emmanuel's old colleagues at the Mission don't believe that the Hawaiians and Chinese should learn English, but I say that our girl ought to have the same chances that a daughter of a Bingham or a Waterhouse does. Don't throw away our girl's hopes for a modern education!"

" 'Our'?" Rulan cried out in anger. Pao An had retrieved their daughter out of the hands of the devious Widow and her *tong* henchmen; now her friend Lucy was threatening to steal her daughter too. "Look at her eyes, her face. She comes out of my body, not yours."

Quietly but firmly, Lucy replied, "I forgive you that cruelty only because I suspect that a mother can hold on beyond reason to a child. . . . But how can she be a fit partner to a man of substance without a modern education?"

"My daughter is Chinese," Rulan repeated. "She belongs with her family, her own kind. A 'man of substance' is a Tang man who owns his own store in Chinatown with a strong wife to help him."

Appalled at how narrow Rulan's mind had grown, Lucy chose her next words with great care. "Molly will have many men to choose from. Even Chinese merchants have to deal with *haole* and Hawaiian suppliers and customers, do they not? And a woman who has both *haole* and Chinese knowledge will be a credit to her husband and her race."

"We cannot afford to send her."

"I have no child. I will pay her bills. School begins in September. Ask Molly. You know she will want to go. She has always been quick to learn."

"She won't leave me," declared Rulan obstinately.

"She has already begun to leave you. Have you seen the way she clutches at the books I bring? Or how she wanders the marketplace looking for someone, anyone to talk to? You will surely lose her if you hide her away." Gesturing at the dusty floorboards and shelves crammed with baskets of foodstuffs, Lucy demanded, "Is this to be the limit of Molly's world? This . . . this shanty?"

"This is my home."

Lucy did not relent. "You left China in order not to be branded a slave. Surely you would want the same measure of freedom for your daughter! If you do not give her up, she will leave of her own accord."

Long after Lucy had departed, Rulan sat listlessly among the sacks of coffee and rice. Lucy's words had stung far more than Rulan let on. She was never afraid for herself. Yet for her daughter, she had towering, uncontrollable fears. Thus with ruthless devotion, she had surrounded the girl with a wall of old customs, values, and assumptions, re-creating the village of her girlhood in the vain hope that the past could safeguard the present. How strange that a mother could do one thing while believing another. Or that she who had held a knife to an imperial soldier's throat was also a mother made weak by love. The matter would have to be decided by Pao An.

With the books from Bosworth's library, Molly was able to indulge her taste for the fantastic: she read Virgil and Homer to learn about war, Malory's *Morte d'Arthur* to satisfy her curiosity about witchcraft, Milton and Coleridge to explore her fears of God and the demonic, Keats and Tennyson to prolong her melancholy. These nymphs and dryads, princesses and demon lovers were vastly more appealing to Molly than the fox-spirits and disobedient daughters of her mother's kitchen fables. Inspired by the poets, she composed stories of her own, confessed the secrets of her heart to the pages of foolscap, printers' paper, provided by Lucy, knowing that this world of words was impervious to her mother's meddling. She worked in the midst of the mayhem of the store, ignoring the noisy chatter of customers, the mother spilling over with aphorisms, the father sharpening tools, the boy dragging crates and pails and tins across the wooden floor. Her world shrank to book and pen, her spirit spilled luxuriantly upon the pages.

*F*oolish girl to have such pretensions, thought the mother. *Haoles* needed quiet and space for their strange habit of writing down secrets on paper, secrets that were best not examined. These were not letters or deeds or descriptions of property or essays or poems copied out to perfect one's script or to cast one's feelings into formulas. These were words written only to oneself. A Chinese girl could not afford such self-indulgence, could not afford to ignore her obligations to the family. But perhaps in this new kingdom to which her daughter would belong, the grieving mother admitted, a Chinese girl might need new knowledge—even ways of being selfish.

"My rascal girl," Rulan complained to the customers who came to call. "Look at the stacks of books she leaves around. She reads so much, she may go blind!" Grumbling was a way of announcing her pride in her brilliant daughter. Yet often, when Molly opened a writing tablet in her presence, the mother wanted to rip it up. At those times, the mother felt that the girl was miles away, her ears deaf to the advice streaming from the mother's lips. What could she be writing down that a mother should not know?

On a day when Molly had gone to Lucy's for more books, Rulan was packing up boxes of clothes to be sent to the new arrivals off the ships. There were piles of her husband's old clothes to be mended or discarded. And Molly's outgrown things that could be made over for another. Bad spoiled girl, Rulan told herself, who never took care of her things. She was always thinking about her daughter, always everything was for her, with not a moment's peace or pity or thanks.

As she passed Molly's pile of books and papers, a stack of foolscap fell across the floor. Careless girl, she scolded the absent Molly, scanning her daughter's crabbed writing with a frown. Rulan could never get used to the way *bak kuei* script went the wrong way across the page. Yet one word stood out. "Mama . . ." And there: two lines in bold black ink. "I won't be like Mama—slave to a junk store and a mean stubborn man!"

Rulan put the paper down, her body trembling. Words set down on paper were prophetic, holy. One could burn them up, rip them to shreds, and still their power prevailed.

Molly returned from Hiamoe to find her mother storming around the house with mop and broom. That night her mother insisted on washing Molly's hair. She scrubbed hard with her nails, hurting her daughter, talking all the while, but Molly knew enough not to protest or to interrupt when her mother was angry.

"Did I ever tell you that one must never put secrets on paper?" Rulan said as she dumped buckets of cold water over the girl's soapy head. "Never, never write anything down or those words will stick to you like the thorn from a *kiawe* bush. There was a man my mother hated. A usurer. She owed him money. The hatred was burning up inside her. She went to the temple, wrote down his name on a piece of paper and gave it to the monk. It cost two copper cash. There was a basket full of yellow papers like ours, hundreds of them, all charms against evil. At the next feast day, the monk burned up the papers. My mother watched the paper turn into cinders, then mixed the ashes with water and drank them down. Even then, the hatred did not go away."

Molly thought her mother's story more bizarre than usual. What an odd, laughable thing to burn up one's words on a sheet of paper and eat the smoky residue! Words were meant to be savored for the sentiments recollected in solitude, even if those sentiments were no longer as true as at the moment they flowed from one's pen.

Pao An was building a henhouse in the backyard with Lincoln. The two were stripped to the waist and sweating in the afternoon heat. They worked silently, anticipating each other's moves. When they stopped to dip their cups into the bucket of hot tea, Rulan drew her husband aside.

"Lucy has offered to send Molly to Queen Emma's school, the one run by nuns from England."

"No," Pao An said, then went back to sipping the scalding tea. He said it without thinking, reacting purely to his instinct never to give anything of his own away.

"Lucy says it will be good for her to know English. It would help in the business."

"Who is Lucy to say anything about this family?"

"The islands are changing. There are things a young girl needs to know."

"Old ways are best for an innocent girl. These islands are full of evil. The *tong* has its fingers in every place where Chinese have gone . . ."

"Once you called Hawaii 'The Blessed Isles'—"

"I was desperate. I knew nothing."

Rulan put her hand over his lips. "Don't reject the man you were. You believed that women should go wherever their hopes might lead."

"Our girl knows nothing about the outside world," Pao An declared. "Look how the Widow's lies bewitched her! How much more helpless will she be in the hands of the deceivers at the Priory! Keep her at home where I can protect her."

"We cannot hide her forever," Rulan replied. "I am sending her away!"

Molly did not go far. Less than two miles separated the Priory from the edges of Chinatown. Yet the crowded warren of wharfside shops and alleys seemed a world apart from the broad thoroughfares downtown. The Priory was situated on a large, choice parcel of land purchased by Queen Emma in the heart of Honolulu's expanding commercial district in close proximity to the Anglican Cathedral and the crumbling old palace where Kalakaua and his queen lived. Molly was suddenly aware of a wider world thrusting itself violently into the islands. Germany had just declared war with Samoa, and, peeking through the Priory gates, the girls counted the diplomats' carriages passing to and from the palace as debate in the legislature intensified over the question of foreign expansion in the Pacific. And there were always rival British and American warships at anchor in Honolulu Harbor with guns poised for battle to preserve the fragile truce between the contending countries.

Yet despite the threat of foreign invasion and the squabbling between native and *haole* citizenry over the constitutional power due the throne, the young kingdom springing up around Molly was enjoying a heady burst of prosperity. The ascendancy of Hawaiian sugar in American markets had made many island families rich and fueled their tastes for things European. Mother Juliana, the headmistress sent to the Priory by the Anglican sisterhood in England, took pains to point out to her girls how much the sugar interests owed to England in the form of money, equipment, and brains.

For the first time, Molly had friends her own age whose fluency in English and Hawaiian exceeded her own. The curriculum was similar to what a girl of good family in England might expect at a private boarding school—languages, history, music, elocution, grammar, moral and natural philosophy, literature—although Keats took second place in the minds of these *alii* daughters to the amorous goings-on at Kalakaua's court, especially the liaisons among the younger royals and the foreign community. The girls were fascinated by young half-Hawaiian men like Robert Hoapili Baker, dubbed the "Hawaiian Adonis," and Robert W. Wilcox, a Hawaiian youth sent to study in Europe at the kingdom's expense and at the urging of Kalakaua's new foreign minister, the volatile Walter Murray Gibson.

It was odd, Molly mused, that after fighting with Hawaiian girls at the common school, she would find her closest friends at the Priory to be all or part-Hawaiian, including one girl whose *hapa haole* mother had married a rich Cantonese. Priory girls considered themselves a new island elite and were, therefore, in the habit of choosing friends without regard to racial background. Her greatest influence at this time was Mother Juliana, who gave her young charges daily and powerful doses of unsweetened Anglican doctrine. After one of Mother Juliana's stirring calls to Christian service, Molly was ready to take Anglican orders and help drive paganism from the islands herself.

9

Easter Feast

The Widow's procession pushed its way through the hundreds of Tang men who had come to the Manoa Chinese cemetery for the spring ritual called Ching Ming. The delegation she led up to her husband's grave was large and splendid, numbering government officials, *tong* elders, and all the hangers-on who had made Liang Mo's widow rich. Although perspiration was soaking the sleeves of their frock coats and satin *ma gwa*, the marchers did their best to ignore the heat and the noise and the rowdy bachelors on holiday from the plantations, taking their dignity from the matriarch, resplendent in tunic and pants of royal blue silk and married-lady's coat of embroidered black satin, who leaned on her daughter's arm.

The celebrants at the graves were young, like the dead themselves, who had been cut down in their prime by smallpox or cholera or bizarre accidents with gunpowder or cane fire. The *tai kung*, or "great ancestor," of Tang men in the islands (so named for being the first Chinese to die on Hawaiian soil) was buried here. Since that first entombment nearly a half century before, the cemetery had added acre upon acre. Now the merchants were applying to the king for incorporation as a burial association.

Hawaii was as much home as China, and its rich red soil was the place where a Tang man might lay his bones, happy in the knowledge that there were clansmen to sweep his grave and feed his hungry spirit at Ching Ming. If a Tang man was lucky enough to have a wife in the islands, she was probably not Chinese but a Hawaiian who had endowed her husband with a *kuleana,* a homestead, and dark-skinned progeny to lay out wine and rice or an occasional roast pig to welcome his hungry ghost every spring after he died.

Yet despite frequent intermarriage between Hawaiian women and Tang men, relations between the two races were precarious. Sugar barons like Spreckels were delighted with the unending source of cheap Chinese labor, yet Hawaiians were increasingly disenchanted. Not only did the Chinese bachelors introduce opium and gambling into the islands, they had also created a labor surplus that threw natives out of work and lately imported another round of smallpox from the China ports, which had devastated Oahu's rural districts in the early months of 1880.

Mindful of the strain, the Widow had invited several Hawaiian officials to the dedication in addition to the king's mercurial foreign minister, Walter Murray Gibson. Gibson had knocked about Asia for years before washing ashore on the small island of Lanai with a band of renegade Mormons. And when that community dissolved, he had declared himself the champion of native Hawaiian interests. In short order, Gibson had acquired a long white beard, remarkable fluency in the native tongue, and a prophetic sense of his own role in shaping the future of the Hawaiian kingdom. His ascendancy on the political scene was spectacular. Having risen to the post of foreign minister, Gibson was energetically courting the leaders of every race except his own, most of which reviled him.

With so many dignitaries in attendance, Mei Yuk did not want anything as commonplace as a roast pig to commemorate her dead husband. This year, to celebrate the success of her business and the upcoming marriage of her daughter, the Widow was dedicating a gate at the entrance of the graveyard in Merchant Li's memory. It was necessary, she judged shrewdly, to burnish her dead husband's reputation if the family enterprises were to grow, for once enshrined as a patriarch in the lore of Chinese Honolulu, the dead Liang Mo would confer on his wife a distinction she could never attain on her own. It was hard enough to be a woman in male-dominated Chinatown, let alone one whose fortune depended on outmaneuvering the newly prosperous merchants a half step away from the plantations. Chinatown was bursting with ambitious peasant-entrepreneurs like the Chens who would be happy to see gentry like herself come to ruin.

The procession made its way over a slight rise into a valley where the new gate, two thick posts of monkeypod wood crowned by ornate crossbeams and shiny with red paint, rose twenty feet into the hazy morning air. Farther up the rocky slope, the grave mounds were spread out upon a bare brown hill dotted with spindly young trees under which the various families were conducting separate Ching Ming rites.

The scowl on Molly's face was ample proof to Lincoln that the girl was spoiling for a nasty theological fight. Wisely, Lincoln had avoided her company on the long walk from their cart to the gravesite, keeping to Pao An's more rapid pace, an enervating feat for one who balanced a whole roast pig on a board on his back. Molly, he was sure, regarded their party as a ludicrous parade, especially when compared to the splendid Li processional.

Once at the gravesite, Molly flounced down angrily upon the ground, her petticoats ballooning around her suntanned legs. "I'm here only because you forced me," she complained to her mother for the hundredth time. "Mother Juliana says it's paganism to worship the dead." She tossed back her dark ringlets with an aggrieved expression and put her handkerchief to her nose so she would not have to smell the hundreds of burning joss sticks stuck into tin cans filled with sand. Heroines in novels always soaked their cambric handkerchiefs in eau de cologne. Since her pocket money went for the novels themselves, with none left over for luxuries like cologne, she sprinkled hers with vanilla.

"Think of it as a family tradition, not a religious ritual," her mother said, while stacking up the bowls and cups for the wooden altar. "We're here to honor the dead, not worship them."

The dissimilarity of Ching Ming to Easter was not lost on Molly, who was burying her head in her Bible to avoid having to handle the tokens of idolatry her mother was putting out on the grave. They had never celebrated Chinese rites in the Bosworths' house, she recalled bitterly. But with her father's return, all their customs had changed overnight. From the age of seven on, she had gone with her parents each spring to the cenotaph that Pao An had set up in memory of his dead father. Although she could not understand why her mother honored her husband's ancestors instead of her own, Molly nonetheless had loved stuffing herself on the special foods, playing hide-and-seek among the grave mounds and pinching her nose to imitate the nasal whine of the flute.

But now, after a year of the Priory's corrective teachings, Molly's attitude had changed. The Anglican Sisters of the Most Holy Trinity had engendered in their newest pupil a deeply morbid strain of adolescent religious sentiment. In bed at the Priory, Molly filled pages in her spiritual diary with long lists of transgressions. There were whole chapters given over to guilt-ridden reflection about her shortcomings at school and especially about her aborted alliance with the Lis, her most serious disobedience so far against her parents, and in some not quite explicable way, against God. It frightened Molly that while she sought God's grace nightly, she was still unable, through sinful pride she guessed, to beg her parents' forgiveness for having shamed them at the Lantern Queen competition. Her mother's intrusiveness and her father's ferocious overprotectiveness made her flee whenever they came near.

Below the Chens' small graveside celebration, the dedication ceremony for the new Li gate had begun with an explosion of firecrackers and a burst of music from the hired musician. When the last notes of the flute had faded, the Widow addressed her retinue in halting English. "My husband die young but he smart man," she said with sad dignity. "Plenty time he say to me 'Lucky I come Hawaii. Work hard, byemby make money, get rich! All Tang men can do alla same like me. Should be all Tang men like brothers, follow Tang men's way. Our way make money is best.' " The Widow spoke so imperiously that some Tang men thought that the patriarch himself was addressing them through the body of his small wife. The Hawaiian guests, on the other hand, thought the Widow quite blatantly mercenary.

Looking up from the shadows of the gate, the Widow spied Rulan and her family laying out their offerings on the side of a hill. "A bad example, those Chens!" she said, switching to Punti dialect so the outsiders could not overhear. "They have no respect for those who, by their wealth, have earned the right to command. I am glad my husband did not live long enough to see how brazen *that one,* our former bond maid, has become. A good thing the council was not taken in by her bad girl's bid for Lantern Queen. See how the ridiculous creature cavorts in *bak kuei* clothes! And look there, how the girl idles when she should be laying out food on the altar. What man would marry such a no-good? I blame the mother for sending the girl to the British school to learn the unfilial ways of the Carpenter God instead of keeping her decently at home!"

The Tang men accompanying the Widow, all *tong* officials, stirred the dead air with their fans as the flute began a long skirl. What would Tang men do without ritual and the Widow to guide them? It was unseemly that the upstart Chens were always seizing on new schemes—first a fire brigade, now *haole* education for a mere girl. Where would their misguided ambitions end?

Great God, Molly thought to herself, all around me are pagans bearing the stamp of eternal curse! The sound of the flute floating up from the crowd at the Li gate was more obscene than amusing, echoing in her ears like the "woman wailing for her demon lover" in her favorite (though scandalous) poem, Coleridge's "Kubla Khan." She hated having to lie to her teachers about going with her parents to put out food for corpses, even though they visited a cenotaph, a mere symbol. No dead ancestor reposed beneath the marble slab. The real grandfather's bones were somewhere in China. Nor was the dead man a true ancestor, but some farmer from On Ting village, a man who had rescued her orphan-father as a child in a field of burning cane. The whole pagan ritual seemed farcical to Molly. Her tough, dour father went softheaded every Ching Ming whenever he approached this nongrave of this nonfather. He got on his hands and knees to brush away with his bare fingers the moss and dirt that had collected over the rainy season and counted out the ritual bowls and cups with scrupulous attention to the required number of articles and offerings on the altar.

Molly kept her attention on the words before her: a chapter from Leviticus denouncing sinners who ate sacrificial food from pagan altars. Perhaps a lightning bolt would strike them all dead, Molly told herself. Or better yet, choose just her for martyrdom. Then she would be vindicated, and her hard-hearted parents would be forced to mourn her all their days. She wondered how she would look as a corpse: beautiful, she hoped, her skin fashionably pale, her lashes pressed like fans against her cheek.

"I don't see why we need to fuss if *he* was adopted into the clan," Molly whispered to her mother who was laying a pair of new bamboo chopsticks next to each porcelain bowl of food placed as offering on the grave. In her angry conversations with Rulan, Pao An was always the nameless *"he." "He's* not really a Chen so why waste money on a dead stranger?"

"Show respect," her mother snapped. "The dead man is still your grandfather. He made your father the child of his heart."

Molly knew enough not to criticize Pao An too sharply to her mother's face. Instead, she turned to Lincoln, complaining in angry whis-pers of the rampant paganism about them. Yet Lincoln surprised her by taking the infidels' part. He claimed, in his offhanded, humorous way, that since he had not discovered a theorem that conclusively proved the exis-tence of God, it was impossible to prove that He would be offended by any ritual, pagan or otherwise.

"Besides," he said, "how could God punish you when He Himself commands that you honor your parents?"

Lincoln's cavalier attitude about an issue that involved the fate of one's immortal soul infuriated Molly. To chastise him, she decided to ignore him throughout the entire graveyard ordeal, as her own father was ignoring her now.

As Rulan made the final adjustments to the altar and Molly retreated behind her Bible, Lincoln wandered off, unwilling to witness the inevitable row that would drive Molly further from them all. Her Priory education had made the girl as mulish as Pao An, with the same prickly tendency to detect scorn where there was only compassion. It exhausted him to be around them both on the weekends Molly came home. Seating himself beneath a spindly palm tree, he picked up the book on mathematics, which he had borrowed from Hoapili. Mathematics was as restful to his mind as a sip of hot tea on a humid day to his body, and he was busily engaged in looking up diagrams and formulas to calculate the area cast by the shadows of the Li Gate, when he saw someone climbing the hill in his direction, a girl whose familiar features he could not quite place in his mind.

"What are you reading, boy?" the girl called out, panting slightly from the exertion of her climb.

"Geometry," he said curtly. He looked down at his book, wishing her away. Dressed in a tunic and trousers of shiny yellow cotton and with her hair neatly braided and oiled, she was far too pretty to be ignored.

"Explain that word *geometry* to me," the girl asked, her tongue tripping on the foreign term. She sank down eagerly beside him on the grass, heedless of what the mud might do to her immaculate clothes.

Lincoln shut his book. "It's just lines and angles and circles and squares." He felt clumsy and ill-dressed beside this delicate creature.

"Then you must be very clever to make sense of it," she observed shyly. Her small white face, tipped up to his, was as guileless as a child's. "I am quite stupid, you see. My mother does not believe a girl should go to a *real* school so she hired a tutor from China who was paid to teach me nothing at all."

"But anyone can learn geometry," Lincoln replied, softening toward her. No girl had ever noticed him before, let alone thought him clever. "Look, I'll explain. All things are arrangements of angles, curves, and lines," he ventured, flipping through the pages of his book to show her first one diagram than another, "so if you understand their relationships, then you can construct whatever you like—houses, bridges, roads . . ."

Lily cocked her head, turning a dimpled cheek in his direction. "Geometry is very useful," she admitted. "A person with such knowledge could build something, sell it, and make lots of money. That's why a smart boy like you studies—to make money, *hai ma*?"

This observation, falling from the mouth of such an ingenuous creature, struck Lincoln as quite bizarre . . . unless the girl had drunk in such mercenary convictions with her mother's milk. Now he remembered where he had seen her before. "You're Lily, the Li girl who rides in the parade," he declared.

Lily's lips parted in a rueful smile. "I haven't been Lantern Queen for years. Mother says I am far too old, an almost-married lady."

The notion of any entanglement with the opposite sex, arranged or freely chosen, official or otherwise—dismayed Lincoln. "That's terrible for you," he said with feeling.

Lily gave Lincoln a sharp glance. "Mother tells me I am lucky—but actually," she admitted, her face darkening, "I am . . . unsure about the man she chose for me. He's old, you know. Older than my mother!" These last words were uttered with such desolation that Lincoln put the book aside in sympathy.

"Then tell your mother you refuse!" Lincoln declared indignantly. "These are the eighties! Hawaii is not China! A woman has choices now—"

"Other girls, not me! My mother has always decided for me . . . my clothes, my friends, what I say, and who I must greet. She says that since all the men in our clan are dead, I owe her the cardinal loyalties I would to them. She is father, brother, and emperor to me."

The girl's passive acceptance of an intolerable fate made Lincoln furious. "You're not a child. Simply tell her that marrying an old man is unacceptable!"

Lily's eyes were shining. "*Unacceptable!* I must remember that word," she said softly to herself.

Suddenly, Molly thrust herself between them. "Are you spying on me?" she demanded of Lily.

"This boy was sitting here, and I had no one to talk to, so . . ."

"The Widow sent you," Molly insisted. "You don't move a finger unless your mother commands it. There's no thought in your head that she didn't put there!"

Lily hung her head, her face scarlet.

"Stop bullying her," Lincoln interjected.

"You're taking Mei Yuk's daughter's part against me?" Molly raged. "Go back to your own kind, Lily! We're not good enough for you!"

Lily began to cry. Putting her hand on Lincoln's shoulder to steady herself, she rose. "Talk to her for me. Tell her I never meant her harm."

"Oh yes," Lincoln whispered, breathing fast. Lily was close enough for her hair to tickle his cheek. He saw that her skin was red from the sun at the opening of her tunic where the swell of breasts began.

"That was kindly done," Lincoln said coldly when Lily had stumbled away.

"You're acting like a dog in heat, panting and rolling your eyes at her," Molly shot back. "She's a fox-spirit, a temptress, like all the Li women . . ." She stopped, realizing that she was haranguing Lincoln in the same manner that her own father hectored her about going with "deceivers." And yet, she told herself, it was perfectly clear that Lily was using him.

Rulan was calling them over for the ceremony. Unlike most heads of families, Pao An did not insist on a long lecture at the grave. As a result, the rites were quite short, consisting of a brief address to his father's ghost, the burning of paper money, the pouring of wine and tea upon the ground, and a few perfunctory bows. When Lincoln stood up to answer the summons, Molly realized that he was no longer a gangly, skinny boy. Sometime during her months away at school, he had grown tall enough to tower over her. It occurred briefly to Molly that Lincoln might be a person in his own right, not someone put on earth to annoy her, a stray puppy come to steal food off her plate. From certain angles, he was quite presentable. She could almost understand why a girl as sheltered as Lily might find him of passing interest.

That night, when the festival dishes were set out for the family to eat, Molly refused to put the food of pagan altars to her lips. She cinched her sash tighter, feeling all the more virtuous for the pangs of hunger that assailed her. Yet her mouth watered for the foods she had always loved: roast pig, sweet pork buns, the fragrant soup made of lily root and chicken. And despite the justice of her cause, she was troubled by the resentment her piety seemed to incite. Her mother seemed hurt, and Lincoln muttered that he would never be educated if it made him narrow-minded and mean. Nor did her righteous example have its intended effect. For the next day, her father went back to sweep the grave and to build a little wall of gravel and crushed seashells around the marble marker as if his daughter's martyrdom only made his heathenism more firm.

10

A Gauntlet of Admirers

After the disastrous Ching Ming holiday, Molly returned to the Priory as much angered by Lincoln's infatuation with Lily as by her parents' persistence in error. The fact that they resolutely ignored her warnings made her worry not only about their salvation but about her own rapidly changing circumstances as well. What had she become? She was a fraud and a freak, she decided. A mongrel with unkempt black hair, dark skin, narrow eyes, and a penchant for Tennyson and Lucy's cast-off crinolines. Thus seesawing between piety and doubt, loyalty to family and a desperate desire to strike out on her own, the bookish Chinese girl was taken up by Sarah Kauhana, the prettiest and most mischievous of the Priory girls.

Only fifteen, the voluptuous Sarah could easily pass for twenty. She was bold and domineering and easily recruited the ingenuous Molly as confederate. Unlike Sarah, Molly had come late to maturity; yet the cloistered atmosphere of the Priory had nurtured in her the intense fascination with the opposite sex that all the girls shared. Yet whereas Molly's relationship with boys was confined to her long antagonism with Lincoln, Sarah's experiences, recounted in titillating detail to Molly, were frantic, furtive encounters with young cadets from St. Albans or sons of her father's friends, complete with secret meetings; stolen kisses; and even, she claimed, a tête-à-tête so erotic she had swooned and was not even sure what had actually happened. She engaged Molly in a heated exchange over whether this paroxysm might have engendered a child.

The Anglican sisters were acutely aware of their charges' romantic natures and tried vainly to suppress the girls' overwrought imaginations with a regimen of fresh air, calisthenics, and prayer. Even Dowager Queen Emma's plan for the school buildings was designed with the girls' moral education in mind, for the Priory was constructed in the shape of a quadrangle with one edge open to the mountain breezes: a walled cloister swept clean of overwarm spirits by Nature herself. Yet the girls found innumerable ways to subvert the high-minded curriculum and the protective fortifications. The sisters were heavy sleepers, and it was amazing how many pages of a forbidden novel could be consumed in the wee hours of the morning or how easy it was to bribe stewards and cooks to pass letters to the missionary sons at Oahu College who were themselves sneaking out on a Saturday lark to the horse races on King Street. No girl was more adept at mischief-making than Sarah, and she soon led the worshipful Molly into launching attacks on order and decorum. If a bird was found beating its wings in the rafters of a classroom, there was little doubt who had enticed it indoors. If the teacher reached into her paper drawer and a wiggling gecko came scurrying out, the culprits were usually the laughing dark-skinned beauty and the quiet Chinese girl who displayed no emotion at all.

Molly's classmates, well-born Hawaiian or part-Hawaiian girls like Sarah hand picked for the Priory by Emma and her circle of Anglophiles, had been enrolled under the assumption that an English education would make them accomplished in all the necessary feminine virtues. Yet Emma's earnest experiment was inevitably shaped less by Victorian precepts than by the particular realities of island life, especially given the scarcity of healthy Hawaiian women in the kingdom. By some mysterious form of communication known only to their sex, men-about-town always seemed to know at what time of the day the Priory girls would emerge to do errands or attend chapel at the nearby Anglican cathedral. At the appointed hour, the girls, accompanied by one or more stern-faced sisters, would be greeted at the Priory gates by a crowd of straw-hatted youths making elaborate espousals of undying affection.

If the attention of local rakehells was the Priory chaperones' greatest affliction, it was the chief source of delight for their charges. Molly, however, quickly saw that the same faces reappeared in the gauntlet of admirers—a junior officer from an American ship, a young waterfront tough, a scattering of schoolboys from St. Albans, two plantation dandies on a lark, all infatuated with Sarah.

"I hate how I look," Molly blurted out one morning as she and Sarah were dressing their hair in preparation for braving the gauntlet on the way to chapel. They were peering into a small hand mirror that Sarah kept hidden in her drawer, for no wall mirrors were allowed in the Priory for the vanity they induced.

"Then don't walk around with your chin tucked into your chest! *Pakes* have this sidelong way of making themselves known. It's fine for doing business, but a disaster if you want to attract a man. Move your body like a *wahine.* There's no shame in having hips and bosom!" Sarah undulated her hips to make her point; she loved punctuating her arguments with various gestures from *hula,* for she had joined Dandy Ioane's *hula* troupe and had set her sights on dancing at court now that Kalakaua had brought native arts into fashion.

"And there again you have the advantage." Molly looked down ruefully at her chest, as flat as a boy's.

"Well, act like you have a bosom, then. Make the men think you're just waiting to be spirited off by a lover."

"Not with Mother Juliana watching . . ."

"Then you will never be kissed by a sailor," Sarah declared.

"I doubt I shall be kissed at all" was Molly's wan reply.

*O*ne day, a few weeks after their conversation at the mirror, a new face appeared outside the gates.

"*Auwe,* this one *pilikia,*" Sarah whispered to Molly in mock-chagrin behind the headmistress's back. "A real fancy man."

Molly's interest was instantly piqued by any form of danger, particularly of the romantic kind she and Sarah read about in novels. Mother Juliana shushed Sarah and hurried them both along.

"Look at that dark one with the extraordinary eyes," Sarah whispered as they skipped along. "The one holding the black horse. His eyes are light enough to be *hapa haole,* I can't tell from here. Oh dear, Molly, hide your face! He's seen us staring."

What struck Molly first about the stranger was not the odd mix of Polynesian features and green *haole* eyes, but his age. He was old! Twenty-two, at least, clean shaven but with the shadow of a beard about his square chin. The horse he rode was as sleek, dark, and glossy as he; his morning coat was expensive black broadcloth tailored to fit his slim frame; his beaver-skin hat was brushed to a high sheen. And unlike the pimply faced habitués of the gauntlet who made hooting noises at the girls as if they were hailing a passing ship, the stranger had dignity: he studied the parade of virgins with the nonchalance of a buyer at a horse auction, while pulling at the reins to quiet his high-spirited animal.

He was outside the gates the next day as well and the day after. Sarah was full of girlish imaginings about her unknown admirer, and with typical energy, she set in motion her extensive network of aunties and cousins to discover the stranger's identity. She was rewarded in a few days with an answer. He was Peter Ikaika Constable, half-Hawaiian offspring of a Kauai planter whose grandfather Isaac had been a "First Boater," one of the original Congregational missionaries to Hawaii. Peter had been sent away at his father's death to boarding school in England by his *haole* half-sisters, who wanted the son of their father's Hawaiian mistress out of reach when the family's holdings were divided.

"Isn't he the very picture of Lord Byron?" Sarah enthused.

"And with the morals of Don Juan," Molly sniffed.

"My cousin Kawika says he's clerking for the legislature. I'm sure with his connections, he's destined for a post in the king's Privy Council. I wonder if he's come looking for a wife . . ."

"You'd best be careful, Sarah."

"I don't want to be careful! I want to be *adored*."

11

TYHUNE'S "NUMBER TWO"

Nalani, who had sworn off men after her second husband died, had fallen in love again. The unlikely object of her affections was a surly Hakka named Tyhune who owned a tobacco shop in back of the Chens' hardware store. The liaison provided rich fodder for gossip in Chinatown where Tyhune, a leader in the Hakka association, was considered a colorful eccentric. The Widow was heard to entertain her *ma jong* companions with ribald accounts of how one skinny Hakka simpleton had been seduced by a *wahine* twice his size.

Liaisons between Tang men and Hawaiian women were so common in the last decade that they rarely drew comment anymore. Tang men were a domestic lot and many entrepreneurs like Tyhune desired not simply an occasional transaction with a prostitute but an authentic family life. They found willing partners among Hawaiian women whose sweethearts had vanished overseas or perished from disease. It was in part the survival of their shrunken race that led many Hawaiian women to take Chinese as mates. This was not the case, however, with Nalani and Tyhune, who had little in common at first but dislike.

Although he had risen to his present high estate through an exhaustive knowledge of the smoker's art, Tyhune was a Buddhist so austere in his personal habits that he regarded all uses of tobacco as noxious. He saw no conflict, however, in selling what he loathed to weaklings willing enough to pay, although he drew the line at women chewing tobacco and placated his conscience by exhorting his customers to restraint in the consumption of his wares. Curiously enough, the more he preached abstinence, the more prosperous his business grew, for his patrons concluded that any man who reviled the very goods he sold would not overcharge. In that regard they were wrong, for Tyhune overpriced his product to penalize customers for their vices.

The romance, if it could be called that, began on the afternoon when Nalani came into Tyhune's shop to buy a plug of tobacco. He glared at her over the massive wooden counter he had bought at auction from a dance-hall bar. "What for you want chew dis kin'?" Tyhune challenged her.

Nalani had plenty of money to indulge her taste for good food, an occasional glass of imported whiskey, and chewing tobacco. She had come to buy, not to endure a lecture. "Shut up you damn face. Give me two plug Virginia," she demanded, throwing her coins on the table and muttering under her breath about the "*damn* nosy *pa-ke.*"

"I no sell da kin' to *wahine,*" declared Tyhune, setting his jaw in a stubborn line. "You go 'nother store!"

Nalani had rarely encountered any personality as obstinate as her own. "Whassamatta my money?" she challenged.

"I like you money. I no like you!" Seeing her start, Tyhune switched to another tack. "For what *wahine* like make da kin' teeth black?" he whined.

Nalani decided to play coy. "I no buy for me," she said, the picture of injured innocence. "I buy 'nother fella."

Tyhune was offended that the woman thought to take him in with such a simple ruse. "You, me, *pau!* Business all finish!" he declared impatiently. "Go 'way!"

Nalani erupted in fury. She grabbed a long twist of tobacco and slammed it down in the jaws of the iron chopper to cut a plug. Just as quickly, Tyhune jerked it out of the machine and snatched it back.

"Goddamn crazy, *pupule pa-ke!*" Nalani shouted and cuffed Tyhune hard on his leathery cheek with her open hand. In an instant, Tyhune had run around the counter and grasped her by the neck of her Mother Hubbard gown, whereupon she yanked his queue and scratched his face with her other hand. He retaliated by squeezing her breasts; she screamed and pushed him off balance but he held on with such grim determination that they both toppled to the ground. With so much tearing of cloth and flashing of bare limbs as they strained together upon the sawdust-covered floor, it was little wonder that what began as a wrestling match soon turned into a more ardent connection. In fact, Tyhune closed his shop early to settle the argument with Nalani in more leisurely fashion twice over in the back room.

Although Nalani disagreed with Tyhune about virtually everything he held dear—meatless meals, austerity in religion, decorum among women—she was sufficiently infatuated to give Lucy immediate notice and move in with her new lover. With characteristic exuberance, she stuck her broad, flat nose into every facet of Tyhune's business, showering customers with solicitude, lowering prices to undercut other dealers, and using her *ike papalua*—her "second sight"—to predict the ups and downs of tobacco economics. The consequence of Nalani's interference was that Tyhune's profits fell off straightaway—which led to more stormy confrontations and athletic reconciliations.

The happier result of Nalani's union with Tyhune was that Rulan and she became neighbors, for Tyhune's store abutted the Chens' backyard. Nalani now had legitimate reason to pour her complaints into the ear of her friend, for Rulan was encumbered with a mate even more infuriating than Nalani's. Yet despite her grumbling, Nalani adored her "stubborn *pake*" because he "no go sea, he no get sick, and work damn hard, you bet." She became a great favorite of the Tang men who patronized Tyhune's store; only Pao An, whom she continued to disparage, seemed impervious to Nalani's charms.

"*I*n five years, Tyhune sell his shop, go China," Nalani boasted to Molly on one of the girl's rare weekends home.

"Doesn't that bother you, Auntie?" Molly asked.

"I no worry. I go China too."

"But he must have a wife back there. All Tang men do."

"He get," Nalani admitted. "But him rich man, can get two, t'ree wife. I number two."

"But that's ghastly. How can you bear it?" Molly was preparing a speech on the feminine imagination for a gala at Queen Emma's summer palace in Nuuanu and intended to emphasize her conviction that women should not submit to men in love or work. Molly could not believe that the brash Nalani would willingly take second place to another wife, let alone marry a Tang man as bossy as her father.

"Easy. Number one my sister," Nalani asserted. "Just like your mother, us two like sisters."

"But why leave Hawaii? Here a woman can own land, open a business.

In the village, it would be like turning the clock back to the days when your grandmother had to eat with the women and hide away in the women's house during her bleeding time."

"Plenny Hawaiian girl marry *pa-ke,* go China live!" declared Nalani with some heat. And she ticked off the names of those women already enjoying the luxury of playing second or third wives to Tang men who had cashed in their profits from selling *poi* or *manapua* buns and returned to their villages as mandarins of trade.

"My mother was a concubine in such a house," Molly warned. "You should hear her talk about the bickering and jealousy in the women's rooms."

"Auwe," Nalani declared in sympathy, although in the next breath she reminded Molly that her own mother's *punalua* marriage with a sister and her sister's husband had been loving and close. Jealousy was not the Hawaiian way, she insisted. "Tyhune number one wife alla time sick, I take care chil'ren. I get my own house, my own *wahine hana* for cook and wash clothes! No more, 'Nalani do this, that.' " She lay her ample hand on her *hanai* daughter's arm, and added, her dark eyes dancing, "No worry me. I get *ike papalua,* eyes can see two ways! I go be rich lady. Lazy all day, busy all night," and with a shrug of her plump shoulders signaled the closing of the matter.

The notion of Nalani as a respectable *Tai Tai,* her considerable bulk stuffed into a married lady's skirt, suddenly struck Molly as hilarious. Yet in the midst of a giggling fit, Molly saw through her auntie's perennial sunniness to the loneliness within. With loved ones carried off by disease, Nalani had made do on the fringes of other women's lives; she was the consummate *wahine hana,* auntie extraordinaire, selfless and ever present, nursing other women through childbirth and disease, settling their quarrels with men, raising their children. Yet all the time she wanted nothing else but a home and *keikis* of her own. Now that she had found a man who loved her enough to give her that home, of course, she would follow him wherever he asked—to China and beyond! Still, her own mother had done the same, Molly reflected. The results of that decision had been the dissolution of will, something Molly herself would never allow!

12

THE DARK LOVER

Peter Constable's next appearance at the Priory gates was on foot, holding his horse by the reins, which induced in Sarah a fit of nervous giggles that she tried to stifle behind trembling hands. Molly, however, cultivated an attitude of haughty disdain. Her efforts were met with an immediate response, for the stranger doffed his hat and made a half-mocking bow, which sent Sarah—thinking the man was bowing to her—into a renewed cascade of terrified laughter and brought Mother Juliana racing back in their direction. With a sharp rebuke, she hurried her young wards before her and took the head of the line like an anxious mother quail. But Constable had mounted his horse and, ignoring the squeals of alarm from the girls, trotted beside the embarrassed Molly as far as the cathedral.

Once safely installed in the school pew, Kealoha, one of Sarah's followers, poured out her envy and excitement. "Good gracious, I swear he was drawn to *you*, Molly!"

"Don't be absurd," Molly whispered back, scarlet with excitement. "He was shielding his eyes from the sun."

"He couldn't take his eyes off you," Kealoha declared emphatically. "He was talking to the caretaker when I turned around. I heard him ask your name! Did you see his eyes when he smiled? They glowed green, as if they pierced your heart!"

"You saw all this from behind your fingers and at such a distance?" Molly shot back.

"I saw that you fancy him as much as he fancies you," Sarah chimed in angrily.

"Then you're as blind as Kealoha!" Molly could barely keep up the pretense of outrage, her heart was beating so.

Sarah, nursing a broken heart, did not speak to Molly for days, during which time Constable vanished from the gates. Yet his absence had a happy result, for Sarah in the interim gained a new admirer who had taken Constable's place in the gauntlet. This infatuation quickly expunged all memories of the old, and Sarah was once again Molly's confidante.

At the end of the month, the Priory girls were taken to tea at Emma's summer palace in Nuuanu Valley, an annual occasion for mingling with the queen's Companions and various sponsors of the school. This year, the ladies were joined by graybeards from the *alii* clans loyal to the Kamehamehas and a contingent of radical young nobles and clerks in the legislature whom the king did not favor; rumors were flying that Emma intended to mount another challenge to her old adversary, Kalakaua, who had not yet been crowned.

The afternoon, to the great delight of the ambitious young men who had come to call on Emma, had rewards both social and political. They sipped tea and lemonade on the spacious *lanai* with Emma's Companions and ogled the Priory girls who were being trotted out to display their skills at elocution.

Dowager Queen Emma was standing under the shade of a canvas awning, a sweet-faced Hawaiian woman in black taffeta, whose light skin and small features betrayed her English blood. Only forty, she had grown stout and melancholy in the years of her widowhood, and was rumored to be consulting a *kahuna* to fend off an imagined curse; yet on this brilliant afternoon, she was once again the vibrant, charming Emma of old. Around her were a half dozen Hawaiian cadets dressed smartly in blue-and-red uniforms with gold braid and epaulets. Molly, peeking out from behind a potted palm with Sarah, thought it ludicrous that youths who had never tasted battle were so elaborately decorated. Yet if passion counted as much as warrior skill, these young men were fully capable of daring deeds, for their hands were moving in vigorous counterpart to their loud voices. The one talking most animatedly with their royal hostess, the only one without a uniform, Molly saw with a start, was Peter Constable.

Then Emma came forward, serene in her widow's weeds, gathered the assembly together and introduced Mother Juliana, who in turn ushered in the youthful speakers. Molly was the fourth to address the crowd. A murmur went up from the well-dressed gathering as Molly strode to the front of the room. She knew they were wondering what she, a charity case and the lone Chinese girl among the students, might possibly say to a gathering of the kingdom's Anglican and Hawaiian elite. She had chosen to speak on imagination and the speech she had written would probably displease at least half of the audience. Still, she meant every word. Nervously, she spied her auntie Lucy, pink cheeked with anticipation, pointing her out to the Companions. In the back of the room, lounging against a wall, was Peter Constable. Molly's mouth suddenly went dry at the realization that his eyes were fastened upon her. *Don't look at him!* she told herself, fearing that the practiced phrases might fly out of her head. Mother Juliana nodded at her to begin.

"Shelley once praised his fellow poets as the 'unacknowledged legislators of the world.' And in whom is the wellspring of poetic imagination most deep? In the frail and slender body of a woman! I say to you that every woman possesses the capacity for imagination. Were not all the muses women? Have not women served as preservers of culture within the family through their powers of recollection? And is not memory, the fount from which imagination and art flow, freshest and deepest in womankind? Hence, we women of the Priory, having been carefully trained in the arts, must exercise the talents given us by God to beautify our kingdom with the flowers of our imagination!"

Molly punctuated each phrase with forceful hand gestures as she had been taught. Looking into the sea of male faces on the veranda, she felt herself carried on the crest of her words by sheer conviction. "I will not dispute those who say that women have no capacity for reason. Rather I assert the peculiar power of the feminine mind. Reason is for men. The imagination is left for our sex to nurture. And the poet Shelley leaves no doubt which faculty is superior. 'Poets are the hierophants of an unapprehended inspiration. The mirror of the gigantic shadows which futurity casts upon the present, the unacknowledged legislators of the world.'

"What did Shelley mean? That *she* who possesses the idea shapes the course of civilization to come. It is to us, therefore, the women of the new Hawaii, through the power of our artistic and poetic imaginings, to disclose the means by which men of reason might build for us all an island paradise!"

The applause and the young men's cries of "hear, hear" resounded like thunder in Molly's ears. *Was* his *voice among them?* she wondered. She thought she would faint from happiness. After Emma had thanked "her girls" effusively, first in Hawaiian and then in English, Molly pushed her way through the laughing, jostling men in search of Peter Constable. But he had slipped away.

A letter arrived in the next day's mail.

> Shelley also said, "The freedom of women produced the po-
> etry of sexual love. Love became a religion, the idols of whose
> worship were ever present. It was as if the statues of Apollo and the
> muses had been endowed with life and motion and had walked
> forth among their worshipers, so that the earth became peopled by
> the inhabitants of a diviner world!"
>   Let the Age of Love come again!
>   —Peter Constable

Reading this, Molly felt a sharp pain pierce her breast. Was this a love letter in the purest sense? There were no compliments, no instructions for rendezvous. Except for the last puzzling line, the words were Shelley's, not his own. How then should she reply? Should she reply at all? While Molly and Sarah were pondering this delicious dilemma, the Christmas holiday came, and the girls made preparations to leave school.

Constable's appearances at the gate and at Queen Emma's gala had not gone unnoticed by Mother Juliana who resolved to investigate. The best defense against the blossoming of any troublesome "involvement," Mother Juliana decided, was to pinch off the bud.

*T*he Christmas holiday yawned like an abyss before Molly. In spite of a ledger of rules and punishments, the Priory was the one place Molly felt free. Home was a series of gray afternoons, whereas the Priory was only sunlight and laughter. Home was where her tyrant father and his equally inflexible consort reigned. And of course, there was no chance of seeing Peter at all.

Sarah, two bulging carpetbags at her side, had bid Molly a long and tearful *aloha*. She was going back to Maui to visit her grandmother for the first time in a year. The channel crossing on the steamer was a slow and sometimes dangerous passage, and the prospect of death by drowning enough to drag out each precious good-bye to each precious friend to inordinate lengths. These schoolgirl fears were genuine; they all had lost loved ones to fever or pox, and any *aloha* might be the last.

Only after Sarah and the rest had finally departed did Molly take out the old blanket Rulan had given her, pile her clothes in the middle and tie it into a bundle. Then she walked out into the street where Lincoln was waiting.

He was never late, always predictable, and as dour as the skinny mule that pulled the rig with which he made deliveries of coral stone or lumber across the island for Pao An. She hated having to ride in anything so disreputable for fear that her friends might see her and laugh.

And there he was, with the mule cart blocking the front gate, so that every girl passing in a buggy to her family's mansion up Manoa or Nuuanu or Waikiki might see.

"Couldn't you pull around back or wait down the street?" Molly said, glowering as she climbed into the seat.

"Why?"

"Because you look like a delivery boy!" She threw her bag in the back where it set a pile of iron implements clattering.

"I *am* a delivery boy," Lincoln replied, and heyed up the mule, who jerked forward into a brisk ungainly trot that set the entire wagon jangling and shaking like a barrel of discarded tin cans.

Lincoln knew Molly was ashamed of him . . . of them all. Whenever she came home, she brought a knife and fork in a napkin stamped with the Priory seal and used the utensils at every meal, even though the fork was useless in chasing grains of rice around the bottom of a porcelain bowl and the bite-size pieces of meat needed no further cutting. Her affectations so infuriated her father that sometimes he would wolf down his food and slam out of the house before the others were done, thus validating his uncouthness in Molly's eyes. And when Molly wasn't cramming her mouth with sharp, forged pieces of metal, she was rattling on about people that none of them knew. All she had learned at the Priory was how to set herself above and beyond them.

Although he chafed at her petty snobberies, Lincoln loved her still. More than before she had left them, for he saw through to the desperation that drove her. Whenever she pushed aside the dish of *mui* her mother bought for her, his heart ached because he knew she craved it so. Whenever she rattled off titles and authors to emphasize the limitations of his knowledge, he memorized the unfamiliar words, storing the sounds at the back of his mind, fiercely determined to know them too. Whenever she provoked her father to erupt in fury, he had to stop himself from grabbing her up and spiriting her away.

Lincoln had known for some time about the *hapa haole* man who had accosted Molly on the way to chapel. There were no secrets in Honolulu, particularly among the young. Gossip about Molly's suitor had come via a Hawaiian boy who worked on Pao An's building crew, a *hanai* cousin of a Priory girl. And which man could fail to notice this sweet, wild, wonderful creature in the crowd of giggling schoolgirls? Of course, Molly would be captivated by a *haole* or a Hawaiian or a half-Hawaiian, anyone not her kind. A forbidden flirtation fit her nature so perfectly. Of course, she would lurch after whatever outlandish lover lured her, run pell-mell along whatever crooked, *kapakahi* path she thought fate intended her to follow. Yet when that road ended and the lover slipped away, when she was trapped on some desolate field, some precipice above the pounding sea, at the point when there was no other place for her to run, he would be there. To stop her. To save her. To bring her safely home.

Lincoln drove on in silence, the cart shaking so hard that Molly was forced to hang on to the wooden seat with both hands. He did not answer when she tossed her long unruly hair and demanded, "What are you grinning for? You look like a stupid monkey!"

13

A CHRISTMAS WISH

A week before her Christmas Eve dinner, Lucy's *wahine hana* took sick. An immediate summons went out from Hiamoe to Rulan which was just as swiftly spurned because of Pao An's dislike of the Bosworths. In her place, however, Rulan sent Molly and Nalani, for she recognized the urgency in Lucy's appeal. There was a huge amount of cooking to be done for Lucy's Christmas dinners normally, and this particular one merited special care. Over the years, Lucy had concocted her own holiday recipes using local produce, and many in the *haole* community who had eaten at Lucy's table swore that her *lilikoi* pies and macadamia nut bread surpassed traditional Christmas fare. This year, Lucy's hospitality was being tested by the volatile mix of guests.

In addition to the usual crowd of Companions, journalists, and entrepreneurs, Emmanuel had invited every legislator who opposed the Spreckels-owned Oceanic Steamship Company. His last editorials were aimed at exposing Claus Spreckels's takeover of sugar refining, factoring, and financing; and Emmanuel was intending to gather at the gala a core of supporters to undercut Spreckels's influence at court. In the past few years,

Spreckels had acquired forty thousand acres on Maui for his own use by finagling the heiress Princess Ruth Keliikolani out of her rights to certain crown lands. He had used the land to construct a village named Spreckelsville where he built the largest and most technologically advanced sugar mill in the world. Now, through his steamship company, he would control transportation to world markets as well. Bosworth intended to mobilize the legislators to oppose Spreckels and loosen his grip upon the island economy and the king, whom he had bought lock, stock, and barrel.

Lucy, bursting with pride at Molly's triumph at Queen Emma's gathering, was grateful for any renewed intimacy with her "dear girl." At one point in the chaotic preparations in the kitchen, Lucy declared that it was "just like the old days," with the jam pot bubbling merrily on the stove, the aunties wrist deep in dough, and Molly sneaking bites of ginger cookies as they came out of the stove.

Neither auntie recognized how much the dear girl had changed. Molly understood now that kitchen-talk was chiefly a means of exchanging gossip and that each of the aunties had her own way of conveying it. Nalani used Hawaiian words for what Lucy's ears could not bear to hear directly, whereas Lucy cloaked meaning behind euphemisms and elaborate obfuscations.

Having found herself in the presence of such gifted gossips, Molly decided to test the name that had been scrawled at the bottom of the note.

"My friend Sarah Kauhana has an admirer," she ventured.

"Who is that, dear?" Lucy asked absently. Sarah's mother, Abby, was one of the Companions, and Abby herself had often remarked to Lucy that her daughter's crushes were as brief as they were preposterous.

"A *hapa haole*. His family name is Constable."

Lucy frowned. "The boy who was sent abroad? I'm surprised Abby Kauhana hasn't forbidden her daughter to see him!" Lucy asserted. Her memory for local genealogy was nearly as extensive as Nalani's.

"Sarah's not exactly *seeing* him," Molly admitted. "She only spoke to him once."

"Then she is a naughty girl for encouraging this unsuitable young man without her mother's knowledge!"

"Why? Because he's not rich enough?" Molly bristled. It seemed to her that adults always found that the suitability of a young man rose and fell with the size of his inheritance.

"Pure rakehell is more the story," declared Lucy. And she launched into a lengthy account of Constable's planter father, who had monopolized the best land on the island and the prettiest Hawaiian girls as well. He had two families at least. Peter was the only son, but "born on the other side of the blanket. Handsome, like his mother—but given the bad report I hear of him, it isn't likely that an island girl with any fortune or decency would take him on. The inheritance is in dispute too. The old land grant is a sorry mess now that there's only the big house left of the estate, though there's money there if the sisters stop fighting. Sarah ought to be warned off the scoundrel. If blood holds true, young Constable won't give up the wild life for domesticity."

Two splotches of color burned in Molly's cheeks. Her mind was consumed with remembered images of Peter Constable: the rakish tilt of his straw hat as he lounged against the wall listening to her speak, the sardonic smile and flashing white teeth, his green eyes seeking her out in the line of girls, the flamboyant signature at the bottom of his note. He was the very sort of spoiled young man who figured in her mother's most insufferable cautionary tales, and moreover, the imperious kind of *haole* whom her father reviled as a deceiver of the worst kind. And already she adored him! She had seen the *haole* and *hapa haole* heirs to the great sugar plantations and cattle ranches, the new *alii* of the islands, on holiday in Chinatown: they would race their thoroughbreds down King Street and order their houseboys about while smoking cheroots and sipping brandy from silver flasks. None had ever shown her, the gawky daughter of Chinatown shop-keepers, the slightest interest . . . until the most dashing among them had discovered in her some hint of beauty or genius she could not yet see in herself. He had liked her speech well enough to respond in kind. Surely, then, some spark of that same imagination she had spoken so earnestly about must be there in him! She thought about the urgency in Constable's note and wondered whether being desired automatically evoked an answering affection.

The Christmas gala at Hiamoe proved a huge success. The guests were royally feasted by Lucy, plied with brandy, rum punch, and cigars and sent home tipsy, replete, and united in their opposition to Spreckels. Bosworth was in an expansive mood when he took Molly home that night. Now that he had scored a victory in one quarter, he had a proposal to deliver to the Chens. Since the experiment in women's education was proving so successful in Molly's case, he hoped to give Lincoln a similar opportunity. The Boston Mission was touting the achievements of Yung Wing, a young convert from China who had received honors at Yale College and inspired scores of Chinese youths to seek Christian training in

America. For years, the various Honolulu missions had been searching among local Chinese for Yung Wings of their own, and Bosworth had high hopes that Lincoln might be one. The boy clearly showed promise and might provide another fine cause for the *Dispatch* to espouse. Lincoln did not seem religious, although Bosworth was certain that the boy would convert out of ambition and need, if not devotion. With polish and schooling, he predicted that Lincoln might make an excellent minister among the Chinese.

"How's Mother Juliana treating you, my girl? Are you sitting at the front of the class or stuck in the corner?"

"The corner, Uncle. All I see are converging walls."

Bosworth roared with laughter. In his estimation, Rulan had raised Molly to be "too infernally good," and he was delighted to know that the girl was kicking up her heels at school. If she aggravated the supercilious Anglican sisterhood of which Lucy was so fond, all the better. "Good, good! Learned some of my best lessons with my nose to the wall. Ample time for moral reflection. Had a horrible bad habit of wiggling. Punished mightily for it. Worst sort of wiggler, I was told. A wanton wiggler. A wiggler who provoked a classroomful of wigglation. Caned twice a month for it, sat in the corner most every day."

Molly laughed to think that her sweet old uncle had ever been naughty and leaned over to kiss his whiskery cheek.

Lincoln was on the porch outside the shop as Bosworth's rig came up the lane. "Ignore him," sniffed Molly. "He'll just growl at you if you try to be nice." But Bosworth called the boy over as soon as Molly had gone inside.

"Reverend Hoapili says he's run out of books for you to borrow," Bosworth said. "Why don't you come up to the house, use the library any time . . ."

"I have to work," Lincoln said curtly.

"Just got in a crate of books you might like to see."

The offer made Lincoln drop his guard. "Is Stephen Douglas among them?"

"Assuredly—and translations of Count de Tocqueville and Rousseau. Hear of them?"

Lincoln shook his head.

"Look, you can't hide the fact that you're hankering after more schooling than the government can provide. The kingdom needs young men like you. I know the family's struggling with the store and your uncle hasn't got the money to send you on to a high school. He's a proud and difficult man, used to doing things alone. He kicked up a holy fuss over

Molly's schooling after Lucy came out for the girl, but in the end, he saw the advantage it offered. You could have the same chance, you know. I can't speak for Oahu College, for they blow hot and cold over anyone without missionary blood and money's uncertain for them these days. An Englishman's son is the same to them as a Hottentot. But a place like St. Albans, which accepts Hawaiians and Chinese . . . You could go there next month, lickety-split. I'll speak to the master if you like, send him to talk to your uncle . . ."

"No," Lincoln said sharply.

Bosworth stopped in surprise. He had expected gratitude, even tears; not a quick, cold rebuff. "If it's money you need—"

"I don't need anything," Lincoln repeated emphatically. "My uncle and I are quite content as we are."

When Bosworth had climbed back into the cart, Lincoln inspected the bundle Molly had left for him to carry. Inside were several mason jars of Lucy's mango preserves for Rulan and enough secondhand dresses to keep a young woman reasonably presentable at a place like the Priory. He took one corner of a skirt and held it briefly against his cheek. It smelled of face powder and plumeria blossoms, and a woman's skin.

Not Molly's skin. Molly's scent was unmistakable: the clean green smell of the sea. When he lay on his narrow straw mattress, he could shut his eyes and will the absent Molly into being; he smelled again the rich, heavy scent of her hair, her breath as sweet as the plums she loved. Lincoln's memory for odors was unusually precise. He could recapture lost chapters in his life by virtue of a single remembered smell. His childhood was shrunk to the dark opium-scented space in which his mother had entertained men. His mother, too, was more smell than image: a sandalwood scent that enveloped him in sorrow. He remembered the dry, fungal smell of the peat into which he and the uncles had pressed seeds with bare fingers. Best of all was the rich meaty odor of the medicinal broth that bubbled daily on Rulan's stove. She made the soup for him—a scholar's food for a scholar's weak eyes—the timeless smell of hope and home.

Lincoln stood a moment on the porch to watch the torches and lanterns wink on in the noodle shops and gambling halls, stamping each pinpoint of light onto his memory as the camera once etched Lucky's brief season of hope onto a glass plate. This was his last night in the house of the only father he knew, the end to his tenuous hold on family life. The severing of his fragile connection with Molly. Lincoln put his head in his hands. Tomorrow, Pao An was sending him to a camp on the other side of the island to be apprenticed to a surveyor of roads. The work would bring in cash for the business and guarantee Lincoln a decent livelihood in years to come. He would do it—anything—for his uncle. But Lincoln wished he could sink into the ocean and disappear.

Far down the lane, Lincoln heard the whining of rusty carriage wheels as Bosworth's rig turned the corner onto Merchant Street, bearing all his dreams away.

14

POETS AND REBELS

Back at school, Molly chafed under Mother Juliana's disapproving eye, which now seemed annoyingly similar to that of her mother. Constable appeared at the gates of the Priory, yet if he was impatient to meet Molly, he gave no sign. He was there every day for two weeks, during which time he neither spoke nor followed her, but simply watched Molly pass, his arrogance emphasized by a pretended show of respect. A most reluctant lover, Molly decided.

"He's a bohemian," Sarah asserted stubbornly. "The kind that prefers the exotic. He's studying you from afar. My brother Jamie says there are young men with querulous tastes who prefer any woman different from the *wahines* they know." Sarah had a new sense of her importance; she believed herself destined for a marriage as brilliant as that of Lydia Liliuokalani Dominis, Kalakaua's sister, whose *haole* husband, the governor of Oahu, commanded as much power as a chief due to the wealth and status his royal spouse bestowed.

Molly was annoyed by Sarah's glib pronouncement; she thought herself neither exotic nor extraordinary in appearance, desiring above all to blend in, rather than stick out of the crowd. If the truth were known, she did not think of herself as wholly Chinese either. The fact that she did not resemble the birdlike Lily no longer pained her. She much preferred to think of herself as a *wahine* like Sarah and the rest of the mixed-race Priory girls.

If Constable made no move to approach her, neither did he withdraw. The constancy of her admirer gave Molly great status among her peers. Sarah offered advice on how to draw her lover out through winks, sighs, and sidelong glances. But when Molly employed these stratagems on the way to chapel one day, she was apprehended by Mother Juliana and sent to bed without supper. The next day, Mother Juliana threatened the girls with reprisals if they fraternized with "men of the street." Molly, the chief offender, was made to scrub the refectory floor, a punishment that she vigorously protested as *ex post facto*. Such impertinence earned Molly a more painful penalty: being barred from the cathedral. Mother Juliana herself would hear Molly's weekly confession.

Yet Constable *in absentia* was even more compelling a lover than Constable in plain sight. Night after night Molly dreamed of him. She was hungry all the time. Sometimes, she would awake with an overpowering craving that no amount of purloined sweets would staunch. Her newly demanding body alarmed her.

On the first afternoon her punishment was lifted, Constable was absent from the band of loiterers. An impatient Molly looked up and down the street, staggered by disappointment. Had he turned his attentions to another? Then she saw a lone horse beyond the knot of noisy bachelors. Not a black stallion but an ancient mare with washboard ribs and a swollen belly. A plump Hawaiian man was at the reins, his bare feet dangling over the horse's ears. She dawdled at the end of the line, but Constable did not appear. Only when she had almost entered the gate did the tired horse with its portly rider came trotting slowly by.

"Eh, wahine, eh," the rider called softly. "Byemby you come *hala* tree outside the yard. Ten o'clock tonight. Somebody like see you." And he passed without another word.

"Ooh, naughty *kolohe* girl, you're going to meet him," Sarah cried in the darkened dormitory room later that night, torn between jealousy and fear. "What if you're caught? Mother Juliana will pack you off home!"

Molly was too busy searching through her trunk to reply. The prospect of expulsion, or worse, a confrontation with her father, could not dampen her excitement. This was grown-up business! A lovers' rendezvous! And she had determined not to meet her first real beau in schoolgirl ruffles. She pulled out a long white silk shift, Lucy's old undergarment, and slipped it over her body. The diaphanous material clung from neck to ankles in a most seductive way.

"You can't go out like that!" gasped Sarah.

"Kealoha dances for the king half naked! At least I'm covered up!" She had once seen the king's latest mistress promenade past the Priory in a similar dress to the noisy approbation of the men in the gauntlet. Running her hands over her slender body, Molly decided finally that the tight dress was probably far more striking on the lady-in-waiting than on her. Her body never seemed to change! She ate as much as her father's workmen, but her chest and hips remained as narrow as a boy's. She would never have the voluptuous figure of the wasp-waisted *haole* women that one saw in dressmakers' advertisements. To distract the eye from her slimness, Molly wrapped a long sash around her hips and stuck Sarah's wide-brimmed straw hat on her head. She pulled the skirt up to her thighs to climb out the window and over the wall, with Sarah playing guard. From the wall, it was only a short barefoot race by moonlight down the rutted road lined with royal palms to where the dark outline of the *hala* tree was painted against the moon.

When she saw him, she was suddenly shy.

He called to her in a mellow voice. A Hawaiian voice. "An odd mode of dress," he observed, helping her into the carriage. "But you're pretty. You can wear what you want."

She found herself blushing furiously in the darkness, wondering if he thought her a slut. Well, she was not as wanton as he imagined, she told herself and settled back into the carriage, fully prepared to resist his advances. Yet he made none. Instead, he commended her speech and told her of the admiration he shared with her for Shelley and the great epic poem he was working on which would match the sublime message of *Prometheus Unbound*. He intended one day to be the poet of the Pacific but in the meantime earned his bread as a hack for the legislature in order to buy time to write.

They rode through the darkened lanes of the sleeping city, up through the mists of Manoa Valley into the hills hung with tangled vines to the edge of the Chinese graveyard. He told her how he had woken up in his landlady's house in London and imagined that behind the fog blanketing the great dome of St. Paul's he could see the mist-shrouded mountain called Waialeale on Kauai. It occurred to him then that he was wasting his time shivering in fog-bound England when true literary greatness lay in Hawaii. For Hawaii had no poet! True, there were the *meles* and the chants of the *kahunas,* but these had never been written down and were fast fading from memory; and the best-educated young Hawaiians of his generation knew the writings of Carlyle and Macaulay better than their native lore. The poem he had in mind to write was an epic setting down the history of his people, from the coming of the first Polynesian settlers from Tahiti on double-hulled canoes to the dance of death of *alii* and commoner in the present . . .

". . . and I had been searching for a way of ending my poem," Constable admitted, "until I saw you." It was clear to him now, he told her, that the poem would end in a mighty clash of nations over Hawaii's soil. He had had no notion how to portray that towering struggle until he had seen her, the face of Hawaii to come. Her words at Emma's house secured his admiration. "The New Woman, more than the New Man, will inaugurate Hawaii's coming-of-age in an industrial era," he told her. To that end, he had made inquiries about her. "I know where you live, who your parents are. I went into Chinatown and found your father's store. I engaged your mother in conversation. I found her a fund of stories, in her own quaint way a person of some eloquence."

He is mad, she thought, flushing with shame at the thought that he had actually gone to that hovel in Chinatown. And yet his attempt to draw her into his scheme was irresistible. Was this how poets worked—mining the lives of their companions for inspiration? Moonlight carved out of the darkness the broad Polynesian planes of his face, the thick Hawaiian nose, the sea green *haole* eyes and thin *haole* lips, a countenance at war with itself.

They met twice more by moonlight. He plied her with questions about the customs of her house, her race. When he commanded her to speak to him in Chinese, she babbled snatches of a lullaby, baby talk, counting rhymes from her girlhood to fill the silence, to hold his interest . . . anything to keep him at her side. He nodded, pleased and excited by the sounds, unaware of her enormous ignorance of all things Chinese.

*T*hen for two weeks, no message came. Molly wept frantic, bitter tears, insulted Sarah and the others when they tried to comfort her. And just as suddenly, the blowsy Hawaiian on the ancient horse appeared in the same spot under the *hala* tree with another summons.

"*D*on't go," Sarah warned. "It's cat-and-mouse he's playing." The two friends quarreled. There had been a girl the previous year who became *hapai* and had to be sent away to bear her baby in shame. Molly swore she was smarter than that. "Only once more," she promised Sarah. "To tell him good-bye."

But it was he who was leaving. "My *kupuna* is calling for me. Grand-mother has pressing family business on Kauai," he told her.

"When will you be back?"

"I don't know. It's wrong for me to lie. Understand that you have my love now." He gave her a kiss, open-mouthed and ardent, to bid her *aloha*.

In his absence, she was undone by love. Had his grandmother really called for him, or was he deceiving her with another? Had she been too slow to show her affection? Was her father right in calling men like him "deceivers"? Her mind was a hollow gourd rattling with suspicions. She dragged herself through the day; sleep eluded her by night. She stopped eating. When Sarah could not wake Molly for morning prayers, the sisters sent her to the infirmary, convinced that Molly had fallen victim to a wasting disease. Sarah told the girls that she feared a *kahuna* had put a spell on her friend.

Sarah visited every day with a bowl of *poi,* pleading with Molly to eat. Molly agreed only if Sarah would read her the sad poems that the sisters disallowed. But when Molly begged to hear "In Memoriam," Tennyson's verses to his dead friend, Sarah became alarmed. Death by drowning, particularly if the victim was young, was so lovely, Molly told the fright-ened Sarah. Mother Juliana visited the sickroom every day at Sarah's insis-tence, but Molly sent back the plates of salt pork and boiled yams and made a pretense of sleeping whenever she came.

One morning, the door banged open.

"Poor dear. She's sleeping," the Anglican sister whispered.

"She's pretending," came Rulan's curt reply. "Get up," she ordered her daughter in Chinese when the door had been firmly shut against the matron. She had put on what Molly called her "warrior face," a counte-nance fierce enough for battle, although Molly doubted whether her mother had been in any battle more fierce than those waged with stingy vendors in the fish market. None of her mother's stories had ever made sense: stories upon stories concocted for a daughter who had no interest in how the lessons of old China applied to present-day Hawaii.

But this warrior mother was formidable enough to make her child shake with apprehension. Rulan looked down at the girl, flesh of her own flesh, blinking up at her from a bed strewn with books of melancholy verse.

"Who is the boy?" Rulan barked.

"What boy?" stammered Molly.

"The boy who is making you act like a fool."

"There is no *boy,*" Molly said sullenly. Strictly speaking, she was telling the truth. Peter Constable was a man!

Rulan peered intently into her daughter's eyes. "Have you shamed me?" she asked finally.

"Mother, how could you!" Molly declared, turning her face into the pillow. She felt her ears redden at the memory of what she had allowed Constable's lips and hands to do.

"Who is he?" Rulan repeated stubbornly.

"I told you!"

"Is he *haole*?"

"No! I mean, there is no boy."

"Then why do you stop eating? I went hungry so my daughter would never know famine! But you starve yourself because it is fashionable for spoiled girls to pine away for a lover. You have no idea how much you shame me."

"And what about me? What other mother wears such funny clothes, shuffles around in slippers and screams like a fishwife, butts into her daughter's business and makes accusations?" Molly had never spoken to her mother in such an insolent way, and now, frightened by her own behavior, she felt tears streaming down her face.

Rulan pinched her daughter's cheek as Chinese mothers do to disobedient children. She too was crying. "Bad girl, cut your head and tongue," she cursed in Cantonese. "Turning away good food! Insulting your mother! Unfilial. Disrespectful."

"You won't let me grow up, Mother," Molly wailed. "Not the way I want to. This is not China, and I am not a small-foot woman like Lily waiting to be sold off for the highest price. I—I'm different. . . . I don't know what I am!"

Rulan fought for composure. "You know who you are, but you are ashamed of it!" Then she stormed out of the room, down the steps, and stood a while, leaning her head against the cool stone of the Priory walls. Loving her daughter was like pouring water onto the earth. A libation lost. Her chest hurt, and she could not stop her tears.

Even Mother Juliana could not make peace between mother and daughter. In the end, it was decided that Molly would go to Hiamoe on weekends, and that if she spoke to any young man, she would be expelled.

*B*ut one night, Molly looked out her window and saw him under the *hala* tree. She climbed out the window and ran through the silvery patches of moonlight scattered on the lawn. Her bare feet touched the cold stones. Shivering in her thin gown, she wept when he touched her. And then he was kissing her cheeks, her lips, her shoulders—wherever her tears had fallen—murmuring endearments in Hawaiian. He took her into the waiting carriage and caressed her intimately as they were borne through deserted boulevards bathed in the glow of shimmering gaslights. When the carriage veered along the darkened wharf to the rooms he kept above a coffee warehouse, he bid her farewell and ordered the driver to take her back to the Priory alone. It was she then who pressed herself upon him. She, upstairs in his rooms, who flung off the thin shift and touched him. It was she again who brought him twice to release. And a third time, despite the blood and the pain, to satisfy her desire to know at last not pleasure, which eluded her, but the shame her mother had foretold.

$\mathcal{M}$olly's malingering had a disastrous effect on her schoolwork, thus prompting Mother Juliana to confer with the girl's mother as well as her sponsor, Lucy Bosworth. The headmistress, with Lucy's and the girl's mother's consent, put Molly to work in the laundry room for board and tuition. They agreed that harsh labor was a good corrective. Exiled from the other girls to a room near the kitchen, Molly would have no opportunity for plotting with Sarah, another mischiefmaker who was being carefully watched for signs of rebellion. Mother Juliana was soon able to report to Lucy and Rulan that the spartan regime had brought Molly to her senses. The girl was made tractable again; her sweet disposition had returned. She was up early and in bed early, and too fatigued from folding and sorting linen to think about the romantic attachment that had made her so unmanageable at the turn of the year. In short, so much had honest labor changed Molly that the girl was begging to spend free weekends studying at school.

In truth, Constable crept through her ground-floor window each night into her bed. These midnight transgressions did more to keep Molly obedient than all the scullery work that the sisters could find for her.

$\mathcal{A}$ terrible shock, the Widow confessed to the women who had gathered in her courtyard at midday to *yum cha,* to drink tea and snack on "small foods." "The gifts exchanged, the clan records certified, the hall rented for the banquet, a new cook brought over from Canton City. . . . Who would have predicted that such a strong man would succumb so suddenly? Surely he must have done something terrible in a previous life! Unfortunate for poor Lily, but better that we were not linked to such an unlucky family. How lucky for us that we escaped catastrophe."

The Widow was entertaining lavishly and often these days in order to stem the tide of rumor that was running against her house. She knew that the women were talking behind her back about Lily. All the years the Widow had held out for the highest bride-price for her girl, and then when a bargain was finally struck with the Tang man who had made a fortune in *poi,* the groom had dropped dead in the office of his factory while being measured for his wedding suit!

"I warned my daughter that her betrothed was too thin. He was a mature man, not *excessively* old, but there might have been a question of potency, one never knows. . . . But no, no, my Lily wanted a good provider. You know how she is, sensible beyond her years, not like some young girls who chase after any man, no matter the family or color of skin . . ."

The young bond maid set out a lavish array of small foods on the round banquet table for the women to taste with their tea: tiny pork dumplings, curried tripe, translucent rice noodles, stewed chicken gizzards, and duck feet steeped in aniseed and soy. This was city food, not the plain fare village women were used to. For a while, the only noises were the clicking of ivory chopsticks and the sounds of chewing as the women "tasted" their way rapidly through the platters of food.

"I say, we must not let Western notions of marriage corrupt our girls," the Widow was saying. She had taken up the teapot and was filling the empty cups herself. "Teach them sense and responsibility, and they will always choose the right way. That Chen girl, for instance, thinks she is too good to show her face on these streets. I suppose she will choose her husband herself! What folly! It is as if one were saying, 'I will spend my life with whatever *la sap* the wind blows my way.' A Tang man who cooks in a restaurant downtown saw her on the arm of a *hapa haole* man! Draped all over him! I heard this from the cook's own uncle. That family has no shame! Well, my Lily has more sense than to go with a man out of harlotry. And a sensible woman will always bring fortune to her husband's house, *hai ma?*"

The women swallowed cup after cup of fragrant tea, picked over the duck bones for the last tasty bits of gristle, then went home to report that the Lis' new cook must be commanding enormous wages and that the daughter, Lily, looked as happy as a cat licking oil out of a warm *wok,* while the Widow herself seemed more devastated than when her husband had died.

Nor could the women forget the image of a groom dying in his wedding suit. "Isn't it odd about the Lis . . ." they told their husbands and sons. "How bad luck always befalls their men."

15

AN EVIL WIND

The inhabitants of Chinatown felt the storm's hot breath by midafternoon. There were odd rumblings, an ominous darkening of the heavens, and a lifeless humidity dragging down the air. Then a sultry wind swept across the channel, gathering speed on its journey inland. This was no ordinary storm, a worried Nalani told Rulan. There was dry thunder, thunder without rain, ample proof that the cycle of nature was awry.

"Bad t'ings going happen," she affirmed darkly. Her life was too good. Tyhune had made an exceptional sale. He had installed a humidor room in Kalakaua's new palace and stocked it with a thousand of the finest Cuban cigars. Nalani distrusted such blatant good fortune, especially after his misadventure with the king.

Tyhune was strutting around the lanes like a mandarin, regaling all who would listen about his foray inside the newly built Iolani Palace. He had described feeling the old fear of going into the *yamen* of the county magistrate in China and how he spat to keep bad luck at bay. The palace itself rose above him like a mountain, an immense square building of painted brick three stories high. There were towers at each corner and a larger tower over each entrance. A six-foot-wide trench encircled the palace to provide ventilation to the basement where the cigars would be housed. In this basement, as Tyhune was busily installing an airtight closet of fragrant wood one afternoon, the Chinaman met up with a frowsy Kalakaua wearing nothing but a *malo* around his loins. At this point in the telling, Tyhune would break out in a wicked grin. "The king just get up two o'clock and already looking for one cigar. He rub his eye and say me, '*Eh, pa-ke!* I like talk you.' 'Yes sir, King,' I tell 'im. He no say nothin'. Take one cigar, cut it, light it, and blow smoke little while. Then he tell, 'Too many you damn *pa-ke,* make too much money. Byemby I bring in Japanee.' 'Oh, not them dwarfs!' I tell 'im. 'They no like Hawaiians, even king like you!' '*Auwe,'* he say, sad like. 'Nobody no like me. Even my own sister.' He talk his sister, get plenny mad. Byemby he say, 'You *pa-ke* like smoke opium too much. Time for make you fella pay.' "

Nalani was aghast at what Tyhune's irreverent account revealed. Like most Hawaiians, she delighted in the court spectacles provided by the royal family and the plaintive music Kalakaua and his sister, Liliuokalani, composed for popular singing. And whereas Tyhune was convinced from his encounter that the king was lazy, Nalani believed Kalakaua's lethargy to be a sign of secret sorrow. The further hint that brother and sister were at odds would mean that Hawaiians, caught up in the feud between Emma and the king, would be split into factions yet again. And Tyhune would be punished for merely bearing the ill news.

On the afternoon that dark clouds massed over the horizon, Nalani came to the hardware store confessing her fear that the storm was an omen directed at her man. "I get *ike papalua,* can see bad t'ings before going happen," she told Rulan. "No good what Tyhune tell about the king, make all Hawaiians look bad. Maybe *kahunas* put a curse on him."

Rulan sent Nalani on her way with assurances that the storm would blow itself out at sea. But by evening, as dark clouds pressed down on them, she made Pao An board up the precious glass windows and sent him out for boxes of candles and metal drums of coal oil, for there was always a run on expensive imported goods after a storm.

Soon the wind was howling through the lanes, and sharp torrents of rainfall were setting off muddy explosions across the yard. Instead of passing over the city, the wind increased in intensity. They huddled in the innermost room as buildings collapsed outside. Then a noise like bursts of gunfire tore through the yard outside. It was quiet for the space of an hour. Rulan ran outside and saw that the blast had shattered the windows of Tyhune's store, lifting the corrugated iron roof like a lid and sending it tumbling end over end down the road. She imagined the frenzy inside the house as Nalani and Tyhune scrambled to protect their precious merchandise from the pounding rain. Then the wind turned and came from the opposite direction, more forcefully than before.

After the worst of the storm had passed, the stunned shopkeepers wandered through the streets poking through the debris to gather what valuables remained intact. But neither Tyhune nor Nalani was to be seen. Alarmed, Rulan hastened next door and found Tyhune's shop in ruins. The wind had wrenched down the doors and torn the sacks asunder, leaving the boards shaggy with wet tobacco; the heavy wooden counter that stood at the front of the shop had been hurled through the wall into the storeroom behind. It was Nalani's leg Rulan saw first: a bare brown limb jutting out from beneath the splintered wood. It took three men to lift the heavy wooden counter from the broken bodies. Nalani and Tyhune were found with limbs entwined, his fingers tangled in her hair, her arms wrapped around his skinny neck, fighting and loving at the last.

Until their kinsmen separated them. Tyhune was buried by his clansmen in the Chinese cemetery up Manoa with the rites due a union elder while Nalani's *hanai* aunties and cousins came to claim her body for the family plot on the other side of the island. Neither side would allow a stranger to lie beside one of their own. Before taking Nalani away, the women wrapped her in one of Lucy's quilts and began a chant in the ancient style.

> Raise up the prayer for life
> Raise it up to the star-studded sky
> Raise it up to the gods who live on high . . .
>
> Hear my prayer of sore affliction.
> These are my troubles. Grant me sacred peace.
> Free me that I may stand and walk again . . .
>
> *Amamu ua noa* . . .

The singers' mournful words rose up to the place where their sister had already flown with her man.

16

THE ROAD

The hurricane proved a boon for Pao An. His was not the kind of inventory that could be spoiled by wind or rain, and now everyone needed hammers and wire nails, lumber and coral stone to rebuild. Roads, dikes, dams, fishponds also needed repairing, thus prompting the king to auction off contracts for a massive public works scheme across Oahu. The grass shacks and wooden tenements built in Emma's reign were proving woefully inadequate to house the foreigners flocking to Hawaii's shores; and Kalakaua, having already depleted his treasury in the building of his brick and iron frame palace, intended to do still more to reshape Honolulu into the commercial center of the islands. His next plan was to construct a road encircling the island so that a man might go from Waianae Beach to Honolulu in less than half a day. With the cost of construction soaring and pitting him against a reluctant legislature, Kalakaua had turned to Claus Spreckels to bail him out of his gambling debts. Already there were critics like Emmanuel Bosworth who mocked Kalakaua's spendthrift ways by dubbing Spreckels "King Claus."

By skillfully underbidding his rivals, Pao An was granted a lucrative contract for the building of a section of the road and promptly hired a crew of Chinamen and *kanakas* to dig the windward end. With Lincoln as surveyor and a road crew led by three Tang men who had blasted tunnels through the Sierras for the railroad, Pao An began by reducing the lava cliffs to rubble, then leveling the roadbed with drag sledges pulled by oxen. On the bluffs, the soil was porous and ashy, the residue of a long-dormant volcano called Kaimana-hila, or Diamond Hill, for the false hopes sparked decades before by crystalline fragments that occasionally winked in the rock. The grading was as tedious as dredging the heavy, waterlogged peat of the deltas of China or California by hand. Although Pao An fell easily into the familiar task of moving earth, he could no longer discount the changes that age and toil had wrought on the powerful body that had once been his pride; his broad back was beginning to bend, and after a day of hauling rock his ribs, knees, and shoulders had pains that sleep could not cure.

Yet despite the cost to his body, moving rock was finally earning Pao An the prosperity for which he had labored so long. Squinting into the harsh light from under the brim of his conical straw hat, he saw the distant shape of Maui across the channel; behind him rose Kaimana-hila blanketed by clouds. Generations of Chens in On Ting village had spent their lives tilling their few square miles of Delta earth before laying their bones there. Yet he, an outcast son of the village, had walked from the southern tip of the empire to the very outskirts of Peking. He, the poorest boy in On Ting, was now turning the red earth of a land his kin knew only in talk story, the place they called *Fusan,* the Blessed Isles. Given a chance, Pao An thought proudly, even he, the humblest of Tang men, might accomplish feats worthy of an emperor. In its own way, the building of this road was as grandiose a project as the wall the first Chin emperor had made to safeguard his empire from northern invaders.

One day, his vendors would travel this road from his lumberyards to small fishing villages on the coast to bring tools and lumber to any man who wanted a store or restaurant or cottage of his own. By then, roads would crisscross the island and buildings made from the Chens' stone and lumber would dot the horizon. He envisioned an Oahu furnished with dwellings to suit every purpose: one-story plantation cottages stuck side by side on stilts so that workers need not sleep like animals penned in a barn but live decently with wives and children and a vegetable garden of their own, dwellings made from clapboard or adobe and thatch like those he had seen along the levees in California, stately edifices of lava stone where bankers and merchants came to trade.

"Someday," he told Lincoln, gesturing at imaginary roads and canals and dwellings as if he were presenting the boy a kingdom, "this business will be yours. Something for you and your sons."

In truth, Lincoln didn't want what his uncle proffered. At least, not this way. He revered the man who had taken him in, but he hated reducing himself to a mindless thing of sinew and bone. He hated the mud and the sweat and the agony of pitting himself against the relentless drift of earth and sea. The summer before, he had steeped himself in the writings of Emerson, Wordsworth, and Rousseau and come away convinced that by meditation, one could cross over at will from the real world into a veritable paradise of the mind. Escape from the drudgery of each day came as easily as thought. He had discovered that any rhythmical activity performed for prolonged periods—the swinging of a pickax, the steady contemplation of the swell of the waves—would create answering interior rhythms that would send his mind soaring above his aching body. In those moments of "transcendings," Lincoln neither heard the cacophony of animals and men nor felt the soreness in his muscles nor remembered his despair.

The Widow had won a contract too, a lucrative franchise to supply the workers' canteen, a natural extension of her fish and vegetable markets. Because her provisions were abundant and cheap, she was soon supplying food to road gangs all over the island. For an extra fee, a laborer might buy a packet of opium, which the Widow's vendors, all brothers of the *tong,* hid inside covered baskets of rice. Pao An had forbidden opium on the job; even so, the Widow managed to do a thriving clandestine business in the drug. The day was coming, she foresaw, when the bankrupt kingdom would reissue the lucrative opium license and assess taxes on the smoking of dirt as other kings had done before. Having heard that Walter Murray Gibson, the most powerful adviser to the king, was pressing Kalakaua to reintroduce the opium license, the Widow was spending a fortune on bribes. When the license was issued, she would be ready for trade.

A week after the crew broke ground, the Widow ordered her driver to take her in an ancient rig to various construction sites to oversee the midday distribution of food. She came dressed in a shiny coat of embroidered black satin and a black Buddhist headband encrusted with seed pearls, making a great show of scolding her workers for not being liberal enough with portions of food.

Pao An saw her coming from the hillock where he was helping Lincoln mark off the section of land for the next day's blasting. His immediate response was to throw her off the site. Yet one glimpse of Mei Yuk fanning herself in the rig while her menservants scurried like puppies to do her bidding brought back a disturbing recollection. He remembered her at their first meeting, a girl of fourteen borne aloft on her wedding palanquin and he a stone-stupid youth teasing the bride on her way along the levee road. When she had peeked fearfully out of her covered palanquin and raised her veil to look at him, he had been struck dumb by her beauty and felt for the first time the meanness of his estate. He was a paddy boy too poor and dirty to touch the hem of her garment and as much an ox as the one he drove through the mud.

Since then, he had risen to battlefield glory, heard his name trumpeted among the Taiping armies, and in time bedded her. Now the remembered heat of their joining touched him like an old sickness that he couldn't throw off. The realization that he was still mucking about in mud made him ashamed. Rather than face her, he grabbed up his pickax and shovel and headed up the road toward the sea.

The Widow, however, had come to waylay someone else. For some time, she had been gathering reports on Lincoln who inspected the food baskets and calculated the invoices from her cooks and suppliers. Her overseers had been grumbling about the scrupulousness of his tallying. Now she watched the tall, rawboned youth oversee the apportioning of food; he had not yet lost the clumsiness of boyhood and was covered with red dirt as dry as powder.

"You, boy," Mei Yuk called. "Come here."

Lincoln sauntered over, preparing himself for a fight. The Widow had her driver pull into the shade of a *hala* tree, the only one in that barren section of rocky ground. "You like crawling through the dirt like a gecko in this heat?" Mei Yuk asked, fanning herself as she reclined under the canopy of her buggy. "Give me a stool in a Chinatown shop any day." She was rewarded by Lincoln's rueful smile. "This work is fit only for *gu li*," she said vehemently. "You are not a 'rough man.' Why do you stay?"

"My uncle needs me," Lincoln replied with what courtesy he could muster. He wondered why others thought this small woman with her pretentious city accent so formidable. Still, the Widow was sensible enough to divine his dislike of dirt and stone and his unease among the rough, crude men. For he did indeed miss the order of the shop, the clean floors and polished wooden countertops, the logic of commerce and inventory and the smooth abacus beads under his fingers.

"How is your uncle going to pay you?" she prodded. "In Kalakaua dollars?" She laughed at her own joke. The newly minted coins stamped with the king's head were considered worthless by the Chinese, who would not accept wages or trade goods in them. Claus Spreckels and Walter

Murray Gibson had beguiled the king into creating the new coinage as a means of skimming money off the treasury.

"My uncle's coins are as good as his word," Lincoln replied.

Mei Yuk went on reprovingly. "Not your uncle by blood! You're more filial to this stranger than his own daughter!" Suddenly Mei Yuk leaned over and said in a conspiratorial tone, "My daughter says you are a scholar. Quit this job and come to me! I could use a bookkeeper who speaks English and Hawaiian as well as you. And I pay in American money!"

"There are twenty Tang boys at the Fort Street Mission who can figure as well as I," Lincoln replied, while secretly delighting that Lily admired him. Since their meeting at Ching Ming, he had thought often of her delicate features and her shy smile, and had quietly rejoiced when her betrothal had fallen through.

"Perhaps, but you are shrewd and my men fear you. So if you decide to do something better than smash stone for a living, come see me."

"I am already learning a trade."

"Pah! Crushing rock is not a trade for an educated man. And any apprenticeship can be bought off," Mei Yuk retorted. "You're old enough to make your own way. How will you get a wife if you have no decent livelihood? And do not tell me you intend to muck about in mud, for you are not built along your uncle's lines. You would surely fail at his business!"

Lincoln shifted his feet self-consciously and looked down at the ground. The Widow was nosy and impertinent, yet she was putting into words the same doubts that had plagued him for months.

"I will pay you five hundred Yankee dollars a year to keep my company's books and oversee the food concessions." When his eyes widened at the princely sum, she continued with a smile. "Tell your uncle about my offer. See if he puts your interests above his own!"

"My place is with him," Lincoln affirmed.

Anger blazed up in her eyes. "*Aiya,* I see you are the consummate businessman," she snapped, "one who intends to set the pace of the bargaining. Well, every man has his price, and I mean to discover yours."

Lincoln left feeling soiled and guilty. The Widow had a way of reaching into the recesses of his mind and dragging out his secret fears.

"The Chens have no breeding, no appreciation for the scholarly mind. I tell you, they are wasting that boy's gifts," the Widow told the council, which was meeting that morning on one of their charitable schemes to impress the government. This time, they were selecting the most worthy youth for further study at a private high school. The training would be at their expense, for any youth who lifted himself up did the same for all Tang people in the islands. It was a shrewd investment too, for if the boy were a brother bound by oath to the *tong,* he would eventually be in a position to pay them back handsomely in the form of favors. "Even the *kanaka* teacher at the common school says Lin Kong should not be apprenticed. A scholar should use his brains, not his back."

The council brother with the smoothest tongue was delegated to convey the news to Pao An that Lincoln had been selected as that year's scholar. But the man had uttered no more than a few sentences before Pao An drove him out of his shop for interfering in matters that were not the *tong's* concern.

In bed that night, Pao An raged at his wife. The man was undoubtedly sent by the Widow who was trying to entice the boy into her employ, for the *tong* emissary had implied that Pao An treated Lincoln too harshly. No man had done more for the boy than he! Didn't these fools know, moreover, that they were sowing the seeds of their own destruction by sending Tang boys to school with the *bak kuei*? The day was coming when there would be no more brave Tang men laboring in earthworks or plantations or fishing boats up and down the coast of California or in the port cities of the Hawaiian kingdom. The builders and the dreamers would be gone. Soon they would all be talking in the strangled accents of the deceivers!

The altercation with the council brother coincided with one of Molly's free weekends, which Molly chose to spend at Lucy's, a decision that greatly distressed her mother. Rulan would have been more upset to know that Molly spent the time in bed with a fever, which Lucy diagnosed as a bladder infection. It bothered Lucy that the child was incurring such ailments before marriage. The malady was not serious, merely uncomfortable, although it required a suppository of ingredients that only Dr. Hunnicut could prescribe. Molly begged Lucy not to let the doctor know her intimate ailments; and Lucy, understanding a young girl's modesty, bought the necessary medications as if for herself.

Pao An's feud with the *tong* and Rulan's agony over her daughter left him with a grinding sense of unease. Late Sunday afternoon, he drove out to Hiamoe, the first time he had been to the Bosworths' cottage since he had taken his wife and small daughter away. He found the house empty except for Molly, who was well enough to rise out of her sickbed to prepare the Bosworths' evening meal. Fish knife in hand, she started when she saw her father.

Pao An marveled at his daughter's skill. She held a slippery red fish in one hand and with the other rapidly maneuvered her knife so that scales flew like drops of iridescent rain into a bucket. She was as beautiful to him as when he had first seen her, with her mother's quick intelligence and bodily grace. Now her brow was as knit with concentration as when she had played with the doll he had made for her out of wood after her porcelain one had broken. She had tried to heal the doll, using the same phrases with which her mother prescribed medicines to customers. He had wanted only to keep his girl safe. Why, then, did she return anger for his protection, deliver coldness for his concern? Why didn't love call forth love?

"You make your mother cry," he told her. "Come home."

"We need a rest from each other," she said coolly. "Anyway, she's used to me being away."

"She misses you."

Molly gave an exasperated sigh. She felt feverish and tired and longed for the coolness of Lucy's bed. "I study better here. Lucy helps me with my Latin and geography and mathematics—"

"Good, good. Mathematics is useful," Pao An interrupted, trying desperately to signal his approval. "You can help Lin Kong with the accounts when you come back next year. . . ."

"I—I'm not coming back," she stammered. "I have other plans."

That declaration shocked him. He was willing to admit that his daughter might run to Lucy's arms when she fought with her mother. And he had known better than to stifle her brilliance by preventing her from going to school. But never, never did he imagine that a girl, *his* girl, would live anywhere but in her father's house. "You belong at home," he declared. "You have no choice."

She put down the knife and wiped her hands nervously on her bloody apron. "Choice is exactly what I do have," Molly explained earnestly. There was a spot of dark blood from the fish on her hand. "That's what the sisters teach at school!"

His voice rose. "They may say so, but do not believe for a minute that the white devils will let you live among them. Unless you want to wash their sheets, carry out their shit pots, scrub their floors . . ."

"I'm going to teach . . ." Molly regretted the words as soon as she uttered them. She had kept her ambitions secret even from Constable.

"Teach? Teach who?" he barked. "Not *their* children."

"Then *our* children," she exclaimed. "Tang children. Chinatown has children now, not just bachelors from the fields!"

"What makes you think you can teach anyone?" he shouted. "No one can teach you anything! Why must you be different from all of us? What's the matter with being like your mother, working hard for the family business, being wife to a hardworking man of Tang—"

Molly's hands were shaking as she picked up the knife. She held a silvery fish in one hand, gutted it with a single stroke, then dropped it into the bucket. "I don't want to be like her. I don't want to be like any of you. . . . I can do better!" Molly stammered.

Pao An slammed his hand so hard against a post on the porch that the girl jumped up in fear. To think that in her heart, the girl had left him long ago. Had he worked all these years only to exchange loneliness for more loneliness?

That night, Rulan came to massage his back, something she had not offered to do in months. They had hardly spoken since Nalani's passing; he was gone on the road, and she was exhausted, shouldering the burden of three in the shop and still numb with grief for her friend. Although Pao An had not told her of his disastrous visit to Hiamoe, it was a comfort to him that his wife sensed his misery without his having to speak. The rich smell of the raw peanut oil made him drowsy, and soon he was sleeping, rocked by her strong fingers rhythmically sweeping from neck to hipbone.

Her talk story roused him. "I met a young man in the market yesterday," she said, as her fingers probed the shelf of muscle along his shoulders. "He had just served his three years on the Chillingworth plantation, and his legs looked as if he had been cut with a knife. From the cane leaves, he said. I told him a cheap medicine to use: squeeze the juice from cane shoots and rock salt through a piece of cloth onto the cuts. He thanked me for saving him money and said he was looking for work. I offered him a job cutting lumber and a bed upstairs, but he said no.

" 'I want to work on a boat,' he told me. 'My father was a farmer and all he could think of was adding another *mu* of land to his holdings. But I am sick to death of the dry world. The best time I ever had was on the ship coming from China to Hawaii. Everyone else got sick but me. I loved the pitch and roll of the ship. The first thing I did was get a *kanaka* to teach me to swim! I want to be a sailor! I will have my own boat one day. I will ride upon the ocean on a long board of *wili wili* like the brown men.' "

Pao An lay facedown on the bed as his wife prodded the soreness from his body, waiting for what Rulan would say about the girl. Every one of his wife's talk stories was an attempt to make clear what perplexed them both about their daughter.

"They are willful creatures, children," she whispered, clinging to him. "You see generations of birds take the same path across the sky, the young bird following dutifully in the wake of the elder. Only men and women fly wherever they please . . ." She began to weep softly then, for the tidy aphorism was no comfort to her either. "What will she do? How will she make her way without us?"

Back at the digging, Pao An saw that Lincoln, in his absence, had pushed the road ahead another mile along the mountain. Yet Pao An was short-tempered and rude to the boy, unable to praise. To mollify his uncle, Lincoln talked about the prospects the road presented for cross-island trade, but Pao An snapped at him, saying that the road would never be completed if he could not stop chattering long enough to lift a spade. When the cook boys came with buckets of hot rice and tea, Pao An saw Lincoln take his bowl to eat rice with the men. The boy was angry with him. And angry at himself too, Pao An concluded ruefully, for pretending an enthusiasm for the work he did not feel. Had never felt.

They worked side by side in edgy silence. Lincoln's anger had burned itself off in the heat of the afternoon. Now memories of his uncle's past kindnesses returned to haunt him: he remembered drinking from his uncle's cup when they worked together on the farm in Antioch. Another time, his uncle had fed him from his own bowl during one lean season on the levees. The memories were as painful as a magistrate's bamboo on the frail flesh of an unfilial son.

"Where have you hidden the book?" Pao An asked Lincoln that night. He had returned to their tent after visiting the privy to find the coal oil lamp relit, the flame turned down low.

Lincoln's face fell, embarrassed for having been caught yet again. "Here," Lincoln said, holding out a well-thumbed copy of Edward Everett's orations from beneath his blanket as if it were an excrescence. He had taken it from a stack that Bosworth had given Molly.

Outside the tent, the men were playing a noisy game of *fan-tan* around the fire. Pao An turned the small volume over in his big leathery hand. "What is in this book?"

"Grand phrases, big ideas . . ." Lincoln muttered. "I don't always know what they mean but I like the sound."

"You would rather read than sleep, wouldn't you?" Pao An asked.

"I don't read while I'm working," Lincoln said defensively.

"I know you don't," Pao An growled. "You work hard. You are the best man of all my crew."

Lincoln inclined his head. His uncle's praise was rare and therefore precious.

"You prefer books to anything, especially this . . . the rock, mud, noise, oxen . . . the *fan-tan* game. The road." The words were more statement than accusation.

The lamp threw Pao An's craggy features into cruel relief—the corners of eyes and mouth dragged down by disappointment, the cheeks sagging from exhaustion and care. Seated on his cot, Lincoln raised a hand in mute resignation. He was convinced that his uncle was seething at having raised a boy to manhood only to have him scorn the legacy of sweat and tears constructed on his behalf.

"So, boy," Pao An said gruffly, throwing the book down upon the cot, "I am taking you off the job."

"Why?" Lincoln wailed, a frightened child again. "How have I failed you, Uncle?"

"You have not failed me. I am the one to blame. I have taken away the thing you love."

"No!"

"Tomorrow you leave me. I will get another boy to take your apprenticeship. Go to Bethel Mission or Fort Street Mission or Mills Institute or wherever clever Tang boys go these days to turn themselves into scholars. But be forewarned. Take what you wish from them but believe nothing the *bak kuei* say."

"But you need me!" the boy insisted.

"No. Not now, not anymore." With a gesture of finality, Pao An reached over and turned the little metal knob that stopped the flow of coal oil. The flame instantly shrank and died.

The next day, after Lincoln had departed, Pao An composed a poem, the first he had made in Hawaii, for the urge to make poems had vanished with his domestic responsibilities. Now faced with the dissolution of his house, he felt words welling up like tears.

The son I have is not my own
Only a shadow, myself in miniature,
Hiding, always hiding.

I offer him the earth,
But he refuses, longing instead for the sky.
I ask nothing of him.

We went together, he and I,
Two warriors to tame a mountain.
Side by side, we thrust shovel and pike into the red rock.

I cannot begin to tell you
What it was that
Made him lay a trail toward the west.

I want a sword
To carve out the mountain before him.

An arrow to mark the distance
He must travel
Away from me.

17

OAHU COLLEGE

"Every place is taken this term, boy! There's no room! You savvy?" the headmaster declared with what he hoped was absolute finality, then clapped his hand on his head with a groan as the China boy planted his stubborn self onto the wooden bench at School Hall. The youth had come for what all China boys desired—admission to Oahu College, the only secondary institution in the islands that prepared pupils for American universities. To the eye of the newcomer, the school was simply a barren farm campus in the highlands of Manoa whose most obvious wealth in dry Honolulu was in water, the fabled Kapunahou spring gushing out of a rocky knoll; yet its rigorous curriculum and tenaciously dedicated, though underpaid, teachers were the envy of other private academies serving the children of old-timer *haole* families. Not that the school purposely closed itself off to other races. Founded in 1841 by the Congregational Church's overseas evangelical board to educate the offspring of its missionaries, Oahu College had widened its original charter to include select scholars of the Hawaiian race and, since 1864, a few Chinese. Since then, one or two sons of prominent Chinese Christians were always passing through the upper grades in any given year. These came to Oahu College via the usual channels: nomination by the Chinatown missions or the powerful societies. For the last decade, the headmaster guessed that he had interviewed every bright hope of every surname society and turned down scores of bribes.

Yet never had a China boy with no money, no sponsors, and no visible signs of Christian piety come forward on his own!

The boy had grit, nevertheless, the headmaster allowed. So much so that the headmaster decided to use insidious means to frighten him off. He launched into a vivid account of how Chinese boys were always struck dumb with terror on Declamation Day, when students gave speeches to the visiting public. To the headmaster's chagrin, the boy seemed mildly intrigued by the ordeal. Even the headmaster's description of the "Punahou swing," the tradition by which newcomers were hurled into the muddy taro paddy near the ancient spring, failed to frighten the boy off. As a last resort, the headmaster gave a detailed report of the grueling examinations in classical languages he would have to pass to gain admittance to the higher-level courses. This tactic seemed to engender the expected response, for the boy slipped off the bench and fled straightaway. Better to dash the boy's hopes from the beginning, the headmaster decided, than let the place kill his soul.

But the next day, the boy was found scrubbing the wooden steps to the second-story classrooms of School Hall. And no matter how often the gardener sent him packing, the intruder was soon popping up like the pesky Hawaiian elves called *menehune*—patching up the *kauna,* the mud walls of the taro paddies, after the girls ran races there; harvesting cane in the school fields; lugging pails of water up from the Punahou spring to the trough where the hogs and chickens were fed. The boy got boxed in the ears by the laundryman who found him tinkering with the linen vats and was swatted with a broom by the gardener who found him asleep in a tamarind tree.

"We can't afford another charity case," the headmaster told the boy after he was caught for what seemed the hundredth time eavesdropping outside the Latin class and conjugating verbs in the dirt. "We aren't like those academies endowed by Emma and her brood of Anglicans and Episcopalians. We're hand-to-mouth every term! We have no library. The roof of the dormitories leaks through the thatch, and the floors are warped and rotten. Our teachers' bedrooms run with field mice. Our science lab has a washtub for a pneumatic cistern . . ."

But when the boy seemed profoundly unmoved by the litany of current woes, the headmaster erupted in fury. "I don't understand you Chinese! We do our best for you. We take in one or two of you and a dozen more clamor to take the test. What more do you people want from us?"

Again the boy slipped away. And again he was found, this time sleeping in a wheelbarrow filled with *ti* leaves drawn up behind the pigsty, a hiding place of apparent long standing.

"You're not leaving, eh?" the headmaster barked after prodding the boy awake with the toe of his boot. "Eh, you little beggar?"

The boy shook his head.

"Why won't you give up?" beseeched the headmaster, utterly confounded by a youth who refused to accept that he did not belong. "You have not a single friend in this place. You have no money to pay for books, no preparation for the kind of scholarship we do. I suspect you can't spell or write English as well as the younger children in our preparatory classes! How do you expect to take the upper-level exam with no knowledge of Latin? Give me one reason for staying on where you will always be an undesirable!"

Slowly, with painful deliberation, the boy sat up on his makeshift couch. He slipped something into his mouth and then made an unpleasant noise that sounded to the headmaster like gargling. His face grew red from the effort, and his forehead was knit in concentration.

The sounds made no sense to the headmaster. Was the boy a half-wit? Was he stricken by palsy? These animal gruntings were humiliating to produce let alone to hear. And then out of the growls and clicks and throaty rumblings came a half-formed word, and another. In Latin! *"In . . . c-c-c-cipe p-p-p-ar-ve p-p-p-u . . . er . . . ma-ma-ma-tre-m."*

The boy's accent and pronunciation were atrocious, and he had left off half the line, but the words were unmistakable. The last phrase of Virgil's messianic *Fourth Eclogue,* which the first-year Latin students had been memorizing: "Begin, small boy," the annunciation of a golden age to come.

The headmaster felt like the Philistine Goliath come face-to-face with a Chinese David. The boy was teaching himself to speak Latin, to orate like Demosthenes, the stutterer, who trained by speaking with stones in his mouth. Crazy *pa-ke!*

The headmaster gave a great sigh and did some rapid calculations in his head. Then with a brisk nod, he put out his hand and jerked the boy to his feet.

18

MONGRELS AND STRANGERS

A week before spring vacation, Peter Constable was invited to try out for a place in one of the king's racing canoes. Kalakaua, a gambler in any sport, had a special passion for boat races. To this end, he had built a huge boathouse on the edge of Honolulu Harbor where he kept a fleet of racing canoes and his private yacht. The banquet room above the boat slips could accommodate a score of guests for *luaus* and was rumored to be the site where whiskey, cards, bare-breasted *hula* dancers, and all manner of riotous merrymaking took place. Constable would make a trial run with the fleet as far as Kona on the Big Island. If he rowed well, the king's favor was ensured. Molly must then decide whether to stay a schoolgirl or throw in her lot openly with him.

It was not marriage Constable was proposing but a union "without legal constraint," in the same manner that all the great minds of the age had taken literary companions instead of mere wives. "You will be Mary Godwin to my Shelley," he declared expansively. "With you to regulate my habits, I'll write a thousand epics!" he vowed.

Worn down by Constable's pleading, Molly looked forward to the Easter holidays for the respite it would bring from him. This time, she vowed not to pine for her lover. Yet when she arrived at the Chinatown house expecting sanctuary, she discovered only enmity. She fought with her mother over the upcoming Ching Ming rites and quarreled with Lincoln over his refusal of a scholarship to the fashionable St. Albans in order to take his chances at passing the Latin examination at Oahu College.

"You are the most shortsighted person I know!" she told him in English at the dinner table. They had just finished their meal, and she had left a portion of *mui* uneaten simply to vex him. When she saw his eyes wandering to the bowl, she plucked the remaining plums out with her chopsticks and popped them into her mouth with glee. "You will always lose what you desire!"

"Everything but my honor," Lincoln replied.

"Speak Chinese in this house," Pao An growled.

"Honor? You?" Molly scoffed in English before switching to Cantonese, not so much to please her father but to make her words more galling to Lincoln. "No one knows you or regards you at all—what 'face' do you have to lose?"

"I said 'honor,' not 'face.' Honor is not dependent on another person's regard. I have my principles," Lincoln responded.

Molly tossed her head and rolled her eyes. "What valor."

Rulan rose from the table with such alacrity that she knocked over her chair. She began grabbing up bowls and platters and utensils, even the chopsticks that Molly still held in her hand. She took a rag and scrubbed the ancient table so vigorously that she scraped her knuckles. "A tree lives by its bark. A decent girl ought to live to preserve her face," she muttered between clenched teeth.

*T*he *rat-tat-tat* of Rulan's cleaver echoed through the house. Pao An and Lincoln had left to order a pig slaughtered and roasted for Ching Ming. Rulan was furious . . . and frightened. There were telltale signs no mother could ignore. A stained handkerchief wadded in the pocket of her daughter's skirt. A lace petticoat torn up one side. Even the languid way her daughter walked was new and knowingly wanton.

They ate pork hash mixed with salted duck egg every night, for Rulan hammered each piece of meat her husband brought home from the market into a pulp with the cleaver. Bowls were thrown in a fury upon the table, chopsticks flung at their owners, dishes seasoned with no thought of balance or taste. The woman for whom food was a measure of love could not eat what she cooked; she stared in stony silence into her bowl. The rice stuck to the roof of her mouth. She could not swallow. Even the girl's touch was an affront. For now Molly made a comical noise when she embraced her mother—*oof!*—as if disavowing her mother's flesh. She called Rulan "Mother" like a conceited *haole,* not "Ma-ma," as a Chinese daughter ought. Who had taught her such disrespect?

Rulan's distress expressed itself in an ever more frantic intrusiveness that inspired in Molly a desperate longing to escape. She guessed that Rulan knew her secret. *Since she already believes me wicked, let her stew,* Molly decided. There was no hope to regain her mother's trust. She would show her mother how bad she could be! Having stepped on the road of iniquity, she would leapfrog her way down to hell! Strip the bark from the tree, throw off what was left of honor and face and good name, and run with open arms to join the deceivers her family despised!

Ching Ming that year was a lonely affair with only Pao An, Lincoln, and Rulan at the grave. Easter passed with no sense of atonement, only more sorrow. When the young people departed for school, Rulan was left with a sense of dread that Lincoln's letters only deepened. He was happy with his classes and confident of passing the Latin exam, but when he went to Sunday services at the cathedral, Molly had not appeared with the Priory girls.

"*I* got it, Mol," Constable crowed, swinging her around in the air. They spun and spun across the grass under the old *hala* tree in the moonlight.

"Quiet!" she said, giggling. "The sisters will hear us. Got what?"

"The appointment, signed by Wylie, the prime minister, and stamped with the king's seal! It was my strong arm in the king's canoe that won his eye! I'm the official translator for the legislature, Molly. Supervised by the great Gibson himself! Business is conducted in Hawaiian and English and every speaker must be heard. So that sets me at the very nexus of power. I control the flow of words in every arena of law!"

Molly kissed his lips and burrowed contentedly into Constable's arms. The rough wool of his coat scraped against her cheek. She felt his hands slip under the thin cloth of her chemise.

"I'll be making a proper salary. Not a ransom, mind you, but enough for two."

"Is that a proposal?" she asked. So far she had refused to quit school and move in with him. And even if he did propose, she had the suspicion that marriage to Constable might be more risky than living in sin.

"I'm not trapped that easily, my girl," he said mischievously, lifting her

off the ground to bring her to eye level. "It's an invitation to utter deca-
dence. We'll lie together every night, and make love until the afternoon."

"Hush," she said, blushing and holding her hands over her ears in
mock-chagrin.

"Admit it! You love it as much as I. And will wear me out in a year."
He put her down with a bump. "Look, Mol," he added in a rush, "you've
got to get away this Saturday. Some friends are giving me a celebration. Tell
the harridans at school that you're going to a church meeting or some such
rot and sneak away for the night."

Molly was thrilled at the invitation. Her first grown-up party in society—and on the arm of her lover! "The sisters watch my every move," she
replied. "But they believe anything about the Bosworths. Maybe if I tell
them I'm invited to Hiamoe for the weekend. I can do Auntie Lucy's hand
quite well . . ."

"Capital! It's settled. I'll buy you a dress that shows you off to advantage. The swells already envy me my position. Think what they'll say when
they see my little China flower on my arm!"

Molly had never heard him use such a phrase before. She smiled
sweetly while bristling inside at the absurd epithet.

The ruse worked. Mother Juliana released her in exchange for a jar of
Lucy's preserves stored in her locker. Constable met her on a corner and
drove her down to his rooms where a dress of yellow silk was spread out
upon the bed. There was a tight stomacher of black satin that cinched her
waist and pushed up her small breasts in an odd and inviting way, black
fingerless gloves, a black feather fan and matching headpiece for her hair,
and a purse of black lace and netting to dangle off her arm. She thought
that the outfit made her look like a trollop, but he assured her that she
looked "smashing."

The broad boulevards of Honolulu glistened with rain as the lovers
rode after sundown in a hired hack to Waikiki. They passed the wetlands
where Hawaiians and Tang men grew taro and rice, then came at last to the
long coastline of white sand curving outward to the tip of Diamond Hill.
Once the exclusive playground of the *alii,* Waikiki had been reborn in the
prosperous era of Kalakaua into a tropical Brighton Beach, where residents
flocked by omnibus in record numbers to escape the heat of Honolulu.
There were public bathhouses for swimmers to take their ease, a racetrack
in nearby Kapiolani Park for betting and sport. And when one grew tired
of sand and races and baseball, there were miles of coconut groves to stroll
through. Many of Honolulu's new moneyed elite had built their mansions
among the groves, the most splendid of which was Ainahau, the seaside

villa of Princess Kaiulani, the king's half-Scottish niece and the only surviving child of the royal clan.

Molly felt giddy and grown-up, her color high from lovemaking. The
night breeze swept like velvet against her bare shoulders. Constable directed
the driver down a narrow winding lane to a beachfront cottage on the
king's estate, which a young chieftain from Kona used as a temporary
residence and a pleasure spot for his friends.

A dozen men, light and dark skinned, and half as many women raised a
halloo when Constable entered. "Here's the new prevaricator," someone
yelled.

"Ganymede, the cupbearer of the gods."

"A toast, a toast!"

The Waikiki cottage had been built in Emma's reign to house the royal
retainers whenever she and her young husband and son wanted to escape
the rigors of kingship. The original grass hut had been torn down by
Kalakaua and replaced by a wood-frame cottage refurbished for royal tastes,
with glistening koa wood floors lined with China rugs, velvet armchairs,
two heavy leaf-style hutches filled with glassware and plates, and large
windows open to the sea. Molly found herself quickly taken up by a trio of
noisy, overdressed women who were as drunk as the men. One woman, a
Hawaiian in a tight *holoku,* had hair that flowed over her shoulders to the
backs of her knees.

"Aloha, aloha," she murmured, rubbing her nose on Molly's in a
Hawaiian-style kiss. She touched Molly's hair and inspected her costume.
"Auwe, so expensive," she said in a lilting, lazy voice, pinching the fabric of
the skirt. "Peter must like you better than the others."

Molly refused a glass of peach brandy and asked for lemon crush
instead. The girl who brought it laughed heartily when Molly grimaced
and commented on the bitter taste. "True, dear," she replied, "the gin's
not the best."

On the other side of the room, Molly saw that Constable was caught
up in what looked like an altercation. He and his companions were shouting oaths while downing glasses of brandy as fast as the servant brought
them.

But when she asked her long-haired companion if Constable was in
any danger, the girl snickered and told her that they were merely discussing
politics. "Soon they'll be talked out and the *welekahao* will begin." The
Hawaiian word, with its delicious suggestion of ribald festivity, made Molly
feel that she had passed from childhood into a realm of sophistication and
adventure.

The room was soon stifling hot and dense with smoke from the men's cigars. Someone began to strum on a mandolin, which prompted the long-haired girl to begin a sensuous *hula* accompanied by the young chieftain, his collar undone, who banged on the table, using it like a drum. Couples disappeared outside, then reappeared again, sleepy and covered with sand. Constable was loudly holding forth in the midst of a knot of men when Molly slipped beside him. He stopped talking at her approach, momentarily distracted, as if he had forgotten who she was. Then he put a possessive arm around her, as puffed up with pride as a rooster at sunrise. He had an opinion on everything and from the approbation of his colleagues was voicing it magnificently. His talk kindled in Molly's mind more insights about Hawaii than she had ever had before, although when she tried to sort her thoughts out later, she was not able to recall what it was that had seemed so profound.

In the midst of a debate over the large sums of money Walter Murray Gibson was spending for the king's upcoming coronation, the crowd around Constable was diverted by angry shouts outside. There, on the sand under the coconut trees, four men were struggling drunkenly with the royal tenant of the cottage. Some men cheered and jumped down from the veranda to join the fray. The women screamed. Then the young chief, bleeding profusely from his nose, staggered out from the pile of struggling bodies and fired a pistol into the air.

"You're all under arrest," he shouted.

The guests thought it a great joke, and the *welekahao* continued with renewed fervor until guards arrived from the palace. At eight the next morning, the police escorted Molly home to Chinatown.

*P*lunged into the comforting routine at the shop, Rulan had gulled herself into believing that her daughter's rebellion was finally waning. The last reports from the Priory sisters were heartening: Molly was putting her mind to books again. Even the girl's attachment to Lucy, Rulan allowed, was a good thing, for if a boy had taken her innocence and broken her heart, at least she was turning to a trusted auntie. And then came the news that Molly had been caught in an act of monumental stupidity. Found in the midst of a drunken riot among court scoundrels and prostitutes! The letter of expulsion was delivered by messenger from the Priory minutes after the culprit was returned in disgrace. Rulan could not recognize the girl that the sleepy policeman brought to their door. Was this sullen, frowsy stranger in a stained yellow gown her child?

And when Rulan demanded to know why Molly had disgraced herself with such *la sap,* the girl declared carelessly that she had done no wrong.

The sin was theirs—her parents', the Priory sisters'—for keeping her from the only man she would ever love: a penniless *hapa haole* with a petty government post.

There wasn't anyone for Rulan to talk through the hurt with. Lincoln was at boarding school on the Kapunahou grounds. Lucy would always take the culprit's part. Rulan steeled herself to bear her daughter's shame, but the mere thought of that was agony when she remembered the terrible things said and done the morning of Molly's return: the way Molly recoiled when her mother tried to touch her, or when Pao An struck his daughter, shouting that he was going to marry her off to the first Tang man who offered for her. And Molly herself foolishly crying that her parents had spoiled her life, suffocated her at home, that Constable was a genius, when any person could see that this *la sap* was poisoning their family like an adder slinking into a nest. Molly went around the house sullen and brooding while tenderhearted Lucy counseled repentance and forgiveness. It was best to let the young man see her, Lucy counseled, best to let the heat run its course. . . . And everyone trying to skirt the obvious: that the girl had been for months with that *la sap,* in taverns and eating houses and in one room with one bed.

Rulan recognized that Molly's actions fit a familiar pattern: never satisfied with what was in her bowl, always wanting more or someone else's share. Always nursing grudges against the ones who meant no ill, preferring the outsider, the enemy, rather than the loved ones close by. The wilfulness was an inheritance from Pao An who, like his daughter, nursed a rebel's heart under the appearance of stolidity. It was silly, it was naive, but unstoppable, this belief father and daughter shared that nothing in the present mattered, no error needed mending. What if today the deal went sour, the crew made mistakes, what if one were branded a whore? Tomorrow brought the glorious dawn erasing the night . . .

*C*onstable was no stranger to Pao An; the man was notorious to downtown tradesmen as much for his vices as for his inability to support them. The two had even come face-to-face in a bizarre and, for Pao An, prophetic encounter six months before.

One of Pao An's work crews had been contracted to repair the broken tiles on the roof of the Honolulu Hotel, a two-story structure with wide verandas and curved porticos where dignitaries and pretenders, newly minted merchant princes, and young *alii* mingled freely (and scandalously) along its candlelit corridors and darkened *lanais*.

Pao An found these swells as abhorrent as their dance music. He himself had neither time nor desire for play. Nor would he countenance such frivolous behavior among the men he employed. His business was always cash poor, the profits from one project used to buy equipment for the next. One misstep could ruin the fragile balance of the whole. Thus, night after night, Pao An haggled with the German hotel manager over the wages due his crew while a stone's throw away, men in dark coats and women in gleaming *holokus* drank brandy and champagne and twirled breast to breast on the outdoor dance floor to the brassy strains of a Vienna waltz.

On such an evening, Pao An had been standing under the boughs of a tamarind tree waiting to be paid his day's wages when a parade of young dandies and their sweethearts streamed off the veranda onto the wet ground, their glasses held high. At the tail end of the noisy throng ran a young woman in a wine red *holoku,* followed by a handsome youth with skin the brown-gold color of tea. "Mapuana," he called, howled, really, as if he were a hound in mid-chase.

The girl named Mapuana darted behind the tamarind tree, coming so close to Pao An that her long skirts brushed over his straw sandals. In his haste to grab the girl, the youth fell against Pao An, and for a moment, both men swayed together in lockstep, like dancers in a waltz, the young man staring wild-eyed into the Tang man's startled face. Then he shoved Pao An aside with an impatient oath, caught the woman by the waist and swung her into the air. The girl threw back her head for his kiss, her long hair brushing the ground.

"Good Lord, Peter. Can't you two wait?" someone yelled.

The youth grinned, showing perfectly even white teeth. But when he bent to kiss the girl's neck, she tore herself loose and darted away, and again the hunt was on. This time when he caught her, he grabbed her by the buttocks and spun her around with a wink at his fellow revelers. Shrieking, she whirled about and to the crowd's delight, struck the man on the cheek. The revelers roared.

In the next instant, the man slapped the girl back, so hard that her head snapped to one side. The party stopped its raucous merrymaking to stare.

The blow seemed to do what caresses could not. For the girl leaned toward her pursuer with a whimper; now it was *her* lips that sought his, *her* hands that roamed across his back. They clung together a long while before stumbling off behind the drunken band.

It was his own fault that his girl had gone bad, Pao An conceded, for he had been soft when he should have been strict, tender when he should have been sharp. And so he had loosed her from his hand. And what had happened? She had made herself hostage to a creature of monstrous appetites who would drain her sweetness, break her body, kill her spirit as surely as Creel had done to Vera. His duty as a father was clear: he would hire the go-between to arrange a marriage with a decent Tang man. The girl would cry, of course, claim that she would die for love and sorrow, but in the end, she would submit. In the end, she would thank him. For what did this girl truly know of love or sorrow, except the lies she had read in the books Lucy had given her? Family, decency, duty—these were more important than a fleeting romance with a brute.

*E*xhaustion settled like a dark shroud over the household. Then Pao An appeared with the go-between, making real what neither Rulan nor Molly had believed he would ever do.

While Pao An stood aside like a prison guard, the go-between put on the table photographs of four Tang men who had offered for Molly: a sugar merchant from Kauai who was looking for a new wife after his Hawaiian one had run away, a foreman from a Big Island plantation, a widower with a pig farm outside Wahiawa, a tailor in Honolulu. "Look, look, all decent men," the woman babbled officiously. "No debts. All good providers."

"And every one a toothless old man!" Molly blurted out in fury.

"*Aaiiee,* what a caustic tongue for a young girl who does not know how much her price has fallen," the woman clucked reproachfully. "Tang girls are like gold in Hawaii, but a bad-luck girl who has lost face for her family is cheap goods. Be grateful to your father for offering half his hardware business as a dowry," she told Molly, "otherwise no man would come forward at all. Of course," she added, "negotiations are off if you are *hapai.* No decent Tang man wants to pollute his line with a barbarian bastard."

"Mother . . ." was all the stricken Molly could say, but already Rulan had snatched up the photographs and, ignoring her husband's protests, propelled the old woman out the door.

After the go-between had gone, the battle between husband and wife raged in full view of their startled daughter, who had never seen her parents fight before. "You're selling our girl," Rulan accused, "like fathers did in starving times! How could you, knowing what was done to me! Knowing that we went to war to end those evil ways!"

"Then the old ways are best," Pao An asserted stubbornly. "The girl is headed for ruin. It is a father's job to protect his own. The girl is too young to know her own mind. This way, I know she will be safe."

"Safe? You have no idea how vulnerable a woman can be if the match turns out badly!" Rulan declared. "How could you sell her off when you and I chose each other freely?"

"We are different," he insisted. "This girl will destroy herself if we let her follow her desires. I have made up my mind. Even a pig farmer is better than that *la sap*. If she does not choose from the four men, I will choose for her."

Pao An made a bed for himself in the store that night away from his wife and daughter. In the morning, after he had left for town, Rulan found her daughter stuffing her school valise with clothes and books.

"He doesn't mean it," she told Molly. "He doesn't know how else to be a father but to scold and threaten . . ."

"Don't make excuses for him," Molly shot back. "He intends to make that awful woman earn her fee."

"Patience. He'll come round. He always does," Rulan pleaded. When Molly continued packing, Rulan blurted out in despair, "There's no going back this time."

"I know."

"But why pick a man who will never marry you? Are you seeking revenge on your father? Because if you are—"

"It isn't him," Molly admitted. "It's me! Even if you could make Father give up his pathetic idea of marrying me off in the old style, what would happen then? I'd still be 'cheap goods' in Chinatown. You can't know what it's like to be different, to look one way and feel another. To hear the whispers and know that people are laughing at you. Peter says that we are both *poi* dogs, mongrels, strangers in our own skin. This is the one chance I have to do something on my own. . . . You'll be proud of me one day, I promise." But Rulan saw that Molly, by going with this *la sap,* intended to pluck herself out of the family, roots and all.

Molly hugged her mother. And there she went, there she went, into the deceiver's arms.

The New
Hawaiian

1

"HE CROWNED HIMSELF!"

February 12, 1883

"A glorious new beginning for Hawaii-*nei*," Constable exulted as Molly reached up to pull the ends of his starched wing collar straight. "And you and I are to play a part in it, Mol. Those stiff-necked, stuffed-shirt, Congregationalist *haoles* who have directed the Hawaiians' destiny so long will have to yield control now! No more calling us savages . . . except in matters of love—" and here he playfully brushed his mustaches against Molly's cheek, eagerly seeking her lips.

His black beaver-skin hat was from San Francisco; his dark morning coat and light-colored trousers were sewn by a Chinatown tailor; his linen and boots were London made; a gold watch was tucked into the pocket of his waistcoat—and he had grown a mustache and side whiskers to look like Curtis Iaukea, the kinsman of the king, who had mastered three languages and would go, directly after the coronation, on a grand tour of the courts of Europe.

Molly thought the whiskers made him look more like the "doddering graybeards" whom he professed to despise. "Be still, or I'll never get this fastened," she said in mock-fury, pulling free of his embrace.

"The hour of the New Hawaiian approaches," Constable proclaimed in stentorian tones to his image in the oak-framed mirror in the vestibule of the wharfside tenement he had rented for Molly and himself. He waved his hands in imitation of Walter Murray Gibson in the heat of debate while Molly ducked and weaved. "The king has a new palace, and I have a new gold watch! He *will* be crowned, and I *will*—for once!—be on time!"

"There!" Molly pronounced, patting the knot of his tie. "Now you look quite distinguished."

"Distinguished enough to turn the heads of every fair *wahine* when I read at the *luau*?" Constable teased. He had been engaged by Gibson, the newly appointed premier of Hawaii, to read an original poetic composition commemorating the Kalakaua dynasty that night at the first of the postcoronation *luaus* and again at the unveiling of the new Kamehameha statue two days hence. Gibson's commission had raised Constable's hopes to unnatural heights; he was convinced that a cabinet post was a poem away.

"No *wahine* will be able to taste her *poi* after gazing on you, Mr. False Pride," Molly said.

Constable clapped his hat on his head and admired his reflection in the clouded glass, declaring himself "too, too bloody *maikai*!" He was lacing his speech these days with Hawaiian slang, for it was the fashion in Honolulu for young bloods to mimic the neo-native style of Kalakaua and Kapiolani, his queen. This meant decking oneself out in British fashions in public while lounging on *hala* mats at home; singing the king's compositions to Western guitars; and mixing into the old *hulas* a few waltz turns. Kalakaua's resurrection of native song and dance in defiance of the long-held strictures of the Christian community had enormous appeal for Constable, who had tried the white man's ways in England only to be made to feel a "black imposter in a frock coat." The translating Constable did for Gibson in the legislature had brought him into what he called "intimate association" with the king although, if truth be told, that intimacy had happened only once, when Constable substituted for an absent regular in a high-stakes card game. He had not yet been invited to the new palace, a slight that bruised his pride; certainly he had not penetrated the inner circle of trusted *alii* around Kalakaua, which was rumored to be planning a return of the ancient priestly rites of the *kahuna* as a way of appeasing whatever gods were allowing the native people to die out at an alarming rate.

Molly had pulled her unruly hair away from her face into a fashionable bun at the back of her head and anchored it with hairpins and combs. It was a grown-up hairstyle, as neat, smooth, and controlled as her newly minted image of herself. Eager to please her lover, she had planned her coronation outfit to the smallest gusset and pleat, yet her sentiments regarding the occasion were more complicated than his. She was uneasy, not only about confronting familiar faces from the Priory or from Chinatown but about the huge sums of money Constable had spent to outfit them both.

"I still don't know why the king's doing this when he's been ruling for nine years," Molly grumbled, echoing the sentiments she had read in her uncle's columns in the *Dispatch,* an anti-Gibson publication Constable had banned from their house but that she read on the sly.

"*Auwe,* girl!" Constable declared in exasperation. "You sound like Blunderbuss Bosworth, always counting pennies! This is a king who will someday be head of an island federation in the Pacific, a future empire of Oceania! Kalakaua can do what he likes! Besides, great nations love ceremony and splendor! And what else but a coronation would attract an Indian maharajah and an emissary from the emperor of Japan to these islands?"

"Will Emma come?" Molly asked nervously while buttoning her gloves. Confronting the disapproving stares of the dowager queen and the Priory matrons was the one thing that marred Molly's joy in her daring new costume, which she had copied off a visiting Frenchwoman's *carte-de-visite.* Despite the high piecrust neck frill, the gown left nothing to the imagination, for it hugged the body from neck to knees. Nor would the Priory matrons approve of the color—virginal white—for one as steeped in sin as she.

"Emma and her dour retinue have refused the invitations," Constable replied, brushing a speck of dust from his boots. "They're so jealous of the king's relations, they can't stand watching them preen." Constable put his whiskery cheek next to hers and whispered, "Any regrets for being made a fallen woman?"

She hugged him so hard that the stiff new wool of his jacket scratched her bare arms. "There was nothing for me till now," she whispered into the warmth of his neck. "With you, I have a place in this grand new kingdom!"

He swept her up in his arms and twirled her round and round in the small vestibule. "Oh, what wonders are in store for us, Mol!"

By the time the hansom cab had dropped them at the edge of the palace grounds, Molly was as giddy as Constable. Iolani Palace sat like a great white Florentine wedding cake in the midst of the royal park: an edifice three stories high surmounted by towers at each corner with galleries running along the sides. It had cost triple the sum the legislature had initially set aside, but to Molly's eager eyes, the splendid stone structure was worth every coin!

They ran hand in hand across the boulevard from Aliiolani Hale, the government building where Constable labored each day, through the gates of the palace. Hundreds were already milling about the open yard, hundreds more climbing over the bleachers for the choicest seats in the front rows. Grizzled grandfathers in their one good pair of trousers leaned on the shoulders of young girls in home-sewn *holokus*; youths in straw hats and suspenders with coconut-husk cigars clenched between their teeth strolled arm in arm with their sweethearts. Many Hawaiians wore strings of *maile* or *pakalana* or fanciful *hoku*-style garlands sewn with varicolored berries, blossoms, and vines. Folk from the rural districts hastened in from the direction of Kapiolani Park where they had set up a makeshift camp to enjoy the weeklong festivities.

Constable led Molly to a shaded section of the bleachers cordoned off with rope for the families of legislators and government officials and left her amid a sea of Hawaiian matrons and their children.

"As soon as the benediction is pronounced, run straightaway to where the cab dropped us, and we'll go together to the *luau*. I need you to bring me luck." He kissed her hand, a gesture that set the women in the stands twittering.

Proudly, Molly watched him stride away, conscious of female eyes following Constable's tall, lithe form. Without looking around, she sensed the precise moment when the eyes shifted to her, scanning with envy and dislike her tight dress, her hairstyle, every movement of her body. She had stolen away a promising *alii* youth at a time when Hawaiian women of marriageable age outnumbered their men two to one. Well, she would show all Hawaii that Peter Constable had not erred in allying himself with the daughter of Chinatown shopkeepers! His cause was hers, his future her own. It was a matter of time before Peter would be tapped for office by Kalakaua, who was in the habit of dissolving his cabinet whenever a new face or a new cause seized his fancy. Even now, Peter was taking his place among the top-hatted officials massed around the crown-shaped circular pavilion where the coronation was to take place. *Haoles* overwhelmed Hawaiians in those sections, and their mood was grim.

From her perch in the stands, Molly caught sight of Lucy's bright head. Her aunt had arranged her hair in masses of old-fashioned curls and plaits and was wearing a high-necked dress of shiny striped black stuff, which despite its elaborate ruching and the gold chatelaine wound around her waist gave the appearance of severity. Bosworth was standing a few feet from his wife in a state of high indignation. His arms were pumping as he harangued a native legislator and a pair of Royal Guards, his face as red as an overripe mango. Her uncle would choose to mar this glorious occasion with political disagreements, she told herself impatiently. If only he were not so disapproving, so combative, so . . . *haole*! Yet what struck Molly more than the discomfort of the couple was how old Emmanuel and Lucy had grown. When had Emmanuel's hair turned from copper to gray? And when had dainty Lucy grown a waist rounder than the brim of a man's straw hat? Molly regretted the months she had avoided their company. The breach with her parents had been extended to the Bosworths, whose politics Constable despised. The enmity between Bosworth and Walter Murray Gibson had grown particularly bitter over the last months, for Gibson was the chief architect of the coronation; and for once, the faction-ridden *haole* community had come together in vociferous opposition to the vast sums of money spent on it.

Molly soon lost sight of her uncle and auntie among the thousands who were now rushing across the grounds and into the stands. A blur of dark and light faces passed before her. The heady perfume of flowers clogged her nostrils. The din rose to a deafening pitch. Just as the noise became unbearable, the Royal Hawaiian Band struck up a tune, the crowd quieted down, and in marched hundreds of students carrying the pennants of their schools. Molly craned her neck to catch sight of the delegation from Oahu College and saw a slim Chinese youth proudly holding aloft the blue banner emblazoned with a gold *hala* tree. When had Lincoln grown so tall and his step so assured? Her excitement at seeing him was heightened by the storm of cheers and whistles from the young men in the crowd. The Priory girls were coming! The young women made a striking appearance in white *holokus* with garlands of orange *ilima* blossoms threaded through their long hair. Then a contingent of Tang men marched forth in black coats and skullcaps and took their seats in a corner cordoned off for them in the theater. Pao An, undoubtedly, was among them, for Molly had heard how he had gathered a delegation of Hakka and Punti from the Chinese Union in honor of the occasion. A pity, she decided, that the man who brought reconciliation to a feuding people was the agent of discord in his own home!

By eleven o'clock, the sun poured down on the palace grounds. Babies were wailing, dogs barking; the band was sweating through thick layers of wool. Several singers in the Hawaiian choruses had fainted and were passed over the heads of the crowd to Emma's hospital.

At first, no one in the noisy crowd heard the long, low pulse of sound that came from the direction of the palace. The conch trumpet came again, the ancient instrument that summoned the coming of a king. *"Ka moi! Ka moi!"* came the cries of those closest to the dais. "The king!" A moment afterward, the choir burst into song. Mellow Hawaiian voices filled the great dome of the theater, winding in complicated harmonies to the very sky. "Almighty Father, hear!" the choir sang. "The isles do wait on thee."

Then the great doors of the palace opened, and through the portals stepped the royals like a line of peacocks in full plumage.

Awesome when carried half-naked on the shoulders of commonfolk a century before, the *alii* were magnificent still. Western finery made them appear more splendid and huge.

Kalakaua wore the scarlet-and-blue uniform of the Royal Guard, although no guardsman sported such a thick mustache or such a wealth of gold braid or walked with more dignity than the first of the dynasty Keawe-a-Heulu, who had defied the *haoles* by the very grandeur of this occasion and given his surviving people back their pride.

Slowly, he stepped across a long white bridge to the pavilion constructed in the shape of the very crown that would grace his head. There, in the pavilion, the tokens of native kingship were put into his hands by the queen's sister: the *lei niho palau,* the whale-tooth pendant hanging from a necklace of human hair; the *kahili,* the kingly standard; the *puloulou;* the *kapu* stick. Then the red-and-gold cloak of the first Kamehameha, fashioned of thousands of feathers from nearly extinct birds, was placed over Kalakaua's shoulders.

When the oath of office had been delivered, the conch sounded, and Hawaiian voices were once more raised in song, a prelude to the coronation itself. The conch sounded. The velvet-and-gold crown was passed from president to chancellor until, without warning, the king put his hand onto the maltese cross at the top of the crown and in one swift movement clapped the crown onto his head. Then with his own hands, Kalakaua placed a smaller crown, identical to his, on the head of his queen.

The conch sounded again. Cheers rose and fell and rose again in great throbbing echoes as king and queen knelt before their people. And now the noise was so deafening that in the crowd, the babies wailed in alarm, for with the cannons booming, they could not tell the difference between war and celebration.

The benediction came all too soon; and Molly, making her way through the throng in search of Constable, found herself swept along with the thousands in the amphitheater who rushed forward to catch the last sight of their king crossing the bridge into the palace. A perfect moment except for what she heard in the hush between the cannons' roar: a voice behind her, unmistakably British, muttering in indignation, "Cheeky black bastard! He's crowned himself, like Napoleon!"

Suddenly, Molly heard a familiar voice crying "Help him! Help him!" over the hubbub. All thoughts of her rendezvous with Constable flew out of Molly's head. "Auntie," she called, frantically pushing through a knot of men. Molly quickly saw that the danger did not lie with Lucy but with the crumpled form of Emmanuel Bosworth.

"Don't die," Lucy begged her husband, while Molly struggled to loosen his collar with trembling fingers. "Don't leave me alone!"

To his credit, Constable did indeed wait for Molly a brief while, except that his comrades soon drove by in a huge cane wagon they had commandeered. He told himself that Molly would find her own way to the *luau* and climbed in beside a score of revelers packed like cattle in the wagon. Even before the driver had flicked a whip across the team's flanks, they were passing around a bottle of home-brewed *okolehao* and calling out to a pair of comely *wahine* to join them.

A mighty stream of merrymakers now clogged the streets. The Hawaiians were shouting their joy at claiming their rightful place at the head of the islands of Oceania. Among the loudest was Constable, who declaimed his verses all the way to the boathouse *luau* to the enthusiastic applause of his companions.

Yet the triumph Constable anticipated did not come to pass. He stumbled badly in the reading of his poem and saw the acclaim that should have been his go instead to a troupe of young dancers from Dandy Ioane's *hula* school. This humiliation led to a strenuous bout of angry drinking, followed by hours of recrimination. He returned to Molly sober enough to blame her for his failure. She had deserted him in his hour of need! He had no sympathy when told of Bosworth's perilous condition. Stroke and paralysis were the natural consequences of age, he told her. That she had chosen an ailing old man over him made her betrayal more heinous.

"You never meant for me to succeed!" he raged.

Molly was forced to sneak visits to the sickroom at Hiamoe to avoid another row.

2

A WRITER IN DISGUISE

Contrary to the pessimistic prognosis of Dr. Hunnicut, who attended him, Bosworth neither withered nor died. His speech was slurred by the stroke though not nearly enough to render him less opinionated. Lucy ruthlessly policed the conversation in the sickroom, fearing that any account of the coronation galas would excite him to apoplectic outrage.

After the first week's feasting, the merrymaking had continued with the coronation ball; a regatta on the canal; races at Kapiolani Park. The Chinese Fire Department (with steam engine in tow) made a splendid showing at the coronation parade, winning applause for their colorful display of triangular yellow banners, their new uniforms and the precision of their marching. Even baseball, an outrageously dull game played with a wooden stick and leather ball, brought crowds to Kapiolani Park to watch, the sons of American and British dignitaries play. Constable yearned to join the British team but had not been invited. The height of public frenzy was the coronation *luau,* a lavish feast for five thousand revelers that began at noon and lasted into the night with dancers swaying to the stately *Kaulilua;* the name-chant of the king, and *Au'a ia,* the prophetic chant that

the king had appropriated for his house, both sacred *meles,* which had not
been performed since the temples were razed by missionaries.

As what he called the "coronation abominations" ended, Bosworth
became his old self again, except for the fact that his right arm and leg were
virtually useless. Furious at having to lie abed with sin running rampant in
the streets, the patient made plain his readiness to return to the newspaper—"pushed about in a wheelbarrow if necessary." But Hunnicut forbade
the servants to carry him a step beyond the door of the sickroom.

"How's the *Dispatch* to be published then?" Bosworth croaked, kicking
up his bed covers with his one good leg.

"Without you" was Hunnicut's blunt reply.

If Hunnicut was severe, Lucy was immovable. With both doctor and
wife united against him, Bosworth laid elaborate plans for escape. But the
trail of overturned furniture in his wake was too easy to follow and when
his third attempt to sneak away to his downtown office was foiled by the
new *wahine hana,* he declared himself shorn of his right of free speech and
gave himself up to gloom. Lucy smiled triumphantly, tucked the covers
under her husband's chin and planted a kiss on his furrowed brow.

It was a sympathetic Molly who acceded to Bosworth's secret strategy
to circumvent his wife's policing. Molly would serve as her uncle's aide-de-
camp in the war of words with his political foes. "You go in and out of
Aliiolani Hale, where the legislature meets, all the time. You are known to
Constable's colleagues—Gibson and William Auld and the younger set
besides. You will listen and tell me what they say on the floor of the
house . . ."

His offer incited a warm response in Molly. While reporting was not
poetry, both Shelley and Byron had made political discourse and advocacy
a noble calling for poets!

"You will be my eyes and ears and legs about town and in the Hale!"
he enthused. Yet he cautioned her not to tell "that reprobate Constable"
what she was reporting. "I am afraid I have compromised you, my
dear," he told her, "but no more than you have done yourself."

So he acknowledged the worst . . . and still loved her, Molly
thought. Would that her father could do the same.

*P*ao An had banned the mention of Molly's name in his presence, a
stricture that his wife, with characteristic stubbornness, refused to obey.
Rulan reminded him of his role in inciting their daughter's departure with
such maddening regularity that there was no harmony between them. After

every quarrel, Pao An stormed off to one of his construction camps outside Honolulu and slept in a tent with his men.

Rulan tried to kindle his pity. "Yesterday Lucy told me that Molly borrowed money. The *la sap* is spending far more than he earns. There are debts to his tailor, to the landlord, to his gambling friends. I do not know how he maintains our daughter—"

"I have no daughter," Pao An snapped, pushing the air with his hand as if to erase the memory of Molly from his house.

"You cannot mean that!" Rulan blurted out. "If she were drowning, you would rush into the sea to save her, *hai ma*?"

"She wants to drown," Pao An retorted and turned away.

*L*incoln walked from the Manoa campus to the Chinatown store on Sunday afternoons, an envoy caught between two enemy camps, unable to broker a truce. Husband and wife kept ruthlessly to their separate spheres: one inside the store, the other in the yard. Yet for all Rulan's fussing in the medicine-kitchen or selling floor, he observed that she moved with a heavy tread and the house bore an air of abandonment. By contrast, Pao An worked in a kind of frenzy. Every project took the form of war: a door warped from heat and rain that had to be mercilessly shaved down, a rotten section of stairs that had to be ripped apart. When he discovered in renovating a cottage in the Mission Compound that termites had eaten through the wallpaper of an entire wall, he mixed wallpaper paste with pepper to drive them away. Soon his hatred for these voracious island pests took the form of a violent vendetta. He spent hours concocting poisons to pour onto termite nests; and when those failed to stop them from burrowing into wood, he burned the nests out with kerosene.

Lincoln found his uncle's campaign against the termites absurd. "Your business cannot thrive without termites," he reminded Pao An. "You build up what they tear down."

But Pao An muttered, "They are a pestilence, a scourge against nature. All they do is destroy, destroy. How utterly useless for such creatures to exist in this world." And although there were no signs of termite damage to his own house, Pao An made Lincoln help him dig up the corner posts on which the building sat, pour turpentine into the holes left in the earth, then sink new wooden pillars coated in tar on top of the coral block footings. When they had finished, the two men sat together in uneasy silence gulping down bowls of hot tea.

"This house is getting old . . . like your uncle," Pao An declared with a tired sigh. "Maybe I die soon."

Lincoln's hands froze with the bowl halfway to his mouth. He put it down gently. Pao An was talking about death more and more.

"When I die," Pao An went on doggedly, "auntie will be alone. I want you to build another house—"

But Lincoln stopped him with an impatient hand. "You have a daughter too."

Pao An flushed scarlet. For a moment, Lincoln thought his uncle might strike him.

"You have a daughter," Lincoln insisted. "You grieve for her. The house is empty, your days are empty. And so you tear down what is still whole and scare yourself with thoughts of dying and fight this stupid, useless battle against innocent insects."

Pao An stared at the new pillars coated in shiny black tar. "I should have hewn the posts out of lava rock . . ." he muttered to himself. "If the termites eat wallpaper paste, they will eat through the tar, break through to the wood . . ." He envisioned everything he had built falling down in ruins.

$\mathcal{M}$olly told herself that her contribution to Bosworth's journalistic diatribes was benign, not a betrayal of her lover. She wrote down only what she saw and heard, the raw matter of experience, which Bosworth shaped into opinion. Yet on reflection, she realized that if made public, her association with Bosworth could easily compromise Constable's position in the Hale as Gibson's protégé. Walter Murray Gibson, the king's eccentric mentor, was the very man Bosworth was hoping to expose as "a two-penny anti-Christ," a "heretic so brazen he had been excommunicated by apostate Mormons." Molly convinced herself that she was apolitical and, therefore, above all factions; but in fact, it was the danger of her situation that excited her most. So she continued her weekly visits to the statehouse gallery to observe Constable behind the podium as he translated the *haole* legislators' English into Hawaiian and the native delegates' Hawaiian into English. How vulnerable he appeared on his little stage, turning and twisting as the words surged through him, a weather vane spun by opposing winds.

She recognized how much power Constable wielded on the floor of the Hale. For he gave his own twist to the arguments, without regard for which party he offended. She wondered if her own scribblings were similarly tainted. For when she read what Bosworth wrote, she was troubled at how extensively her uncle used her copious notes.

Yet she loved the power that wielding the pen bestowed. Each morning in the backyard, where the sunlight fell through the tangled limbs of a tamarind tree, Molly worked in a notebook with a volume of Shelley or Tennyson at her elbow. For the simple act of taking notes in the Hale had prompted a burst of creativity on another front; on those mornings when the government was not in session, she began to write poetry. Those early hours passed with uncanny swiftness, and she would race through the housekeeping in order to get back to her notebook again. Did this mean she was unhappy? she wondered. Her life with Constable was filled with adventure and delight. And yet she could not ignore the emptiness of her existence. She knew scores of important people but had not a single friend. And except for a week's stint taking home piecework for a dressmaking establishment, she had done nothing of consequence until her secret writing life began, for her status as Constable's mistress had closed off her former hopes of teaching children.

And although it hurt her to admit it, there had been the further problem of Constable himself. For Constable, despite his boldly advertised bohemian opinions, was surprisingly conventional as a mate, demanding that Molly devote herself entirely to him. She accused him of being an autocrat, more British than the British themselves. Miffed by the rebuke, he encouraged her to "scribble," holding the example of Mary Godwin before her. But Molly quickly saw that in this, as with everything else, he expected to play the principal part—Percy Shelley to "poor Mary."

Then when she proudly announced that she had been writing poems all along, Constable seemed more angry than elated. He demanded to see every page. And since every page was filled with error to his critical eyes and every line arrhythmical to his sensitive ears, she lost heart. She stopped writing poems, but continued with a spiteful spirit to labor for her uncle. She had her excuses: Bosworth needed her, and they needed the money he paid for her services. And she wrote faster and more easily without Constable's permission than with it.

In the two years she labored secretly for her uncle, Molly's most widely read assignment in the *Dispatch* was also the most painful to report: the solemn funeral procession of Dowager Queen Emma in 1885. The grief Molly felt was tinged with guilt. Emma had been one of her sponsors at the Priory, and Molly had paid back that kindness in base coin. And yet romantic Emma would have been the last to keep a girl from the man she loved. From her post on the sidewalk along King Street, Molly watched two thousand mourners file by on their way to the Royal Mausoleum in Nuuanu Valley to lay the queen to rest next to her dead husband and son. The Companions, Lucy among them, passed by in a carriage draped with black. Molly described in her notes the close precision marching of the all-white volunteer militia, the Honolulu Rifles; the muted, insistent beating of the drum corps. She watched the king ride by in solemn dignity upon a prancing black horse. She did not mention in her report to Bosworth what everyone in the kingdom knew: Kalakaua was free of the last and most beloved of Kamehameha's line.

The death of Molly's royal patron severed a key link with a girlhood circumscribed by custom and convention. She *did* love her new life with Peter, Molly assured herself, even if loneliness was its price.

"We'll rent a hall, Mol!" Constable cried in elation. "You'll sell tickets, I'll palaver. We'll be rolling in coin of the realm and good, strong currency from the San Francisco mint. Think of it! We'll pay our debts in an instant and use the remainder to play!"

"It takes money to rent a hall," Molly replied severely as she cleared the table of the breakfast crockery. She had scraped the last ounce of China tea from the canister into the teapot that morning and stretched white flour with a bit of mashed sweet potato to make biscuits.

"My credit's still good!"

"Your credit is as bad as your reputation!" she scolded. Constable was earning more from translating in the Hale and writing Gibson's speeches than he ever had in his life; yet the money was vanishing in an avalanche of debts. Constable had already thrown hundreds of dollars away on a useless engine that purported to make seawater fit for drinking, owned shares in a still nonexistent silkworm farm on the Big Island, and had bought into a plan to run tours for Californians to view a live volcano. At his urging, Molly had held back a part of his salary for a nest egg; yet after months of penny-pinching, he had spent the lot on a new lounge suit done up by his tailor.

"*Auwe*, my girl," he clucked in reproach. "None of your Angel of Doubt anthems. We new Hawaiians must be true-hearted from the start or we fail of our own leaden despondency. Keep up an Emersonian spirit!"

This, Molly reflected sourly, was Constable's tongue-in-cheek version of the hopeful counsel she herself uttered to jog him out of his dark moods. His fits of morbidity would arise as suddenly as a Kona storm, only to be superseded by a state of frenzy out of which more grandiose projects emerged.

"Sam Clemens came to Hawaii from San Francisco in '66 a disreputable journalist peering at us savages like a naughty boy at a circus. Claimed he caught a 'boo-hoo fever' here. Probably the clap. Look at him now! He makes a fortune lolling about a lectern and telling his lunatic brand of lies!

In Boston, I hear, they turned thousands away when he came to lecture. I propose to follow the same route as he.''

"Mr. Twain has novelty on his side. He plays the Western fool among Eastern dandies. Who can resist a prophet from another town? Besides, his audience was already prepared by his writings in the *Sacramento Union*.''

Constable looked the picture of injured dignity, dark eyes flashing, mustache quivering. "And who am I? Surely I am capable of more than the exaggerations of a scoundrel like Clemens. You forget that my mouth frames the very speeches that become law. Before Gibson addresses the people, he comes to me!''

"But nothing you write is your own! You make your living dressing with fine figures of speech the bare bones of other men's ideas!'' That she herself was guilty of the same transgression made her frustration more keen.

Constable's face fell. He drummed his fingers on the table, saying nothing.

But Molly was sighing, already defeated. "Well, I still want to know how we are going to afford a hall!''

"Damn me," he erupted, "if you aren't acting like a wife, Mol." Bereft of practical solutions, he leaped up from the table, caught her roughly around the waist and stole a kiss, and then another. And so they went around and around, two puppies pulling on opposite ends of a bone, until their ire turned to rambunctious play. In moments of painful clarity, Molly knew she was the instrument that allowed Constable's profligacy to flourish. Yet she could neither change nor leave him. For every argument engendered heat; and heat quickly turned into passion; and in remarkably quick order, the most eloquent appeals to reason were undone by her own frail flesh. This quarrel ended like many before, with anger melting into desire.

Afterward, he slept as if drugged, and Molly berated herself for being made a fool so easily! In the morning, he awoke committed wholly to this speaking scheme, which she was convinced would only lead to trouble and more debt. Try as she might, she could not bring him down to the level of everyday common sense; nor could he succeed in making her breathe the rare ether of his enthusiasms. Were all pairings between men and women so rife with contrarieties of character? Molly wondered. Emmanuel and Lucy were gloriously mismatched; Tyhune and Nalani had been comically so. And her own parents were battling opposites: her father the dour warrior, nursing old wounds and fighting a desperate rear-guard battle against change. Her mother the perennial Moon Lady, the eternal *yin*, taking into herself the scorching heat cast by her husband, trying always to placate her husband's enemies.

That very day, her opposite hired a hall, the main room of O'Brian's Inn, which boasted a piano, a stage, and a theatrical curtain; and by borrowing from Gibson at usurious rates, was able to pay O'Brian part of the cost while pledging a portion of the receipts for the rest. Then he took pen in hand to write the speech that would make him a second Samuel Clemens and fill his pockets with gold.

3

FINE PALAVER

With typical foresight, Lincoln had gone about acquiring the necessary items to make life endurable at Yale. His cheap green steamer trunk contained one heavily inscribed Latin dictionary, a collection of history books with dog-eared pages, and a spartan scholar's wardrobe. His clothing consisted of one dark, single-breasted morning coat with matching waistcoat; two pairs of light-colored trousers; four starched white shirts with detachable collars; several nightgowns; a narrow, four-in-hand tie and another that knotted at the neck in a flat bow; and last, a bowler hat. His underwear had been painstakingly double-stitched by Rulan to last the entire four years until graduation. And she had reworked one of Bosworth's old woolen frock coats, adding a lining of thick cotton batting against the harsh New Haven winters. Pao An secured the trunk with the best-quality rope sold in his store and gave his adopted son a parting gift, a silver pocket watch from Leland's Emporium.

Yet Lincoln would have gladly given away his new belongings if Molly had offered him reason to stay. He had not had word of her in months. Constable, on the other hand, left signs of his passing everywhere. Handbills announcing his upcoming speech were tacked up on trees and fences and decorated half the town. And half the town—the *haole* half—was outraged! Constable's chosen topic, as printed on the handbills, was "The New Earthly Paradise: What Future for Hawaii-*nei*?," a proposition designed to offend a population already divided by skin color and national loyalties into bitter factions, all of whom believed that the future of Hawaii-*nei* was theirs alone. To Constable's misfortune, his speech coincided with a journalistic war over the sugar treaty. Vitriolic essays in *The Hawaiian* castigating America for attempting to run the Hawaiian planters out of business and the planters for undercutting Hawaiian labor by hiring Chinese at cheap wages were widely believed to be authored by Constable himself at the behest of his mentor, Gibson. Overnight, Constable had become the object of every party's discontent. No one trusted the mouthpiece of the despised premier. Lincoln had heard one student at Oahu College warning that Constable intended to call for an end to the sugar treaty with the United States and for a special protectorate under Great Britain and thus drive a wedge between the Hawaiians and the planters. Some hot-headed missionary grandsons were purchasing seats for the purpose of harrying the principal speaker off the stage and throwing him into the canal. Lincoln didn't care if the white devil drowned. It was Molly he feared for.

On his way to Molly's rooms to say good-bye, Lincoln passed a gang of youths merrily ripping down handbills advertising Constable's lecture. At that moment, with the boys' jeers echoing in his ears, a splendid hope took shape in Lincoln's mind: What if Molly herself secretly desired rescue? What if she were clinging to Constable out of loyalty, not love? And who better to save her than the one who had been doing so from the time that they were children! If Molly gave him the slightest reason to hope, there would be one less passenger on the steamboat *Mahealani* tomorrow. She trusted him, that much he was sure of. And trust might prove a foundation for love . . .

*M*olly stiffened with alarm when she answered Lincoln's knock. "Is something wrong at home?"

So she still cared about her parents, Lincoln thought, still referred to Chinatown as "home." Yearning soared. "Only good things," he told her. "I'm leaving for school on the mainland tomorrow, and I came to bid you *aloha.*"

Her face crumpled. "Leaving! I never imagined. . . . I thought it would be I who . . . Well, never mind. Come in," she urged, wiping her face quickly with her apron. "I'm alone until six." She glanced quickly behind her, a nervous housekeeper, and led him out of the vestibule into a large sitting room suffused with sunlight as thick as cream.

It pained Lincoln to see how beautiful another man's love had made her. She was rosy, voluptuous, and far more assured than the wild, dark girl who had left Chinatown for the Priory. And unlike the squalor he imagined, her world was governed by order. There was no sign of inattention in the three sunny, flower-strewn rooms. He saw shiny wood surfaces. A small kitchen with implements hung neatly on the walls, a mirror of her mother's pristine cooking space. Floors scrubbed clean. Doilies scattered on ancient, scarred chairs. Framed pencil drawings of wind-bent palms. Silhouettes of herself and her lover side by side on a small table. And in the next room, behind the closed door, the bed she shared with Constable. How foolish, he thought to himself, to expect that she would leave the reprobate who kept her so well for the penniless scholar whose love had never wavered.

"I've interrupted you—" he blurted out in dismay, spying the papers heaped on a chair outside.

"No, no. I was sitting in the sun writing notes . . . to myself," she said quickly. "Nothing as grand as what you turn out every day for your schoolmasters. I've been away so long from the classroom that I have no idea what passes for distinction. But I'm rattling on about me, and you're leaving, really leaving! Tell me where you're going."

"To Yale. To study classics. There are those who would pay good money to turn a heathen Chinese into a Christian gentleman. Naturally," he added wryly, "they may cut the suit, but I have my own way of wearing it . . ."

Molly's laughter was shrill. "How marvelous! I envy you because . . . because you'll see snow! I always pictured something like the silvery dust of butterfly wings, only colder. How will it feel to hold it in your hands, I wonder, the ice crystals seeping into your skin? The freshness on your face, neither mist nor rain, as we have here, but a bone-white chill. And the way it must transform the light . . ." Her hands moved over her dress, her face, her hair, checking to see if she were intact.

This time, the manic chatter and the fixed smile did not fool him. The order of the rooms was a delusion. Molly herself was the butterfly beating the dust from its wings in a vain attempt to be free. The "bone-white chill" she imagined was real.

His silence seemed to distress her. She drew her chair closer, took his hand in hers and said, "Tell me what you are to do in that place of ice."

He found himself confessing what he had confided only to his journal, simply to prolong the intimacy between them. "Remember the mute little boy you used to tease?" he told her. "I was silent so long that I want to make up for the lost years, perhaps by speaking for Tang people who cannot speak for themselves. There are thousands of us, more Chinese than *haole*! And why have we no voice, no vote? Because we are still bound to a vanished world and thus refuse to accept responsibility for our day-to-day lives! Too many Tang men think 'I can abide anything because this life is not real. I am going to die in China.' But they stay on in a land they haven't claimed as their own. And after fifty years in the islands, they are still not heard!"

"You make me ashamed," Molly whispered. "It seems that I do not *know* you."

To Lincoln's ears, attuned as they were to the cadences of Scripture, the word was excruciatingly intimate. She was close enough now for him to see the sheen of sweat on her upper lip. . . . She drew closer still, laying her head against his new white shirt. Lincoln went rigid with amazement. Molly had never touched him before except to slap his head or kick his shins or trip him when he was running. Yet her body felt entirely familiar. Had dreaming made it so? In wonder and awe, he put his arms around her, felt with his hands the fine thin bones beneath her skin. How fragile she was in the flesh when in his imagination she filled his whole world! His fingers worked their way into the thickness of her hair, and breathless, he bent his head to kiss her. . . .

"Well, I'm keeping you, and I shouldn't," she said, a deep blush coloring her breasts and neck, and flew away from his embrace into the kitchen, leaving his body tingling and bereft. Her footsteps were so light he could not hear her tread upon the bare wood floors. She returned clutching a plate of biscuits, breathless, her color high. The biscuits were dry and overcooked, but he ate every one. The scent of her hair and skin clung to his fingertips.

Molly nervously chewed at her lip, her hair askew. He supposed she was bewildered by the heat that had sprung up so suddenly between them. He, however, was filled with joy. His mind worked furiously, sketching out the words that would bring her back into his arms. He pulled a mutilated handbill out of his pocket and placed the pieces on the table. "I caught some roughnecks tearing these down—" he ventured.

Instantly, she was the old Molly again: stubborn, petulant, proud. "Did Mother put you up to this? Did she order you to sweet-talk Molly, then yank her home?"

In helpless agony, Lincoln watched the wreckage of his hopes in her stormy eyes.

"You think I'm weak," she accused. "Molly and her stunts! Well, little Molly has her pride—"

"Hang your precious pride!" Lincoln exploded. "The word is that hooligans have been hired to stop Constable from speaking! Permanently!"

The retort died on Molly's lips. There had been incidents over the past weeks that she couldn't ignore. Rocks pelting their door. Toughs who had tried to bait Constable outside the legislature. A scuffle in the street, which Constable made light of. Shouting matches in the Hale with opponents who protested the tenor of his translations.

"What have you heard?" she asked in a small, tight voice.

"The planters' faction and the annexationists believe that Gibson has put Constable up to this. Let him mention home rule or affiliation with Britain or changing the sugar treaty, and roughnecks in the front rows will storm the stage. They're carrying pistols . . . Best cancel the lecture."

"He'd never agree to that," whispered Molly.

"Then you, at least, must not attend! Living with him so long, you must know by now that the man's a fool. You're the brilliant one, not him!"

Hot tears filled Molly's eyes. She put her hands to her ears. "I don't want to hear it!"

In a heartbeat, Lincoln had flung his chair aside and had pulled her close. "Leave him," he begged, prying her hands from her head. "He shouldn't let you come to grief, shouldn't let you share his shame. Not if he cared for you as . . . *we* do . . ." Why could he not say the word? Claim her by simply saying *"I"*?

Slowly, she extricated herself from Lincoln's arms. "It's too late. He needs me."

Her words fell on him like hot ash. Yet he put his agony aside because he saw that Molly's terror was real. "You don't have to go tonight," he reminded her.

"But I'm supposed to sell tickets," she said, wringing her hands in dismay. "I've given my word . . ."

"Not speak? You must be daft!" Constable roared. "I've sunk every penny I have into this. You should have warned me earlier before the handbills were put up and the tickets printed."

"Don't take your anger out on me, Peter. This speech was your idea, not mine."

"God, I know! Gibson has warned me off too. If only that damned uncle of yours and his infernal rag hadn't poured vitriol on Gibson. He's frying me in that same oil!" He slumped down at his desk where the pages of his speech lay in disarray.

Molly was flooded with guilt. Why had she persisted in gathering information for her uncle to hurl at the man she loved? She put a hand on Constable's shoulder and pressed her cheek to his thick curls. This trouble *was* her fault. "Peter," she began, "I must confess—"

But Constable had shaken free of her and was pacing the floor. "Dear God," he muttered in rising hysteria, his smile grotesque, "I paid that thief O'Brian one hundred seventy-five dollars in advance and promised him ten percent of the take. At two dollars a person, I'll need a hundred people to break even. The place holds three hundred. . . . Now if every annexationist buys a ticket, we'll walk out of this with our pockets stuffed with gold!" Then in the next breath, he wailed, "But if they all come, they'll riot. Gibson will throw me to the lions, and Kalakaua will turn his back on me. I'll be ruined!"

"I don't care about the money. I don't want you dead."

"Well it's damned if I do, damned if I don't, then, isn't it? Typical of me! Idiot! Dreamer! *Kanaka!* Oh, Mol, what am I to do?" He slumped in a chair holding his head in his hands as if trying to squeeze escape out of his overwrought brain. "I spent a month writing my speech . . . and no one will listen! They'll get me onstage, in the street, wherever I go." He rose, whirling about the room. "I've got to get out and think. But you go early! As soon as the hall is filled, take the coins home and hide them. Hide yourself, for that matter—"

"But I . . ."

"Dammit, *wahine!* Do it! . . . I can't stay here. I've got to walk," and he shrugged on his coat, grabbed up his notes and rushed out the door.

*A*t fifteen minutes past eight that night, Molly stood behind a wine cask set on end inside the door of O'Brian's Inn, handing out tickets with one hand and collecting silver dollars in the other. Lincoln had brought a horse to the rear entrance of the inn for a quick getaway and for the last hour had stood beside her like a brother (although, she thought, he *had* behaved in a most bizarre manner that afternoon, so unlike his typical stoic self). He had also managed to placate O'Brian who had been threatening to clap "that reprobate and his concubine" in irons if the event proved unprofitable.

Lincoln had spent the afternoon stowing his gear aboard the *Mahealani* and eating the farewell meal Rulan had prepared in his honor. His ticket was tucked in the pocket of his waistcoat; there was nothing now to tie him to the islands.

By eight o'clock, it appeared that whatever the lecture cost Constable in reputation, the evening itself would not prove the financial disaster that Lincoln anticipated and Molly feared. Gangs of men were streaming through the door, and the innkeeper soon lapsed into contented mutterings, while filling glass after glass at the bar. O'Brian had tripled his business in liquor alone. Soon the room was filled to overflowing, O'Brian was purring with satisfaction, and Molly was steeped in fear. The minutes were ticking by and still the main speaker was not in sight. "If he doesn't show, the mob will tear this place apart!" she whispered to Lincoln. "But if I pay the audience back, O'Brian will sue us! Either way, we're lost!"

Haoles and *kanakas* crowded the aisles, lolled atop the long tin-topped bar, sprawled drunkenly in chairs and windowsills, leaned against every open surface and taunted each other. One wrong note and O'Brian's would become a sea of flailing fists and flying bottles. Yet there was money to be made, all right. Molly had counted up the take as the men filed past: over six hundred silver coins. She had filled the chatelaine around her waist with coins and stuffed the rest of the money into a pair of saddlebags borrowed from O'Brian. Well over a year's salary for Constable. *If* he arrived—and *if* he survived the hostility of the crowd!

At half past the hour, the air had turned stifling from the sweating bodies. The audience had gone from restive to ugly, stomping and booing and hollering insults at the closed curtains of the stage.

"Come on out, you bastard! Let's hear you cry Britannia now," someone jeered.

"Black coward!" shouted another. These taunts were followed by angry outbursts from the score of pro-Gibson Hawaiians who had come to applaud their comrade. A chorus of jeers was followed by angry voices calling for the return of the ticket money. Molly did not realize that she was holding Lincoln's hand until he squeezed her fingers in reassurance. He left her momentarily to make a survey of the street outside, and came back, tight-lipped, to announce that Constable was nowhere in sight. The *la sap* had abandoned Molly! The thought filled Lincoln with righteous anger, and a soaring emotion akin to hope. Molly might yet be his! And at that moment, a series of chords were played on the barroom piano behind the curtain. Every head swung toward the stage where Constable was playing a run with one hand, while holding the curtain aside with the other. There was a deafening chorus of jeers.

Molly ran in Constable's direction. "Something's happened. He's hurt himself," she shouted over her shoulder to Lincoln, who could see even without Molly's prompting that Constable's suit was muddy and torn. Somewhere he had found a crushed top hat, which perched on his head. His tie was undone, and one of his coat sleeves was ripped clear through. He stepped awkwardly to the front of the stage, carrying no notes, no papers, no speech.

"Dear Lord," Molly moaned, stopping suddenly. When Lincoln caught up to her, she clutched at him blindly, saying, "He's staggering drunk!"

Having come to that realization themselves, the rowdies in the front row were now hurling bottles at the stage. The rain of insults and debris did not dampen the man at the piano, however. Constable drew himself up like an offended preacher and shouted over the din, "Gentlemen—and ladies, if any are present—a condition that would be a notable first in O'Brian's. Let me say as someone once did, 'Let him without sin, go . . . fetch me a gin.' " He stepped away from the piano and bent from the waist, a perfectly executed bow except for the tremors caused by a spasm of hiccups. The audience howled their scorn.

"He is ruined," Molly whispered. Constable's modest position in the legislature, of which he was so proud, would be snatched away as soon as Gibson heard how his man had made himself a laughingstock before the enemies of the king.

Oblivious of the danger that he courted onstage, Constable was stepping as delicately as a ballerina across a floor strewn with broken glass, putting down each foot with exaggerated care. When he achieved his destination—the podium—he cleared his throat and began again. "Gentlemen . . . and ladies," he mumbled, then stopped and reached for his battered hat, realizing that that encumbrance still perched on his head. But in trying to remove it, he knocked it to the ground. Three hundred men taunted him. Yet the object of their scorn continued to ignore the rude display and carefully stooped to retrieve his fallen hat. Slowly and with great dignity he extended his arm, farther and farther, until he was bent in half like a nutcracker. One more inch . . . and he fell flat on his face among the broken bottles and puddles of beer. Applause rang through the hall.

Molly buried her face in Lincoln's shoulder. "He's destroying himself."

"Look again," Lincoln said in a voice that seemed strained and remote. "He's not as drunk as you think!"

Constable picked himself up off the boards and groped once more for the hat, which remained maddeningly out of reach. He had to step beyond the podium to get it, yet when stepping forth, kicked it farther away. The audience hooted in derision. After two more fumbling attempts to catch hold of the hat, he held the offending object in his hands. Then with a grave flourish, he returned it to the top of his head to rousing cheers. Then he swung his legs in stiff, marionette fashion back to the podium.

"Gentlemen," he began again, "and ladies . . ." He rolled his eyes upward, remembering his hat again. This time, he grasped it with both hands and forced it down upon the podium as if it were a living thing about to take flight. He must have hooked it on an unseen nail, for it hung, defying gravity, at a precarious angle at the edge of the podium. He pointed at it with a warning finger. The defiant hat seemed, from the audience's perspective, a sly bird keeping to its perch only by dint of its owner's will. *"Stay,"* Constable intoned, and glared at the hat he intended to tame. The assembly of rowdies and political antagonists cheered his forceful command.

This time, Molly laughed too.

Curious now, the audience returned to their seats in a state of heightened expectation. Constable assumed an air of exaggerated dignity. "My topic tonight, refined en route to O'Brian's, is 'The Future of Hawaii-*nei* Transformed by Beer' . . . *ahem,* that is, 'Bliss,' or 'What Shall We Make of Paradise?' A noble prospect and an ideal to which we all aspire." Constable cleared his throat as the laughter died down. "We have different notions, images, utopian imaginings gleaned from the poets and the book of Genesis to guide our thinking. But what is paradise to you and to me who enjoy at firsthand this island oasis in the midst of the blue Pacific?" He nodded sagely to a line of sniggering youths. "Our present situation reminds me of the old miner, one of the original Argonauts in the California gold fields who died and went on to Paradise."

"Ain't never one of those made it yet," someone yelled from the back of the room. "Hell, I know! I was there!" The house guffawed at this commentary.

"Well, at least this one did, and white-bearded St. Peter, a replica of our own St. Gibson"—he paused to allow the catcalls and boos to die down—"met him at the pearline Gates and asked him his occupation. 'Panner, sluicer, and hard rock gold miner,' said our newly deceased friend. 'Well,' said St. Peter, 'there's been a few of your persuasion come up here lately, and we do not have room for another miner.' "

"Musta been a bad barrel of rotgut," the same man in the audience called out.

Constable quieted him with a hand held high in stern reproach. " 'Well now,' the miner said to St. Peter. 'If'n I thin out the ranks, might you have a bunk for me?' The good gatekeeper said he might arrange that with the proprietor."

Now the audience was caught up in the story, eagerly anticipating where it would lead. "So the miner hightailed it around until he came to the mining camp section," Constable continued. "Men were sittin' around telling old stories and drinking first squeezing of the grape." He paused for laughter. " 'Where's the camp office?' our friend asked. And when it was pointed out, he went there because he knew he'd find the assayer. Once inside he asked the man if he could speak in complete confidence. 'Of course,' the assayer said. 'This is Heaven.' "—more guffaws—" 'Now I want this to be just between you and me. Before they let me in up here, I was prospectin' down below, and they just hit a major vein in the last circle of Hell.' 'Really!' the assayer said. 'Well, your secret's safe with me.' Our friend went aside to take a short nap and a half hour later the camp was empty. He went looking around and there wasn't a soul. A day later, St. Peter comes by. 'I see you have the place to yourself.' 'Yep,' said the miner, 'but I'm thinkin' of headin' down there meself.' 'But why?' St. Peter asked. 'Well now, I know'd I started that rumor, but there just might be some truth to it!' "

The room rocked with laughter. "Hell, yes!" the old forty-niner in the back of the hall yelled. Men were slapping each other's backs in delight. It took a minute or two for things to quiet down enough for Constable to continue.

"Gentlemen," he said, "I warn you that like the miner in Heaven, there is no truth in what I have to say tonight!" Cheers rang out, and he proceeded with his next story.

Molly began to breathe again. She saw Constable's daring plan: to say nothing of substance and thus steer their ire away from him. So he went on in a digressive manner, choosing as his targets all the issues roiling the islands, espousing none of them while mocking those leaders who did. In Hawaiian and in English, he did wicked imitations of a fatuous Gibson, the arrogant American envoy, an apoplectic Bosworth, even the royal *hula* master. No one escaped his sharp tongue, not even the king. The audience never stopped cheering, stomping, and laughing for the two hours of his performance. When the curtains were closed, three hundred drunk and happy men spilled onto the streets, some wiggling their hips in ribald *ami ami* and repeating the ridiculous things Constable had said or done and declaring the speaker "better drunk than Sam Clemens sober." Annexationist, nativist, and British sympathizer went away from O'Brian's equally entertained by the man at the podium.

They were rich, Molly realized, as Lincoln piled the heavy saddlebags over her shoulders. At least until the next crisis of debt came along.

Molly pushed her way across the inn toward the stage, conscious of the glorious weight of the coins, then turned at the foot of the stairs. She had forgotten to thank Lincoln! Good, dependable Lincoln! He was still standing where she had left him and studying her in the intense way he reserved for geometry diagrams. Then his face hardened, he gave a perfunctory wave and disappeared into the crowd.

Moments later, Molly was pulling back the curtain, eager to salute the man who had turned disgrace into triumph. But she found the champion of the evening slumped on the piano bench, his face shiny with sweat and tears, crumpling his hat between his hands in relief and mortification.

4

THE LETTER

"I know you will discount my good advice," the Widow said belliger-
ently to the *tong* council. "I know you will make excuses, saying that *that
girl* does not deserve our attention. *That girl* has left Chinatown and if she
goes whoring with a brown devil, that is not our concern. Yet I have risen
from my sickbed to tell you that her evil has come back to haunt our
door!"

Each council member gathered in the private, second-floor meeting
room of the *tong* hall groaned inwardly, preparing for yet another of the
Widow's diatribes against the Chens. Her complaints were old and familiar
and, therefore, not of pressing consequence, just as the Widow herself was
an embarrassing relic of a previous era and no longer of consequence to the
present age. Especially since profits in the Li enterprises were falling off.
The Widow had had to sell a block of choice real estate to raise cash, and
her daughter's inability to win a rich husband had become a community
joke. And all because of the mother's last attempt to betroth her daughter
to the China-raised son of the wealthiest rice factor in the islands. Who
would have guessed that the son, so handsome in the marriage broker's
photographs, would prove an imbecile in the flesh? There were rumors that

the daughter had threatened to shave her head and join the gray-robed nuns at the Kwan Yin temple if her mother hired the go-between again. And now the Widow herself was ailing, growing visibly weaker.

Having witnessed Chen Pao An's success as a builder and in organizing the Chinatown fire department, the council members were beginning to believe that they had put their stake on the wrong player. Despite the fact that immigration from China had been restricted to twenty-five that year because of the unfortunate outbreak of smallpox traced to a Tang man that had spoiled the king's coronation and turned Kalakaua against the Chinese, businessmen in Chinatown had continued to prosper, among them Chen Pao An. To his credit, Chen had not tried to cut in on the most lucrative services the *tong* operated, namely burial insurance, opium distribution, and loans to compatriots from their home districts.

Mei Yuk reacted to the subtle disaffection of her colleagues with heightened complaints against her enemies. "I know you think your founder's widow foolish to condemn *that girl's* licentious relationship with the *hapa haole* who babbles in two barbarian tongues in the legislature," she continued with shrill conviction.

The men made feeble protests against the rebuke. "The girl is indeed corrupt," one of the men said soothingly. "On that issue we agree. Only, what can the *tong* do if parents ignore the bad behavior of their child?"

"*Aiya!* You do not listen!" Mei Yuk cried. Angrily, she struck the table with her small fist. "I tell you that the Chens have not really broken with that girl. These are devious people! They were insurrectionists who brought down my husband's house from within, *hai ma*? They work best in secret. Or has Hawaii made you so soft that you forget how rebellion begins! You know how the king has turned against us, cutting down on immigration! How the Hawaiians blame us for bringing disease! How the sugar planters look to Japan to supply cheap labor! Times are hard. Brother turns against brother to protect the profits of his house . . . and a shrewd businessman like Chen knows how to kill off the competition. How does a landowner ensure that the emperor's official is in his camp at tax time? What does a merchant do to secure a government license to transport salt? He bribes the man who can grant him a favor with whatever is in his power to supply! Money, property, services . . . even daughters!"

The men looked at the Widow with puzzled faces.

Mei Yuk exploded in rage. "The opium license! The king needs money and wants to make legal the opium trade again. But only *one* Tang man can be granted the license. You and I have paid the necessary bribes to win back the license, but do we have Gibson's ear? Can any of us speak Hawaiian or English well enough to address the officials who make laws?

So who will get the prize? The one whose daughter sleeps with the favorite of the king!"

Cries of outrage rose from the men at the table. "What can we do?"

"Beat the Chens at their own game," Mei Yuk replied. "The king will need money now that he has spent his gold on roast pigs, parades, and racing canoes. He will not refuse us if we open our purses to him. Bide our time. Spread our money around like manure across a paddy. We should offer the same assurances—in secret, of course—especially to the princess, his sister—for who can trust a king who favors Japanese over decent Tang men? We will have to be single-minded. We cannot smile and hope the Hawaiians and the *haoles* will leave us in peace or lift the immigration quotas out of love for us. Tang men are turned away from the islands while barbarians from Japan and Portugal are given houses and cash gifts to bring wives to help pick cane! Tang men are taxed more than any other people in the islands! Why? Because we have neither the *kanakas'* claim on the land nor the power of *bak kuei* gunboats nor young men who can speak or write in the languages in which laws are made! We must find men in government with empty pockets who will act in our behalf. And we need to do this now, before *that girl* steals the opium license away."

$\mathcal{M}$onths after Constable's lecture at O'Brian's, a letter from America arrived by morning post. Molly shoved it in the pocket of her skirt so Constable would not see from whom it came. Even before Lincoln had left for Yale, Constable had taken a violent dislike to him, dubbing him "the Pedant" for his untoward interest in Western philosophy.

When Constable had gone off to the Hale and Molly was safely in her walled garden, she pulled out the envelope and tore it open eagerly. The letter was dated a month before and written in Lincoln's sprawling, angular hand.

Dear Molly,

First you must note this special watermark—a snow crystal melted upon the page so that you may see in its ethereal state what I see from the third-floor window of my rooming house: the world magically decorating itself out of thin air! Rooftop and cobblestone, lawn and hedgerow are blanketed in ermine white. Through the shifting, powdery mist looms the spidery outline of the tree in the courtyard where the masters' children have hung their swing. Beyond that lies a vast whiteness, which has swallowed up the entire limits of my world—the enclosed courtyard, the arched brick walkways, the walls and corridors on the opposite side of the cobblestone square where doubtless another man peers out from a casement window straight at me. I cannot convey how silent and cold this beauty is! Colder than the loss of all I love. And not at all as you imagined, although I suspect that your genius for turning a phrase might transform even this frigidity into a thing of beauty. Like the "dust of butterfly wings."

I have written uncle and auntie many times. They have said nothing about you, so I gather that you have not made your peace with the family. You must not separate yourself from them! We are bound by our origins, and their affection is unwavering, even if unspoken. Of that I am certain.

So far I have resisted all attempts to turn me into a facsimile of a white man. I do not care to be trotted out to local ladies' societies as proof of the Congregationalists' success at civilizing the heathen. When the master quizzes me, I am purposely vague on the question of theology. I sit docilely at chapel, take tea with the master and his wife. But I keep my own counsel. And in truth, I have no idea what I believe.

My classes here are more difficult than I imagined. I am decent enough at Latin and Greek, but am no Hebrew scholar. Milton called it the language in which the angels sing. I am afraid I must become one before I ever master the sound and the syntax. My favorite activity may surprise you—debate! Yes, this tongue-tied orphan is judged by his peers to be an orator. So my plan goes forward by spurts and starts. I remember even more clearly in this snowy landscape the field laborer who speaks only rural Cantonese and the merchant who converses with his customers in ill-chosen oaths in Hawaiian and the shop owner who smiles and smiles at the tax collector and cannot make plain his rage at the unjust assessment. I know by heart their aspirations, cry out condolence for their defeats, claim boldly their rights to be free men in a new land. Tang people need a voice especially since even "good" citizens in the islands are demanding their exclusion, and I am audacious enough to believe I can speak for them.

You need not write back. Only let me write now and then to you. The thought that we are tied still by the same string of fate will give me pleasure indeed. I will ask nothing else except the hope that this letter creates in you some fond recollection of . . .

Lin Kong

That simple inscription at the bottom of the page brought back memories of the half-starved orphan who had been mute, forlorn, alone. She had almost forgotten that he had a name other than the one his Hawaiian schoolmaster had chosen long ago! How ironic that the grown man clung as tightly as the small boy to the idea of family after that family had in fact ceased to be. She put the letter beneath the half-finished poems in her notebook and watched a green folded mantis waiting, waiting upon a flower stalk for its prey. But she did not make peace with her mother and father.

On the long train ride east, America had unfolded itself to Lincoln in vistas of frightening proportions: dry golden hills and blue rock stretching to the horizon, mist streaming off the rank marshland into the clouds, endless prairies. Only the eastern edge of America seemed to him fully settled, exhibiting by the very design of its cities the triumph of mankind's industry and ingenuity over nature. New Haven was what Honolulu might one day become: a city of machines set in motion by thousands of immigrant hands. A traveler to New Haven proceeded via canal boat or rail past factories that churned out every manner of useful article from eyeglasses and clocks to chaises, carriages, and firearms. From the dockside, that same traveler might take one of myriad trolleys that wound through the bustling city to the city's historical and commercial center, the Green. Here on one side was a long row of red brick buildings, the very Acropolis of this American Athens, Yale College, where, Lincoln hoped, his febrile mind could find rest.

He had set for himself a mission of self-improvement, and was thus delighted to find a ready-made self thrust at him. The role of Yale Chinaman was such an easy one to fill. Simply by showing up at chapel, by keeping his linen spotless, by pronouncing his words with exaggerated care, he became an exotic tamed. In short order, his alien features became a mask that rendered him invisible, and he was left alone to read and think what he chose.

He took his classes in Divinity Hall, one of the four buildings on Old Brick Row, and rented a small third-floor room in a boardinghouse for students near the corner of Chapel and College Streets. The bedroom was drafty and small, barely accommodating a table and bed. But there was a fireplace and a rooftop retreat: all in all, palatial conditions for a youth who had never been granted his own space. Better than the privacy was the view, for the casement window looked out onto a leafy margin where students sprawled under the ubiquitous elm trees that dotted the city to read or doze on fall afternoons.

His schedule was spartan and invariable: a ten–hour round of lectures and study and meager boardinghouse fare, except for Sunday afternoons when he walked eight long blocks to the home, just off elegant York Square, of a local Congregational minister named Bainton, who provided Sunday dinner for the Hawaiian Mission's charity cases. Zealous in guarding his privacy, Lincoln had dreaded this meal with strangers, until the minister's daughter, reed–slim and with gray eyes framed by pale lashes, greeted him on the porch the first evening and boldly proffered her hand.

"I am Heloise, your Christian sister," she told him in an excited whisper and plucked off the bonnet that was already sliding off her silvery hair.

Lincoln saw immediately where Heloise had inherited her flaxen good looks. Reverend Bainton was a slight, compactly built man of about fifty, whose blond handsomeness was an asset in New Haven's sea of churches and preachers. But his voice, like his intellect, was disappointingly thin; and his sermons thudded with platitudes. His wife, by contrast, was plump, short, and acerbic, with garrulousness and wit for two. If the household seemed prosperous at first glance, it was due to Clarice Bainton's skillful housekeeping. Only later did Lincoln fully realize that the simplicity of the Baintons' table was due not to a natural asceticism but to a paucity of income. The family's fortune seemed to reside chiefly in Heloise, a girl as brilliant as quicksilver and as difficult to contain. Whenever Heloise headed a young people's charity brigade, even the most self-indulgent town youths fanned out in her wake to plant trees, take up alms for the orphans' asylum, or (after a nip or two) decry public drunkenness.

Heloise Bainton made known her fascination with Lincoln on the first evening he came to dine. She peppered him with questions. Where had he learned to use a fork? How had a Chinaman learned Latin? In what language did he think and dream?

Lincoln had never considered that any young woman might find him interesting, let alone one as attractive as Heloise. At dinner that first night, he willingly surrendered intimate details of his history, reminding himself that Heloise's inquisitiveness, though rude for a Chinese hostess, was proper given the *bak kuei's* odd predilection for conversing while eating. Lincoln found himself describing events and places he had not thought about in years: the China camp in the gold country around Sacramento, the starving years with his uncles on the Delta, the rains that had engulfed the levees in 1872. His narration seemed to impress his hosts, judging from the upraised forks, the girl's gray eyes shiny with astonishment, the mother's rosy face made rosier still by skepticism, the reverend nervously chewing the end of his pipe.

In his delight at finding a new friend, Lincoln failed to perceive the Baintons' disapproval. They had raised Heloise according to the evangelical ideals of the Second Great Enlightenment. As a child, she had accompanied them to temperance meetings and societies on moral reform. It had been a mark of particular pride for the parents that Heloise attended the School of Art, the first of the Yale colleges to open its doors to women. Yet they were shocked when their daughter put the principles of civic justice into practice. It was one thing to admire the *idea* of a Christian Chinaman, and quite another to demonstrate an immoderate interest in one. Yet as much as Lincoln discomfited Bainton and his wife, neither would relinquish him to another family. Bainton's conscience would not permit it; nor would his wife abandon the chance to play hostess to a Chinaman, a proof of social as well as heavenly grace. Foreign students were a considerable asset for a hostess; Lincoln was the Baintons' Chinaman, and he would have to do.

For all Heloise's warmth, however, she could not assuage Lincoln's homesickness. Luckily, he found two ready-made uncles living in ramshackle quarters beside the oyster factories near the docks. These Tang men had ventured east after their contracts with the railroad had ended and stayed to work in the lucrative oyster trade in the frigid waters of the Long Island Sound. Cut off from Tang men in the cities, the uncles were as hungry for company as Lincoln was for the comforting sounds of his mother tongue and food more palatable than Clarice Bainton's viscous baked beans and dry brown bread.

Lincoln also found friends among his fellow first-year students, redfaced farm boys from western Connecticut and Maine and pale patricians from New York and Providence. The former had Christian earnestness bred into their thick bones; the latter arrived with grave doubts about their vocation. No matter; Lincoln listened to their spiritual wrestlings, read whatever tract they put into his hand. Caught up in impassioned discussion with his new comrades as the fire in the boardinghouse hearth crumbled into ash, Lincoln felt that knowledge was a bottomless pool from which he could drink, and drink again.

Despite his friendship with Heloise, Lincoln longed all the more for Molly. He wrote letters to her describing the wonders of this metropolis and his dreams of rebuilding Honolulu into a "new haven" built along modern industrial lines. Molly wrote back only once. It didn't matter. Molly silent was a more tender confidante and more real than the gray-eyed young woman who greeted him on ever more frequent evenings at the door of her parents' house.

5

Dangerous Enthusiasms

At the year's end, Pao An's companions in the union pleaded with him to return to active leadership. The unpopularity of the Chinese meant that every strong Tang man was needed to shore up their power in the islands. With planters turning to workers from Japan and the Portuguese Azores, there was more necessity for societies like the Chinese Union to take care of the thousands of Tang men who had completed their field contracts and were now flocking into Honolulu, some of them too sick or too poor to leave. The union would need a new clubhouse to fit their expanding role as the foremost charitable association in the community, and commissioned Pao An to construct it. So Pao An turned his attention to organizing field hands to build the Union Hall, a splendid edifice he intended to make impervious to fire.

In China, divided by rank, birthplace, and clan affiliation, they might have been enemies; now, however, they marched as brothers under the union's triangular yellow banner emblazoned with the imperial dragon. The men sat on wooden benches under the sky and listened to their leader speak, and when Pao An was finished, each man took a shovelful of earth from the hard ground to mark the place where the Union Hall would rise.

Pao An had convinced the union brotherhood to spare no expense in the building of the new hall. The finished clubhouse would contradict the *haole* assumption that Tang men were opium-smoking bachelors who brought disease into the islands, then ran back to China as quickly as their contracts expired. No, the men of the union had as great a stake in the affairs of the islands as any citizen of Hawaii. They listened now to Pao An because he had built a business in the face of the kingdom's new policy on exclusion and without kowtowing to any *haole* banker or *tong* gang; this too in defiance of the more conservative older Chinatown societies. And on the strength of sheer conviction, he had helped create first the fire brigade and then the Chinese Union itself.

"How many fires in the last year?" Pao An harangued his cadre of twenty-five volunteer carpenters. "Thirty? Fifty? All small. But Chinatown is a tinderbox now that so many Tang men are crowding in!"

Others joined in the chorus of complaints. "My landlord let a cracked keg of kerosene leak for days."

"The blacksmith left his fire to put a number in the lottery."

"Every man in my bunkhouse is an opium smoker. At night the bunkhouse glows with lighted pipes. But when I told them I'm afraid to fall asleep for the fire they might set, they said I was foolish to worry over a few heaps of ashes!"

"*C*hinatown is built from driftwood and *pili* grass," he told Rulan that night. "We have to teach Tang people to take better care or tear down the tenements and build new."

"Not everyone wants to put money into fixing what is not broken," she said while setting out a plate of steamed flounder on the table.

"Why not?"

"Most Tang people live day to day. The old is comforting."

"Most people are fools." He tore a choice piece from the tail and plopped it into her bowl, the first time he had displayed such husbandly affection in a long time.

He threw himself into the building of the new Union Hall. He ordered expensive wood paneling from the Philippines and brass fixtures from San Francisco and hired artisans from China to carve fanciful designs along the edges of the roof and onto the enormous doors. Into the half-built rooms streamed wooden screens decorated with mother-of-pearl, hand-painted porcelain statues of gods and goddesses, jade inkwells, and tables and chairs of burnished teakwood—all donated by union members. At the same time, he proposed that the union send teams of inspectors to canvass every building in Chinatown for fire hazards. The inspectors would levy fines, which would be allocated for renovations.

"And if the landlords refuse?" Rulan asked.

"They dare not" was his confident reply.

Yet rather than winning compliance, the scheme drew scorn, particularly from the *tong,* whose suspicions were whipped up by the Widow.

"I know the rebel general named Chen," she warned the council. "Blocked on one front, he opens up another. He was known in the Taiping wars as a sapper, one who dug tunnels under walls and lay gunpowder under the city while it slept."

"But how can he harm us with this plan?" one man asked her. "I have had good reports of the new fire engine. Checking for fire is a safe thing. . . ."

"Who cares about an engine? I care about their 'fives and twenty-fives.' That's how the Taiping rebels organized their squads of soldiers. How do you think Chen has organized his inspection teams? Two battalions of fifty, divided into twenty-fives and fives! Cadres of men who obey him and his union, not the clan societies or the *tong!* Let his inspectors into our midst, and we bring rebellion within our walls."

Thus while outwardly complying with the Chinese Union's plan for fire safety, the *tong* found a hundred ways to thwart the inspectors, particularly when their own clubhouse was judged unsafe. Certain warehouses were locked on the day the inspectors came to call. Bribes were offered in exchange for wiping a record clean. The Widow brought all her powers to bear on a massive campaign of resistance.

At the same time that her father's scheme for community safety was being thwarted by the *tong,* Molly's plans for prosperity were being similarly undermined. She was miserable, for Constable was in the grip of an enthusiasm more dangerous than his brief turn at public speaking.

He had returned from a Sunday afternoon outing—his usual excuse to visit an opium house—in great agitation. "I took the horse tram to Waikiki and had the most extraordinary revelation while walking along the sand in the king's coconut groves. Two boys had sneaked past the guards down to the sand and were climbing the trees to steal the green fruit. It was like a scene from the old days! They were barefoot and wearing nothing but *malos* and had tied a hemp rope ankle to ankle to scoot themselves up the trunk. And at the very moment that one boy grasped the coconut, I saw forwards and backwards in time, as if my ancestors had sent a message straight to me!"

"You mean to begin your epic?" Molly asked hopefully. She had finally given up writing for Bosworth in order to play the role of muse. Yet after Constable's prosperous foray into public speaking, he seemed to have set down his pen and taken on commercial aspirations. Anti-Gibson fervor was currently sweeping the islands, and Constable, fearing for his own future, was talking lately of jettisoning politics for business.

He blanched at her suggestion. "No!" he said, indignant. "Our people will never advance until we accept the fact that tending a shop is as noble as writing a poem or chanting a *mele*! I am referring to something that will transform the agriculture of our island, make us less dependent upon sugar cane! First there was sandalwood, and we cut it all down and sold it to the British for a pittance. Now there is cane, which we sell to the Americans along with sweat and our souls. Where is the next fortune to be made, Mol? I have asked myself that question a thousand times. It took a barefoot rustic in a *malo* to prove that we have been sitting in the midst of treasure!"

"What treasure?" Molly asked dubiously.

"The Pharaoh's nut! The ancient condiment for soaps, perfumes, cosmetics that adorn the faces of women everywhere. . . . And here it grows under our noses—or rather over our heads! Coconuts can be our second sugar crop! The very essence of the islands!"

Molly exploded into gales of laughter. "Oh Peter . . ." she gasped. "You are too fantastic!"

He clamped his teeth together in fury and went out into the heat of the garden to sulk and smoke his pipe. But she knew that another scheme was hatching in his febrile mind, one that would undoubtedly leave them poorer and with a single convert to his cause: herself, the perennial handmaiden to his madness.

A few nights later, Molly accompanied Constable to a gala following a concert at the Hawaiian Hotel, the one bright spot on the dreary downtown streets of Honolulu.

Throughout the evening, Molly had observed Constable approach prominent businessmen, pressing his coconut scheme on potential investors, she supposed. And judging from the numbers of men who came away shaking their heads in annoyance, he was failing miserably to impress. Molly hated parties. Her race made her conspicuous and alien, despite the fact that most of the guests were foreign-born interlopers, and she the true child of the islands. Her unmarried estate only complicated her role as the sole Chinese woman to penetrate the more bohemian circles of society. By contrast, however, displaying his mistress only increased Constable's bachelor allure. Women flirted and fussed over him, while avoiding Molly, particularly those former mistresses who had been elevated to the status of wife. The only ones who approached her were rebellious daughters, the occasional foreigner who mistook her for a courtesan or a lady's maid, and predatory males. She had removed countless hairy hands from her knee, deflected several drunken propositions, and refused to carry away a score of dirty glasses. Now at parties with Constable's colleagues, Molly had revived her childhood habit of letting her mind fly away from the present moment, of seeming to be engaged when in reality she was thinking of nothing at all.

She had been staring with a benign expression for long minutes into the sparkling ruby depths of a crystal punch bowl when she heard Constable embark on a now-familiar routine. He had found a receptive audience at last! From across the room, Molly heard him hold forth to a young couple—a *haole* rancher from the Big Island and his Hawaiian wife. Their match had set tongues wagging for months—the girl was the daughter of his mother's *wahine hana* and the youth had threatened to shoot himself rather than marry the *haole* girl his parents had picked for him.

"Sugar to be sure," Constable was saying energetically. "Sugar is king, yet it is an adopted child of the islands. Shouldn't we be building our economy on native plants? Coconuts to be exact! The palm tree is the vegetable equivalent of *puaa,* the native species of pig! Useful from nose to toes or, rather, roots to crowing leaf. A fact our forebears understood but which we, in thrall to modern manufactured conveniences and products, have forgotten. The fibers from the husk make mats, brushes, and ropes and can be burned to repel mosquitoes. The meat when young is rich and nourishing, the milk sweet, succulent, and pure as that from a woman's breast. . . ."

The bride, blushing scarlet, tried to excuse herself, but Constable trapped her and her husband in a corner and continued. "The roots of the palm make a medicine for dysentery and sore throats. When the coconut meat is aged and dried it can be sold as copra . . . that's the major trade. But squeeze the dried copra well and you render an aromatic oil for soap, lotions, and candles. You appreciate the business side of things," he told the planter's son. "We do ourselves in these islands a disservice. We send the raw material, the natural wealth of our land, abroad for others to manufacture and thereby lose the rich rewards."

"Peter is inspired by all those stinking unwashed he lived with in London," one of his drinking friends suggested for the benefit of the small crowd who had gathered to be entertained with another of Constable's humorous speeches.

"But copra's never been Hawaii's trade, sir," a merchant in the crowd declared emphatically. "Not enough trees for it. That's southern Oceania."

"All the better, *sir!* We can fulfill our duty to our sister islands, as Kalakaua himself intends. Make Hawaii the center of oil extraction and manufacture. Extend our commercial lines of power throughout the Pacific. We share the wealth of the coconut with other struggling island nations."

"*Ae, ae,*" a soft Hawaiian voice said in agreement. Hearing her voice in the momentary lull of debate, the rancher's young wife blushed again and hid behind her husband's back.

"Squeezing a fortune out of coconut is as crazy as Kalakaua trying to make an empire out of black atolls and heaps of coral!" the merchant jeered. "Poppycock!" And turning in the young wife's direction, he said in Hawaiian, moving his finger in a circle around his temple for emphasis, "*Pupule!*"

*U*nable to convince anyone at the hotel gala to invest in coconuts, Constable had drunk nearly a full bottle of brandy, so that when the young rancher from the Big Island knocked at the door the next afternoon, Molly had to drag Constable out of bed. He stumbled to the sitting room in his robe, holding a wet rag to his aching forehead and grumbling mightily to himself. Mercifully, the visitor stayed only long enough to hand Constable an envelope and shake his hand, explaining that he had left his wife outside in the carriage and that it was she who had insisted he come.

Constable looked into the envelope and sat down on the battered sofa, which Molly had covered with lace doilies, his legs splayed out before him, his jaw agape.

Molly rushed forward in alarm. "What did he give you? Is that a bill, Peter?"

With a laugh, he turned the envelope upside down and let a slender piece of paper flutter out onto his lap. Molly snatched it up: it was a bank draft for five thousand dollars, more than was needed to outfit a small factory for the manufacture of soap.

*I*n defiance of Molly's warnings, Constable quit his job at the legislature and flung himself maniacally into commerce. The enterprise was a partnership, sixty-forty, with the young rancher and his wife contributing money and Constable running the day-to-day business. He rented a dilapidated three-story brick structure near the harbor that had once served as a warehouse for an outfitter in the now defunct whaling trade. When profits from whaling plummeted, the owner had added a wooden extension at the back of the warehouse, which he rented to a Chinatown merchant who opened a saloon. The place had done a lively trade for years among certain segments of Chinatown who came not for gin or beer but for the opium and gambling in a room hidden behind a false wall at the back. A quick renovation by Constable's building crew transformed the capacious hollow shell where masts and spars once stood as thick as a California forest into a soap-rendering plant, with offices above and chemical vats below. The original iron staircase, which zigzagged up a back wall like the thread of a drunken spider, now led to a catwalk running along the third floor thirty feet above the ground. From that perch, one entered a row of offices opening directly onto the upper balcony from which Constable reigned over his kingdom of coconuts.

He made contracts with a British syndicate running ships in the copra trade and began buying up quantities of green coconuts and dried coconut meat. He dealt with chiefs from rural districts on the outer islands and British and Dutch exporters of copra from as far away as Sumatra. Then he went looking for an expert in soapmaking. He found a Swiss chemist who had designed a new type of sugar boiler and claimed to have expert knowledge in rollers, vacuum pans, and steam-driven centrifugals for separating out sugar from molasses. How different could making soap be from making sugar? Constable theorized, and hired the man away from the sugar factory.

The Swiss chemist concocted a recipe that sounded in Constable's ears truly scientific, using ingredients such as sodium hydroxide, glycerol, metallic salts of fatty acids, alkali, and such, all of which had to be imported at tremendous cost. For equipment, Constable scavenged what he could from sugar makers, ship outfitters, and butchers. He found that whale oil kettles from a generation before made excellent boiling vats. Economizing was necessary, for there were expensive casks, drums, tanks, copper coils and bricks for ovens, wooden cooling forms, and molds to purchase. Nor did the odoriferous concoction of coconuts, potash, lard, and meat scraps endear him to his neighbors. In short, Constable soon found that the enhancement of beauty by the exotic essence of Oceania required a considerable mess of expensive equipment and foul-smelling ingredients, and even that was not enough. He had a factory; equipment; and Hawaiian laborers to haul, process, and refine coconut meat—and not a single bar of decent soap.

The recipe was bad, he told his overworked crew. He turned the Swiss chemist out and took over the task of mixing himself, sending to France and England for sophisticated recipes. He railed at his workers for not cleaning their equipment or for tainting the substances with toxic materials. He worked night and day, and if Molly did not share his quixotic dream, she did at least admire his industry.

Then shipments of copra from major suppliers stopped; the natives in the Indies were on strike against their colonial masters. Great God Jehovah as well as the *akuas* of the earth and the sea seemed to mock him, Constable complained bitterly to Molly. In six months' time, Constable had spent nearly all his money and still had not one commercial-grade bar of soap or fragrant unguent to show for his efforts.

Finally Molly decided to consult her mother. Rulan, she remembered, had a fund of recipes for female ailments, including those for soaps and cosmetics. Pride must not stand in the way of survival.

*H*ow difficult could it be to make soap? Molly wondered, amazed at Constable's inability to accomplish something so simple. Nalani and her mother made soap out of plants and tubers when the store-bought stuff was not in stock or proved too costly. She wasn't sure whether or how coconuts were involved, but the woman who prescribed remedies for diseases as complicated as scrofula and asthma would surely know how to make a substance to keep one's body clean! Although it galled her to beg, she decided to make peace with her mother on the chance that Rulan would not let Constable drown in a financial tidal wave if it meant taking Molly with him.

Molly knew her mother's habits so well that an "accidental" meeting was easy to arrange. Rulan frequented the Kwan Yin temple, took tea at Lucy's, made shopping trips to the vegetable stalls in Chinatown with the regularity of the bells at St. Andrew's Cathedral. Molly could visit her at the shop, of course, yet in all these places her mother was surrounded by prying eyes and ears. The only time Rulan was truly alone was on the first of each month when she ventured on foot to the Ala Moana marshes to place an order for live ducks, an excursion that was as close as she came to leisure since it took her out of Chinatown for half a day.

Molly put on her oldest dress, a faded muslin with buttons from hem to throat (lest her mother scold her for becoming too proud), pulled her hair into a tight married-lady's bun and caught the jitney wagon going to the beach. Coming over a small rise, she could see the white breakers around the reef and the sea beyond, and lying between the mountains and the sea the low-lying wetlands on which Chinese and Hawaiians grew taro and rice and did a brisk side business in live ducks. She got off the jitney where it turned toward the pleasure-houses of Waikiki and walked the remaining half mile to the duck farm her mother patronized. The dirt road was wet after the night rains, and her stockings and skirts were soon stained with mud. By the time she reached the duck pond, the midmorning sun burned hot, bright, and blinding. The ripe smells of swamp and manure overpowered the sharp briny scent of the sea.

A skinny Tang man, his queue wound around his shaven pate, was knee-deep in a rice paddy. She called out a greeting. Rulan was expected but had not yet come, he replied with a toothless grin. The farmer sloshed out of the marsh and padded behind her in bare feet, bragging about the extent of his holdings and the fatness of his ducks, whether to impress this strange Tang girl in *haole* costume or whether in preparation for overcharging, she could not tell. After a few minutes, a cook from the Hawaiian Hotel arrived in a brougham for his weekly order of poultry and rice, and the duck farmer turned his attention to negotiating a sale.

Molly found a congenial seat on a gray shelf of rock overlooking the pond and the road, which curved around it. From that spot, she would be sure to see her mother before her mother saw her. Better to prepare her face for the harangue that her mother would unleash when she met her daughter face-to-face. Over her head, seagulls flew in a low, curving loop over the wetlands in search of fish. A green turtle, as round as a bowler hat, lumbered out of the reeds and made a slow, arduous journey across the mud. Sliding into the water, he was all grace and elegance, turning, diving, and resurfacing as easily as the gulls in their empire of air. She giggled when the turtle's beaky face poked above the surface of the pond as if to reproach her for doubting his skill.

"In China, turtles are good eating. For long life," her mother announced abruptly at her elbow.

Molly whirled around in surprise. Her mother seemed to have emerged out of the ether or out of the ground itself.

"Why did you pick this spot to waylay me?" Rulan demanded.

"Because Father would not be here!" Molly replied, her carefully planned speech flying out of her head. She felt ungainly and belligerent, shrunk to the size of a small girl.

"That is the ugliest *haole* dress I ever saw!" declared her mother. "Are you out of money? Is that why you dress like a pauper? Has that *la sap* finally thrown you out?"

"Certainly not!" Molly snapped.

"Then he will when he loses his factory. Everyone in Chinatown complains of the stink he is making. Your father says he bribes the *haole* fire inspector so they won't report him. We see wagonloads of coconuts going in and nothing coming out but cracked shells. They say he is eating them and soon will be as fat as the king."

Molly was too angry to see the fleeting smile pass over her mother's face. "Imagine anyone in Chinatown complaining about stink."

"Be ashamed! Chinatown was once your home. But I forget how

grand you are. You would rather walk around the porches of the Hawaiian Hotel with the dance-hall girls and loose women.''

"I know you hate Peter," Molly accused. "Nothing he does is good enough for you!''

"I'm your mother. A mother tells the truth no one else dares tell you. As for that *la sap,* he doesn't deserve you.''

"A 'loose woman' like me? A *la sap* girl has no reputation to worry about.''

"You think I'm insulted by your language? How come you and I don't understand each other? I was a concubine, too! I ran away with your father. We slept together lots of times before we were married! I don't care what others call you. You are a good girl. I know you don't love that man.''

"I do!" Molly shouted, her face scarlet with embarrassment. She did not want to hear about her parents' love life. It was unseemly for a mother to confess such things to a daughter. "Don't tell me what I feel.''

"Why not? How come you don't know what you feel until you sit down and write it on paper? It made me sick when Auntie Lucy praised you for sitting down to write what happened to you every day. I thought to myself, 'That girl is very stupid. She doesn't feel pain until after she starts to bleed. Then she has to write down how it hurts.' ''

"I can't talk to you! Why do I even try? I wanted to get a recipe for soap from you, but forget it! I'm leaving!" announced Molly, stomping off toward the jitney line.

"All right, I send you my recipes," Rulan shouted after her. "If that *la sap* is so stupid, I help him out! But what kind of soap you want? You want the special kind for women? I know lots of those. Auntie Lucy grew a yellow flower from America to make a soak for her feet. Nalani knew more recipes than any of us. *Hau-a-au* bark for shampooing hair . . . and a kind of *maile* for sweat bath. And *oliwa* for bathing sores—depends what kind of sores, how can I know if you don't tell me— And *iwaiwa* to wash infants so their skin turns soft. . . . Some recipes ask for coconut, but what part of the coconut you want to use? You can use coconut milk for women's organs and eyes, coconut oil for dry skin, coconut meat for—''

Rulan ran out of breath long before her store of recipes was exhausted. By that time, Molly was already out of earshot, having almost gained the edge of the marshland where the jitney took on passengers. Was the girl sick? Rulan wondered. Why was she trembling and tossing her head back and forth in abandon? Her shrewd eye studied the slim figure dancing in the distance, after which Rulan decided that that careless, irresponsible girl of hers was laughing!

6

THE GATE

"Chance rules our lives," Mei Yuk remarked to Lily one evening over their evening meal of rice and salted fish. They ate alone these days, for the young bond maid had been enticed away by another family with an eligible nephew eager for a bride.

Neither Molly nor Lincoln would have recognized the silent girl picking at her food without appetite. Mei Yuk's daughter was twenty-three, already old for a prospective bride, and the beauty that had blossomed before all Chinatown was frozen hard by time.

"She looks like the ghost-faced porcelain dolls the *bak kuei* give their children," one woman observed of Lily as she left Mei Yuk's house after the *ma jong* game. Another spitefully insisted that the Widow intended her daughter to be as blighted as a flower in the dark. How better to feed her own vanity than to have a daughter who was withering before her eyes?

"Did you hear her brag?" another said. Imitating Mei Yuk's mincing tone, she said, " 'My daughter and I wear the same clothes, and I am the one that gets the praise.' "

It did not escape the women's notice that Mei Yuk wore her hair in two braids coiled around her ears like a young girl and powdered her face to look as pale and fragile as her daughter's. Once she actually made Lily take off her tunic and shoes in front of the women guests and slipped them on, twirling with hands on hips to show how the clothes hung on her small frame.

"See?" the Widow had crowed, pulling up the tunic to point to her waist. "Only sixteen inches! My girl is fatter!"

Lily was the object of great sympathy. She was a shadow of the splendid shining Lantern Queen of earlier years. There had been six offers of marriage since the last bridegroom had proved an imbecile and the wedding had been called off; all, including this last offer, had ended in anger and disappointment for the Widow, and in secret, silent glee for the unclaimed bride.

On this evening, as was her habit, the Widow erupted into angry reproaches at her daughter. "Are you my daughter?" she shouted between swallows of rice. "*My* daughter ought to know, as I knew by instinct, a hundred ways to charm a man. I was only fourteen, already a bride, and I had only to show my face for men to fall in love! Two paddy boys tried to kidnap me on my wedding journey. One died for love of me. Then bandits waylaid my palanquin and would have taken my virtue . . ."

The girl sighed and picked absently at a morsel of fish. She had heard the tale before: lies polished into brightness by an aging beauty.

The mother slammed down her chopsticks. "Bad, foolish girl. You have no charm, no grace. You move as clumsily as an ox. How do you expect to attract a husband?"

"The husbands you choose for me are old . . ."

"And money makes them young again! I swear you are as useless as the rest of the Lis! If not for me, the fortunes of this house would have fallen down around our heads long ago. Girls younger than you are stealing the best men away. The greedy Chens are buying up blocks of warehouses for their evil-smelling factories, and all you do is let our luck slide out the door and into our enemies' hands! Cut your head and tongue! For a copper, I would sell you to a leper if he would take you!"

Lily chewed thoughtfully. Slowly and with great deliberation, she replied in her lilting voice, "Perhaps I am not meant to marry, Mother. Perhaps I am meant to end my days an ugly crone like you."

The Widow grew pale and an uncharacteristic rush of tears clouded her eyes. Lily's occasional bursts of malice confounded her. It was a mother's duty to berate a daughter, but against all custom and decorum for the daughter to reply in kind.

Lily went on eating, entirely oblivious to her mother's confusion. Her fingers plucked daintily at a piece of ginger that had stuck between her teeth.

An appalling new notion seized the Widow. Was Lily—dutiful, sub-servient, weak-willed Lily—purposely disrupting the marriage negotiations? Sometimes the Widow wondered if she knew her daughter at all.

If the Widow could have eavesdropped on her daughter's thoughts, she would have had good cause for alarm. Lily was not for sale. She would break every betrothal the go-between made her sign, outwait and outwit the woman before whom all Chinatown quaked. There was only one Tang man in all Hawaii worth marrying, and Lily meant to have him.

Lincoln passed his first winter in New Haven wrapped in firelit comfort in a village smothered in snow. His friendship with Heloise had progressed only as far as her parents and the conventions of the dinner table would allow. Then one gray February afternoon, that friendship took a surprising turn. There was a plan among prominent town ladies to com-memorate the pure, colonial heritage of the city by holding a spring cotil-lion. The idea was to bring together young ladies of "good family" with eligible bachelors from town and from the college. Unmentioned was the fact that some of the most prominent wives were not precisely of "colo-nial" lineage themselves, but a half-generation away from the newcomer Irish, German, Polish, and Italians whose labor in the downtown factories was making their husbands rich.

The very notion of a cotillion sent up a hue and cry from the Yale faculty, who complained that future leaders of government and church must not imitate the frivolous social customs of Boston and New York. Reverend Bainton himself protested to his wife that "dance by its Diony-sian derivation inflames the emotions. Daughter must not attend!" Yet just as the Yale professors proved no match against the alliance of faculty and town wives, so Bainton was made to bow before the ambitious Clarice, who felt keenly her inferior status as wife of a pastor.

The reverend retreated to the airless rooms in Beinecke Library, while his wife insinuated herself on minor dance committees, spending weeks copying out menus by hand and constructing mountains of tiny paper flowers that would eventually adorn the walls and tables of the Tontine Hotel.

One afternoon, Lincoln arrived at the door to find both Baintons gone out, the dinner unmade, and Heloise twirling in the front parlor with a damask pillow to her bosom.

"At last," she cried out, "I have found my partner."

He watched her gliding on the carpet like a skater on an icy pond, a lock of silvery hair stuck to her flushed cheek. She turned and turned, then breathing hard, called out to him again, beckoning him closer.

"I'm no use to you," he told her. "I can't dance."

"Can't dance? How absurd! It's as natural as singing!"

Lincoln's limbs, so weightless and easy a moment before, planted themselves into the ground, anchoring him to the floorboards. He pressed his hands upon his books to stop their trembling. "I don't sing either!" he told her. At chapel, he had merely mouthed the hymns, self-consciousness rendering him as mute as in childhood. Lincoln envied those who sang and danced with such ease. The missionary grandchildren with whom he had studied at Oahu College were mad for Vienna waltzes and flung themselves into the foreign steps with the abandon of young *alii*. Lincoln attributed his inability to sing or dance to the practicality of his race. How could a Chinaman free the body from the all-encompassing mind?

"Put down those books at once," Heloise cried out. "If you cannot dance, then I must teach you! You have only three weeks to learn!" And she tossed aside her pillow and grabbed his hand.

Why Lincoln allowed himself to be dragged onto the Baintons' carpet might be explained by the manner in which Heloise placed his hand upon her waist. Her breasts rose and fell with excitement; her face and neck were burnished with a pearly sheen. Heloise was exactly his height, and she set her gray eyes directly upon his, pushing him in a circle backward around the floor, forcing him to take tiny steps in time to her humming. After a few awkward circuits around the room, Lincoln found himself moving in reasonable accord with his partner. And who could blame him if his fingers occasionally brushed her cheek or his forearm her breast or the front of his leg touched the region of her skirts where her thighs moved. His fingers felt through whalebone and stitching the lively young body beneath. Even a Yale Chinaman, who had steeled himself to suppress all bodily desire, might find his resolve shaken with gray-eyed Heloise in his arms.

The absent Lincoln was more real to Molly than he had been in the flesh. His letters from Yale described his life there with such vividness that she could trace in her mind the lacy patterns of frost on the leaded windows of his rooming house, bend with him under the low stone arches below the stairs through which students passed to their classes. His last letter touched her with his description of his movement from loneliness to tranquility.

How had he managed to build in that frigid corner of New England the kind of freedom which eluded her at home? He wrote:

Dear Molly,

Finally, I am content. I have hibernated all winter beside a fire with a few boon companions and my books. And I have grown rich in spirit, having found, at long last, my place and time. I steep myself in the past with company as eccentric as I and am an orphan no more.

Last week, I took a walk along the frozen river with a pastor from town and his daughter. You, a child of the tropics, cannot imagine how a seminarian closeted behind thick walls yearns for the cracking of river ice, the breaking of snow-encrusted earth by green shoots.

Your father sent me a draft for fifty dollars and word through a scribe: he has organized, as he puts it, "an army to fight fire." War is his natural state. And it is a noble war to draw Hakka and Punti together against a common enemy! All good motives are suspect, of course. I would assume that his efforts are construed by certain parties in Chinatown as a blatant attempt to grab power. He courts danger and sows enmity, but such is the lot of any warrior.

I have known his softer side. I wish you would allow him to know yours.

Your cousin,
Lin Kong

Molly stuffed the letter into the pocket of her skirt and read it many times. She marveled that Lincoln always seemed to know more about her parents than she, although she discounted his warning about the dangers faced by Pao An, having long ago decided that her parents' tangled affairs in Chinatown were mostly imagined and not her concern. No, what made Molly burn with curiosity was the mysterious source of Lincoln's newfound serenity. Who were these "boon companions" of his hearth? The "company of eccentrics" in which he took such pleasure? Did they include the pastor's daughter?

*A*t the same time that Constable was spending money in reckless abandon, Rulan's storefront business had grown so much that she had to hire ten workers and a Chinese *luna* to manage the surge in orders. Hawaiian matrons and a few newcomers from Japan and Portugal found their children passing around bags of *mui* and developed a taste for the sweet-sour fruit themselves. Pao An and Rulan were wealthy by village standards now, and their story was among the dozen tales rehearsed at community gatherings and at banquet tables as proof that the poorest *gu li* could grow rich in Hawaii. Yet prosperity brought no tranquility between husband and wife. Stubborn warriors to the last, they waited in vain for the other to make the first move toward peace.

Pao An gave to lava stone and earth and wood what he denied his wife. He had embarked on a renovation of their Chinatown property. Rulan was used to his efforts to make their tenement safe from fire, yet when he began demolishing the back wall and ripping up the ceiling and floor, she scolded him about the noise, dust, and useless activity, only to have him thrust a sheaf of papers at her with a guttural oath. These were his building plans, stained and dirty from sawdust and grease. And she was struck not only by the age of the sketches but by the magnitude of the project. He was transforming the original tenement and yard into a warehouse and factory—for her! The main floor would be for retail trade. In back would be the area for the preparation and packing of rice, spices, coffee, and preserved specialties like *mui*. Machines would pound preserved fruit into "crack-seed" on one side, and on the other, women at long tables would separate piles of dark, glossy *mui* into individual brown paper packets labeled and tied with string. The basement would serve as warehouse for the barrels of *mui* and crates of spices, boxes of medicines, canisters of tea from China carried off the dock. To move the products from the warehouse to the factory to the selling floor and down again to the vendors' carts in the backyard, he had designed an ingenious network of tracks and carts with metal wheels on which a shipment could travel the length of the enterprise and be transformed from bulk product into a packet tied with string in a single day.

After the foundation of coral block was laid by one of his road crews, Pao An worked alone, hammering and sawing and chiseling by the light of a single kerosene lamp. He ordered the best iron and brass pipes for plumbing and rot-resistant redwood from California for the posts and beams. Slowly, Rulan saw their shabby tenement transformed. By the time Pao An began building a gate for the fence that surrounded their property, there was enough of the factory completed to make plain the structure he carried in his head.

Late one night, while slicing green mangoes for pickling in vinegar and sugar to sell in the store, Rulan saw from the kitchen window her husband putting a coat of red lacquer onto the gate, an elaborately carved affair standing higher than a man's head, like the gates of wealthy families in China, an incongruous item given the spartan style of the building. The kerosene lamp burned brightly, gleaming off the bright surface of the paint. His brow was knit in concentration and filmed with sweat; his hands were dyed a lurid red. There was a curious sound thrumming in his throat like the droning of bees, and she realized that her silent, inarticulate husband was singing! All these years they had slept in the same bed, dipped their chopsticks into a common dish, tallied the accounts with a single mind and she had never heard him sing. Selfish man! she whispered to herself with a smile. Hoarding your song like a secret coin!

She remembered a strong young voice that years ago had promised her paradise. The acid in the fruit stung the cracked skin of her fingers. She put her knife down, tossed the last handful of mango into a pickling bucket, and rinsed off her hands at the pump before going into the yard.

"It's a strong gate," she told him. Her shadow merged with his upon the glossy surface.

He went on painting, holding in his head the image of the small girl swinging on a gate, the first sight he had had of her. What was a gate, after all, but the weakest part of a wall and, therefore, a place that must be continually fortified. Gates were always a problem for warriors defending a sanctuary, for they provided quick access to the unwary inhabitants within. He had shut tight the portals of his house against marauders, but he felt old now and was tired of being afraid. Was it weakness to open himself up to the perils of the world again? To let down his defenses to the one who had wounded him so? He was building the gate for his daughter. But what if the gate stood open, and she never came home?

When Rulan took the brush from his hand, red paint smeared her fingers. For a long moment, they swayed together, two longtime lovers caught in a flickering corona of light.

7

A WHISPER OF FLAME

Chinatown, 1886

There was a *fan-tan* parlor hidden behind a false wall in a wharfside tavern owned by the *tong*. Gambling was the society's most lucrative business, and this particular gambling parlor was worth the exorbitant rent the Hawaiian tavern keeper paid. Or had been until the noise and smells of the soap factory adjoining the tavern had driven customers away.

The stench seeped through the brick wall into the airless space where the Tang men gambled. The manager of the gambling rooms burned joss sticks, but nothing helped. He had complained to the authorities but to no avail. The room was spartan in the extreme, containing only the barest necessities for gambling: four round tables covered with green felt, a high cabinet stocked with tiles and chips and ivory buttons, ceramic opium pipes, crates of tea and jars of imported Chinese spirits. The lottery and money exchange cage was built against one wall, its front window covered with chicken wire. Against the opposite wall hung the painted visage of the warrior-god Kwan Kung, the patron deity of the house, under whose fierce stare the games of chance went on. Below the portrait a narrow wooden table served as an altar where votive candles lit by hopeful gamblers burned throughout play.

The games went on until the early morning hours, when an agent from the *tong* collected the house winnings and gave the manager his share. One evening, when the smells from the factory had been particularly fulsome and business unusually wretched, one of the *tong* leaders, the owner of the gambling house, came in person to collect the winnings from the manager. Fearing retribution from his employer, the manager babbled a stream of imprecations against the owner of the soap factory next door whom he blamed for bad business, but the owner seemed uninterested in plunging profits, expressing instead the curious desire to light a candle to Kwan Kung for a *ma jong* game on the following afternoon. That the owner, though a woman, was a dévot of Kwan Kung, a man's deity, did not surprise the manager in the least. No, he thought to himself, rubbing his neck with relief, the one who commanded the loyalty of *tong* ruffians would not have offered housewifely prayers to the goddess of mercy.

Once alone, the owner took a fat red prayer candle from its box and carried it into the wire-covered lottery cage where the manager stored a mound of papers. She set the candle in a wooden box filled with thin rice paper lottery tickets and watched the heat make the paper curl. Soon they would turn brown and puff into flame. Her lips were murmuring what could well have been a prayer.

Only then did the owner glide on tiny, cloth-shod feet through the curtained doorway. Outside, she heard the engines stirring the vats of coconut oil grind into life in the factory next door.

Perhaps the flame would falter and be snuffed out. Perhaps not. "Chance," the Widow murmured to herself with a smile, "rules our lives."

At first, the flame was as insubstantial as a whisper. Hidden away inside a box, inside a cage, inside a room, inside a building. Lost in the general miasma of the wharf, it sputtered faintly in its lonely corner in the locked lottery cage in the back room of the tavern. Until it found air. Then it sucked in fresh life. The tiny flame spread out into fiery fingers, igniting all it touched: a spider's web hanging against the wall, a splinter of wood, a box of discarded tea leaves, a chair, a wall, a roof, a building—all things became fire.

*P*ao An was sleepily entering his shop at cockcrow when he heard the block captain shrieking the alarm. In seconds, he was sprinting half-dressed through the narrow lanes to the firehouse where a team of men was stoking a small fire in the belly of the engine to make steam. Bucket brigades were already running toward the harbor. Women hurried sleepy children before them toward the mountains. It was still quiet; neither Chinatown nor the fire itself was fully awake.

By the time the engine was hitched and driven to where the blaze burned hottest, fire had engulfed three buildings. Then it leaped across the lane onto a tinder-dry stairway where it snaked across the shingles of a roof and fell upon a grass storage hut, which exploded into flame like a torch dipped in oil. The brigade had worked quickly, handing out hoses and buckets and shepherding the crowds through the streets. Yet the fire was spreading too fast. Another building and another fell to the flames. Pao An directed the squads to set back fires, hoping to keep the flames contained on one block. But the wind, blowing inland from the sea, helped the fire jump across the narrow lanes onto new blocks of buildings. Soon they were running short of men and water and had to let their panicked team of horses go. And so the brigade pulled the little steam pumper by hand into the heart of the blaze.

The Widow shivered with pleasure when the clanging gong of the fire brigade echoed down the lanes. Luck had fallen in her direction. For she *was* the goddess of chance: strong, prescient, invincible. Let the goddess's enemies beware!

So when Lily lost her calm, crying out to the servants to throw buckets of water to wet down the roof of the house, the Widow pulled the coverlet over her ears to drown out her daughter's squalling, secure in the knowledge that Chance would have her way.

Lily ran into the bedroom carrying thread and scissors. "Get up, Mother," she ordered. "Give me your jewels to sew into our clothes!"

The Widow closed her eyes, delighting in the din below. "The fire is far from here. Do you doubt your mother? Let the brave men of the fire brigade do their job!" She dismissed her daughter's gibbering and the servants' terrified wails. Peasants were always frightened by what their betters faced with aplomb. She alone in this household had had the foresight to ensure that events ruled in their favor. She had waited thirty years to punish those two, the agents of all her sorrow. And now Chen Pao An would be made to suffer the consequences of his defection. Let his house and his woman burn . . . and if the flames took a stray victim or two, it was unfortunate, but it could not be helped. A superior person left nothing to chance alone.

The racket rose from below. The Widow decided she must discipline the groom who was doing something bothersome to their horse, judging from the clatter of hooves on the coral flagstones of the courtyard. The stones were Belgian block set just that summer into the red earth, a sign that her house had put down roots into Hawaii. Never again would a Li call China home!

She tried to cleanse her mind of ugly thoughts. And yet the sounds nagged at her. A whinnying horse. The cries of gardener and groom. Small-feet women running up and down stairs. The crash of boxes thrown off a balcony into a courtyard. Irksome, familiar noises. Nonsense, she told herself. I have left all that behind.

And then she heard the voice of China. The terrible roar of a people gone mad, the wordless hum of myriad voices fusing into a single scream. She had heard the cry of the mob when it broke down her grandfather's house in Canton, looted it of treasures, and did unspeakable things to the old man. She had heard its voice again at Abundant Spring Mountain, her husband's cliffside mansion, echoing like thunder from heaven. And the Widow saw in her mind the flames leaping from terrace to terrace down the mountain; the servants jumping from the Lower House into the oily brown river. But that fire happened long ago, she reminded herself. This is Hawaii, where the will of the Widow holds sway.

Footsteps clattered on the veranda outside. "The fire, Mother! We must get away!" cried Lily.

"Cut your head and tongue," snapped the Widow. "I have arranged everything. This fire will pass us by." The Widow glowered at her daughter, who had made herself as ugly as a hunger-marcher. The girl was wearing several layers of clothes, which bulged around her hips and waist.

"The fish market is lost! And now the roof is ablaze—"

A small, skinny hand jerked out of the quilt and slapped the girl on her cheek. "Be ashamed!" The Widow's eyes shone huge and black. She looked around the room serenely, counting up her treasures. "The fire will not come here."

Lily ran from her mother's room into the courtyard. Cuffing their heads, she forced the gardener and groom upstairs. She would need them to bear witness to the crucial moment when her mother's "indisposition" began. Her cheeks were burning, not from her mother's blow or the heat of the fire, but from the intoxicating feeling of liberation sweeping through her even as the flames raged outside their gates.

Lily's first act as *Tai Tai* of the Li clan was to order her mother bundled into the quilt and thrown like a sack of rice over the shoulders of the groom. Her second act was to open her mother's safe. She had already sewn their jewels into the linings of her tunic and tied bags of coins around her waist. In minutes, she had secured the best of the treasure: deeds, rental agreements, and leases as well as contracts binding individual Tang men and whole societies to the Li clan in a network of secret debt and obligation for generations to come. Then she led her mother and a handful of servants around the expanding circle of fire to the harbor and the safety of their fishing fleet.

Sweating, cursing, Pao An's men struggled on, laying hose, retreating and laying hose again. They fought through their exhaustion. One man climbed to the top of a ladder with a hose, when suddenly a second-story window blew out, vomiting fire in his direction. He fell, screaming, in a flaming arc to the dust below. One by one, the men succumbed to the heat and the smoke and were led off by friends, spewing up ropes of black mucus. The red monster came on, and what was safe at one moment was quickly consumed in the next.

Pao An took some comfort from the knowledge that the fire had veered away from the wharfside area where Molly lived. Yet the blaze might shift at the slightest change of wind, and the clanging gongs in the distance told him that the fire was still spreading beyond the block of factories and warehouses where it had first burst forth.

And now the fire created its own wind. It sucked air down through the valleys and up from the sea, sending sparks shooting into the atmosphere, where they hovered and eventually fell in a fiery rain all over Chinatown beyond the center of the blaze. Pao An and his brigade retreated street by street toward the harbor while the fire pursued them like a vengeful foe, cutting off this route, collapsing that avenue of escape with an avalanche of disintegrating buildings.

They had worked their way around in a wide circle, and Pao An soon found himself at the place where the blaze had first broken out, staring in anger and astonishment at the soap factory whose brick walls rose above the blackened timbers of the *fan-tan* parlor, whole and strong and untouched by the flames.

The streets were clogged with rattling carts and frantic Tang men dragging valuables hastily tied up in rice sacks or blankets, the remnants of unearned riches, the detritus of dreams.

Rulan pushed against the swelling human tide, one lone woman carving her own path against thousands of Tang men bent on escape. Pao An, she knew, would be in the heart of the furnace fighting the blaze, and it was to him, not to sanctuary, that she ran. Burning cinders swirled above the heads of the fleeing multitude like fiery demons' eyes blinking at the holocaust below, and in her ears sounded the roar and crackle of the flames, devouring all.

"Crazy woman, you're going the wrong way," shouted a man bent beneath a shoulder yoke. In his haste to push past her, his exertions set his baskets rocking, and he knocked Rulan down with one wooden end. In a heartbeat, the terrified mob swept over her. Kicking and shrieking and struggling for air, she fought against the onslaught of boots and limbs and pulled herself upright against a hitching post, bleeding from the temple where the yoke had struck.

This is China again! she thought to herself in disbelief. The same fleeing masses. The same face of terror multiplied a hundredfold, the same brutish scramble through the streets. And on the heels of the multitude, the enemy—war or hunger or drought or fire.

Even though the fire had moved away from the area where Molly lived, Rulan knew it might shift at the slightest change of wind.

Three men from the fire brigade, their noses and mouth blackened by smoke, ran past, carrying lines of new hoses coiled around their shoulders.

"Chen Pao An—where is he?" she shouted at them.

"Commanding the steam engine," one replied. He pointed to where a cloud of purplish smoke billowed into the sky.

"Take me too," she cried, rushing after them. But at that moment a burning brand fell against her, sending up a shower of sparks that ignited tiny fires in her hair and skirt. Spying a horse trough, she quickly slid into its depths, leaning back to drench the scorched ends of her hair. Her clothes hissed and steamed. Then she climbed out, ripped off the hem of her tunic and held the wet rag over her face, cursing herself for having lost time. The firemen had already disappeared into the throng. Fiery jets of air seared the cloth to her face in seconds. Holding the flimsy mask to her nose, she ran onward in the direction the firemen had gone.

On the block beyond, the windows of a building exploded as if a giant bellows had burst within. Blue-white flames flashed up the brick facade. She hastened past the burning shell and discovered to her terror that she was trapped in a landscape as alien as the inside of a volcano. All about her was leaping flame. Behind her, the gutted shell of the brick building bulged outward as if pushed by an invisible hand and crashed into the street in a shower of fiery debris. Ahead, two lines of hissing flames were swiftly moving together from opposite directions. Once the fiery streams met, she would be trapped inside a funnel of whirling gases. The water had long evaporated from her clothing, and the very air was afire, streaming out of the burning buildings like the breath of dragons. Rulan had just enough time to run between the swiftly moving rivers of fire. The flames rose up with a mighty roar as she passed through. Now she was cut off from Pao An as surely as if an ocean divided them. She had passed beyond the worst of the blaze to the very edge of Chinatown at Nuuanu Stream.

Half-sitting, half-floating, half-crawling upon the slippery rocks, she came in due course to where the stream poured into the harbor. There beneath a hanging pall of smoke, a flotilla of boats bobbed on the waters. Each boat was crowded stem to stern with Tang men, women, and children, wailing and praying, as Chinatown crumbled into ash.

*P*ao An's men had been fighting the blaze for hours and had saved nothing. Tenements, shops, warehouses, market stalls, and smithies—all were lost. Nothing remained now of the wooden structures except for one incongruously obstinate edifice: the evil-smelling soap factory owned by the *hapa haole* who had corrupted his daughter. And now the fire had spread past to the edges of Chinatown, threatening Honolulu itself. The air seared the eyes and lungs of those firefighters who remained whole enough to fight the blaze, and these helped Pao An drag the engine down a rubble-strewn path toward the water.

Yet he could not help turning back for one last look at the brick building that mocked him. Even now he could hear the machines inside grinding just as the terrified workers had left them. A high whine rose above the clank and hiss of the engines. Puffs of steam billowed through an opening in the brick. The vats of oil were still being churned.

Pao An told himself he was fully justified in what he intended to do. Otherwise, that monumentally stupid man would survive the conflagration and go on to build a fortune while holding his daughter in thrall! The brick outer walls had protected the factory, but the interior was still vulnerable to fire. Why should this deceiver profit when the livelihoods of thousands of decent Tang men had been destroyed? He picked up a burning post and made his way across the smoking debris toward the factory, signaling his crew to take the engine farther down toward the edge of the wharf where the smoke was beginning to dissipate. Puzzled at his actions, the men were nonetheless eager to fill their lungs with sweet, pure air and rushed onward without him.

Pao An mounted the singed, rickety steps, squinting against the smoke, and shoved the burning end of the post like a lance through a pane of glass. Hot air belched from within. Good, he thought. There was fire inside already. He threw in the flaming brand, and noted with pleasure the clang it made when it fell against a metal vat.

Then he heard a cry.

Pao An peered into the interior of the factory and glimpsed a white shape climbing up a darkened staircase at the rear of the building. He craned his neck upward. There it was again—a pale form running along an interior balcony on the third floor. A woman swaying like an injured dancer across the parapets of a stage, her long hair flying out in sharp points above her head.

Suddenly, with a terrible grinding of metal brackets, the staircase pulled loose from the brick wall and collapsed, sending the slim figure reeling backward. The staircase rocked to and fro and then broke apart, collapsing upon itself. A shower of sparks erupted on the floor below and ignited smaller blazes all around. The broken balcony, bereft of its center support, listed downward; and the iron crampons that held it to the brick face thirty feet above the burning factory floor squealed and ground on their moorings. The figure upon the iron gratings grasped desperately for support along the wall and turned her face toward the street.

"Daughter!" Pao An whispered. The word was agony to him.

The girl gripped the broken railing of the balcony, her eyes wide with terror.

Pao An kicked open the door and dashed into the burning factory. Fed by the air that followed in his wake, the fire took on new life. Open vats of oil sent up varicolored flames like witch's brew that burned blue and green and white. The girl hung by both hands high above the burning vats.

"Peter, is it you?" Molly screamed, when she saw him burst through the gloom.

"Don't move," Pao An commanded and raged about like a trapped bull looking for a way to get to her.

"Father!" she cried in confusion and alarm. Her mind was spinning, and she was dizzy from the fumes. How had her father appeared out of nowhere? And where was Peter? She thought she might be dreaming, except that the heat that rose from below was all too real.

Pao An raced to the far wall where an exhaust pipe ran up through the ceiling above and began to climb the pipe like a rope. Burning cinders fell upon his hair; hot air filled his lungs. Black smoke billowed up from below, trailing him on his journey upward. He had to lean far out to grasp the balcony rail. Below him, jets of tallow and oil spewed liquid fire into the air like a lake in Buddha's hell.

Pao An seized the rail, swung over, and pulled himself up. The balcony was now broken in the middle and a gap of ten feet separated him from his daughter.

"Father!" Molly cried. "I'm afraid!"

Without hesitation, Pao An ran along the tottering balcony and leaped over the gap, crashing to the iron grating on the other side and sending a shudder through the precarious structure. He pulled himself forward just before a section of the balcony sheared off and plunged into the fiery pit below. Drenched in sweat and covered with soot, he crawled toward his daughter. Hot tears coursed down his blackened cheeks. A searing pain ripped from stomach to chest. Something had broken inside him, and he felt himself an old, old man. He wanted to stop. To rest. To die. But Molly still hung there!

"You knew I was here," she sobbed in amazement. "You came for me." Tiny sparks hissed in the folds of her skirts; already her dress was burned at sleeves and hem.

Pao An scanned the fires below and spied a small patch of floor not yet aflame. "Take off your dress. We'll make a rope. Quickly."

Molly stripped off her outer gown and helped her father tear it into strips. He doubled some strands together, knotting them tightly. While they worked, the fire spread. The balcony broke in another spot. The wrought-iron fasteners that anchored it to the brick wall were loosening in the heat. There was not enough time, not enough fabric to make a rope long enough to reach the ground.

Pao An tied the cloth strip around his ankle. "I will hold on to the rails," he told her. "You climb over me and down the rope."

Molly nodded. Only after he had climbed over the balustrade did she realize the danger to him. "But you'll be trapped—"

"I'll pull the rope up, tie it here, then climb down. I can manage the drop."

"You'll be trapped!" she repeated dully.

"Go! Now!" He was perched on the outside of the balcony rails motioning to her to begin the descent.

"I won't leave you!"

"Are you my daughter?" was his stern reply.

She had asked herself the same question a thousand times before. By way of answer, she climbed over him, grasping first his strong neck, his muscular shoulders, his waist, his legs, clinging to the cloth swaying high above the inferno below. She worked her way down the makeshift rope until her feet were eight feet off the floor. It seemed a mile. She looked up and saw him dangling above her. His hands were clasped around the base of the bannister rails, his face was turned down, following every inch of her progress.

"Let go!" he ordered.

She released her hold and fell in a heap beside a bubbling vat. Aching, she rose, her ankle throbbing, hobbled to the window and looked back to see her father straining to pull himself upward. His arms were quivering with the effort, his muscles stretched taut. By arching his body, he had managed to lift one leg up to the level of the catwalk. But his strength was ebbing. Slowly the leg sank down. Slower still his arms unfolded and he hung now like a man on the crossbeams of a ship in a roaring gale, twisting like a flag upon the parapets of a burning city.

"Oh Lord, no!" she screamed. The balcony began to disengage from the wall like a ribbon, one iron fastener at a time giving way with a piercing, screeching, wrenching lament.

"Go!" he yelled. "Leave me!"

Molly backed toward the window just as the interior collapsed in a roar of smoke and flame. The force hurled her backward, screaming, through the shards of broken glass onto the street.

Lily had directed their small party through the only street left open to the harbor where the last boat they owned at the dock awaited. The boat drifted out to the reef where they anchored alongside a bizarre armada of fishing vessels like their own as well as double-hulled canoes, makeshift rafts, even a washtub filled with three squalling babies and their terrified nursemaid. Each ramshackle craft dragged up its share of ragged, hollow-eyed Tang men struggling in the waves.

When the Widow spied Rulan in the stern of a nearby canoe, she spat and shrieked out over the waves, "*That one* did it! Destroyed my house, pulled it into the fire! *That one* and the traitor Chen Pao An! Throw her out, let her drown!"

No one listened. Not even Lily.

Thirty-seven acres—the entire Chinese sector of the city—was destroyed. Every building, every tree, lamppost, boardwalk, fence, and signboard was reduced to smoking wreckage. The Chinese firemen were heaped with ridicule in the press.

"This calamity would not have transpired if *regulars* had been summoned first," trumpeted the *Polynesian,* although Bosworth's editorials in the *Dispatch* asserted that the tragedy had been years in the making and that the Chinatown fire department was the "lone voice trumpeting safety in a wilderness of Chinese indifference."

Gone was the meeting quarters of the *tong;* gone too was the new clubhouse of the Chinese Union, less than a year old. Within the community, bets were placed as to whether the alliance of Hakka and Punti would split asunder, and whether the union would disappear and the Chinese separate themselves into warring factions again.

Six thousand Chinese and Hawaiians who had inhabited the wharfside tenements were made beggars. The Hawaiians took shelter with kinsmen in rural districts, while the Chinese camped on the grounds of the immigration depot in tents provided by the king. Some Tang men, however, saw a way of turning ruin into profit. A barrel of clean water cost as much as a whole roast pig. A simple needle went for a silver dollar. The Widow's daughter was the first to suggest that claims be made against the kingdom for their losses. With records lost, who would know the full extent of any Tang man's holdings? The Li properties alone included tenements, shops, the fish market, and several gambling houses. When the king balked at the idea, talk went round the tents of a mass lawsuit against the kingdom.

The widow of Chen Pao An showed no interest in banding with the others to make a claim. Nor did she exhibit the typical signs of grief: no wailing, no tearing of hair and clothes, no prolonged sieges of prayers and fasting. A callous woman, Chinatown gossips concluded.

8

THE DANCE

After several Tuesday afternoons of dance practice in the Baintons' parlor, Lincoln still moved as lumpishly as ever. Heloise, on the other hand, had mastered intricate twirls and dips, sometimes bending her body backward so low over his arm that her hair brushed the ground. Lincoln found Heloise's lack of inhibition astonishing. Molly, he remembered, was even more reserved than he; to his knowledge, she neither sang nor danced in public. It touched him that Heloise remained convinced of his inherent grace, so much so that she was now insisting that Lincoln escort her!

"No," Lincoln returned. "I don't like parties." Practicing alone in her parlor was one thing; appearing together before New Haven society was another. The risks were as obvious to him as to Clarice Bainton and the good wives of New Haven. He marveled that Heloise could be so naive.

His refusal made Heloise furious, and she was haranguing him one afternoon with warnings about the dangers of a "hermit life" when a noise on the veranda stopped them in the middle of a dance turn. They looked up to see three youths from town, all members of her father's congregation, staring at them through the porch window into the parlor.

"Hello, Willie," Heloise sang out to a freckle-faced youth with a shock of carrot-colored hair.

Willie turned brick red at the greeting. "Howdy do. Reverend home?"

"Gone out to campus," Heloise replied, falling with exaggerated exhaustion onto the chesterfield. She had caught Willie hanging outside the house several times before. "Sweet on you," Clarice Bainton had observed to her daughter.

Willie stomped over and stood inside the doorway, mashing his felt cap between his hands; his eyes swept from Heloise to Lincoln and back again, taking in the chairs moved back against the walls, the cups of half-drunk tea, the empty house. "Shouldn't be home by yourself," he growled, glaring at Lincoln. "Not with foreigners roaming 'round town, putting on bulldog airs, butting in where they don't belong. Better you send that Chinee home and let me set with you till Reverend gets back. We—I—got to ask you something . . . about the dance coming up . . ."

Heloise's pale skin flushed crimson at the slight to Lincoln. She rose from the couch and strode toward Willie with the arrogance of an advancing army, sweeping the floor with her skirts. "Thank you, Willie," she said with a brittle smile, "but Lincoln here's keeping me most proper company." Her crinolines were so wide that neither Willie nor his friends could squeeze through the doorway without knocking her down. "Funny you should mention the dance. You're terribly late. I've filled every dance but two and I'm insisting that Lincoln take those. Sorry . . . !"

Willie sucked in his breath sharply, then turned and stomped off the porch as his confederates butted into his back like sheep. "Wha'd I tell you?" Lincoln heard one boy mutter. "Two of 'em alone in the house!"

The dance lesson went badly that day, even for the unflappable Heloise.

The following Tuesday, every young woman of good family had received the long-expected invitation to the cotillion by afternoon post. All except one. That afternoon, Mrs. Bainton was stopped at the butcher's by a woman from her husband's congregation who congratulated her for allowing her daughter "to go so far in Christian charity" as to make a "Chinee" her mission project, but warned Mrs. Bainton that certain bluenoses in town were not of the same mind.

To her credit, before Clarice Bainton confronted her husband with the disastrous results of their hospitality toward Lincoln, she prayed for an hour, her forehead pressed down on her open Bible. When her husband came through the door, she was quite composed.

"Daughter has been much offended, Henry," she announced from the top step. And after explaining the circumstances, she outlined her plan. "She *shall* go to the dance. And her mother shall stand by her chair!"

Reverend Bainton knew better than to chip away at his wife's Maine-bred granite. That stubbornness seemed suddenly to have surfaced in his daughter, whose flightiness he had always bemoaned. Because Lincoln could not be persuaded to go, Heloise went to the dance escorted by her plump fury of a mother. Both women sat alone, Mrs. Bainton abandoned by her feminine peers and Heloise ignored by the wall of young men in somber black. And when the last waltz was announced, both women put on their cloaks, quit the brightly lit hotel, and were met by the reverend who had been waiting for hours in the softly falling rain.

The evening after the dance, Lincoln was pelted with rocks by five youths from town on his way back to campus from the Baintons'. The next day, he was followed to the river by two dozen men. Goaded by their leader, they fell upon him at the spot where the women workers discarded the empty shells of shucked oysters. There they struck him down and pommeled him with fists and heavy boots. Lincoln was certain that they would have killed him if the two uncles had not rushed out of their house brandishing knives used for gutting fish.

Having been kicked to unconsciousness, Lincoln could not later attest to the actual commission of a crime, although there was ample evidence of a mob run amok. For the uncles' shack was burned to cinders, and the battered bodies of the Chinamen were found thrown atop a mound of oyster shells, ankles bound and queues knotted together. And yet, no witnesses to murder could be found, no motive rendered except the inexplicable explosion of evil in the midst of decent folk.

On the Sunday following the deaths of the two Tang men, an ecumenical service of penitence was held. Bainton, by virtue of his association with the overseas missions in China and Hawaii, was invited to offer a meditation. Heloise sat with jaw set, her gray eyes darting between the white cloth of the altar to Lincoln who was seated across the aisle, his head swathed in bandages. Clarice Bainton never lifted her gaze from her husband's slight form beside the other divines on the dais. And when Bainton entered the pulpit, the somber purpose of the service gave new power to his reedy voice. He called upon his friends and neighbors to make "private contrition and public remonstrance." He reminded the congregation that all that lay between them and barbarity was the "fortress of civilization, the keystone of which is Christian conscience. If the keystone slips, all fails, all falls."

Yet a certain red-haired individual was at that moment seated placidly among the worshipers, his eyes fixed on Heloise's bright head, his conscience securely at rest.

At fireside colloquies that week, the first-year students dissected the case of the two dead Chinamen with the fervor of scholars unraveling a particularly crabbed text. The talk was of the efficacy of New Testament forgiveness over Old Testament law, the necessity of corporate repentance for individual acts of violence. They commiserated with Lincoln for the misfortunes that had happened to "your kind."

As his comrades dithered, Lincoln's mind fixed on a certain red-haired town youth. He had learned from Bainton that Willie was the son of a prosperous tradesman named Prior, the town cooper and a part-time member of the local constabulary. More troublesome news came from Heloise, who reported that someone had been following her home from choir practice and lurking under the trees outside her bedroom window. She suspected it might be Willie.

As soon as his bandages came off, Lincoln hastened to the police station to check on the investigation. But the constable in charge declared that the case was closed. No one had come forward to identify a single citizen. Without witnesses, there was no case.

"I am a witness," declared Lincoln. "I told you that William Prior was there. He was the one who kicked me—"

"You had a concussion, which means you saw nothing at all," the constable returned gruffly. "And young Prior has an unassailable alibi. He was home playing whist with his pa that night."

"He's lying!"

"Mind your tongue, boy! You may have weaseled your way into Yale, but that don't give your kind the right to set yourself over decent folks. Willie and his pa are as right as a church door. Give it up, or go back where you come from."

Lincoln walked for miles past the wreckage of the dead men's hovel up into the hills overlooking the college, then back along winding paths overgrown with bracken and rotten foliage down the Boston Post Road through lanes shrouded with the serpentine branches of dogwood and elm. Daylight was fading; lamps in the parlors were being kindled into a rosy glow. Behind the thin curtains, shapely silhouettes moved, laying down suppers for husbands and brothers and sons. Not for one such as he. It was past dark when he found the Prior cooperage, a two-story storehouse and a dimly lit shed near the railroad tracks. The place was empty of workers except for a lone figure rolling a barrel down a ramp to a dark mountain of kegs set against the side of the warehouse. The man hoisted the barrel onto the pile, stepped into the open doorway of a shed, placed his hands on the small of his back and stretched his arms skyward to unkink his sore muscles. The light cast by the gas lamp turned his hair to flame. Willie.

Lincoln did not have long to wait before Willie blew out the lamp and stepped outside the shed, whistling and jingling a ring of keys. Some animal instinct made him pause as he turned the key in the lock. He squinted into the gloom, lips pursed, his eyes sorting through the shifting shadows.

"Alfie? Dave? That you?" When Lincoln emerged, a grin spread across Willie's freckled face. "Got me a foreign guest. Guess my work ain't over yet." Still whistling, he walked over to a large barrel filled with loose staves, rummaged through the slats and plucked out a wide, flat piece of oak longer than his leg. Then he tested it like a baseball bat, cleaving the air with savage force.

While Willie was selecting his weapon, Lincoln was making his own preparations. First he hung his coat over a hitching post. Then he took off his shoes and stockings, rolled up his trousers and sleeves, and began to bend and twist his body in fluid movements that struck Willie as ludicrous. As a child on the Delta, Lincoln had joined his uncle in practicing the complicated choreography of *t'ai chi ch'uan,* two warriors battling gnarled trees and stands of corn. Yet this was no ritual combat against a phantom foe. There was a blood-price to collect for two dead innocents. Lincoln slowed his breathing, suspended all thought, and concentrated on the nexus of power in his gut. Soon, the only sound that filled his ears was the roar of blood. His span of vision had shrunk to the barrel stave swinging like a scythe in Willie's hand. Lincoln stepped toward Willie, splay-footed, bent-kneed, his palms sculpting tiny circles in the air.

Willie charged; the barrel stave swung wide and clipped Lincoln on the elbow, thus setting in motion a series of swift, practiced movements. Lincoln pivoted, slammed his foot hard into Willie's groin and as Willie doubled up in agony and surprise, Lincoln struck Willie's neck with the side of his hand.

"Yellow bastard!" Willie screamed. "Shoulda knowed you'd fight dirty!" Shaking his head to clear it of pain, he swung the stave from side to side as if threshing grain, but Lincoln pedaled backward, easily eluding the weapon's insidious arc, so that Willie was forced to stumble to and fro across the hard ground. Impatient now to draw his enemy into battle, Willie began to hack at Lincoln's head. But as he raised the stave, Lincoln leaped inside the deadly swing and punched Willie in the chest. Air exploded from Willie's lungs. He reared back, and in that moment, Lincoln thrust two fingers into Willie's throat.

Three kicks broke Willie's jaw and teeth. A blow to the ribs was rewarded by the dull snap of bone. Two more kicks and the big square cooper's son was curled on the ground like a worm in a cocoon. Another kick to the base of his chin flipped Willie on his back.

Lincoln put his heel on Willie's quivering throat. One quick stamp and the cooper's son would go the way of the dead Chinamen. Yet with his foot poised to extinguish his enemy's breath, Lincoln felt the world shift. He heard the gulls crying overhead, the faraway clatter of the railroad. Frigid night air stung his nostrils. Looking up, he saw pressing down on him the great bowl of the sky shot through with stars, their light so bright that it pierced his eyes. He saw that his fingers and toes were smeared with blood—his own and Willie's. And now his mind stirred, probing, weighing, assessing the consequences of the last half hour. Killing Willie would not bring back his two uncles. Yet some flaw in the moral order had been set right. A man who had dealt out pain with a careless hand had been repaid in kind. Justice had been served, an ethical equilibrium worthy of Confucius achieved. Slowly, Lincoln lifted his foot, dressed himself, and limped out of the cooperage.

On the long walk through the labyrinthine streets of New Haven to his boardinghouse, Lincoln wept over the wreckage of his scholarly hopes. He had entered the temple of reason to discover that those who preached justice did not do it; those who counseled mercy had none; those who bestowed learning were themselves unwise. And Heloise, for all her sympathy, was not the woman to heal the wounds he had suffered in a place more hell than haven.

9

REBUILDING

Out of tragedy, one small miracle arose: mother and daughter came together again under the Bosworths' roof. Rooms were in short supply; the homeless slept in tents or on the ground. Constable, along with other well-born Hawaiian youths, bunked at the king's boathouse. He would not have set foot in Bosworth's house in any case.

Hiamoe, the house of refuge, became a house of pain. Molly screamed out her guilt in dreams, declaring herself a hateful thing for surviving when her father lay dead. She called for Constable, alternately cursing him for abandoning her, then cursing herself for having driven him away. The river of recrimination mounted until Rulan and the Bosworths kept a watch on Molly out of fear that the girl would take her life.

Rulan felt her daughter's affliction more keenly than her own. The girl's tie to Constable was more complicated than she had realized—not simply infatuation or lust but an obsessive need to abase herself, for even in absence, he dragged the girl down. What had she and Pao An done to have so twisted their daughter that she clung to this weakling like a helpless blind thing?

Bosworth sent word to the boathouse to summon Constable to Pao

An's funeral. No answer came. Nor was he present at the ceremony in Manoa when Pao An's remains were placed into the ground, although Molly delayed the graveyard services for a day in the hopes that he would arrive.

Molly was in black despair when they returned to Hiamoe. Bosworth took her aside while the others went into the house to prepare the funeral feast. "Come," he told her. "I want to show you something."

Leaning on his walking stick, he limped to the horse barn while Molly trailed behind. The old mare was stabled there alongside an ancient carriage, which Molly remembered riding in as a small child.

"See that beam?" Bosworth asked her. "Never told anyone the story . . ."

Molly listened stonily. Sorrow had hardened her heart to her uncle's loving admonitions, and she felt her spirits sinking at having to endure yet another sermon. The image of her father's grave yawned in her mind, the hole wide, black, and inviting. One could find ways to climb down into that pit to escape from despair. She tucked that notion into a corner of her mind. If only Bosworth would leave off talking . . .

". . . you were a babe when Lucy got the pox," her uncle was saying. "Caught it off an infected woman's dress that Lucy begged me to buy. My fault really," he sputtered. "You see, I loved her more than any man ought to love any creature. And she didn't love me back. So I spoiled her, tried to buy her love with trinkets, and ended by making her a frivolous creature who counted her worth in beauty.

"No one dared come near us. On the twelfth day of her ordeal, she began to sink. By then, the pox had scarred her horribly. I came out here. Took the reins and threw them over that beam. Got up on that barrel there and tied the traces round my neck." He was staring at the window above the hayloft. Specks of dust spun like flecks of gold in a narrow band of light. "Even if she'd survived, she'd be a ravaged thing. Couldn't face that . . ." The old man snorted, took off his spectacles and wiped them energetically. "Your mother stopped me. Made me ashamed; no end to guilt, child"—he coughed—"except by grace."

"But you and Auntie love each other now—" Molly blurted out, unwilling to believe that the Bosworths' perfect accord had been a sham.

Bosworth sat down on the very barrel on which he had once stood to end his life. "More, child. More."

She turned away, shaken. Nothing was as it seemed. What was the point of loving if one suffered so? How could love blossom out of indifference?

The old man caught her hands in his own. "Your father and I were never friends. But he would say as I do now: face your sorrow, child. Beat the devil at his own game—"

So Molly put aside her grief, swallowed her pride, and hastened to the boathouse to confront Constable with his neglect. She found him splashing ankle-deep in the surf clad in the tight striped shirt and black knee pants of Kalakaua's official boating crew, launching one of the king's racing canoes. In place of the blubbering wreck she remembered after the fire, he was sleek, rested, fit and clearly enjoying the camaraderie at the boathouse, which seemed more a jovial fraternity than a ward for victims of the fire.

"Poor Peter's got to tend his hens," she heard one of the stripe-shirted young bloods on the shore tease.

The plural grated on her ears. She was spoiling for a fight by the time Constable ran up the beach in her direction. He ignored her protests and caught her up in an embrace that left her breathless and drenched with seawater then steered her to a sunny spot on a rock overlooking the harbor with as much gallantry as if he, not she, had initiated the meeting. Behind them lay the plain of ashes where Chinatown once stood.

"He's not going to sue," Constable blurted out.

"What are you talking about?" Molly replied, enraged at the lightness of his mood. He was obviously happier now at the boathouse than he had been in months. Happier with his comrades than with her. His green eyes flashed with good humor, his body was hard from exercise.

"My partner," he replied. "He turns out to be a most farsighted young man. He had taken out insurance on our business—in his name entirely, of course—and on *my* life as well. Ha! Had I died, he'd be wallowing in dollars."

"It was his money," Molly pointed out and waited for Constable to acknowledge the death that had actually transpired, the same one that had left her so thin and wan.

"And he's recovered it all . . . and more! He made money on my losses, and left me with nothing. That's the way *haoles* do business!"

"Are those sentiments yours or your current roommates'?" she retorted. "I don't remember that you had such scruples when you accepted the money for the soap factory."

"Molly, I've been a fool for more years than I care to remember. Living with my brothers—my true *kanaka* brothers—has opened my eyes! Diplomacy, friendship—all that has failed us. To create a new Hawaii, force is inevitable!" He raised his voice for the benefit of his comrades watching from the balcony of the boathouse.

The fire had neither defeated nor changed him, Molly observed; he had simply shifted his energies toward another hapless goal. It was useless to rebuke him. He had no recollection that her father had died or that she ever had a father at all. His mind was filled with canoes, races, comrades, all the things that made his present situation amusing. Seeing this, Molly could not help taunting him. "Since you're half-Hawaiian, perhaps you will be allowed only half a share in this new Hawaii." When he bristled, she goaded him further. "And will I have a portion too? My people have mixed their bones into the soil. You see the evidence there—" she cried, pointing toward the ash heap that was Chinatown. "Are we entitled to anything, or do your comrades propose to keep it all and pack Tang people back on boats?"

"Be reasonable, Mol. Your share will come through me."

"I want my own!"

"Auwe!" he cried with a grin, pulling her close. Everything she said he interpreted as flirtation. "Pushy *pa-ke*! How is a man to succeed with such a woman?"

"By helping that woman to what is rightly her own!" She was struggling out of his arms, turning her face away when he tried to kiss her. "Stop pawing me, Peter. I'm tired of your games and your useless schemes. Tired of living like a pauper. Maybe I should stay at Hiamoe until your plans are clear. Auntie Lucy has made over my old room for me, Uncle can find me work at the *Dispatch* . . ."

The alcohol was wearing off and with it Constable's giddy mood. This was not the compliant mistress he had bragged about to his brothers. He expected that his comrades would play out a ribald version of this scene over their *poi* tonight. Even more than being jilted, he hated being laughed at! "You find me at a disadvantage," he murmured testily, "for at the moment, I have neither bed nor roof to call my own, let alone *useful* schemes to augment *your* future, and I am committed to racing practice today . . . if I'd known . . . if you had given me fair warning—"

"*La sap,*" Rulan was heard to mutter when Molly described Constable's behavior. Bosworth erupted in a flood of oaths and proposed to take a whip to the rogue's back for "leeching off our do-nothing king." Molly announced that she had purged her lover from her life.

A few weeks later, he surprised her with an announcement by afternoon post that he had rented rooms in the city house of a rural chieftain. Just two, all he could afford. "I have set my mind back on poetry and have no money for brandy. Come to me now," he begged.

To Rulan's relief, Molly tore up the summons. Empty promises, she told her mother, from a failed writer whose unborn poem would go the way of his aborted ventures in government and business.

*O*ne afternoon, while drowsing under a mango tree over a book of verse, Molly was roused from slumber by the barking of dogs down the lane. Raising her head, she saw in the shimmering heat a Tang man coming up the road from the direction of the harbor. He was tall, thin to the point of emaciation, and walked with a loping, exhausted stride. His pants were stained and travel-worn, and his leather boots grimy from the dust of the road. She recognized him even before he reached the gate.

"Mother," she called excitedly. "Look who's come!"

A moment later, she was staring up at a stranger wearing Lincoln's face. He had grown taller since his departure, and had taken on the complexion of the New England snows. He wore spectacles too. And there were other, subtler changes. Suffering had aged him, and yet he bore himself with such dignity that Molly felt a child by comparison.

Then Rulan was running toward the gate, wiping her wet, red hands on her apron with a look of mad expectancy that tore at Molly's heart. Lincoln noticed the bizarre quality of Rulan's actions before Molly did. He saw how Rulan stopped, stepped around him, saw the awful alteration of her features at the sight of the empty road stretching behind him.

"*Aiya!*" she said softly, and seemed suddenly to shrink into her body. And to Molly's chagrin, the woman who had not shed a tear as her husband's bones had been placed in the ground was pommeling her adopted son with her fists, demanding in fury, "Where is he? Where did you leave him?"

Only then did Molly realize that her mother's icy calm had been an act of supreme denial. While others were mourning, Rulan had been waiting quietly, hanging the clothes on the line, expecting in some obscure corner of her heart that Pao An would come up the road one day and call her name. She had clung to the notion that if he had survived battles in China, if he had endured misfortune in Gold Mountain, surely he would survive fire. Even death! Now her strangled words became a cry of pain.

*A*ll the time he had lived in New Haven, Lincoln wrote scores of letters to Molly, most of which he did not send, for he was ashamed to reveal how desire for her had deepened the longer he was away. Most of all, he would not have her know how he had suffered at the hands of the deceivers. In the days following his assault on Willie, he limped to class, wearing his wounds like trophies of war. He had taken a brass letter opener and sharpened the point to a razor's edge. This he carried in his pocket as he walked through the village alone, showing himself brazenly in the shops and sidewalks, daring Willie's gang of thugs to take their revenge. He would not go down into death alone. And because he sought death, death eluded him. For Willie was no longer seen at church or outside Heloise's window, and the youths who had followed him melted away before Lincoln's silent presence on the streets.

Anger now organized Lincoln's days, dictated the books he chose to read, the way in which his ears shaped the professors' lectures. He refused the Baintons' invitations to dine, existing on stale bread, tea, and potatoes roasted in his fireplace. When Heloise came herself to his rooms, he shut the door against her pleas. Molly was the only source of heat and light that last interminable winter. In his dreams, she wrapped him about with hair and limbs of fire. He hoarded the one letter she had written like the foodstuffs Rulan sent by ship, devouring the pages of spidery script like a starving man come at last to dine. And when news of Pao An's death finally reached him, Lincoln, in his towering anguish, had no thought to spare for himself, only for Molly.

And now that he beheld her in the flesh, this Molly was nothing like the girl he remembered. She was neither the proud creature who had sent him away nor the voluptuary of his dreams, but a wounded child. He wanted to catch her up in his arms, join his voice to the terrible wailing of his uncle's widow, for Molly's loss was his, her people his own. Except that he could not bear it if she pushed him away again or offered her cheek for a brotherly kiss.

"I'll take care of Auntie," he told her curtly.

"Yes," she replied and wondered why she had not thought to help her mother before.

*W*ithin hours of his arrival, Lincoln was making an inventory of the family's losses, sent word to Pao An's customers that the business would continue under his direction and redrew from memory Pao An's plans for a new factory. He frightened Molly with the urgency of his actions on Rulan's behalf. She felt usurped. The adopted son was proving far more filial than the flesh-and-blood daughter. Whenever Lincoln came near, words flew out of Molly's head; she was as tongue-tied and unsure as in the days when she had aped and envied Lily. If he asked her opinion about the business, she grew mute, conscious of her lack of schooling in comparison to his and of how much she fell short of the women in New Haven. Moreover, she could not bear the reproach in his eyes: she was the one responsible for the death of the man he revered. Guilt drove her back to Constable.

So she packed her valise and fled Hiamoe for the two small rooms near the Hale where Constable was playing the poet. Kalakaua now concurred with Constable's self-assessment, confiding to Constable one night at the boathouse that Hawaii needed a poet laureate. Constable took that pronouncement as a promise that the king would see him through the publication of his projected epic. He searched his old notebooks for half-finished verses, which he rewrote as compliments to the king, and refused Gibson's new offer of a post as government scribe. Yet there were landlord's notices to pay and bills for food and the tailor. Since Constable would not stoop to "clerking," a job less prestigious than the translator's post he had enjoyed before going into the coconut business, Molly sent word quietly to disappointed clients that she would take on whatever he refused. She was paid a pittance to start, but her work was accurate and fast; and in due time, orders mounted, thus providing them a small but dependable source of income.

To his credit, Constable was more productive than he had been in years. His poetic tributes to the king, for which he was paid in invitations to the palace rather than in coin, occupied a prominent place in Walter Murray Gibson's newspaper and earned him a period of local renown. Encouraged by the attention, he was reviewing his notes for his epic on the islands and was making promising scratches here and there. Molly watched him carefully for any new sign of procrastination, for some unforeseen enthusiasm that presaged a radical change of course.

Lincoln, too, was gaining a measure of fame. After initial rejoicing in some quarters that the "Chinese problem" had been solved by a "fiery act of God," it soon became clear to nativist factions and *haole* laborers alike that the Chinese would not be dislodged from the islands. For here was the sudden and irksome appearance of a Yale-educated Chinaman popping up in the corridors of the Hale complaining about the new restrictions on Chinese immigrants and in better diction than his benefactors! Despite having reaped the benefits of a Western education at the Hawaiian Mission's expense, this former indigent, it seemed, lacked sufficient humility to keep his place. Indeed, he appeared to have surpassed his dead foster father in pigheaded ambition. Thus when Lincoln organized work crews to begin the massive rebuilding of Chinatown with the restoration of the Chinese

Union Hall, a hue and cry went up in drawing rooms and taverns and bankers' offices.

Lincoln ignored the criticism and went about rebuilding. He cajoled the leaders of local churches and schools for emergency funds for housing, went hat in hand to his former classmates at Oahu College for donations, made plain to the officials in the legislature the Chinese community's familiarity with law courts. By playing upon widespread guilt for the plight of the Chinese, he built a complicated structure of loans and grants from public and private agencies and individuals, enough for any Tang man and woman rendered homeless by the fire to begin anew. For although public blame for the fire was laid on the Chinese themselves, many *haoles* privately acknowledged that the Chinese were proving themselves an indomitable lot. There was no looting or discord in the tent cities. Instead, gardens were growing in the spaces between cooking pots and washing lines, and life was proceeding apace. Peddlers slung their wares in baskets on long poles as they had done before the fire, this time trekking inland to the rural areas to hawk vegetables or cloth, fresh fish or *poi*.

Had the king's agents known that the *tongs* and clan societies were also receiving aid from their confederates overseas in Gold Mountain, Kalakaua's suspicion of criminal conspiracy might have dried up the well-springs of charity. Yet Lincoln kept Chinatown's secrets, argued for what he believed was his people's due. Switching easily from English to pidgin, Cantonese to Hawaiian, he brooked no condescension from *haoles,* could catch an *alii* in the midst of an evasion, and had an eagle eye for a faulty figure or clause. It was inevitable that such a person would become the lightning rod for accusations both inside and outside his community.

"Sneaky little pedant," Constable fumed to Molly. "People are saying that rebuilding the Union Hall is a scheme to funnel government money into his friends' pockets. I never trusted your so-called kinsman when he was leeching off the missionaries at Oahu College! Having gotten grand at Yale, he thinks he can talk his way into a seat in the Hale by buying off his union cohorts!"

Molly's spirited defense of Lincoln made Constable's denunciations more virulent. To her profound embarrassment, Constable invited Princess Liliuokalani's personal bookkeeper to the building site to expose Lincoln's perfidy, only to have Lincoln throw open the building's accounts for the man's inspection. Not a single cent for rebuilding had come from the public coffers! The new hall was being funded by the members themselves, each of whom contributed a private treasure: a silver dollar saved from the fire, a sister's gold bracelet, a China-bound ticket turned into cash. The workers labored for free, claiming that they would gladly bend their backs for an organization that served Hakka and Punti, Hawaiians and Tang men, and for the foster son of their dead comrade. The Hawaiian bookkeeper went away praising Chinatown's newest leader while Constable reiterated to Molly his conviction that her race had a devious streak.

Shops and dwellings were not all Lincoln intended to rebuild. He, more than anyone, had helped Rulan repair her broken life. Hard work was his antidote to their shared grief. Rulan had been the first woman to join the renovation crew, appointed by Lincoln to direct the volunteers at the cooking station. She was aided by a dozen union wives who lugged baskets of steaming rice and jugs of hot tea among the men. Neither she nor Lincoln expected Molly to contribute to a cause that had meant so little to her in Pao An's lifetime. So it was a shock to them when Molly came one day, put on an apron, and stayed.

"No soap here, only dirt," was Rulan's acerbic greeting to her daughter.

This was not the speech of welcome Molly expected to hear. She was openly defying Constable by coming to this place and neglecting her own work to play the obedient daughter! Surely her mother ought to say some word of affirmation for the sacrifice Molly was making for her father's sake. But Rulan had already passed her by. Grimly, Molly stoked up the fire under the *wok* and began to chop a knob of gingerroot, which was soon hissing in the pan.

By the end of the first day, Molly's frock was ripped and filthy. Her hair had come loose from its pins and sprung back into its natural wild state; her fingernails were torn from lifting coral blocks, and her arms were marked with angry blisters where hot oil had splashed up at her. Ugly, ugly, she told herself, bent by the weight of the jugs dangling from her carrying pole. She might carry an ocean of tea on her knees to every Tang man in the islands and there would still be penance to pay for all the times she had brought her father shame.

Sometimes she heard Lincoln from a distance. His was the voice that carried over the hubbub ordering the men about in various tongues, shouting village epithets in Cantonese, cajoling them in lilting Hawaiian, poking fun at them in ribald pidgin. At dusk, when the workers and their women had gone home for their evening rice, Molly stayed to share Lincoln's and Rulan's small supper. They ate what remained of the day's rations: a bit of fish or meat, odds and ends of vegetables, the crusty residue in the rice pot. By then, exhaustion had etched lines onto their faces and their fingers were so stiff, they used chopsticks like shovels, holding their bowls up to their open mouths.

When Rulan went to plunge the utensils into a vat of boiling water, Lincoln groped for the teapot in its straw caddy. As he was pouring tea into his empty rice bowl Molly saw a telltale bulge in the pocket of his shirt, not unlike the one in a pocket of her apron. A small book.

What had it cost the scholar to return? Only his dreams.

In the glow cast by the oil lamp, she took note of the hands that held the bowl. The fingers were marked with blisters and calluses: the hands of a rough man, not of a scholar. Those same hands, she supposed, only months before had wielded an instrument no heavier than a pen.

He swirled the hot liquid around in his bowl and gulped it down, then rose and walked to where she sat. "No use hiding it," he said, looming over her.

She stared at him blankly, so he wiggled his fingers. "The book . . ." he ordered.

When she gave her book up into his hands, the lines of exhaustion lifted from his face and a smile touched his lips. He was turning the dog-eared pages, scanning the script. "You surprise me. I thought you too worldly for Mrs. Browning's sonnets," he observed wryly. Then with a rueful laugh, he pulled out the book in his own pocket and waved it in the air. "Lost my faith in poetry somewhere up at Yale. Now I read only authors with common sense." His was a bound leaflet, part of a two-volume study of the American character written by a visiting French nobleman named de Tocqueville half a century before. Lincoln considered the work a surprisingly accurate assessment of "us Americans."

"Us?" shot back Molly. "You, the leader of Tang men?"

"—*and* Gold Mountain born," he reminded her with surprising heat, "*and* as restless, ambitious, and impatient with impractical philosophers and poets as de Tocqueville claims all Americans are. Yet in this one observation de Tocqueville is wrong," Lincoln asserted. "We Americans do feel what he calls the 'deepest emotions of the heart'—" He stopped, embarrassed.

"How you must miss your life at school," she observed quietly.

He made a rude sound. "You going on about the 'scholar's life' too? Whenever I visit the Lis on business, Lily lectures me about abandoning my books. She hates me to come to her with dirty hands. I would have agreed with her once, but now, never! I like the men," he said thoughtfully, "and the clarity that labor affords the mind."

Lincoln had put on his spectacles and was studying her as if she were a column of figures. The result bathed Molly in shame. How could he ignore the greasiness of her hair, the cracked and dry skin at the corners of her mouth, the ungainly body—long of leg, bony at hip, the wide feet stuffed into cheap leather shoes? So Lily and he had found each other again! Not surprising considering their childhood affection. It was the perfect partnership: wealth with wit, good name with raw ambition, intellect with beauty—and sealed, moreover, by the "deepest emotions of the heart."

10

CHANGING PARTNERS

At Christmastime, the king's sister, Liliuokalani, threw open the iron gates of her Washington Place mansion for a welcome-home gala for several young Hawaiians who had just returned from countries as far-ranging as China, Japan, Italy, and England. Of particular interest to the princess was a dashing young *hapa haole* from Maui named Robert W. Wilcox, whose flamboyant clothes and elegant waxed mustache proclaimed his newly acquired European sophistication. Even before he had gone at government expense to military school in Italy, Wilcox had been an ambitious political organizer with a fiery oratorical style. The nature of his politics varied with circumstances and mood, but Wilcox could always be counted on to attract a following. He had been a leader in the "Hawaii for Hawaiians" movement in the previous decade and an early ally of the now deposed Walter Murray Gibson, in exile and dying of tuberculosis in San Francisco. Gibson had been ousted in a swift, bloodless "revolution" by the all-*haole* Hawaiian League and their private army of mercenaries, the Honolulu Rifles, which took control of Honolulu for three days in the summer of 1887, and left Kalakaua a monarch in name only.

As welcome as Gibson's fall was to many citizens, the ascendancy of the antiroyalist Reform Cabinet plunged the kingdom into greater disarray. The Reform Cabinet's first action after wresting power from the king was to force Kalakaua to put his name to a new constitution which greatly extended the political privileges of alien residents of American and European descent while drastically curtailing the power of native Hawaiians to rule themselves. Nor was this "Bayonet Constitution" of 1887 a boon to the Chinese; they were still denied the vote, and became even more vulnerable targets of a soaring wave of anti-Chinese agitation.

Wilcox had returned to the islands with a new set of European ideas, an Italian contessa as bride, and pitifully few prospects. Kalakaua did not warm to the youth, and the Reform Cabinet quickly branded Wilcox an agitator. Yet Liliuokalani, the king's heir, was sufficiently charmed to take Wilcox under her wing (and, as malicious tongues said, into her bed). She moved him and his wife into her mansion in the Palama district, and in a few weeks, Wilcox had taken Honolulu by storm.

Wilcox was the very "new Hawaiian" that Peter Constable longed to be. In short order, they became fast friends. Wilcox himself had secured Constable's and Molly's invitation to Liliuokalani's gala affair, having anticipated the advantage such a friendship could bring him. The "Chinese question" was being hotly debated in the legislature, and parties who were bitterly opposed on every other measure were united in a campaign to reduce a population believed to have driven down workingmen's wages. Wilcox, however, had made himself a champion of the Chinese, especially the wealthier ones. Hence the inclusion on the guest list of Constable's "China dolly" in addition to the "better element" of Chinatown. Wilcox was calculating that the hostility of wealthy Tang men toward the new regime offered him an opportunity of unparalleled scope for raising revenue for his own ends.

To suit the occasion, Molly had powdered her face to a fashionable *haole* paleness, crimped her front hair into a fringe of curls and pulled the rest into a loose chignon secured with sandalwood combs. Two weeks' wages had gone toward the purchase of a rose-colored gown, which hugged her body from bosom to thigh and billowed at the back in a profusion of tucks and flounces.

As evening fell and the lights of the mansion winked on, a parade of carriages rounded the great circular drive. Wilcox stood beside the stately Liliuokalani, who was known in *haole* circles as Mrs. Lydia Dominis, on the portico of the mansion to greet the guests. He was as splendidly arrayed as the princess, having put on formal fitted frock coat, top hat, embroidered waistcoat, and four-in-hand tie. Once the party was in full swing, Wilcox devoted his attention to keeping the king's loyalists well apart from the supporters of the princess, who blamed the king for relinquishing power to the Reform Cabinet.

Molly even found an old friend to keep her company: Sarah Kauhana Machado who was waiting with three young matrons in an alcove screened by potted palms for the dancing to begin. Sarah was a married lady now, plump and respectable, having recently wed a middle-aged rancher from the Azores who had spotted the girl's flashing brown limbs and white teeth among the line of *hula* dancers at Kalakaua's birthday jubilee in 1886. Senhor Machado's ardor was heightened by the fact that winsome Sarah had inherited acreage in the Kohala district of the Big Island large enough for a coffee plantation. Since her marriage, Sarah no longer performed in local *hula* exhibitions but spent her days doing good works and teaching the *hula kui* to small girls. The dance, popular in court circles, combined the ancient style with steps from Western ballroom dancing.

There was an unavoidable tension between the two women as a result of Sarah's marriage: Machado was an advocate of Portuguese immigration whose voice was often raised in the Hale against the Chinese. The malleable Sarah had absorbed her husband's anti-Chinese biases, yet she could afford to be kind; Molly, after all, had not done as well as she. Sarah was heartily apologetic that Senhor Machado insisted on spoiling her so. Her gown, a confection of figured velvet with high kick-up sleeves and a collarette of jet beads, had cost her husband a small fortune. "A dreadful waste," as Sarah made a point of complaining.

"How I envy your blissful privacy! I neither bathe nor dress myself. The one thing Mother Juliana praised me for—my sewing—is done by a maid. . . . Tell me," she blurted out, "do you actually *earn money* by doing copying? Doesn't Peter feel hurt with you taking the part of a man?"

*B*y eight o'clock, the ices were consumed, glasses of champagne punch were being handed round by Hawaiian footmen in scarlet livery, and the conversation in the small alcove had gone from houseboys and dressmakers to the omnipresent specter that haunted every Hawaiian woman of childbearing age. Two confessed that they had recently lost a son or daughter to pox or fever, and Sarah, to her great sorrow, had been unable to provide Machado with an heir.

Just as the talk turned maudlin, Molly spied Constable's dark head bobbing next to Wilcox's well-trimmed curls in a crowd of admiring women. When Constable spoke, she saw the women's heads turn and the flutter of ostrich-feather fans. Her heart sank. There was another fruitless scheme afoot! The signs were all there. The boasting. The flirtations. The manic swings of mood.

Couples began to drift toward the tables set around the dance floor as the orchestra struck up a tune in the brassy Teutonic style of the Royal Hawaiian Band. One by one, the husbands claimed their wives until only Sarah remained beside Molly.

"Look there—" cried Sarah mischievously. "This is a social first! Mr. Wilcox is broadening the princess's circle of friends!"

The crowd parted to let a party of Chinese through. Molly recognized several of the Tang men taking seats at tables farthest away from the dance floor.

"I thought your women stayed penned up at home! Someone ought to have kept *that* crone under lock and key," jibed Sarah, who pointed to a small woman with scarlet lips and nails, complaining in strident Cantonese to a slender girl. The Widow was dressed with more ostentation than the princess herself, in a blue silk tunic appliquéd in the "curling cloud pattern," which swirled across shoulder and back and fastened at the collarbone with a red button shaped like a peony. By contrast, Lily's dress was severe: an ankle-length column of pale yellow silk cut in the style of a Manchu court robe. The gossamer-thin silk shimmered as Lily walked, making her as ethereal as the Moon Lady gliding across a patch of night sky.

Senhor Machado, a stocky Portuguese with a white beard and a self-important air, came to claim his wife for a dance. He frowned at Molly and whispered in Sarah's ear as he danced her away. Finding herself momentarily alone, Molly glanced through the lacy fronds of a potted palm, searching for one particular face among the Chinese. She spied Lincoln in heated conversation with a stocky young Chinaman. Both had short hair and wore the Western lounge suits coming into fashion among young professional men, yet Lincoln inhabited his costume with ease, whereas his companion was pulling uncomfortably at his tight wing collar and tie. Molly observed that austere black and white became Lincoln's slim body and suntanned face. He passed from person to person with a greeting, stopping to bow to the Widow as Lily hid her face behind an ivory filigreed fan. The older woman erupted in a burst of high-pitched laughter that carried over the hubbub.

A hand gripped her shoulder. "Finally, I have found you," Constable scolded. "Robert has been asking for you."

As they threaded their way across the dance floor, she saw with alarm that they were headed straight for the contingent from Chinatown.

"I won't go there," Molly declared. This was not a simple social engagement, but a prelude to another disaster! "Tell your precious Wilcox to find another marionette."

"Confound it! For once, put aside your unnatural feuding with your kind and act in my behalf! Robert needs you to smooth the way with the old dragons of the *tong*." He squeezed her arm. "Please, Molly. There is a larger purpose here!"

Wilcox had insinuated himself among the Chinese and was energetically holding forth. Yet he had ignored the two headmen of the union, a gap-toothed Hakka and skinny Punti in identical threadbare tunics, and was mistakenly paying elaborate court to the most ostentatiously dressed couple among the group: a fat pig farmer and his stout wife. The Chinese were bestowing upon Wilcox an affability as enormous as their contempt. Constable pushed Molly forward.

"You can see how dearly I hold my friendship with you Celestials," Wilcox was saying, taking Molly into the circle of his arm, "if I count among my closest companions this precious flower of your race. Molly, here, has my ear, my trust, in short, my highest regard . . ."

"Pletty gel," chimed the Widow shrilly from the next table. "I know this one."

"Splendid," roared Wilcox and pulled Molly close, kissing her hand.

Molly had not been away so long from Chinatown to forget how Tang people deplore public displays of affection. Lily giggled; the pig farmer's wife pursed her mouth in a small, scarlet O. The Widow murmured, "Good gel, good gel." Wilcox beamed at Molly as if she had just accomplished a feat of astonishing diplomacy. Molly wished the ground would swallow her whole.

At that moment, the orchestra struck up a sprightly tune, and the attention of the table shifted away from Molly, red-faced with embarrassment under her powder, to the sea of bobbing bosoms and flapping headdresses. Molly suspected that every Chinese woman, from the pig farmer's wife to the Widow, was laughing uproariously to herself at the exertions of the dancers, a sight only slightly more ludicrous than a girl of their own race embraced in public by a brown devil.

Lincoln was leaning against the wall with his hands in his pockets, quietly observing Wilcox's performance and Molly's discomfort. She was trying vainly to wriggle out of his grasp. But Wilcox did not intend to lose his "flower" so soon. He slapped Constable on the back, his voice booming over the throbbing of violins. "Ladies and gentlemen, I give you proof of the natural harmony between our two races—this handsome, happy pair! Romeo and Juliet, if you will, but with a glorious ending!

Every day we see the offspring of these unions springing up around us like blossoms out of Hawaii's fecund soil. You must encourage your own daughters to such alliances! Well, let them lead the dance!" he enthused.

"I most certainly will not!" Molly snapped, but Constable had pulled her up roughly by a strong arm and was hauling her onto the dance floor.

"Not another word!" he hissed with a tight smile upon his lips. "You want to spoil it for me? Robert's promoting a cause, looking for contributions! I won't let you sit down until you calm your temper!" Constable squeezed her waist so hard that she could not breathe.

The orchestra was playing a polka, a dance Molly disliked for its odd ungainly rhythm. Impatiently, Constable prodded Molly across the floor while she stumbled against him, speechless with chagrin, stepping on his feet and tripping a woman behind her. Molly's inability to dance was a thorny issue between them, for Constable was an expert in both Hawaiian and *haole*-style dancing, and was convinced that Molly's clumsiness was another proof of the inability of her race to mold themselves to a foreign culture.

"Try not to dance like a bloody *pa-ke*! The polka is an infernally simple step," he said through clenched teeth as they galloped around the room. "Heel, toe, one-two-three! You Chinese don't trust your bodies. It's always think, think, think, so that your mind won't let your feet move as nature intended."

Molly felt forty pairs of Chinese eyes inspecting her. What did they see? A bad girl. Stuffed like a sausage into a dress that revealed naked shoulders and bosom, and jumping around in the most indecorous way in the arms of a barbarian. Grimly, she concentrated on her feet and found herself prancing in reasonable synchrony with her partner.

"Finally!" Constable exclaimed. "I knew you had it in you if you tried. Even the old harridan with the mutilated toes is smiling like a chimpanzee. Probably never saw civilized dancing before. . . . Let's give the old lady a show!" And as the last brassy note died away, he bent Molly backward and planted an ardent kiss on her mouth. The dancers around them burst into applause.

Molly pushed him angrily away as the orchestra began a waltz. All of Chinatown was laughing at her now. Constable had soiled her before her enemies with a single kiss—and stepped blithely away to renewed applause to draw Liliuokalani herself into the dancing, leaving Molly stranded on the ballroom floor.

A strong hand spun her round just as she was about to burst into tears.

"Don't bolt and run," said Lincoln quietly. "Never give your enemies the satisfaction."

"You don't have to rescue me," Molly retorted through her teeth. "We're not children in the schoolyard anymore."

"You're right. This is a good deal more vicious."

"What are you doing?" she hissed as he pulled her close. Angry tears blinded her. "Chinese don't dance."

"Oh, I daresay we Chinese can't polka," he replied laughing, "but we devious devils *have* mastered the art of turning."

All around them, couples were twirling to the sprightly strains of a Viennese waltz. When Lincoln pressed his hand against her waist, she spun easily with him, sensing immediately where he intended to take her.

They made a circuit of the room in silence. The king loved Vienna waltzes and the court party surged onto the dance floor in a dazzling display of gold-braided uniforms and bright satin *holokus*. Gradually, the tension in Molly's body eased. She felt the guiding pressure of Lincoln's hand, and for one brief moment, his breath upon her forehead.

The violins soared, or at least it seemed so to Molly. With scores of couples packing the dance floor, it was necessary now to tuck her head under his chin, to press her bosom against his shirt. The ceiling spun round—pink and gold and ivory, lit by flickering candlelight. Images flashed in dizzying succession: the red-and-gold uniforms of Kalakaua's courtiers, the bare brown shoulders of the women, the men's dark heads, lacy petticoats swirling. She seemed to know instinctively how Lincoln would turn and glide and dip and was intensely conscious of his fingers at her waist and of her hand resting upon his upturned palm. She had not thought that there was so much grace in him.

"Where did you learn to waltz?"

"Here. Just now. With you," he replied, his eyes fixed on the opposite wall. "Before that, I merely practiced a few winter afternoons with a girl who was kind. . . ."

When he returned her to the table, Robert Wilcox had moved away. The Widow was engaged in a furious and one-sided quarrel with her daughter, prodding Lily in the chest with a long fingernail, while Lily retreated into her vacuous amiability. Flushed from her waltz, Molly felt a passing sympathy for Lily. Poor girl, thought Molly, to be so bullied by a shrew of a mother. To be excluded so completely from the company of men.

Constable reclaimed her and took her to where Wilcox was engaging a *tong* elder in a plea for funds. Out of the corner of her eye, Molly saw that

Lincoln had drawn a pink-cheeked Lily into a corner to teach her the steps of the waltz. But Lily was unable to move her feet in the patterns of the dance and stumbled so badly that Lincoln was forced to catch her in his arms. He held Lily close, both of them succumbing to a fit of merriment.

Once again, Molly felt abandoned on the ballroom floor, this time with no rescuer near.

11

PARADISE IN FOUR STANZAS

"You're holding me back," Constable accused Molly. Her penny pinching put a damper on his natural sociability; her obsessive need to work made him look lazy. Worse, her indiscriminate friendships with *haoles* like the Bosworths and with Westernized immigrants like Lincoln were embarrassing him in the eyes of Robert W. Wilcox, whom he desperately longed to impress.

Why couldn't she mold herself to his teachings? When he ordered her to abandon Western literature for the *mele* and *hula,* the "one true poetry" of the islands, she stubbornly stuck her nose into her dog-eared volume of Tennyson. He admitted he had once loved Tennyson, but that was before his enlightenment as a new Hawaiian. "Like all white men, Tennyson's afraid of his own flesh. A thing can't be a thing with him. It has to be pure idea."

"I read what I choose," Molly asserted and threatened to rip up his manuscript if he tore up her books as he typically did those works by authors whom he envied and despised. He had lately shredded, bindings and all, Molly's copy of *Kidnapped* by Robert Louis Stevenson, who was on a well-publicized tour of the South Seas.

"You mark me," he told Molly, "that cunning Scot intends to steal Polynesia's stories and pass them off as his own!" He was convinced that the popular taste for the maudlin, of which Stevenson was master, was the fault of "whiners" like Tennyson. "Why do you cling to that doddering graybeard?"

"—as an antidote to you!" she shot back. "Whenever you tell me I am incapable of writing, Tennyson reminds me 'to strive, to seek and not to yield!' "

The line from Tennyson's "Ulysses" had the expected effect on Constable. He rolled his eyes in disgust.

How had their life together become so contentious and mean? she wondered. Lately they had been arguing over matters far more crucial than poetry. His soaring expenses. Her coldness in bed. His moodiness and unexplained absences. Her success as a copyist with the very customers he refused. Molly matched his rages with violent demonstrations of temper. She had thrown a full teapot at him once when he asserted that since she did not value his prowess as a lover, he had found women who did. The knowledge that he sometimes came to her from the caresses of others brought back the old feelings of ugliness and inadequacy she had known as a girl. And she was the only one burned by the tea.

Stupid! she accused, scolding herself as her dead father would have done. She had thrown her youth away on a *la sap* whose genius lay in failure. And she was as much a deceiver as he, shedding identities as a snake slips its skin. She wore bonnets and flounces when Constable acted the English gentleman, put on *holokus* when he turned mournful Hawaiian, aped Lily's serenity when he needed a Chinatown dolly to display on his arm. Worse, she deceived herself, daydreaming of writing while copying out the words of others.

She should leave him. But what if her leaving led to his ruin? And if she quit his house, where would she go? Not to Chinatown! Not to universal contempt.

Constable had no notion of Molly's unhappiness. All he cared about were his new friends. Bored with the job the king had given him in the public waterworks, Robert Wilcox had departed for San Francisco to seek more suitable employment. He had put Constable in charge of raising members and funds for two fledgling organizations: the Kamehameha Rifles and the Liberal Patriotic Association. Membership had swelled without much urging, and suddenly, Constable found himself in command of a huge "army" of dissidents and a large trove of cash.

"Good Lord, Peter! You haven't robbed a bank, have you?" she said when he burst through the door with a jeroboam of champagne and a brand-new morning coat and straw hat.

He gave a short, sardonic laugh. "All donations from friends . . . mine, not yours."

This secrecy was troubling to Molly because it was so uncharacteristic. "Where is all this money coming from?" she demanded.

"You'd be surprised . . ." he snapped. "Some of them are acquaintances of yours," and he refused to divulge more.

When Constable announced a mysterious mission to Maui with a few *hapa haole* "brothers" from the corps, Molly was terrified. "Wilcox is returning from San Francisco with plans to prick the conscience of the king," he exulted as he bade her farewell. "Our luck is changing!"

Molly, who did not believe in luck, stood at the doorway, a block of ice as Constable embraced her.

"Dear girl," he whispered, his voice thick with irony. "Try not to miss me so."

*M*idwinter rains blanketed the city. On rare sunny days, Molly took walks along the bay of Honolulu and watched the canoes of local fishermen crossing the reef after gathering in nets of red *kumu,* gleaming black mullet, and the parrot-beaked *ulua.* She drifted along the borders of the new Chinatown rising from the ashes of the old in the same slapdash, haphazard fashion—a situation that Lincoln had publicly condemned, but was unable to prevent.

Constable's absence gave Molly an excuse to embrace solitude and fling herself into her work copying documents. Only the far-off bells of the cathedral and the Fort Street Mission penetrated her isolation. Mornings, she worked through piles of new copy, breathing in the dryness of parchment and acidity of ink, deaf to the squawking of Indian mynah birds on the persimmon tree outside. She stopped only when hunger cramped her stomach and would wolf a cold sweet potato or leftover rice. Evenings, she sprawled on the rug in a corona of lamplight, the only sound the scratching of pen on paper.

She slept curled up in a quilt surrounded by inkwells, sputtering lamp, broken pen points, wadded-up papers. She felt bereft only when the pile of papers shrunk and the messenger bore the finished documents away. How to fill the bits and pieces of her days? It was not money but mindless toil she craved.

When she was not copying, her head was bent over Tennyson's "In

Memoriam," the poet's tribute to a dead friend published forty years before. She had read it with Sarah in maudlin adolescence while contemplating dying for love. Now the poem seemed entirely different, not simply a meditation on the union of two human souls but darker musings on suffering. Certain stanzas in which the poet meditated on grief brought her to tears after remembering her own dead father and the way in which her mother mourned. Whereas Rulan continually communed with her husband's spirit, Molly was forced to admit that her love for Constable lacked the spiritual element entirely. Its most compelling feature was sensuality, which now was lost. She remembered hot Hawaiian afternoons entwined with her lover, slippery sweat on naked skin, the gasping ecstasy that curled her body like a bow. What kind of love had she thus tasted? Wasn't the dissolution of mind into pure sensation as much love as the merging of soul with soul?

She sat in the parlor with her notebook propped up on her knee, her skirts covered with ink stains and toast crumbs, and set out to write a justification for the only love she knew. After false starts and awkward experiments with rhyme and rhythm and meter, she produced a passable line. It was wooden and weak, glaringly imitative of Tennyson . . . yet the message was hers. She kept scratching at the page and produced two stanzas of four lines each using Tennyson as a guide. She added another stanza, then another, and fought her way to the end.

And having striven and caught that inner music on paper, she fell asleep nestled among her pages. She dreamed of a man bending over her as one peers at one's reflection in a lake. His face was drenched in shadow. Yet she recognized his smell, his touch, the slim, elegant fingers. Dreaming, she felt light, feathery kisses on those features she most despised—her suntanned cheeks, her oddly shaped eyes, her wiry hair, the hands that were too ungainly and large. She tried to call out his name, except that she did not know what lover, ideal or real, could desire a woman as ill-favored as she.

When Constable returned from Maui, she proudly laid her notebook in his lap.

He had just sat down at his desk, intent on writing a new poem in honor of his brothers and their secret cause. "What's this? More bills?" he demanded. "You know how doing the accounts kills the imagination."

"Oh yes, I do," she replied tartly. "But I've taken your example to heart and neglected the bills to make a poem while you were away."

"Really?" he said, not bothering to disguise his vexation. "I thought you had put aside that old notion to write. You have all your other projects to keep you busy. . . ." He referred to her copy work as "projects," as if she dabbled in painting or embroidery or collecting castoff clothes for the needy.

"I'm quite serious about it."

"Yes, well, good . . ." Constable took out the pocket watch he had bought for the king's coronation, studied its face and shook it vigorously to make sure it was running.

"Aren't you going to read it? It's less than a page. Four small stanzas."

Constable opened the notebook and studied the sheet of paper on which Molly had copied out her poem. She had drawn a border of acanthus around the verses. The title was set down in elegant script: "A Map of Paradise."

Constable closed the notebook with a sigh. "But I have my own work to do, Mol!"

"It won't take a minute to read," she insisted.

He opened the notebook again, frowned at the page as if he were indeed perusing a bill. Then moving his lips and murmuring the words in a singsong rhythm, he made his way quickly to the end. "Fine," he pronounced, shutting the book. "Damned good!"

Molly beamed. "Do you really think so? Is the imitation too slavish? Does the lost seafarer/soulfarer come through clearly? I tried to get the stanza pattern right, but . . ." When he did not reply, she ventured, "You do recognize the model, don't you?"

Constable rubbed his chin vigorously, read it through a second time, squinted at the page, and held it at arm's length as if distance would enhance his understanding. "Hmmm," he muttered. "Wordsworth's 'Excursion'!"

"No, no!" Molly exclaimed. " 'In Memoriam'! Tennyson's stanza pattern is unmistakable!"

"Of course!" Constable's smile was kind. "Should have recognized that old chestnut. I'm a beast for not seeing the image behind the shifting shadow. Yours is a bit riper than old Alfred's though." He winked at her. "Don't you wonder whether he had a bugger's interest in his school chum?"

"But is it any good? Are there any decent lines?" She stammered, anxiously awaiting his opinion.

"Oh yes . . . that one," he replied, running his finger down the page. "There . . . 'some star I needed, a trident clear.' "

"You like it?"

"Of course I do," he said. He thought a moment, and blurted out, "Because it's from *you*."

Molly rose, trembling. "Don't patronize me," she shouted. "If it's bad, tell me!"

Constable heard the squeak of the bedsprings and the storm of weeping on the other side of the wall. "Poets!" he grumbled, furious with Molly for spoiling his concentration on an evening when the words had seemed likely to flow. He tossed her notebook onto a chair, then he opened a drawer, took out his notes, and picked up a pen. He stared at the top sheet of paper. The pen remained poised above the page for several minutes, after which he went to the sideboard where the brandy flask stood half-full, poured himself a glass, drained it, poured another, and went back to his desk to sip the amber liquid while rereading the half-finished octave of a sonnet that refused to emerge out of the cacophony in his mind. The gathering on Maui with his comrades had buoyed his hopes for the rescinding of the despised constitution. They had passed their days with an old *kahuna* learning the chants and sacred dances and practicing ancient warrior skills. And he had returned joyously in touch with *Ikaika* Constable, his "real," that is, Hawaiian self, the side he had denied too long. A pity that the row with Molly was taking the edge off his excitement. He hoped she had not ruined his impulse to write as well.

Finishing the glass, he rose to get another, sat down and drank it slowly while rolling the pen between his fingers. Then he wrote the word *shoals* upon the page, and slowly, deliberately, crushed the nib of the pen into the paper until the ink flooded out and the point was smashed.

12

THE POET OF POLYNESIA

On a rainy January morning in 1889, Robert Louis Stevenson sailed into Honolulu on the schooner *Casco* and for the six months' duration of his stopover was taken to the bosom of Honolulu. Stevenson's visit, coming shortly after the Christmas holidays, had provided the somber king with a round of welcome diversion. Even the most ascetic Congregationalists were wild to meet the man out of whose fertile imagination the *Strange Case of Dr. Jekyll and Mr. Hyde* and *Treasure Island* had sprung. Those fortunate enough to see king and poet together were amazed at the tender affinity between them despite the fact that the two were manifestly different in all physical particulars. Stevenson was an emaciated Scot with the fine long face and fingers of a Van Dyke painting. While sensitive and aesthetic to the extreme, he possessed an enthusiastic and guileless interest in everyone he met. Kalakaua, by contrast, was a brown, squarely built Polynesian, whose preference as a youth for British customs had been superseded in his cynical old age by a desperate passion to preserve all things native. He was the seasoned politician, as hardened as Stevenson was dreamy and soft. Yet one essential thing drew them together: both were dying. That made all else superficial.

Each man, too, was compelled to perform the very activity that exacerbated his illness. Stevenson wrote obsessively, sometimes staying up three nights in a row, working in his pajamas until he coughed up blood and fell exhausted across his own manuscript. The king, plunged in gloom, drank until his kidneys rebelled in pain. Stevenson understood the tragedy that the king was playing out before his people. The drinking and the gambling were the gestures of a king who refused to slip quietly into oblivion. Both were engaged in a battle to constrain time: one by placating it with words, the other by obliterating it with music and drink.

On one memorable February afternoon, the king brought the writer aboard his yacht to hear poetry and song in the native style.

There were *haole*-style chairs and eating utensils aboard for the comfort of Stevenson and his wife, Fanny, and a complete selection of Western spirits, although it was widely known that Stevenson and his wife were perfectly amenable to swallowing raw *opihi* barnacles or drinking *okolehao* or sitting Polynesian-style on the floor. The king's attendants had brought aboard an abundance of local delicacies for an afternoon *luau* aboard ship: raw crab, various kinds of salted and dried fish, baked breadfruit and sweet potatoes, quantities of fresh bread, and the requisite *poi*. Yet those who knew Kalakaua intimately recognized that his fussing over Stevenson's visit was, like the continuous round of galas and balls and *luaus,* another way of filling the empty hours that would only be spent brooding over the Bayonet Constitution that had left him for two years a legislative puppet with a crown. In the past, when faced with a cabinet that refused to yield, he would simply call up another more amenable one. Now his enemies had grown too powerful. Like his late political nemesis, the Dowager Queen Emma, Kalakaua had modeled his rule on the British monarchy, but that form, while revered by certain factions of his people, was despised by the American *haoles*. And now the pro-American party had made a pact with the pro-British party to stand against him, while the chieftains from whom he derived his power were dying at an alarming rate. The "Merry Monarch" had grown taciturn, despondent, and all too aware that his vision of a new and stronger native dynasty would never come to pass. For once having set foot upon Hawaiian soil, every foreigner expected to own it. And now Kalakaua's nephritis was growing worse, and although his doctors warned him that alcohol was bad for his kidneys, he continued to drink champagne and gin punches in order to forget that his people were dying and his kingdom depended on the will and the purses of the *haole* usurpers he loathed.

When the king's invitation came requesting Constable and his companion to join the Stevenson party on the royal yacht, Hawaii's sometime poet was guarded. Since the ouster of the minister Walter Murray Gibson, Kalakaua had shown no interest in Constable. Constable worried, too, whether the overture might be a trick. For although the Kamehameha Rifles and the Liberal Patriotic Society made public statements in support of the king, Kalakaua had doubtlessly heard rumors that they were backed by his ambitious sister. Nor did Constable have any real wish to meet Stevenson, whom he regarded as a literary rival.

Yet Constable's sanguine nature reasserted itself. The invitation indicated a turning point in his relations with Kalakaua. Since no one had put Constable's name forward, Kalakaua must want him there for himself alone! "Finally moved a step beyond bohemian distinction and set foot into the royal circle!" he told Molly, waving the creamy white envelope before her face.

"But don't you owe money to the king?" Molly asked.

Constable had always kept the exact sum of his gambling losses secret from Molly, but the invitation had put him in an expansive mood. "Kalakaua already owes hundreds of thousands to Spreckels and the British bankers. He's never going to clap me in irons for a few hundred here and there!"

"Few hundred!" Molly cried in alarm. "Where are you going to get such a sum?"

"Trust me this one last time," he pleaded. "A poet cannot flower in the dark. Kalakaua must need me, so he parades me to Stevenson as proof that art can flourish on this rock. 'See?' he will say, marching me forward. 'We aren't all *tapa*-wrapped savages and gin-alley whores' sons. We're an ancient nation of heroic singers!' And we are! Or were . . . Once he realizes the importance of poetry to our national character, Kalakaua must perforce make me poet laureate—and why not?" he bristled in response to her frown.

"Show some sense, Peter! You're squandering your talents to make yourself a sycophant to the king!"

"I am intending by my efforts, dear girl, to secure *our* future! I say 'our' because all my ventures are for your sake!"

"Ah," sighed Molly. "I am to blame again for your losses since these projects were undertaken to benefit me."

The quarreling went on, the same as always. Over her suspect loyalty and his wasted abilities. Over her stinginess and his profligacy. Over her asceticism and his derelict habits. But now their quarrels rarely ended in lovemaking.

·   ·   ·   ·

Molly did accompany Constable to Kalakaua's yacht; not because of his expectation of preferment but because she was afraid to stay home while he gambled and drank. She would go to safeguard him, she told herself. Yet she was also curious about Stevenson and his wife, Fanny. For if the writer was famous, Fanny Osbourne Stevenson was notorious. The two had been lovers before their marriage. Rumor had it that Fanny—ten years his senior, with a full-grown son and daughter and a perennially absent husband—had seduced Stevenson in France in a bohemian community where she was studying art. Smitten, the young Scot pursued her to her home in Monterey, California, where he laid siege to the already deteriorating walls of her marriage. Immediately after her divorce, forty-year-old Fanny married her Louis in San Francisco and took on the role of nurse-protector, fiercely guarding his privacy and his health as he penned the verses and stories that would make him famous and both of them rich. Since then, they had encamped throughout America, Scotland, and England; and at each place, he nearly died of pulmonary bleeding. The only place he claimed to feel whole was the sea. After enduring repeated bouts of hemorrhaging and speechlessness, he set sail with his wife in search of a congenial climate for his delicate lungs, a voyage that had taken him thus far to New York and Canada and across the Pacific.

Constable had been in an agony of indecision about what poems to bring along, for it was certain that Kalakaua would expect him to recite. Should it be a page from the unfinished epic? Should he write something new just for the occasion? The week of the excursion, Constable drank too much and wrote too little and missed two meetings of the Patriots from worry. As a result, he was petulant and hungover on the carriage ride down to the dock, and carped at Molly with unusual bitterness.

Molly recognized Stevenson immediately. The writer was standing at the prow of the ship, hatless and dressed in a suit of white linen. His white shirt hung open to the middle of his thin chest, a wreath of *maile* leaves was entangled in his long hair, and over his shoulders hung a *lei* of flame-colored *ilima* blossoms, a garland given to persons of great rank. His was a most romantic pose, until he turned to cough and spit over the side.

Kalakaua was reclining on a chaise longue behind the wheelhouse, dressed like a British gentleman on a seaside holiday in a white straw boater, morning jacket, and light-colored trousers, a four-in-hand tie, and two-toned shoes. Stevenson had returned from his promenade on deck to sit beside the king. He crossed his long thin legs and took up a Chinese fan, which he waved before his face in dilatory fashion. Behind his chair stood Fanny, a stout, unsmiling woman in her forties with a dusky complexion.

The king hailed Constable, who walked quickly in the direction of the small group with Molly trailing behind.

"This is the young man I told you about," the king told Stevenson. "Peter Constable, London trained and island born. One of our best new writers."

"A pleasure!" Stevenson rejoined and offered his hand. The poet's skin was pale to the point of transparency, and in spite of the courtesy of his words, he seemed overcome by lassitude. He turned toward Molly and smiled. "And this is . . . ?"

Before Molly could reply, Constable interrupted. "My friend, Miss Chen," he replied, then nudged Molly behind him as if he were holding back an ill-behaved child.

"My sister told me you were hiding away a Celestial," murmured the king.

"Charming," Stevenson said, and took Molly's hand to draw her aside.

The sailors cast off and a good wind bore the ship out of the harbor and into the channel. The plan was to sail to the bay of Hanauma where colorful fish were clearly visible among the clear waters inside the coral reef and where they might go bathing. But the waters were rough, casting enough spray aboard so that before long, they were soaked with salt water and forced to take shelter inside. The temperature quickly rose in the cramped and humid lounge. The men took off their sea-dampened coats and the women fanned themselves vigorously. Molly had no idea what to say to Kalakaua's personal retainers, all female relatives of the king who were preoccupied with court gossip. Fanny Stevenson was another matter altogether. She said little, content to watch her husband's movements with an anxious frown.

Soon the men were lighting cigars and smoke was filling the room with a pall as sulfurous as a volcano. Fanny whispered in her husband's ear, but he waved his hand in a languid gesture, and went on aimiably puffing his cigar.

Fanny glowered at Kalakaua and, beckoning Molly, went outside to brave the spray. She needed an audience for her frustration and Molly was closest at hand. "Louis would rather suffer anything than refuse his friends. He is only strong-willed in his work. Once a story takes hold of him, he must write until he collapses."

"But he does not seem ill, only merry," Molly ventured.

"Don't let him fool you. I have dreams of him dying while telling a jest."

Fanny explained morosely how her husband had once tried to finish a story in the midst of spitting blood. He had insisted that his pen and paper be kept beside him on a pillow for the odd moment when he felt strong enough to begin again. "He should not be in that room breathing such poison," she blurted out, her anger rising. "He spends a day in bed after every one of these outings, but what am I to do? Gentle as he is, he will not disallow himself good company."

The stateroom was a mess when the two women finally went back inside. The men had been playing cards and there were poker chips scattered upon the round gaming table, with a large mound before the king, a smaller one in front of Stevenson, and a minuscule stack in front of Constable, which he covered with a hovering hand. The talk went on in a cloud of cigar smoke while the boat pitched and splashed through the huge waves and made no headway at all, until finally the king ordered the ship turned around so they could make Honolulu before nightfall.

Fanny had no qualms about scolding a king. "Surely you must stop now," declared Fanny to Kalakaua. "You shouldn't be puffing cigars in such high seas anyway. Amuse us ladies for a moment and not just yourselves."

The king was winning and in high spirits and willing enough to please the *wahines.* "A capital idea. Let's get on with literary pursuits!" he said, and pushed his chair away from the table to signal the end of the game. "Tell us, Louis, what you have been writing so feverishly that you couldn't come before the end of the year!"

"I've been feverish, it's true, but terribly unproductive. Since our stay in Saranac Lake, I've only rewritten a story by my son-in-law and done work on this grim little novel I call *The Master of Ballantrae.* And a small poem or two."

"Then we must have the poems. . . . The smaller the better. It won't addle the brain in these seas," the king said. He got up unsteadily and went to pour himself a glass of gin punch. To Molly's chagrin, Constable followed the king's example.

Stevenson mopped his face with a handkerchief and wiped his mouth, and after conferring quietly with Fanny, told the small audience that he would give them a poem about the highlands. And closing his eyes and swaying his thin angular body to the cadences of the verses, he brought to life the "country places" where "lovely music / broods and dies." The "old red hills" and "low green meadows" and the "valley hollow" filled with lamplight bright as stars, ending with the quiet lament,

O to dream, O to awake and wander
There and with delight to take and render,

Through the trance of silence,
Quiet breath!
Lo! for there, among the flowers and grasses,
Only the mightier movement sounds and passes;
Only winds and rivers,
Life and death.

With barely a pause, he flung himself into another lyric, a childlike chant whose joyful, singing rhythm belied its distressing theme.

Under the wide and starry sky,
Dig the grave and let me lie.
Glad did I live and gladly die,
And laid me down with a will.

This be the verse you grave for me:
Here he lies where he longed to be;
Home is the sailor, home from sea,
And the hunter home from the hill.

Eyes closed, heart pounding in her ears, Molly tried to set the words to memory as he spoke them. When she opened her eyes, Stevenson was staring at her with interest, pleased at the intensity of her response. He recited two more poems from memory, then without warning, he was seized with a hacking cough.

"No more!" Fanny told her husband sternly.

"Rest yourself, Louis," the king replied genially. "We have poets in our islands too. Modern, philosophical poets who are well versed in the British masters as well as our native *mele*. I refer to Peter Ikaika Constable— British schooled but Hawaiian to the core!"

Molly saw Constable stiffen and touch his breast pocket.

". . . a better poet, I dare say, than a poker player. Come now, Ikaika, give us your latest poem!"

Constable cleared his throat. He had matched the king glass for glass and his hand shook when he drew a folded paper out of the pocket of his waistcoat.

"I do not have Louis's formidable memory," Constable said nervously, his voice scratchy from alcohol and tobacco. "I have been laboring over this trivial piece for some time now, and it has been through so many versions, reversions, and animadversions that I had to write it down to remember its last face."

Recalling how Fanny's attention had lent power to Stevenson's recitation, Molly leaned forward in her chair, willing Constable to excel. But he seemed fixed on an interior struggle, and so ill at ease in the hot, smoke-filled room that he appeared physically sick.

"Please," Stevenson said, urging Constable with small motions of his long hands as if pushing a frightened child on a swing.

Should she rise and stand by his chair as Fanny had done? Molly wondered, cursing her shaking knees. She was so nervous for him—and so proud.

Constable cleared his throat and began to recite in a rasping voice. "I call it 'A Map of Paradise.' "

Molly felt as if she had been hit by a rogue wave rising out of the deep. Slowly, apologetically, Constable spoke the lines she knew so well.

Without a chart, blind, forfeit, lost,
    I sailed earth's farthest shores alone,
    A human semblance hung on bone,
A soul forlorn who'd paid life's cost.

Some star I craved, a trident clear
    To mark my way through sea and shoal
    Round rocky headlands toward some goal
No matter tempest, time or fear.

She forced herself to look away, to watch the listeners instead of the man she thought had loved her. The king sat, chin upon his breast, half-drowsing. Fanny's eyes had narrowed to mere slits, studying Constable. Stevenson, however, was rapt, his body swaying to the cadences of the lines.

Then thou, confounding reason, came
    Revising every law therein,
    Surfeiting senses, washed in sin
And thrust me far from guilt or shame.

Stevenson turned toward Molly at these words and smiled. He surmised that she was the *object,* not the author of the poem. She blushed, her senses surfeited by anger, not by shame.

Now in thine arms the stars arise.
    Adrift in night, I wake to grace

And find my compass in thy face.
Thy flesh: my map of Paradise.

"Marvelous, marvelous," Stevenson shouted, jumping up and clapping Constable on the back. "A wonderful, sensuous turn upon Lord Tennyson's dreary spiritualism." To his host, he asserted, "This young man does your people proud!"

Kalakaua seemed as pleased as if he himself had made the poem. He called for another round of champagne, despite the fact that he had already downed the equivalent of three bottles himself, and was no worse for it, to Stevenson's amazement. "A toast," he declared, "to Hawaii-*nei,* our paradise." Constable gravely accepted the accolades that followed. And when the king launched into a lengthy tribute of the innate lyricism of his people, it was to Constable he turned as chief example of "our talented young *alii.*" Kalakaua seemed as exuberant as on the morning of his coronation, shaking his leonine head in merriment and regaling the party with stories. Inevitably, when in the grip of emotion, the king was moved to song. Like his brother and sisters, he was a gifted musician, and he gave the company a love lyric of his own devising, as a female attendant strummed a *braguinha,* a tiny four-stringed Portuguese guitar. He sang with eyes closed, full-throated, his rich tenor gliding up the scale to high falsetto notes. This was a vocal technique used by mountaineers in Switzerland, Constable told the amazed Stevenson; Heinrich Berger, the leader of the Royal Hawaiian Military Band, had taught it to native singers, who had in their turn, adapted that style to native patterns of harmony.

The song ended with a falsetto embellishment that soared from bass to soprano. Stevenson seemed mesmerized by this last exquisite run which he called "as sublime as prayer." In order not to break the solemn mood, Stevenson spoke quietly. "Come now, King David, give us a sacred song as the psalmist did of old," he said. "A lyric from the ancients to make the gods come down."

Kalakaua needed little urging to perform again. Yet this time, a different king seemed to emerge before their eyes. Not the lyrical lover but a warrior crying out with all the savage fervor of one about to do battle with unseen forces. Molly recognized the chant: *Au'a ia,* the sacred *mele* praising the great Kamehameha, appropriated by Kalakaua for his own house and routinely sung and danced on public occasions by local *hula* troupes. The chant contained the well-known prophecy of the coming of Kamehameha, a message of triumph. Yet as performed by the king, the chant had become pure lament, the words a warning to his people to hold fast to their heritage as change swept over them all. The accompanist slapped the back of the miniature guitar like an *ipu,* a hollow gourd.

> *O ke Kama, Kama, Kama, i ka Huliau,*
> > *Hulihia ke au ka Papahonua'o ka Moku*
> > *Hulihia . . .*
> Thou child, child, child of the turning tide,
> > Overturned are the foundations of the land,
> > Overturned . . .

For a brief moment, there was no yacht, no prince in white flannels, no foreign visitors come to call. Only the boards of an ancient temple, a priestly dancer swaying, a drum beating, and the dirgelike chanting of a dying chief.

By the time the rented cab dropped Molly and Constable off at their rooms, the magic of the evening had melted away. Once inside their rooms, Molly railed at Constable, "It wasn't enough for you to take away my confidence. You stole my words too!"

"I hit a block, Mol! I'll make it up to you . . ." he pleaded, "only let me borrow this trifle of yours until I find my spark! You saw what that poem did. It made Kalakaua young again! Who knows? Maybe I'll be laureate after all!"

"For a poem you didn't write!" She flung his perfidy in his face, calling him thief, plagiarist, and idler, until—shamefaced—he tried to appease her with rough kisses.

She let him make love to her—because she deserved it! She had chosen her own punishment. He fell asleep instantly, believing himself forgiven.

13

IF THE KING WILL NOT RULE

Honolulu, 1889

Stevenson set sail for Samoa four months later, and Kalakaua's febrile mind veered to more pressing matters, none of which required the expertise of a poet. Constable's messages went unanswered. There was not even an invitation to an evening of whiskey and cards for the would-be laureate of the islands. So when Wilcox returned from California, Constable gave his entire attention to politics. He slept most of the day and spent evenings drilling with the Kamehameha Rifles or attending meetings of the Patriots, which ended in late hours at O'Brian's Inn.

Still furious at Constable for stealing her poem, Molly did nothing to assuage his wounded dignity at being ignored by the king. Her copywork was their principal means of support. There were bills to pay, and she had no time to waste on idle dreamers.

"Kalakaua dislikes men of vision because he can see no farther than the end of his cigar, no deeper than the bottom of his champagne glass," Constable complained to Molly on one of his rare evenings at home. "He is misled by every fool with a kettle to bang on to attract his attention."

Molly had been busy at her desk, trying to meet a deadline that night. She tapped her pen with ill-disguised impatience. "Is this the same Kalakaua whose praises you sang to Louis and Fanny?"

"Mock me now! But I mean to have my way in the world with or without his help."

"Then do so," Molly said resignedly. "You don't have to be *preferred* to rise!"

"Exactly," he effused. "It is grander work I'm after, nothing less than a plan to turn the hearts of every Hawaiian to the truth!" ·

"What truth?"

"That Kalakaua must be deposed!"

Molly was stunned. Such words were treason.

"Wilcox has seen the outside world," Constable continued. "He knows what one man—the great Garibaldi—did in his day to revive a faltering people. If the king will not rule, then let him step aside—"

Molly turned back to her work. "I promised to have this finished for the messenger at ten—"

"*Auwe,* the daily bread." The clock chimed seven times. Constable blinked, then declared with a start, "Why am I dallying with you when I'm due at O'Brian's in fifteen minutes?" and bolted from the room.

Grimly, Molly picked up a fresh sheet and began to copy out a document in the fine, small hand of a Priory scholar, racing to meet her deadline.

*T*hroughout the last weeks of June, Constable kept up a furious pace, for Robert Wilcox inspired in him a grandeur of purpose he could not muster on his own. They were gathering new recruits to their private militia and to the Patriotic Association, having tapped a dozen streams of discontent. In public, Wilcox professed the goal of restoring the king to the same powers he enjoyed before the takeover of the Reformers. Yet behind the king's back, Wilcox was whispering abdication, and Wilcox's friendship with the king's sister was stirring up gossip. When rumors reached the king's ears that Liliuokalani had gone too far in encouraging Wilcox's band of troublemakers, Kalakaua called his sister to the palace to examine her on this provocation, but she denied any treasonous intent.

On a whim, Molly asked Constable over breakfast the next morning if Wilcox had enlisted the Chinese in his effort to unseat the cabinet.

"Interesting you should ask," he replied through a mouthful of baked breadfruit. "Wilcox wanted your help at Liliuokalani's gala on that very account and was horribly disappointed when you took such an aversion to him. But damn me if he hasn't already become a favorite of the *tong.* Everyone knows your people have piles of gold hidden in Chinatown!

Why shouldn't we have some of it for our purposes, and you have a party to make your case known!"

Rumors were racing through a divided city, igniting old hatreds, fomenting new fears. It was whispered that the Reform Cabinet was planning to strip Kalakaua of the veto, his chief remaining power under the Bayonet Constitution. That Liliuokalani was secretly plotting to force her brother off the throne. That American warships in the harbor stood ready to put marines ashore. That the British were intervening on the king's behalf to thwart American interests. That the old chiefs were calling upon Kalakaua to rise up against the cabinet, while *hapa haole* firebrands like Wilcox and Constable whispered insurrection. That the king himself was willing to sell crown lands to the highest bidder and escape to England. Overnight, it seemed, Peter Ikaika Constable was second in command of a grassroots movement that threatened to topple both the king and the *haole*-controlled cabinet.

Late one night, Molly was roused from a deep, unhappy slumber by scratching noises. She awoke to find the lamp turned down low and Constable brushing his boots to a high sheen. "Where are you going at this hour?" she murmured.

"Only another gathering of the Patriots. Go back to sleep."

She was instantly alert. "If there's trouble, Peter, you must tell me!"

"The Patriots are planning a small protest," he said primly. "Merely a symbolic act of defiance to the Reform Cabinet to restore the monarch's rights."

"Who's backing this—the king or his sister?"

"Both," he said, smiling like a fox with feathers in his mouth. "Or neither . . ."

"So it is Wilcox, playing both ends against the middle!" Molly asserted.

Constable was indignant. "You malign a true patriot! Robert has persuaded our coward king to let us take over both government buildings tomorrow morning to force the return of the monarch's full powers."

"You, who despise Kalakaua, want his power restored?"

There was an uncomfortable pause during which Constable brushed his already shining boots with assiduous care. "I didn't say Kalakaua," he muttered. "I said 'monarch!' " His ebullience had turned sour.

"Wilcox will get you hung!"

"Robert assures us that not a drop of blood will be spilled. July thirtieth will be a historic day! A pity we could not hold our protest as planned for the thirtieth of June! That would have been three years to the day when the Honolulu Rifles stole the monarchy from us. The Kamehameha Rifles were going to take it back, but—"

"But what?"

"But the Rifles did not have the proper . . . attire."

Molly started up from the bed in alarm. "You were buying guns all summer—" she accused.

"Target practice!" he interjected without looking at her.

*T*hunder burst like gunfire when Molly ran up the stairs to Lincoln's rooms. Her frenzied knocking caught the young man unawares, for he came to the door with bare feet, his work shirt half-buttoned and one edge hanging lower than the other.

His small apartment included a galley along the back wall. A side door led to a sleeping cubicle hidden behind a curtain. The main room, like its occupant, was without adornment, though suited to a young man of some means. A wooden stool and a large leather chair were positioned next to a table on which rested a new and expensive gas reading lamp. In one corner, fixed upon a tripod, was an accordion-pleated camera. On the walls were five framed photographs of New England winter scenes and a painted Chinese scroll depicting a tiny pilgrim climbing a mountain draped in clouds. The central features that gave the room its distinction were the hundreds of books, the sum total of his fortune, arranged on floor-to-ceiling shelves, each one crammed with volumes of leather and dark cloth.

Molly read in the lineaments of the room the story of a life not unlike her own: spare, self-sufficient, alone.

"I wouldn't have come," she said, embarrassed, "if not for Peter's newest, maddening escapade—" and burst into tears.

A shadow passed over Lincoln's face. "I've been hearing rumors for weeks, ever since Wilcox came back."

"They're planning a protest against the cabinet to support the king and his sister. Merely symbolic—"

"One hopes, but I have my doubts. The Liberal Patriotic Association is armed and claims to have an army of eight hundred. Hawaiians are saying that Wilcox is the king's man. But in Chinatown, one hears that Wilcox is planning to put Liliuokalani on the throne!"

Molly twisted her hands, saying nothing. She dared not implicate Peter in this treason, not even to Lincoln!

Lincoln's eyes narrowed. "Your silence confirms what I already know. Wilcox has convinced his hotheads that they can revive the old kingdom as Garibaldi did in Italy. The Rifle Corps wears red shirts like the Italians, so there's little doubt who fashions himself the Garibaldi of Hawaii!"

"And having played every role of Let's Pretend, Peter now plays at war," whispered Molly, dabbing at her eyes with a handkerchief. "Peter must be stopped before the whole thing turns bloody! You know he will make a colossal mess of this!"

"Leaving you to clean up the wreckage?" Lincoln asked. His slim fingers drummed nervously on the polished wood table, belying the steadiness of his voice.

"Help me—" she begged.

Lincoln did not answer, saying instead, "I was making tea when you knocked. Auntie sent over a new batch."

Molly laughed. " '*Aiya,* drink, drink,' " she said, imitating her mother's accent. 'Good for an ailing heart . . .' "

Lincoln went quickly to his small galley to conceal his own sickness of heart. Molly was resting her head on the brown surface of the table when he returned with the pot. Her thick, wiry hair had sprung loose from its pins and fell across her shoulders in a dark wave. He eased himself into the leather chair and set out the tea things between them. What a mystery that the girl who had slept separated from him by one thin wall was unreachable still. He longed to feel the weight of her hair in his hands, to gather it to his lips, to touch the bronzed cheek. He did not dare. More than once, he had detected an answering spark in her, as on the evening when he had held her in his arms in the great ballroom of Liliuokalani's mansion. And then she had closed herself off, doused the incipient fire between them. What did she fear—the explosion of an uncousinly passion? But he was not a true kinsman! Well, he was done with waiting. "Come," he ordered her. "Drink up."

Molly lifted her head, rubbed her red eyes, and blew her nose on her handkerchief, as Lincoln slid the round cup across the table.

"This is oolong, plain black tea," he said stonily. "I have no medicine to cure what ails your heart."

She blew upon her cup and watched the curling plume rise, obscuring his face. "No, I suppose not," she said. "I should be like you—calm, controlled . . . a heart wrapped in . . . what? New England ice?"

Lincoln gripped the cup with both hands, scalding his fingers through the glazed porcelain. "I am not without feeling."

"I didn't mean that—"

"I have emotions—"

"—entirely worthy ones! Noble sentiments, noble goals—" She was teasing him, falling into the patterns of childhood.

"Ignoble desires!" He placed his hands upon the table and she remembered how hers had lain in his palm as they danced. She remembered, too, the heat that flared up between them momentarily. . . . But that was just dancing, she told herself uneasily. This was Lincoln! Faithful, stolid Lincoln. . . . It amused her to think that he might indeed have the same passions as other men.

"The Lis have proposed a match between me and the Widow's daughter," he blurted out. "They have offered a dowry. No bride-price is required."

Somewhere in the region of Molly's chest a sharp pain cut deep. She felt nauseous. Perhaps it was the tea.

He watched her through a curtain of steam.

Molly's smile was brilliant. "I should congratulate you," she whispered. "I know your ambitions—"

"You believe that ambition drives this bargain?" he replied bitterly. "You think Lily does not summon in me the same desires that Peter has for you . . . or you for him?"

"Then desire goes hand in hand with money—a fortuitous match!"

"The astrologer's charts have not been cast, but yes, fortune smiles on me," he said flatly.

"This will give you power in Chinatown." Her hands shook as she sipped the scalding tea.

He acknowledged her words with a brisk nod. "I could help your mother . . . and you."

"No one can help me," she replied wearily. She set the cup down, making ready to go. "It was unfair of me to draw you into my problems now that you have . . . negotiations to carry out—"

"Stay!" he blurted out. "Stay here until . . ."

"I can't. They're meeting tonight at Liliuokalani's house in Palama—I have to stop him before he ruins himself! I'll sneak in . . . put on a disguise—stop the meeting somehow—"

Lincoln sprang out of his chair. "Ridiculous! You can hardly pass as a man! You've listened too long to your mother's stories about women in China disguising themselves in war!"

"Then you *will* help me?"

Lincoln felt like winding his arms around her slender neck . . . to embrace her? Better yet to strangle her! After a pause, he said, "I'll find a way to get in. Another Chinese contributor to their cause. One Chinaman looks like another to their eyes. My face and my money should open the door for me."

"Promise me you'll watch over him—I dream such monstrous things!"

"I'll be his shadow, if that is what the lady desires!" replied Lincoln curtly.

"Not his shadow, his reason, since he seems to have lost that."

.   .   .

*C*onstable was working feverishly at his desk when Molly returned. At her entry, he put aside his papers and pressed her to share a glass of brandy with him, an unaccustomed gesture of conviviality after months of estrangement. He talked animatedly about returning to his unfinished epic now that he had a crucial new story to tell, and after refilling her glass one more time, pulled her onto his lap. And to her own surprise, Molly found herself opening her gown to him, turning his head down to her neck. Lincoln's announced passion for Lily that afternoon had unsettled her. She was drunk, she realized, on two glasses of brandy and three dollops of fear, and even the attention of a man she no longer respected was proof that someone loved her still! His lips and teeth were on her breasts, and Molly found herself responding as keenly as a glass bell being struck. In minutes, her petticoats were cast aside and his hands, now tender, now rough, were making her ready for him. He took her on the couch with her bare legs locked around his waist, thrusting against her so that she felt that she might break apart. He brought her rapidly to the edge of release, then quickly withdrew, ignoring her sharp cries; then entered her once more, only to deny her yet again. She lost track of the passing of time. She heard the distant bells of the cathedral and forgot to count the hour; her heart was pounding, her eyes heavy, and her mind afloat with images of open mouths stained with wine. Afterward, she fell into a slumber so deep that she did not see him take a red shirt from a parcel in the wardrobe nor hear him leave.

*C*onstable was late to the meeting at Liliuokalani's mansion in Palama. He was sluggish from brandy and lovemaking, and the plans that had seemed so clear earlier in the evening were now murky and obscure. "Bloody hell," he blurted out when a familiar figure pulled him into the vestibule. It was Molly's relative, the implacable pedant, who proceeded to attach himself like a barnacle. "Who invited you?" Constable demanded.

"You did. . . . I am here to see that the *tong's* money is well spent," Lincoln lied. It worried him that he had penetrated the cabal with such ease. The bank draft in his pocket, made out to Wilcox, was enough to get him past the two men guarding the door.

Constable threw Lincoln a disgusted look and pushed his way past. But Lincoln doggedly followed, saying, "If you're counting heads, there's one conspicuous absence. The king's sister."

"Of course she's not here!" Constable shot back. "You think you're so clever— No room for pedants here. Stay out of the way if you're not going to pick up a gun."

Down the hall, the dining room had taken on the atmosphere of a war room with Robert Wilcox sketching out battle plans on a piece of butcher's paper pinned to a velvet curtain. Wilcox was dressed in the crimson-and-black uniform of an Italian officer complete with cloak, gold epaulets, sword, and a brace of revolvers. He was busily drawing a crude aerial view of the two government buildings across the street from the palace grounds. Arrows indicated the approach the "army" was to take and the points at which it would break into various columns once the men entered the buildings.

Lincoln was appalled. "The Americans would never abide an insurrection," he whispered to Constable. "Why else is the *Adams* staying on when she was scheduled to sail days ago? Liliuokalani is *still* hiding her hand. If she feels you hotheads are running amok, she'll back off. Who will Wilcox turn to then?"

But Constable had no interest in pursuing such hazy particulars. He was busy studying the thick black line that Wilcox had drawn upon the brown paper.

Liliuokalani's house smelled of whiskey, cigars, and masculine bravado. Emotion, not organization, Lincoln observed, was the Liberal Patriotic Association's strongest suit. For even as Wilcox sketched more lines on the thick paper, men gathered in disparate groups to challenge his strategy, as if debating the theories of a war long past rather than a battle about to be joined. Quarrels were spreading throughout the crowd, widening eddies of recrimination in a river of fear.

"If the princess withdraws support, how can we prevail over Kalakaua? He's *still* king!" came an anguished shout.

A youth named Kimo, whose red shirt was too tight for his husky body, raised his voice in protest. "I say Kalakaua's already signed away his powers when he put his name to the Reform Constitution. Because of that act, no *alii* can truly be king now!"

"Hear, hear," echoed Constable. "Kingship is a matter of character as well as blood, and Kalakaua by his weakness to lead has lost his *mana*! Without that mandate from the gods, he has the look of a dying man. And I refuse to perish with him!"

Back and forth went the debate with the supporters of the princess drowning out the handful of Kalakaua loyalists. As the hour approached midnight, the stream of oratory ran dry. Panic was spreading through the crowd. "It's foolhardy to move tonight," one man cried. "Better wait until the Americans set sail!"

"There *always* is an American or a British or a French ship in the harbor!" shouted Wilcox at the dissenter. "Every Western power is waiting to gobble us up. If we back down, that's the excuse any foreign nation needs to secure its interests with cannon! Swiftness and surprise are our weapons! We cannot waver!"

Perfectly done, observed Lincoln, as he studied Wilcox. The arrogant posturing, the studied shake of the head that spoke volumes about human weakness and the ephemeral courage of those less visionary than he. Except that Wilcox was not succeeding. The men were clearly retreating from boldness into fear.

Wilcox turned to Constable and hissed, "Talk to them. Make them listen, Peter!"

The terror on Constable's face made Lincoln suspect that Wilcox's second-in-command was reliving another impromptu speech at O'Brian's Inn. But his general had ordered him forward, and Constable soldiered on. He climbed up on a chair beneath the glistening chandelier and shouted for attention. Slowly, grudgingly, angry muttering gave way to silence.

"Now—" Constable stammered, "is the hour when will becomes action—" His throat was dry, and he broke into a fit of coughing. Sweating profusely, Constable wiped his forehead with his sleeve. He felt naked. He wished he had a hat, a cane, a gun—any prop to hide behind. "Who among you doubts . . . ?" he began earnestly. A sea of hands rose, and Constable glanced at Wilcox in panic. Words flew out of his head. The sound of impatient feet scraping the wooden floor was magnified in the cavernous room. "Quite so, quite so," he hemmed, "what man is ever without doubts, whether over women or war?" A wave of nervous laughter rippled through the room. Constable frowned. He had not meant to amuse. His voice took on a harsher, more strident tone. "These islands are awash in womanish talk—I suspect that there are those prone to believe it. For yes, we are few, and face insurmountable odds. You have heard it said that we do not have the arms, the skill, the means to challenge the cabinet or the sleeping giant behind it, the United States of America!" There was no trace of hesitancy or stuttering now. Ikaika Constable had caught the men's longing for clear, sharp words to guide them. "How can we withstand such might, you say? Are we not condemned to weakness by our small size? Isn't victory as impossible as a man walking on water? You have heard these things and repeated them in your hearts and in repeating doubts, you become afraid!"

Constable had recounted the men's worst fears and in so doing tamed them. Even his own! When he began again, his mood had turned contemplative. "I too have fears . . . and yet I believe that this is the hour when the new Hawaiian must put aside selfish cares for the good of this sovereign nation . . ." And here his voice began to rise in force and conviction. "Are we not people of the sea? Just as our grandfathers walked upon the roiling deep on boards of *wiliwili,* let us catch the wave of history as it breaks, and ride its crest to victory! We are Hawaii's future. Let us grasp hold of these islands and recast upon these ancient stones our map of earthly Paradise!"

The Patriots shouted their joy in one voice. The cheers were heady music to Ikaika Constable's ears. He was a fool and a follower no longer but a man of power! For in this place and at this moment, he was uttering words that were propelling men to fight and love and die! Forging words that altered history, as Shelley claimed great poets should!

Amid the clamor of approval that erupted, Lincoln remained unmoved. Rhetoric, however fiery and fine, was no shield for cannon or rifle.

"Why wait?" Wilcox shouted, leaping to Constable's side. "We will go now and seize the palace while Kalakaua sleeps! He expects us to take the government buildings by day. We will surprise him in his bed by night! What loyalty do we owe a man whom we intend in the end to remove? Each squad will secure a strategic point," he announced. "We reassemble in the courtyard and position the cannon to command the four gates. Once the palace is secure and the guns are in place—I would estimate well before five in the morning—we go on to seize the government buildings and send delegations to rouse the cabinet ministers from their featherbeds. If they resist, they will discover that the palace is impounded, the king nullified, and every Hawaiian rallied to our cause. The traitors will be forced to resign!" Reaching into his pocket, he waved a tightly rolled-up document. "Here is the new constitution to restore power to the monarchy," he shouted, waving the scroll above his head. "With this sword, I will chase Kalakaua from the throne!" The assembly cheered.

Constable raised Wilcox's arm higher and began to chant the forgotten creed of Kamehameha III. *"Ua mau ke ea oka aina ika pono!"* he cried again and again, and the crowd joined in, turning the fifty-year-old dictum into a battle cry. "The life of the land is perpetuated in righteousness!"

The improvised army surged out of the princess's house and into the boulevards armed with rifles, rice-bird guns, revolvers, their torches gleaming, their crimson shirts warming the darkness. At King Street, they picked up their pace, giddy with fear and delight and as much intoxicated with the heroic vision of themselves as with the drinks they had filched from Liliuokalani's private stock. A wind was blowing in from the sea, carrying the harbor smells of salt and sewage. Constable's stomach tightened convulsively. He had an overwhelming urge to defecate, which he blamed on drink. Not fear! While Lincoln ran along at the edge of the crowd, Constable marched resolutely at the head of the throng shoulder to shoulder with Wilcox, ignoring the turmoil in his belly and urging the others to a faster pace. Their footsteps thudded in the soft dust of the road: an army of eighty, one-tenth its rumored size.

At the corner of Richards Street, the red-shirted Patriots broke into an excited trot, then sprinted down Palace Walk, having formed themselves into neat rows, three men abreast. Constable signaled for silence; then brandishing his sidearm, ran up to the sentry at the palace gate.

14

THE BATTLE

Iolani Palace loomed before them: a massive, ornate rock pile behind an eight-foot-tall perimeter wall of coral stone. The government buildings across the street were dark, but lights still burned in the palace on the third floor and in the basement. In 1887, when the Hawaiian Rifles had first shown their power, Kalakaua had stripped the gaslight fixtures from the walls and wired the palace for electricity to flood the yard with light in the event of a night attack. It pleased him now to keep a few lights burning as a sign to would-be intruders of his vigilance.

Wilcox had insinuated his own men into the palace staff. The sentry at the *mauka,* or mountainside, post was a loyalist, so it was an easy task for the Patriots to file into the darkened palace grounds via the unlocked gate. To their delight and surprise, the guardhouse was dark—"lazy bastards are sleeping," came the whisper passed by Wilcox down the line. In the northern corner of the yard stood the Bungalow, a two-story building where Kalakaua and his queen had lived during the building of the new palace. Days before, it had been lit up for a party; now it was as dark as a tomb.

Wilcox raised his hand, bringing the column to a halt and made a series of rapid gestures that sent the men scattering to their respective positions.

Constable took a squad to secure the guardhouse, while Wilcox hastened to the palace to rouse the king from slumber. Wilcox's confidence was catching. The Patriots could hardly stifle the cheers that gathered in their throats. Already they were halfway to capturing palace and king without a shot fired!

Constable kicked in the guardhouse door with guns cocked, feeling every inch a warrior. "In the name of the Kamehameha Rifles and the Liberal Patriotic Association, surrender!" he shouted. But instead of finding slumbering guardsmen, he encountered only empty cots and shadows.

"The cowards have fled!" he cried.

"Or are hiding . . ." observed Lincoln warily. "Or repositioned for an attack. Why are the sentries missing from their post?" The very ease of their entry had instilled in him a horrible premonition that they were walking into a trap.

Constable frowned. The notion that events might go awry was an affront to his faith in the man who had planned the attack. "Damn suspicious Chinaman!" he muttered. Still, Lincoln's observation was worrisome enough for him to dispatch his squad in haste to the armory adjacent to the guardhouse where the next phase of operations was to begin.

In the armory were four cannons mounted on wooden wheels and rounds of shot. Constable's men executed their mission with the skill of seasoned combatants: the cannons were dragged into the yard and positioned at each of the four entrances of the palace in the direction of the government buildings. Quickly then, Constable's small squad began handing out purloined arms and ammunition among the main force.

"They move well," Lincoln observed of Constable's men, "but how many can load and shoot the big guns?"

"The two British over there," Constable replied. "Both were seamen on a frigate."

"Those are old men," declared Lincoln in alarm. "How long ago did they fire such a gun?"

"There will be no need! We train the guns on the government buildings, and the cowards in the cabinet will give way!"

Still, Lincoln noticed that Constable brought his best men to the two former British sailors in charge of the cannon for an impromptu lesson in the loading and firing of the guns. Lincoln himself seized a revolver that was offered him and loaded it with shaking hands.

The sound of hurried feet on the gravel walk halted the troop's feverish preparations. Wilcox was returning in haste from the palace, his face drained of color by the flickering torchlight. "The king's gone! I didn't plan . . . I didn't foresee. . . ."

"Perhaps he has decided to keep out of the line of fire," Lincoln said to Constable.

Constable swore under his breath. Wilcox's announcement was being passed swiftly from man to man. He could feel their confusion mounting. "Lucky for us the king's run away," Constable said loudly enough for all to hear. "Nothing's to stop us now from seizing the palace!" Ragged cheers spread through the ranks.

Wilcox seemed oblivious of how his behavior was affecting the men. "But that's just it—" he stuttered, "the guards are holding the palace! The king put his best man, Waipa Parker, in charge and withdrew to the queen's house in town. Parker says Kalakaua's left orders that if we enter the palace, his men are to shoot us down!"

The cheering stopped.

Wilcox pulled Constable aside. "I swear I had assurances! I had his compliance! The king was supposed to be passive at our entry. I explained to him thoroughly our intent, our sacrifice in his behalf. . . . I'm sure he believed me!"

"You negotiated in secret with the king about our plans for taking the palace?" Constable stammered in disbelief. "Why?" The man before him had suddenly shrunk in size. "Whose man are you, Robert, the king's or his sister's? Or are you even a man?"

"The military annals counsel a general never to commit to a single line of action . . . to hold open a private door," Wilcox babbled, more to himself than to his second-in-command. "I never thought . . . I always intended . . ."

"And having attacked hours too soon, we are betrayed by the very one *we* intended to betray! Beset from the rear and exposed to attack from outside the gates," Constable hissed to Wilcox. "We have no choice but to use the cannon against the palace or be shot like rats in a cage."

Wilcox groaned, stupefied with indecision.

"Our plans are the same! We occupy the palace grounds and take the government buildings," Constable declaimed to the men with as much aplomb as he could muster and was rewarded with a barrage of questions by the terrified crowd.

"What about Parker's guns?"

"How can eighty men defend the Hale, the Kapuaaiwa Building, *and* the palace?"

"Can't we call the princess for reinforcements?"

"Liliuokalani won't help if it means taking a public stand against her brother," replied Constable. "Kalakaua has forced our hand. We have no choice but to reaffirm our loyalty to him to keep the people on our side.

You go to him," he ordered Wilcox. "Tell him our hopes for the kingdom and the new constitution."

"I can't . . ." Wilcox stammered. "As leader, I shouldn't expose—"

"We can force the Reform Cabinet out if he stands with us," assured Constable. "He can't deny the symbolic power of our protest. The people will rally round him—"

Wilcox backed away, shaking his head. "No, no—"

"Stay with the men then! Take the government buildings. I'll go to him myself!" Constable stomped off toward the livery stable, but not before berating a group of reluctant Patriots back into position near the *mauka* gate. He was struggling to subdue a frightened horse when a pair of slim hands slipped the bridle over the horse's head. Constable gave a short, ironic laugh when he saw the face of his would-be accomplice. "You're a damned stubborn son of a bitch, Chinaman, I give you that."

They hitched the horses up in silence together, and when the rig was ready, Constable motioned Lincoln onto the driver's seat and entered the velvet interior of the carriage. The Hawaiian youth Kimo, who had doggedly followed Lincoln from Liliuokalani's house to the palace grounds, leaped onto the seat beside Constable, and the three set off through the darkened streets of Honolulu—a boy, a poet, and a failed seminarian—in the ebony-and-gilt splendor of the royal coach.

*M*olly was jolted awake by the sudden rattling of glass. Birds, she thought groggily. Sunlight streamed through the windows. She was sprawled on the couch exactly as Constable had left her, her temples throbbing in pain. The hands of the clock pointed to ten. Suddenly, a thunderous explosion shook the ground. Another shattered a windowpane. Not birds. Not firecrackers. But the roar and rumble of cannon.

She dressed groggily. Outside, the empty streets told an ominous story. Molly saw that the people were hiding, terrified of the grave new peril engulfing the city. A child wriggled under a curtained doorway and waddled into the lane just as a line of soldiers in United States blue came trotting briskly in the direction of the American diplomatic building, guns carried at port arms. Immediately, its mother ran out and snatched the screaming child from the path of the heavy boots as cannons boomed in the distance.

Molly ran alongside the stony-faced marines, her heart pounding in concert with the distant barrage of gunfire. A riderless horse cantered across their path and was quickly lost from view. Soon the soldiers had passed her by, and Molly had to step across cabbages and breadfruit and coconuts, which had tumbled from abandoned wagons into the muddy streets. On the boardwalk fronting the shuttered stores, she spied a basket of laundry dropped in haste. A stained shirt and muddy pair of trousers spilled across the walk like the crumpled body of a man.

*C*onstable's encounter with the king was brief, disappointing, grim. He hurried back to join the troops, but the battle was already joined by the time the carriage rounded the corner toward the government buildings. With a sinking heart, he saw that the Reform Cabinet had not sat idly by as the protest unfolded. The ministers had stationed their own militia, the Honolulu Rifles, on the rooftops along King Street across from the palace. The Patriots had dutifully followed Wilcox's original plan, one that had invited the present disaster. For having split their ranks, half were now trapped by Parker inside the palace grounds, half were in the government buildings pinned down by gunfire.

A volley of bullets peppered the coach as it careened past the Opera House through the gates of the Hale. Constable threw open the carriage door, and he, Lincoln, and Kimo raced inside. All was bedlam within. The very Patriots who had won prizes for parades and drills now struggled awkwardly with their weapons, firing at random from the windows. Wilcox had taken refuge in a back room with paper and chalk, sketching out more battle plans on paper.

"Where's Kalakaua?" Wilcox demanded.

"Wouldn't come," Kimo replied in disgust.

"But without his aid, we will be perceived as—"

"—traitors!" asserted Constable. "He accused us of conniving with his sister, an accusation I could not deny."

"Preposterous!" Wilcox exclaimed. "Liliuokalani approached me!"

"He saw through our lies," Constable said with a shrug. "His worst insults were for you."

Wilcox swallowed hard. "What exactly did he say . . . about me?"

Constable could not stand to look at him. It was Lincoln who answered in a level voice. "The king said, 'Tell that bloody bastard I'll see him hang.' "

Wilcox staggered as if clubbed from behind.

"We waited down the street from the queen's house," Constable said at last. "A carriage came round, and the king and queen hurried inside. Their servants were carrying things wrapped up in blankets. Then they set off toward the harbor. To the boathouse, I suspect—a handful of men could defend it indefinitely. And Kalakaua was crafty enough to install that phone line to the palace when he put in electric lights. He can direct Parker's operations at the palace and never expose a hair on his head. . . . I recommend we cut the line!"

"Yes, yes—should have done so already . . ." echoed Wilcox.

"Except we've got to cross over to the palace first," reminded Lincoln. This was not about Molly anymore, but about this man Constable. There was a grandeur now about him that reminded Lincoln of the uncles in the *hui* when they went to do battle against the rain. Lincoln would see this through to the end.

"Well, we shall—and might yet persuade Parker and his men to join us!" babbled Wilcox.

That idea was greeted with contempt from Constable and a volley of gunfire from outside. The cabinet militia was attacking the government buildings with renewed force. Worse, sharpshooters on the roof of the Opera House had a clear view into the palace compound and had already cut down one of the seamen manning the cannon, driving the rest behind trees or into the Bungalow for cover. Now the cannons were impotent and the sharpshooters raked the buildings with a continuing fusillade.

At noon, the cabinet militia rushed the government buildings, and Constable decided to rejoin their divided forces and move into the Bungalow, the only available fortress, for a lengthy siege. The Patriots retreated under heavy fire across the street in the direction of the Bungalow. The withdrawal was so disorderly that Constable could only stand helplessly by as thirty men broke ranks, ran straight into the palace, and surrendered.

*M*olly arrived outside the palace just as the Patriots made their chaotic flight into the Bungalow. At the wall nearest her, she witnessed a bizarre scene. Twenty men from the Reform Cabinet's militia were tying nails around sticks of dynamite. Among them was the son of the British Consul, a tall husky youth who had played baseball Sunday afternoons in Kapiolani Park. The young man had stripped off his shirt and was flexing his arms.

"Think you can do it, Wodehouse?" his companion demanded.

The young man nodded and continued rotating his arms in circles as Molly dashed across the road.

"You there, girlie," Wodehouse's companion yelled. "Get away from there. Can't you see there's a war going on?"

Molly shook her head as if she didn't understand English, and walked faster.

"It's Constable's woman," Wodehouse shouted. "Stop her!"

Molly turned and ran. A bullet whizzed overhead, but she was already through the gates and into the safety of the Bungalow.

Inside, red-shirted Patriots ran up and down the stairs in terrified disarray. Two men lugging a huge mahogany table stared at Molly in confusion before jamming the table in the doorway to block further intruders. Wilcox ran past with a leather valise clasped to his breast, darted into a corner, and fell to his knees, pouring out papers, a compass, a revolver, a bar of soap onto the floor. Before Molly could accost him, Lincoln bounded down the stairs followed by a handsome half-Hawaiian boy carrying a handful of ancient Hawaiian spears.

"You! Of all the stupid . . ." blurted out Lincoln. "Of course, things were not bad enough. You had to wade into this quagmire!"

"Where's Peter?" Molly shouted.

Lincoln dragged her up the wide dark stairway, and there, in the long gallery, she found Constable shouting directions at riflemen stationed at the windows overlooking the palace yard. The Hawaiian youth who had carried the spears took up a brace of spent rifles and began to reload them.

"Bloody hell," Constable shouted at Lincoln, "why in God's name did you bring her!"

"She brought herself," Lincoln snapped.

"Outside"—she stammered, pointing to the wall—"behind the Bungalow, men with dynamite. That pitcher on the baseball team—the British Commissioner's son, Wodehouse—he's among them."

"They're lobbing homemade bombs!" Constable declared. A disturbing new thought made him pause. "The cannons we left in the yard . . . if they turn those guns upon us . . ."

"Then stop now! Convince Wilcox to give up!" Molly pleaded. "You've made your statement! No one will fault your courage!"

"Can't surrender," Constable affirmed breathlessly to Molly. "The curtain's just gone up. Got to play until it drops. Don't be so cynical. Plots such as this often turn in the last act by some heroic deed. Besides, I've finally discovered my métier. Not poetry, after all, but war."

"Why throw your life away for such a vain cause?" demanded Molly.

"How else will my people be made whole again if not by some utterly vain sacrifice that makes them look up from their bowl, their cup, their guitar—all the visceral pleasures by which they forget how quickly they are passing away? Better to die for an idea than live in indignity!"

Just then a burst of gunfire from the neighboring buildings hit the Bungalow, driving Constable's riflemen from the windows in a hail of splintering rock. Seconds later, a mighty explosion sheared off a section of the roof not twenty feet above them. Windows, mirrors, vases, porcelain bowls shattered everywhere. Wood splinters and nails came flying through the room. A man fell screaming, writhing on the floor, clutching at his skull. His hands brought back a bloody husk, fragments of bone and flesh covered with matted hair, his eyes already glazed in death.

Constable pushed Molly to the ground. "Back at the windows," Constable ordered his men. "Give me cover!" And he raced downstairs.

"I don't understand. Where's he going?" Molly cried.

"To get a cannon," Lincoln said. "That'll stop Wodehouse from lobbing more bombs and drive the sharpshooters off the roofs."

The handsome Hawaiian boy crawled out from under a teakwood table and gave Molly a crooked grin. "Don't worry, lady. Kimo is Ikaika's shadow."

Another explosion shattered a portion of the upper story, raining shards from the ceiling on their heads. When the clouds of dust and plaster had settled, Molly crawled to the window and saw Constable emerging below. He dashed toward the nearest cannon thirty yards away, while the riflemen above protected him under a blanket of fire. The afternoon light was unusually clear, shining down on the only moving object in the yard, highlighting the reddish glints in Constable's hair, the crimson shirt. Constable did not head directly to the cannon, but darted at quick, odd angles toward his target, the way a wild boar runs through *pili* grass to confuse pursuers. Bits of earth bounced around him, for the sharpshooters on the rooftops had spotted him instantly. Again the Patriots threw a shield of bullets around their brother. In seconds, Constable had reached the cannon and held it by its splayed-leg supports. With a great heave, he boosted it up and leaning his weight against the gun, made his way with agonizing slowness toward the Bungalow. Twenty yards from the door, the heavy cannon stopped, its wheels stuck by a small divot in the grass. Molly saw Constable strain against the metal, but the iron gun would not move. Then Kimo was running toward him. Together, they wrenched the wooden wheel over the obstacle and pulled it forward. They were nearly to the door when rifle fire tore at Kimo's leg. The cannon stopped. Constable quickly hoisted Kimo up under one arm. Bullets from above and across the street rained down on them as Constable dragged Kimo toward safety.

Lincoln flung the door wide, firing over Constable's head, and in the next instant, pulled the wounded boy inside. Kimo's right leg was shattered; bits of bone poked through the torn cloth and bleeding flesh. He would never run or dance or swim or ride the long board upon the waves again, but he was alive!

"Good man, Kimo," Constable said tenderly, then turned back for the cannon. And at that instant, a sharpshooter's bullet cut through his neck.

So great was the force of the bullet that Constable in his agony toppled backward, knocking Lincoln and Molly onto the marble floor. For a moment, he seemed unaware of his wound. He rose unsteadily, perplexed by Molly's screaming, one hand extended in sympathy. Except that the smile he gave her ran red.

Molly screamed and screamed as Constable's life spurted away in a great arcing stream.

Moments later, Wilcox tied a sheet to an ancient spear and signaled surrender.

*N*o native jury would convict the surviving members of the Kamehameha Rifles and the Liberal Patriotic Association of treason. As Constable had predicted, they had become heroes to the Hawaiian folk simply for opposing the hated *haole* cabinet. Lincoln, who had successfully passed himself off as a reporter for a Chinese newspaper, was fined two hundred fifty dollars and released. Molly was never taken prisoner. The militia thought her a palace servant who had wandered into the fray unawares. And Wilcox quickly emerged as the most popular new leader in Hawaii. Liliuokalani, however, disavowed him. So, of course, did the king, whose health took another turn for the worse. A short while later, on his doctors' advice, Kalakaua sailed to San Francisco for advanced medical attention. He would die there in two years, ravaged by overindulgence, his heart burst by sorrow.

Constable had once confided to Molly his desire for a native burial. She gave his body to his grieving brothers in the Rifle Corps who brought it to a *kahuna* to be preserved according to *alii* tradition: the flesh melted in the fire, the bones wrapped in sacred *tapa* and buried in a secret place. In this way, Ikaika Constable returned to his native Kauai not the poet he intended, but the warrior he proved.

15

GHOSTS

Spring 1890

By defying the Reform Cabinet with its anti-Chinese agenda, Lincoln had inadvertently become what he most desired—spokesman for his people. He claimed, however, that that power was garnered not by wisdom but error. Thus his first reaction to his notoriety in Chinatown was to spurn the requests for counsel that came his way, until Rulan convinced him that the authority others invested in him could be exercised for the good of all. Many in Chinatown urged him to side again with Wilcox, who, after the aborted rebellion of 1889, was organizing an independent party against the royals. Wilcox's new goal was to end the monarchy and see himself elected prime minister of a new republic. In this way, he would accomplish with Hawaiian votes what he could not do with guns.

Lincoln would have nothing to do with Wilcox. "The man's a coward and a fool," he warned the elders of the Union, the surname societies, the *tongs*. "The era of kings is over. We should prepare our people for the day when a foreign nation claims Hawaii as its stepchild." So he opposed the continuation of the opium license and the national lottery that Kalakaua's designated successor, Liliuokalani, was advocating to fill the crown's depleted treasury. "Buy a license and you buy the corruption of your sons," he cautioned. "Build farms, build shops, build trade!"

Lily profited by Lincoln's counsel. Now that the fish market was rebuilt and the secret income from opium was pouring into the *tong,* she sold her share of the license at immense profit. Lincoln was her most trusted adviser and so frequent a guest at her house that she kept a set of chopsticks inscribed with his name. She was seen riding with him in an uncovered carriage—unheard of for an unmarried woman!—except that she was rich and he powerful enough to do as they wished.

Presents bearing the chop of the Lis began arriving at the construction site of the *mui* factory outside Chinatown where Rulan lived in temporary quarters: bolts of silk cloth; embroidered slippers; gold coins tucked in red paper; and festival cakes at every new cycle of the moon. Rulan neither acknowledged the gifts nor gave offerings in return but handed them out among her Hawaiian neighbors along the lanes. She knew too well where the gifts were leading: dowry negotiations. The lavishness of the presents accentuated the immensity of the Li fortune and the value of the bride-to-be.

One afternoon, a horse-drawn taxi pulled up at the portion of the building site that served as Rulan's living space. Lily climbed out and daintily stepped between the stacks of raw lumber and bricks of coral stone. Behind her a manservant lifted an old woman out of the taxi and set her down on tiny bound feet. It was Mei Yuk, her skinny frame engulfed by the voluminous folds of her stiff jacket and skirt. Her back was bent, and she leaned on a cane to walk. Yet her voice was as strident as ever and her mouth the same slash of crimson in an immaculately powdered face. Only her eyes, darting fearfully from side to side, betrayed the tumult within. She stabbed her cane at the coral block foundations, infuriated by the vastness of Rulan's property and of the factory that would eventually rise upon it.

The manservant brought the women into the section that served Rulan as dining room, sitting room, bedroom, and selling space for her trade in dried fruit and herbs. Everything was makeshift. Goods were piled in wooden crates; a cot made do for sitting and sleeping; a length of threadbare cotton cloth separated the outdoor kitchen from the room itself. Yet there were unmistakable signs of wealth. Hand-painted porcelain rice bowls and teacups were stacked atop a round mahogany table. A grandfather clock of solid cherry stood in the corner next to a rolltop desk.

Lily politely called Rulan's name on entering. Mei Yuk, failing to offer a greeting, received none in return. Instead she planted herself on a mahogany chair and blurted out caustically, "You Chens are like termites—always digging and piling up dirt. Your man is dead, and still you build more out of jealousy."

"Forgive her," Lily murmured. "Her mind wanders nowadays."

Mei Yuk's eyes swept the room. "A pigsty, like the village. And you have no mirrors! You are afraid to look at your own face, *hai ma*? And no wonder—your face is old!"

"I have no desire to be young," Rulan replied.

"Aiya!" Mei Yuk cried. "Who would not wish for youth? You may deceive my daughter with your simplicity, but not me!"

"My mother wishes to propose a transaction," Lily said quietly. "You remember, Mother?"

"I remember everything!" Mei Yuk retorted. "I remember what *that one* did to me!" Her small body began to rock rhythmically in a practiced ritual of grief.

"That time is past," Lily interjected, but Mei Yuk had already begun her lament.

"It was yesterday that she lay beside your father in the great bed in the house of Li. An hour ago that she destroyed our home! A minute past when she tried to steal the Lantern Queen crown from your head—"

"She does not know the difference between dreaming and waking," Lily murmured as the Widow droned on.

"I know!" protested Mei Yuk shrilly. "I remember! And in spite of the evil done to me, I come to give you money that you don't deserve—money that you will undoubtedly use to build and build and build. And after all your building, you will never be as rich as me! My wealth is in gold, yours in wood! Gold will last. Wood rots! So I offer up my daughter to your worthless foster son for five thousand dollars dowry. Five thousand dollars for the privilege of changing his worthless name to Li!"

Rulan had not given the women tea or "small foods" even though her cooking space was stocked with edibles. "It is not enough" was her retort.

"Aaiiee! Not enough for that piece of *la sap* that passes for a man? Chinatown pretends he is the god Kwan Kung come to life when all he did was get himself arrested! Only a madwoman would refuse a dowry for a no-name man, a criminal! He should be put in a cangue like that other no-name man who plucked him from the road!"

"Five thousand dollars is generous, I think," Lily maintained. "If Lincoln takes our name, his sons will inherit a line of ancestors that reaches back a hundred generations. . . ."

Rulan's mouth hardened. "Money cannot buy what was lost in the fire."

"That one wants me to kowtow, to beg! Never, never, never will Li Mei Yuk bow down to a slave! Am I to blame for your bad fate? No, *you* are

the evil one, the thief who stole my man away! I was the beauty, not you! And still you stole him away. What foul means did you use? Prayers? Witchcraft?"

"Mei Mei," Rulan replied softly, using a name she had not uttered for more than thirty years. "You drove them both away."

With an anguished cry, the Widow tottered forward, her nails raised to slash Rulan's face, but Rulan caught her thin arms and held her fast. "I want nothing from you, Mei Mei," she said firmly. "If you desire peace of mind, go to the Kwan Yin temple and beg the goddess for forgiveness. You have done much harm."

That answer rocked the old woman back on her tiny feet. "I curse this house," she wailed, spittle flying with every terrible word. "I cursed your daughter at birth and all my words have come to pass! Who is the beauty? My daughter! Mine! While your bad girl has no home, no ease, no man! May you both die unmourned! May your house be without sons, burned to the root! I curse you, curse all your—" Choking on her own words, her face an ugly, mottled red, Mei Yuk would have thrown herself on the floor in a fit of fury if Rulan and Lily had not pushed her onto the chair.

When the rage had left Mei Yuk's body, the manservant carried the tiny woman out to the taxi. Mei Yuk was quiet now, her eyes staring blindly.

"Tai Tai," Lily ventured, white and shaken. "Take the money. It is not hers anymore, but mine to bestow. This marriage is a good thing. It will bring an end to the ugliness between our families. And . . ." she murmured, her voice thick with emotion, "I desire Lin Kong most dreadfully, you see."

The girl had spoken with unusual candor, observed Rulan. Lily had used the word *desire,* the closest word the Chinese had to the Western *love*.

"I do not doubt your sincerity. But I cannot take your money. This is not China and Lin Kong is not my son. He must decide."

Tears clung to Lily's dark lashes, and her face was suffused with joy. "Then you will not stand in our way if we marry?"

"Lin Kong will do as he chooses."

Lily, visibly moved, put her palms together in gratitude. Despite the older woman's indignant protests, Lily prostrated herself upon the floor, and in the time-honored fashion of daughter-in-law to her husband's mother, struck her forehead again and again on the ground until Rulan lifted her up.

"No!" Rulan said firmly. "I lived my life in such a fashion that no one should have to do this!"

"A small payment, *Tai Tai*," Lily replied with bitterness, "to discharge a debt that a selfish old woman refuses to pay."

*F*or a fortnight before the spring ritual of Ching Ming, the fine, incessant drizzle that the Chinese call "plum rain" had watered the hills above Manoa Valley where the dead lay buried. By noon on festival day, the curtains of vapor had lifted and Tang people surged across the steaming ground to the skirl of flute, the *dok-dok-dok* of wooden drum, and the ear-splitting explosions of "lucky" firecrackers. Women in colorful holiday clothes darted like bright birds among the dark-suited Tang men while scores of small children leaped back and forth over the grave mounds, munching pork buns and waiting for the rites to begin. Gravestones dotted the hills—hundreds of them now—decked with flags and flower *leis,* incense sticks and red prayer candles stuck in boxes of sand, and low tables set with offerings of food to welcome the wandering spirits of father, uncle, brother, and cousin for their brief, yearly sojourn among the living.

The largest group of celebrants were gathered at the Li Gate where a *tong* official was chanting the praises of Merchant Li, the founder of the Li clan. Presiding over the festivities was his only surviving child, Lily. She stood next to the official, the ritual paper *bau* offering smoldering in her hands. It was rumored that she had bypassed the go-between to negotiate her marriage with the foster son of Chen Pao An, dead in the fire four years before. Older women with no love for the Lis were scandalized by Lily's immodest wooing of the bastard son of a Gold Mountain whore. Yet the girl's supporters in the *tong* defended her choice, arguing that the bridegroom was a leader of the Chinese Union and a scholar who could wield ax or shovel as well as any *gu li,* "rough man." The marriage would not only end the old feud that had split Chinatown into rival camps but give Lily access to the lucrative Chen enterprises as well. Chen Pao An's wayward daughter, it was said, had forfeited her claim to the business, and the mother now favored the foster son over her own girl. Moreover, Lily was permitted liberties due the new *Tai Tai* of the Li clan for restoring the ailing family fortune to health. No one could doubt that the Widow was unfit to run a business. Tang wives whispered around the *ma jong* tables that the Chinatown fire had triggered only the final deterioration of an already unsound mind. And yet, to her credit, the daughter displayed perfect filiality in allowing her mother freedom despite her bizarre behavior. On that Ching Ming morning, for example, the Widow tottered on "lotus bud" shoes from grave to grave, plucking food from this stranger's plate and that

family's basket, and screaming at whoever got in her way. Her eccentrici-
ties were suffered because of the daughter, whose shrewdness, it was said,
was even greater than her mother's had been.

Molly had come alone to the Manoa cemetery by public omnibus,
arriving well after Lincoln and her mother. She found her father's grave, a
grassy mound on the highest slope marked by the new granite headstone
she had commissioned. Lincoln hailed her as she climbed the hill. The
building trade was proving lucrative, she observed, for he had managed to
obtain a whole roast pig, a costly offering when Tang men were still
husbanding their cash to replenish stock and acquire properties lost in the
fire.

"Joining us heathens?" Lincoln said with a lopsided grin when she
approached. Molly had not attended a Ching Ming festival since her Priory
days. Her last encounter with a religious rite had been at Constable's
funeral services. Conducted at the seaside in the native tongue by a Hawaiian priest, those rites had been as incomprehensible to her as this Chinese
one.

Lincoln had put on formal Chinese dress for the occasion. His narrow
chun sam tunic was of fine-quality polished cotton fabric with a pointed,
turned-down collar and fastened with five cloth loops over hard rubber-
tipped toggles. A black satin skullcap, soft fabric shoes with white pigskin
soles, and tight Western pants completed the outfit, tailor-made at considerable expense—the traditional gift of bride-to-be to her future husband,
observed Molly with a sinking heart. Molly had to admit that the costume
was not unattractive on Lincoln. Whether in work clothes or *haole* evening
dress or in Chinatown businessman's attire, he was a man at ease in his skin,
not a collection of warring selves like Constable had been until dying made
him whole. She had mourned Constable, though not as bitterly as those
comrades who loved him better than she. And after the shock of his death
had passed, Peter Ikaika Constable had melted from her life like ashes cast
upon the waves.

"I'm only here to inspect the headstone! I didn't come for the rites!"
And I didn't come for *you*! Molly wanted to add even as her eyes followed
the movements of Lincoln's slim body. Rulan barked a greeting and continued setting out joss sticks on the altar. *My mother never changes,* Molly
observed ruefully, *whereas I put on a new face for every stranger.* She could
predict Rulan's every move: counting out the ritual five settings of cups
and bowls and chopsticks on the low wooden altar, measuring out portions
of wine and tea and rice. Rulan could now afford tailor-made garments of
satin, yet she persisted in sewing tunic and pants from the same crude silk
cloth bought from the same traveling peddler. Nor had her mother ac-

knowledged that the worldly young man at her side had any other name but "Lin Kong," as if he were still that mute little boy who never shed a tear.

To avoid helping her mother, Molly made a great show of studying the headstone, a granite slab far more costly and ornate than the one marking the grandfather's plot. She had paid the graveyard organization to engrave it with Pao An's name and date of death in Chinese and English and to set it into the ground. The phrase *Beloved Husband and Father* had been chiseled at the bottom, a liberty taken by the engraver (who claimed the phrase was an honorific among the *haoles*) to boost the price, she supposed. Molly had let the words stand although that label could never wholly define the life of the extraordinary man beneath the ground. Why not Peasant, Rebel Soldier, Seafarer, Canal and Levee Builder, Road Digger, Firefighter? And although she did not believe this, Lincoln had once hinted that Pao An was a poet as well.

She turned from inspecting the stone to discover that her mother had begun the rites without her. The paper money was ablaze in the oil cans, and Rulan was kneeling before the low altar, pouring out libations of wine and tea on the earth. For a moment, Rulan's slender hands shook, her steely calm cracked. But she quickly regained her composure and put her head to the ground, touching the earth with her forehead again and again, chanting softly. A formulaic village response most likely, Molly supposed. She waited for her mother to rise and for Lincoln to take his turn at the wine jar. Instead, Rulan remained on her knees, her breath coming in sharp pants, her eyes fixed on empty space as the paper money burned itself into ash.

She thinks she sees him, Molly observed in dismay. My father's ghost!

To Molly's further chagrin, Lincoln—rational, Calvinist-trained Lincoln, the shrewdest mind in Honolulu—chose that moment to address the grassy mound. "I greet you, Uncle," he said aloud, as if resuming a discussion only lately interrupted. "The Union Hall rises again. The firemen come together to perform the drills you taught them, but the people are already growing complacent at protecting themselves." His voice rose in agitation. "To save money, they are building their shops and homes in the same rickety fashion and out of shoddy materials. And if another fire comes, they will be swept away again! So I have changed your plans for Auntie's shop. This time we are building outside of Chinatown. I have found a block inland a mile from the Canal on the old street that winds up to the grape arbor the Spaniard Don Marin planted sixty years ago. Marin's grandsons have let the vineyard go to seed, but the name he chose for this street of vines stands. Around the corner is the old mansion of Princess

Ruth and beyond that the district where the new ambassadors are building their houses. Nothing else our side of Vineyard Street except homesteads and banana patches. There's room on our block for a good-size factory. The wind-and-water sage examined the site and pointed out the most propitious placement for doors and the angle of walkways. Not exactly what you planned, but bigger . . .''

Hearing his calm voice, Molly could almost accept as reasonable Lincoln's display of superstitious mania! Why was Lincoln able to walk in so many worlds when she did not belong in any? She had a place neither in Chinatown nor in the violent, unstable kingdom lurching toward revolution. The Chinese notion that the ghost lived on forever to guard its living kin was as absurd to her as the Christian heaven. Certainly, her tears had already washed away the image of the man whose bed she had shared for seven years. And yet she recalled countless details about the father whom she had fought and reviled and revered. She remembered the lines etched into the corners of his eyes, the mouth that was both tough and tender, the calloused hands that with a dismissive gesture could reduce her to tears, yet held her in a grip of iron, safeguarding her from the flames. So her father had perished while she lived on in sorrow and confusion and regret, unable to make sense of his self-immolation. By dying in her stead, he had bequeathed her a legacy of terrible uncertainty. How unfair! The man her father despised was exorcised from her life; to whom could she turn to now?

By the time the rites were over and they had found the horse cart Lincoln had rented, afternoon shadows slanted across the graves. Now the cobblestone lane leading out of the cemetery was clogged with wagons of tired pilgrims bound for an evening of feasting. Molly folded herself into the corner of the wagon next to the roast pig while Lincoln and her mother rode up front. The rites had left her dizzy and confused, and her mother's chanting filled her head like the far-off thunder of the sea. She could smell the roast pig's oily skin, feel its glassy eyes fixed on her as Lincoln turned under the Li Gate and guided the cart on the long trek across the valley toward town.

Yet as soon as they approached the flat expanse of the valley floor and the mountain breeze stirred against her cheek, her senses sharpened. Molly was suddenly alert to the beauty of the countryside through which they were journeying. They were on the outskirts of the city in a rural area where Hawaiians still lived on homesteads, parcels of land ceded by a former king. Molly saw the lines of crumbling stone walls which marked the edges of drained and abandoned taro patches, for *poi* was a Chinese industry now and city-bred Hawaiians rarely grew or pounded their own taro. Inside the walls were pigs grazing, pens of the barkless breed of dogs Hawaiians raise for eating, narrow homes on stilts, groves of breadfruit and bananas. She spied an *ohana*, or clan, erecting a house in a small grove of papaya trees. A half dozen men and boys swarmed around a flimsy wooden structure. And in the next yard, an elderly Hawaiian was hammering together a chicken coop out of mesh wire and discarded boards.

At the curve of the road, two brown-skinned boys were knee-deep in a roadside ditch full of rainwater, building a network of streams, jetties, levees, and dams with rocks, leaves, and sticks. One, a Tang boy with no queue, stood up to survey the small earthworks, shouting at his Hawaiian companion to move a twig that had blocked the passage of a wood-chip canoe. Spying their cart, the boy yelled a warning. Too late, for the horse's hooves had kicked up a small avalanche of pebbles that demolished a tiny fortification. Molly looked back to see the Tang boy frowning, his brows knit in concentration, already planning to rebuild. His face was a small copy of Pao An's.

And suddenly, her father was with her, nearer than her breathing, closer than her beating heart. And Molly saw, as Pao An had, that the land about her was alive! *Chi,* the vital breath of the cosmos, molded the earth through the workings of wind and water into mighty *yang* mountains and fertile *yin* valleys and streams. Fingers of mist rose above the rain-sodden earth reaching for the sky; a rainbow sped from the base of a waterfall, leaped across the valley and disappeared into the clouds. Rocks stood forth like warrior sentinels guarding their kin. Even the distant hills were spread across the horizon like slumbering gods and goddesses awaiting an age of new believers to summon them to life. Each ramshackle cottage shuddering in the wind was a living thing conceived and crafted by an *ohana,* board by precious board. She saw too the shadows of a Hawaii yet to come: *mauka* to *makai,* from mountains to sea, the islands were alive with the dwelling places of men and women like her father who struggled and built and dreamed.

As soon as she alighted, Molly tried to take Lincoln aside to tell him of her vision, but he put her off with a restless shake of his head. The drive had taken too long, he explained, and he was late for a meeting. He snapped the reins on the flanks of the horse, leaving the women to prepare the festival feast alone.

Molly guessed to whom Lincoln was rushing. This would be the last Ching Ming the three of them would share. Molly had no doubt that Lily intended to purge the memory of Pao An from Lincoln's heart. Next year, Lincoln would be offering up the eulogy at the Li Gate as head of Lily's clan, not talking to a solitary spot of earth as if it were alive. Still, the edges of the vision remained with Molly, bathing everything about her with new colors. Molly understood the idea that informed the building Lincoln was constructing for her mother. It was a comfort to her that only the first section had been finished; Lincoln could not cut ties with them completely until he brought to fruition Pao An's legacy for the women he loved. Molly felt her father's presence in the bare boards of the floor and walls, in the coral stone foundation. Fragments of stairways rose eerily into the air; Pao An was there too, filling the emptiness with the elegant idea of the structure to come. The building would be as he had intended, the living quarters connected by wide verandas and external walkways to offices and shops, warehouse, and factory on levels above and below. Only the kitchen and one room had been built so far: the heart of a family compound around which warehouse and factory floor would rise. Lincoln anticipated that the city would eventually spread inland toward the mountains, making this cheap property valuable in years to come.

Their long wait for Lincoln was interrupted by dozens of Tang men who made the trek from Chinatown to their end of Vineyard Street to inspect the shell of the unfinished factory and to bring small food gifts to Pao An's widow and daughter. Had her father touched so many Tang men's lives? Molly had forgotten in her exile from Chinatown that the roast pig was a gift to the living, not simply the decoration for a grave. For after laying out the pig in the courtyard, the men chopped it into slabs, which Rulan wrapped in *ti* leaves and brown paper for every visitor to take home.

"Next year, my good luck, my pig," went the men's refrain, a promise of beneficence when prosperity came again.

By the time Lincoln returned, stars peeked through the skeletal beams of the factory and hot night breezes carried the sharp, scent of overripe fruit from the dead Spaniard's sprawling jungle of vines. The last of the visitors had long departed with his bundle of meat. Molly was famished. While her mother rattled in the kitchen preparing the festival meal, Molly placed the rice bowls and teacups on the table with scrupulous precision. In the space of an evening, Lincoln had become just another visitor, and this a feast of farewell. Even if she wanted to, she could not make a claim on the man she had always badgered and ignored, could not order him about as she had as a child. Molly began to doubt that she ever had the power to bring this uncompromising individual to the point of tears. So she did not protest when Rulan put a chair between Lincoln and herself in the place formerly occupied by Pao An. She could not bear to sit beside Lincoln anymore. He was, after all, betrothed to another.

Rulan might have been acting out of a similar anticipation of loss, for the meal she prepared was more lavish than the usual Ching Ming fare. In addition to roast pig from the gravesite, carved into slivers, the crackling sticky and sweet, there was a braised duck stuffed with barley; a mound of pork buns with red designs stamped onto the skin; and a meatless Buddhist-style stew made of bean curd, black mushrooms, and translucent rice noodles—a favorite of Lincoln's.

Molly was the perfect hostess, pressing the choicest morsels on Lincoln while taking little for herself despite her enormous hunger, for she was shy of him now. And yet as she toyed with her food, she was struck by the conviction that Pao An was beside her in the empty chair, bidding his kin to eat their fill however brief their time together.

Lincoln seemed to have discarded his earlier ebullience along with his formal dress. Over the course of the day, he had gradually grown more disheveled, unbuttoning his tight collar, stuffing his skullcap into the pocket of his *chun sam* and doffing his pigskin clogs for an old pair of cloth shoes Rulan kept on hand for him. He was silent and withdrawn, too, and ate even less than Molly.

To Molly's eyes, the boy of memory could not easily be found in the face of the man who had taken his place. This man's forehead was wide and clear, a scholar's brow. His eyes were long and narrow behind wire-rimmed spectacles. His hair was parted in the middle and swept the high cheekbones like two dark wings. His nose was long and shapely, the mouth was wide, the square chin covered with a hint of bristle. For all their scars and calluses, the fingers were slender and beautiful, capable of wielding pen or tools or chopsticks with grace and deliberation. Capable, too, of patient caresses. With such a man there might be no sadness after love.

Rulan collected the plates of uneaten food and disappeared into the kitchen. "You must forgive this family's peasant tastes," Molly said with strangled courtesy.

"What's that you say?" Lincoln pulled nervously at his earlobe, a habit she remembered from childhood.

"I was only apologizing for not giving you the food you desire."

"I gather I am being obvious," he sighed, running his fingers in distraction through his hair. "My mind is on other things. I have been with Lily and her people all afternoon, you see."

His words aroused in Molly a savage impatience to see the deed done. Let him go to Lily! The perfect Chinese beauty would make the perfect Chinese wife! And yet, Lily had taken only what Molly herself had cast aside: the one man who had been consistently faithful, enduringly kind.

Lincoln dipped a fingertip into the teacup and traced the rim with a wet finger. "My business with the Lis has been concluded . . . unsatisfactorily in their view."

Molly frowned into the bottom of her rice bowl. There were loose grains sticking to the sides. She counted them one by one.

"Amazing how a simple decision has consequences for the future . . ." He paused, then blurted out, "I have turned Lily's offer down. I had entertained the notion of marriage to Lily, I admit. A man would be blind not to acknowledge her gifts. But she and I are from different worlds! She is the product of generations of gentry inbreeding. I am Lin Kong, son of the camp woman Phoenix. Should such a one as I forswear my mother's name, the only thing I have of her? Ask me rather to cut out my stomach and heart! Besides," he added, "this offspring of a woman bereft of choices is foolish enough to believe that families are made by choice, not duty. Chinese believe love sends fissures into the rock of filial piety, makes rich men poor and poor men weaker still. But God help me, I cannot escape it," he said with a wistful smile. "Though love has left me poor."

Yes, he had lost a fortune in refusing Lily, thought Molly. But if not Lily, then *who* did he love?

Lincoln poured tea from the straw caddy into his cup and drank silently, his brows knit in reflection. "Lily was quite distraught. She cursed me."

There was an interminable pause, as if he were waiting for Molly to speak. But what could she possibly say? Molly could barely contain her own unruly emotions let alone interpret his! Did he expect her to offer condolences? Affect a reconciliation with Lily? Draw him a map for some imaginary paradise where an unknown Eve awaited? And, blast the man, who *did* he love?

At that moment, Rulan burst through the curtain that separated the eating space from her kitchen. "More to eat!" she announced brusquely. "Here's *mui* from the last shipment. A new kind to try, *eh?*" She chattered about prices and cargoes and weights while prying open a crock of *mui* with one of her husband's iron tools.

Molly waited, her eyes fixed on the plate of *mui* Rulan slid before them. Crazy woman, how could anyone eat now? Her stomach churned, and the thunder of her heart echoed in her ears. Would Lincoln go back to Yale, to a young woman who had beguiled him on winter afternoons with a European dance step? And, oh!—if he left this table never to return . . .

He was staring past her into an imaginary landscape, bringing, no doubt, a scholar's tidy mind to the problem of what to do for the rest of his life. "Well, then," he blurted out. "It's late. The ghosts have departed, and so must I." Lincoln rose, his forehead furrowed. And he would depart, and there would never be another moment with the three of them alone together.

"Lin Kong! Don't leave me!"

Lincoln paused for the space of a heartbeat, then eased himself into the chair with a small sigh. Wordlessly, he extended a hand and picked up the bamboo chopsticks with practiced skill. Molly watched in terror and hope as Lincoln took a plum from the plate. Then with the deliberation of a *gu li,* "rough man," setting down the first stone of his house, he dropped the plum into her bowl, took another *mui* in his chopsticks and put it to his lips, a gesture more intimate than a kiss.

"Eat, eat," Rulan urged in a peremptory voice, frowning as mothers do when faced with children they cannot command.

Mui, Molly thought. Plum. Girl. Me! He loves me! With joy exploding like New Year's brightness, she picked up the plum with her fingers and hungrily placed it in her mouth. The *mui* was coated in powdery salt. Briny, hard, sharp to the tongue. But sweet at the very core.

GLOSSARIES

GLOSSARY OF HAWAIIAN TERMS*

ahana.   Taunting chant used by children.

akuas.   Gods, spirits.

alii (ah-lee-ee).   Hawaiian ruling class.

aloha.   All-inclusive word signifying greeting, farewell, friendship, love.

ami ami.   A *hula* movement involving the rhythmic circling of the dancer's hips.

auwe.   Exclamation of grief.

hala.   Pandanus plant whose leaves are cut and woven into mats, baskets, sails for canoes.

hale (ha-lay).   A house or a building.

hanai.   Foster (child).

---

* Hawaiian words are generally pronounced as they are written, except that a *w* is pronounced like a *v*. For easier reading, I have formed plurals by adding -*s* to nouns, as English-speaking Hawaiians do nowadays when lacing their conversation with Hawaiian terms. Someone speaking entirely in Hawaiian, however, would form plurals by adding special prefixes to an invariable noun.

haole (how–lay).   Originally a term referring to any foreigner; later referring specifically to a white person.

hapa haole.   Person of part–white ancestry.

holoku.   A formal garment patterned after the "Mother Hubbard" or missionary nightgown. *Holokus* fit close to the body and have a circular
train that is spread out on the floor when the wearer dances the *hula.*

hui.   Organization in which members pool capital and profits.

hula.   Traditional Hawaiian dance using distinctive body movements to
denote the dancer's relationship to a natural world permeated with
metaphysical meaning. *Hula* has many forms, among them, the ancient
temple or sacred dances performed by men *(hula kapu);* the transitional
or Kalakaua-era *hula kui,* which used women dancers, stringed instruments, and nineteenth-century European dance rhythms and cos-
tumes; and the *hapa haole hula* used to entertain tourists in this century.
A remarkable revival of the ancient discipline of *hula* has occurred in
Hawaii since the 1960s, resulting in the flowering of *halaus,* or dance
schools, under master teachers, with annual dance competitions.

ikaika (ee–kigh–kah).   Strong, powerful.

ike papalua.   The gift of second sight; ability to commune with the spirit
world.

kahuna.   Priest, shaman.

kanaka.   Human being; a person of Hawaiian descent.

kapakahi.   Wildly crooked or distorted.

kapu.   Holy, forbidden.

keiki.   Child.

kolohe.   Mischievous, naughty.

kupuna.   Grandparent.

luau.   Hawaiian-style feast.

luna.   Overseer, boss.

maikai.   Comely, attractive.

mai pa-ke.   Leprosy ("Chinese disease").

makai.   Toward the sea.

malo.   Loincloth worn by males.

mana.   Divine energy flowing from the spirit world to *alii,* thus empower-
ing them to rule.

manapua.   Chinese-style buns hawked by street vendors.

mauka.   Inland toward the mountains.

mele.   Oral lore; songs and chants.

menehune.   Mythical race of pygmies who worked by night to build roads,
temples, fishponds.

ohana.   Clan.

okolehao.   Potent distilled liquor made from *ti* root, rice, or pineapples.

ola.   Life, breath.

opihi.   A small shellfish found clinging to rocks. Much prized as a delicacy when eaten with *poi.*

pa-ke (pah-kay).   A Chinese person.

pau.   Finished, completed.

poi.   Starchy paste made from cooked taro corms pounded until smooth and thinned with water; staple of the Hawaiian diet.

punalua.   Sharing a spouse.

pupule.   Insane.

tapa.   Cloth made from pounded tree bark.

wahine (vah-hee-nay).   Woman.

wahine hana.   Domestic ("woman of work").

welekahao.   Merrymaking.

GLOSSARY OF CHINESE TERMS (MOSTLY CANTONESE)

bak kuei.   A Caucasian ("white devil").

bao.   Bun; round paper object holding incense.

chun sam.   Narrow, long-sleeved tunic favored by modern, young Chinese men in the 1880s and 1890s; worn with Western pants and shoes.

fan-tan.   A game popular among Cantonese immigrants using brass cash pieces.

Fusan.   An overseas utopia visited by Chinese seafarers two thousand years ago whose location is veiled in myth. In his version of *Fusan,* Pao An also drew on accounts of another elusive paradise, the "Fortunate" or "Blessed" Isles inhabited by Taoist immortals.

gu li.   "Rough man for hire" in Cantonese; less pejorative phonetic rendering of the Tamil term *coolie.*

Hakka.   Guest people; one of two feuding tribes in Kwangtung. The Hakka speak a dialect similar to those in the north and do not bind their women's feet as do the Punti. Rulan is Hakka, and Pao An is Punti: an impossible union in China becomes viable in Hawaii.

la sap.   Rubbish.

Lin Kong.   Lincoln's Chinese name was chosen by the Fiddletown pharmacist at his mother's request as a way of forecasting her son's future. The first character conveys unity, family, singleness of purpose; the second evokes all the properties of light: keenness, brilliance, distinction.

ma jong (ma jeok in Cantonese).   Game with four players and 136 dominoes, or tiles, used like cards. At the beginning of the game, the players make a square courtyard of tile walls. Each player draws a hand of 13 tiles from the walls, picking and discarding in his or her turn and making sets or sequences based on the designs on the face of the tiles, as in poker.

Mei Mei.   Little sister; Mandarin term of endearment.

mu.   One-third of an acre, the basic land unit in China.

mui.   Girl, sister in Cantonese dialect; preserved plum flavored with various spices.

"pig" trade.   A colloquial Cantonese term for immigrant Chinese labor; the phrase refers to the custom of carrying pigs to market in round baskets, not unlike the ferrying of *gu li* in the holds of ships.

pi pa.   A balloon-shaped guitar.

Punti.   Old-timers of Kwangtung who were themselves a population formed from the mixing of northern Han settlers with indigenous southern tribes. Bitter old-country rivals of the Hakka.

sam fu.   Woman's costume consisting of tunic and trousers.

Tai Tai.   Honorific used to address a married lady.

Tang.   A dynasty in China (A.D. 618–907) during which the southern province of Kwangtung achieved imperial prominence. The people of Kwangtung refer to themselves as "people of Tang" to distinguish themselves from the Han, the dominant people of China, who claim a different lineage and ethnicity.

tong.   A club or society; here used to refer to Triad secret societies known as Hung Moon or Chee Kung Tong, which were often linked with illegal activities such as opium and gambling. The *tongs* in Hawaii were suspected of helping to finance the Wilcox insurrection.

ya hoo lam.   Inexpensive polished cotton cloth, dyed robin's egg blue, used for everyday wear by Chinese families in late-nineteenth-century Hawaii.

About the Author

Linda Ching Sledge was born in Honolulu into a Cantonese family with a long history in the Hawaiian Islands. Her immigrant ancestors include a cook for a missionary family on Oahu, a founder of a *mui* factory in historic Honolulu, a builder of levees in the California Delta, and a runaway wife. She holds a B.A. from the University of California at Berkeley and a Ph.D. from the Graduate Center, City University of New York, and is currently associate professor of English at Westchester Community College in Valhalla, New York. She lives in a suburb of Manhattan with her sons, Timothy and Geoffrey, and her husband, Gary, an editor at *Reader's Digest*. Her previous historical novel, *Empire of Heaven,* was set in China.